LEGENDS OF ZITA THE SPACEGIRL

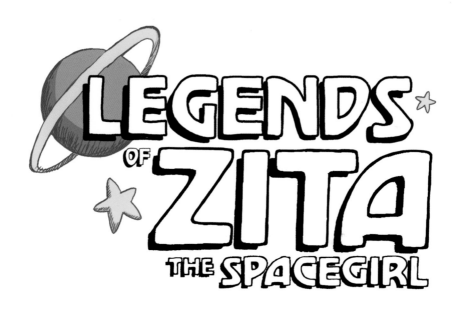

First Second
New York & London

Text and illustrations copyright © 2012 by Ben Hatke

Published by First Second
First Second is an imprint of Roaring Brook Press,
a division of Holtzbrinck Publishing Holdings Limited Partnership
175 Fifth Avenue, New York, New York 10010

Distributed in the United Kingdom by Macmillan Children's Books,
a division of Pan Macmillan.

Cover and interior design by Colleen AF Venable

Cataloging-in-Publication Data is on file at the Library of Congress

Paperback ISBN: 978-1-59643-447-9
Hardcover ISBN: 978-1-59643-806-4

First Second books are available for special promotions and premiums.
For details, contact: Director of Special Markets, Holtzbrinck Publishers.

First Edition 2012

Printed in China by Toppan Leefung Printing Ltd.,
Dongguan City, Guangdong Province

Paperback: 20 19 18 17 16 15 14 13
Hardcover: 10

LEGENDS OF ZITA THE SPACEGIRL

Ben Hatke

First Second
New York

Much after a beginning is difficult, as everybody knows who has crossed the sea, and as for the first step a man never so much as remembers it...

...The first step is undertaken lightly, pleasantly, and with your soul in the sky; it is the five-hundredth that counts.

—Hillaire Belloc

Chapter One

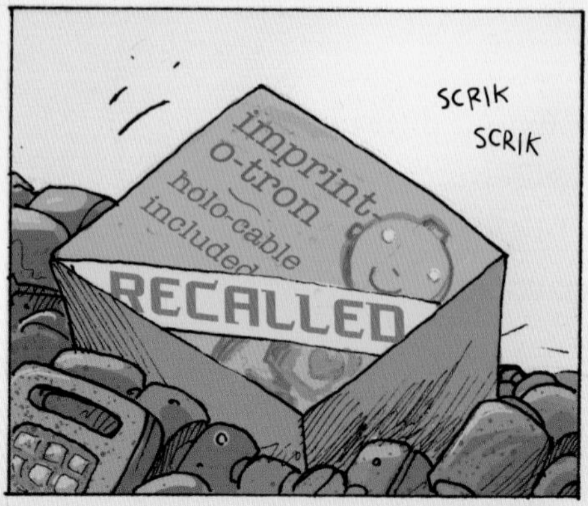
imprint-o-tron
holo-cable included
RECALLED
SCRIK
SCRIK

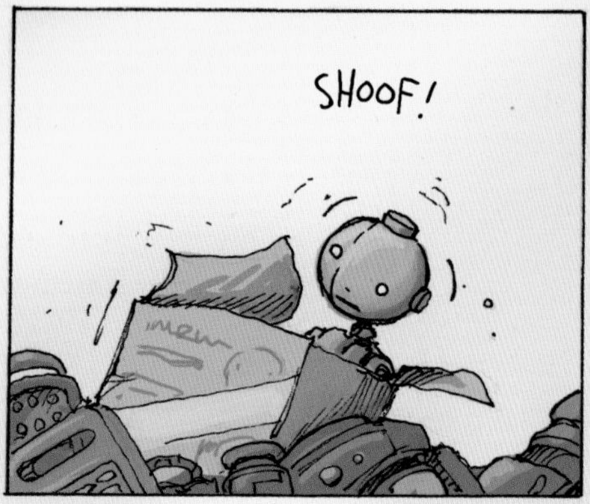
SHOOF!

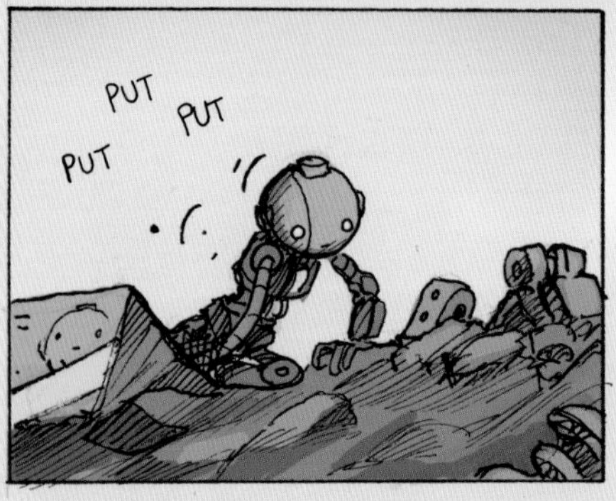
PUT
PUT
PUT

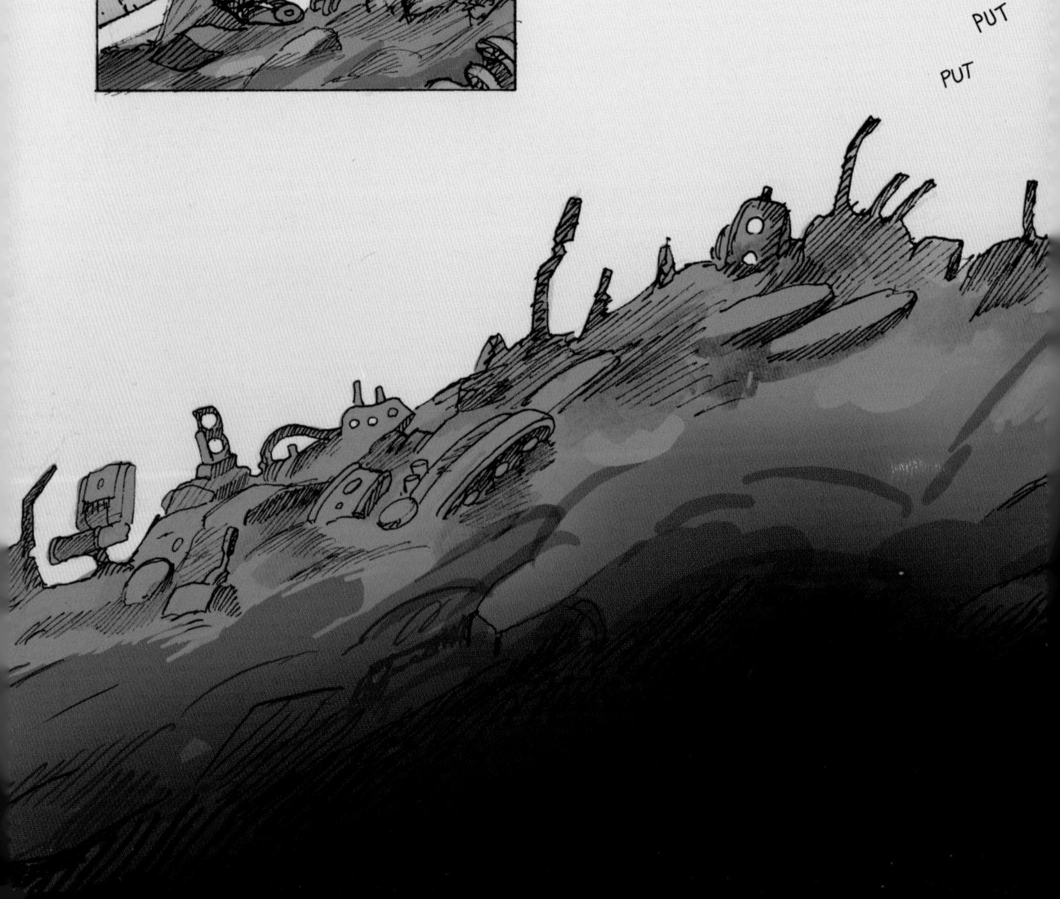
PUT
PUT

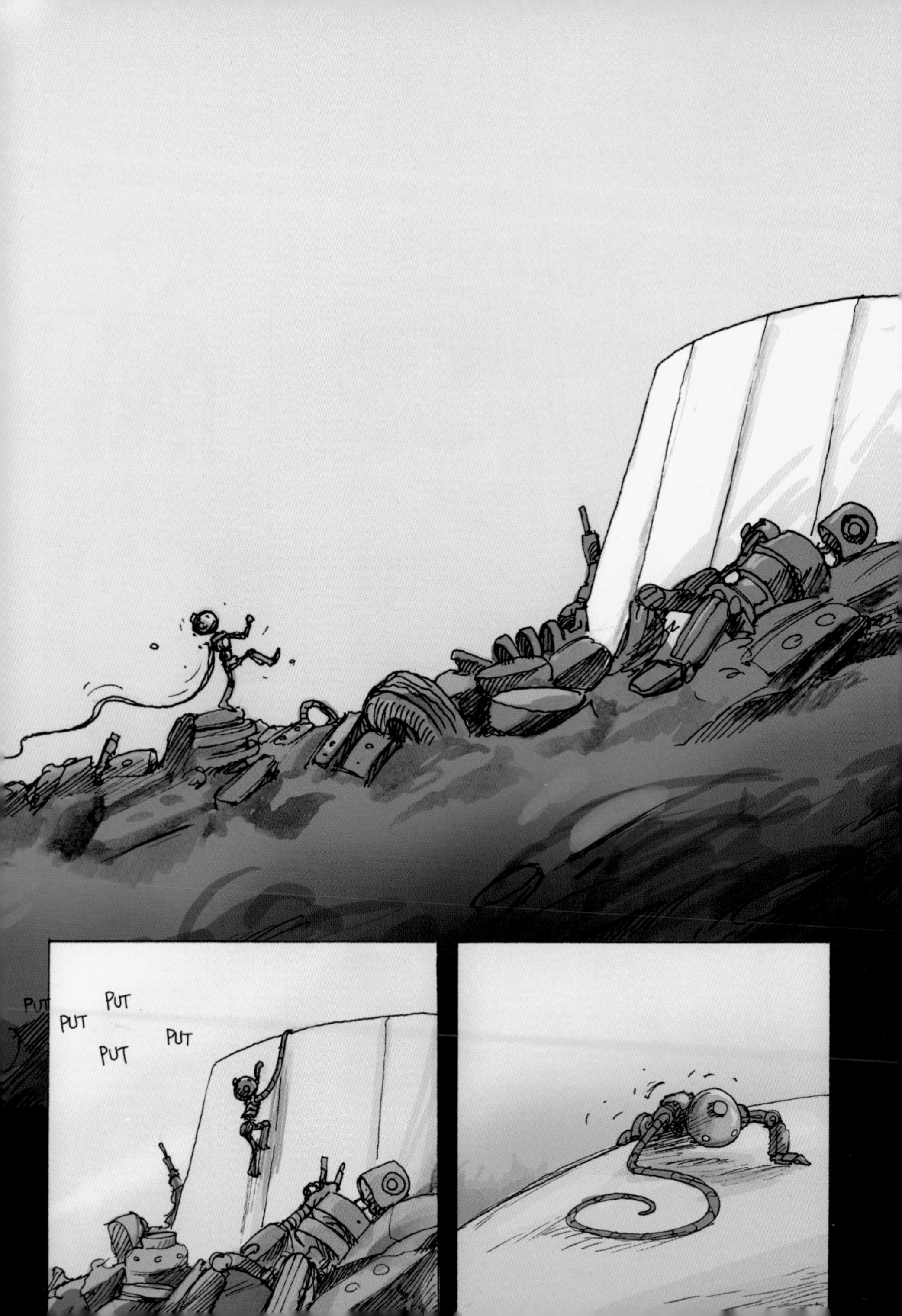
PUT
PUT
PUT
PUT
PUT

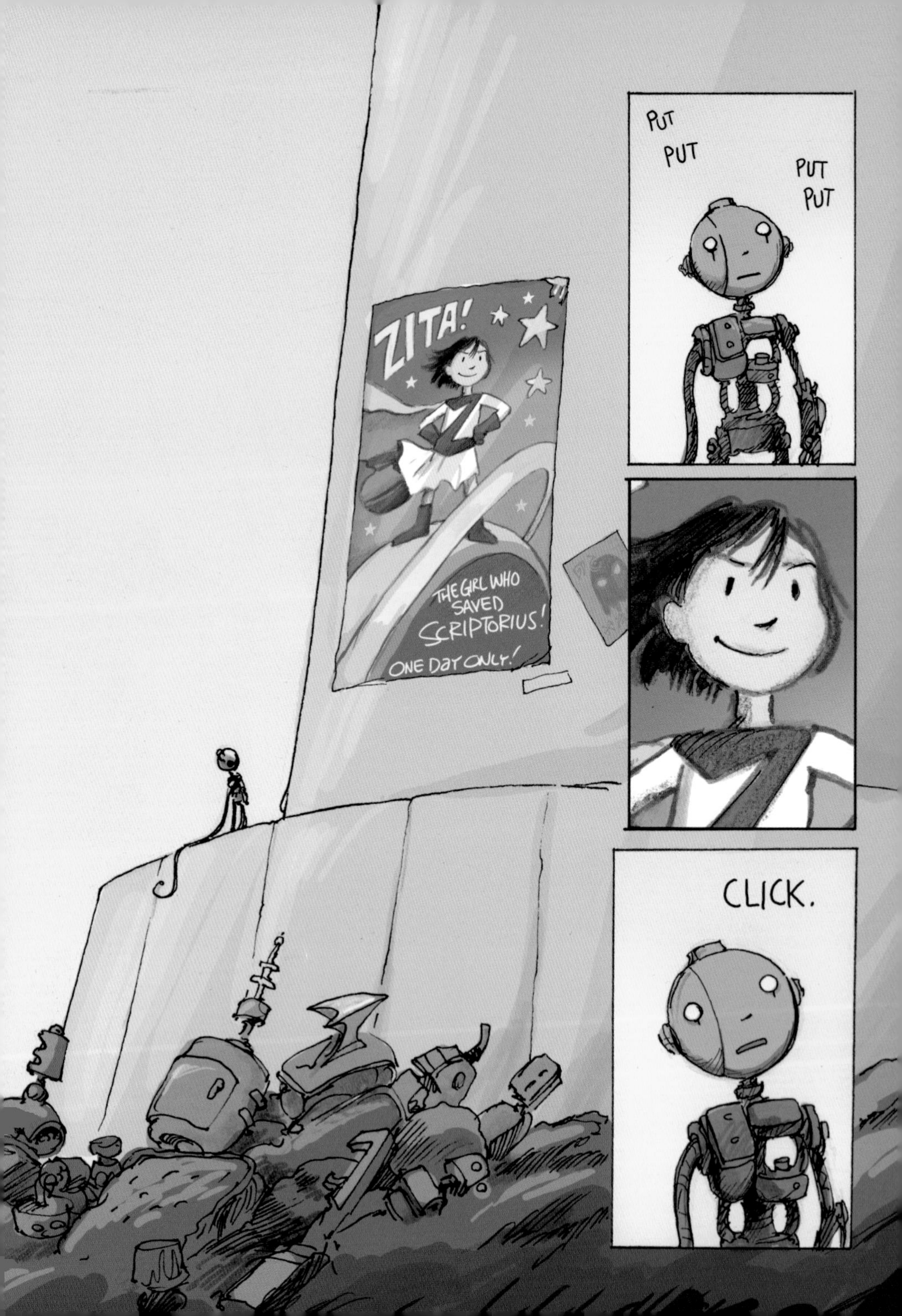
ZITA!
THE GIRL WHO SAVED SCRIPTORIUS!
ONE DAY ONLY!
PUT
PUT
PUT
PUT
CLICK.

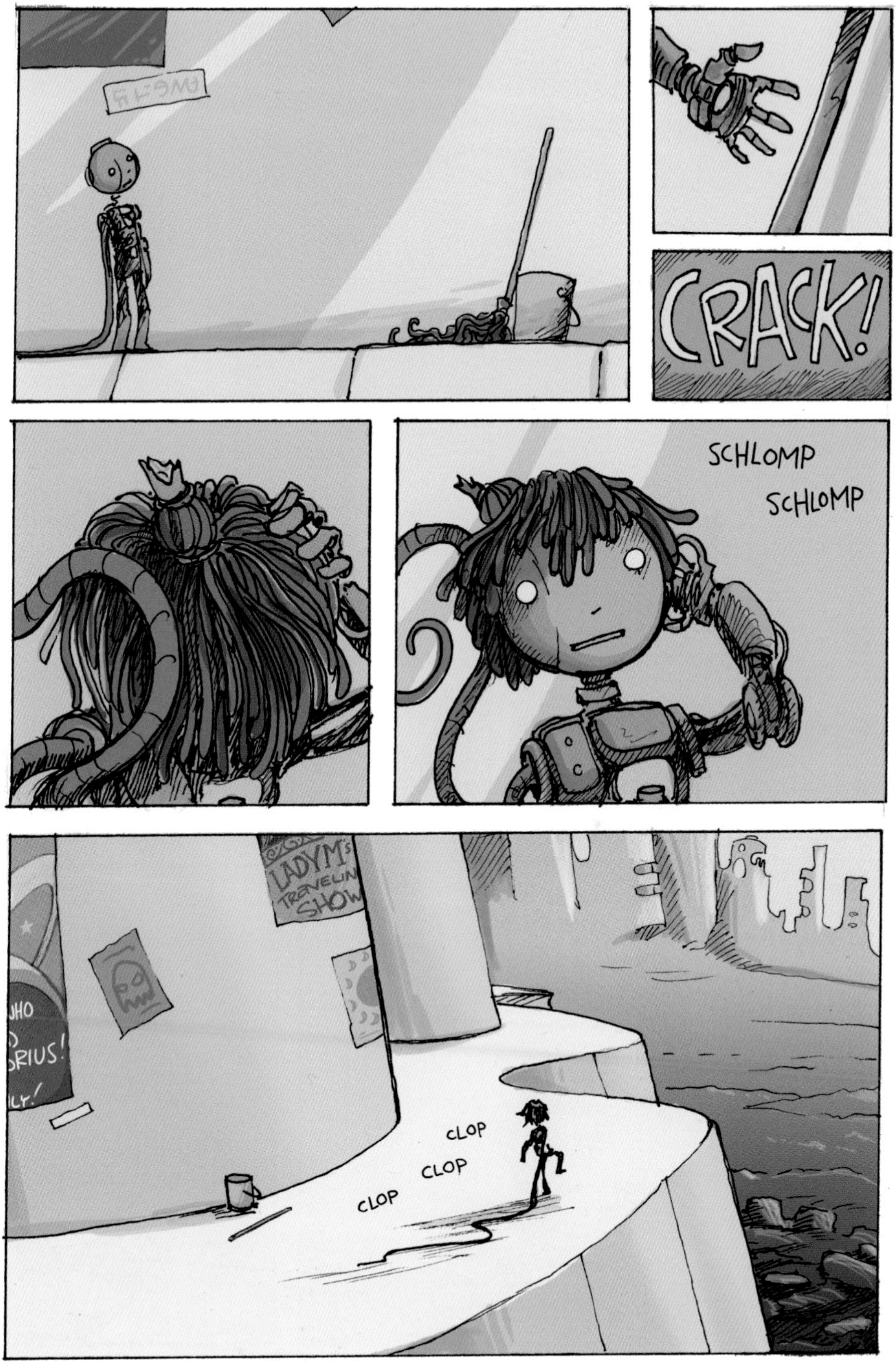
CRACK!
SCHLOMP
SCHLOMP
LADYM'S
TRAVELIN
SHOW
CLOP
CLOP
CLOP

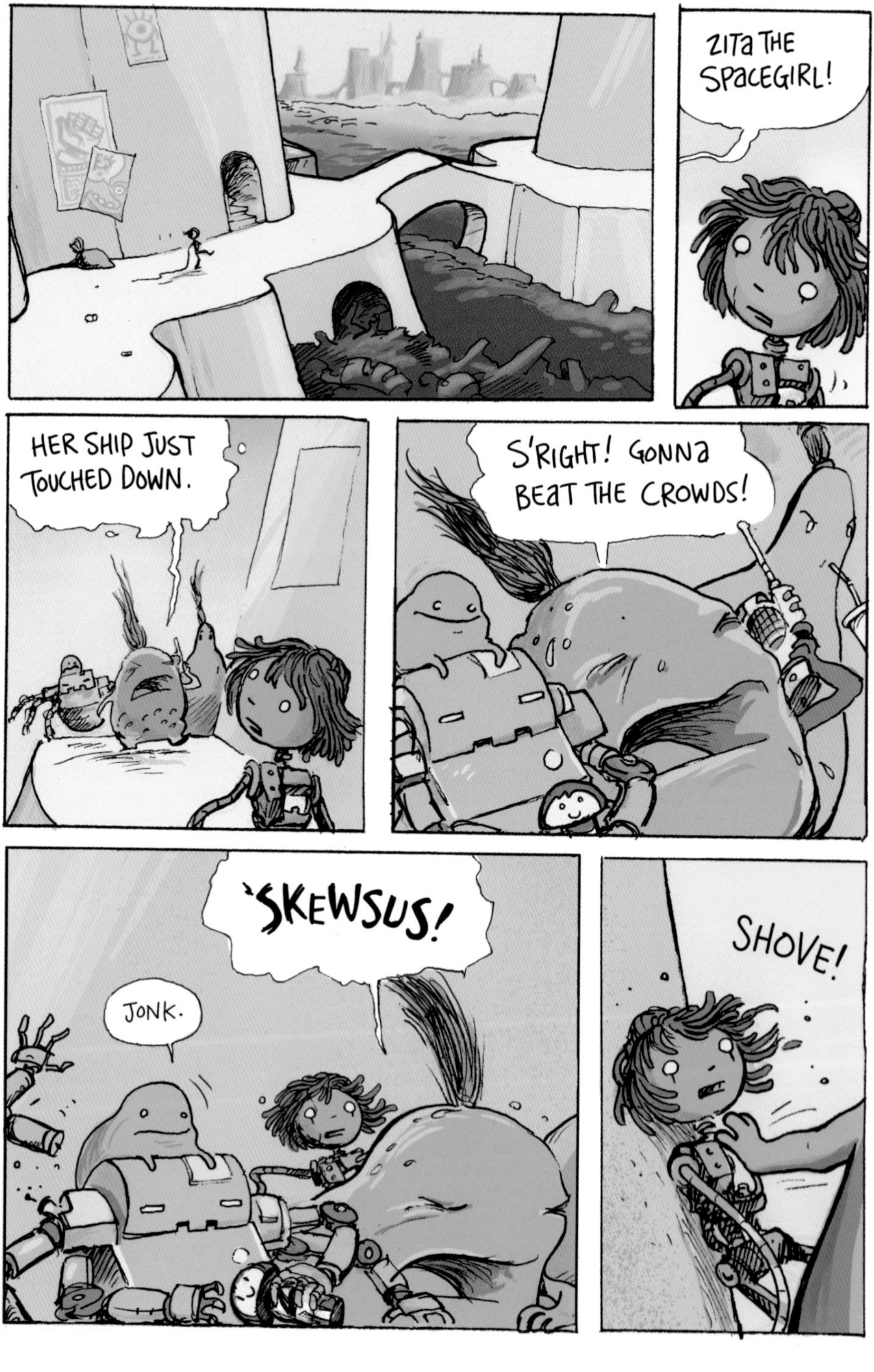
ZITA THE SPACEGIRL!
HER SHIP JUST TOUCHED DOWN.
S'RIGHT! GONNA BEAT THE CROWDS!
JONK.
'SKEWSUS!
SHOVE!

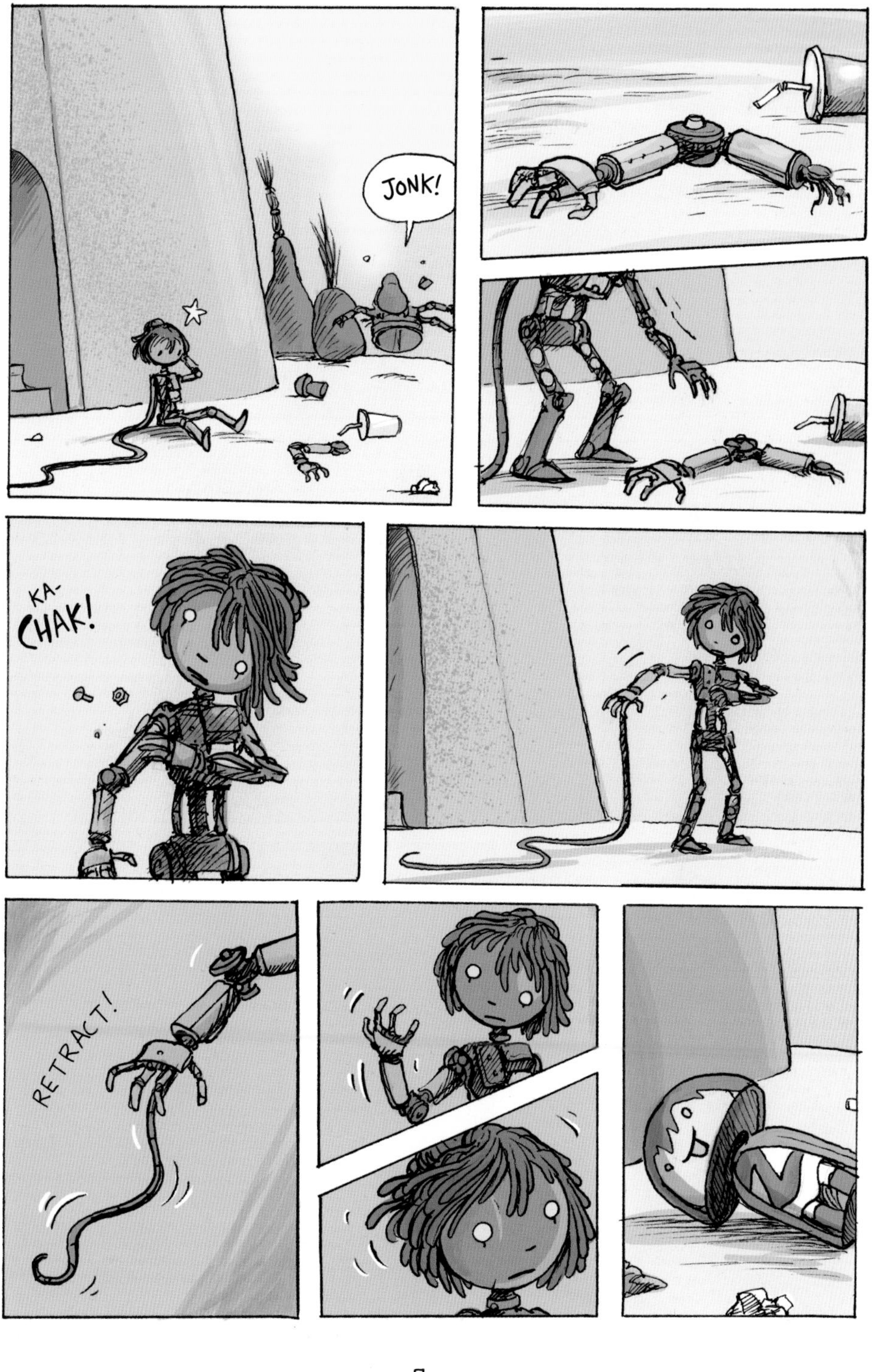
JONK!
KA-CHAK!
RETRACT!

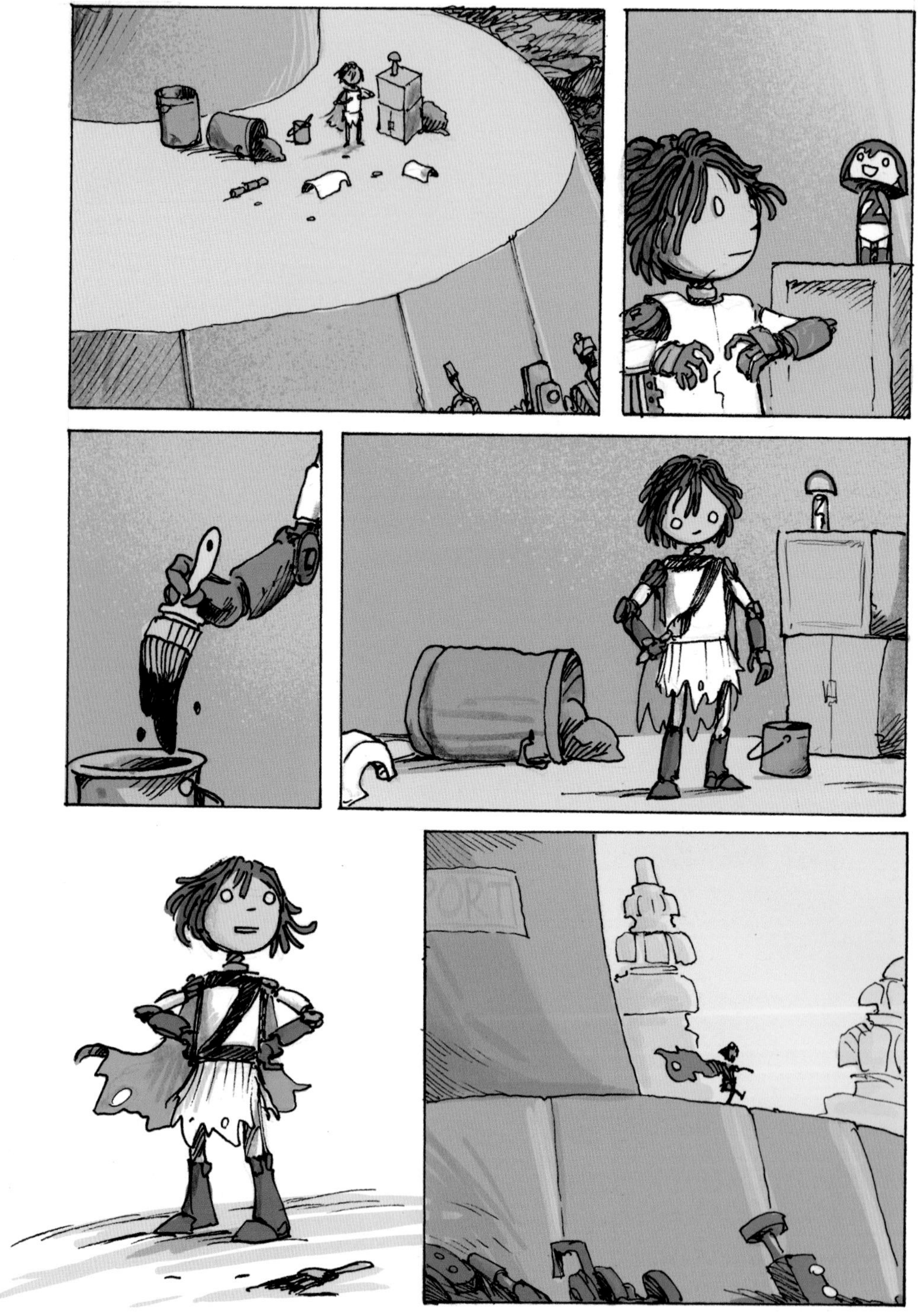

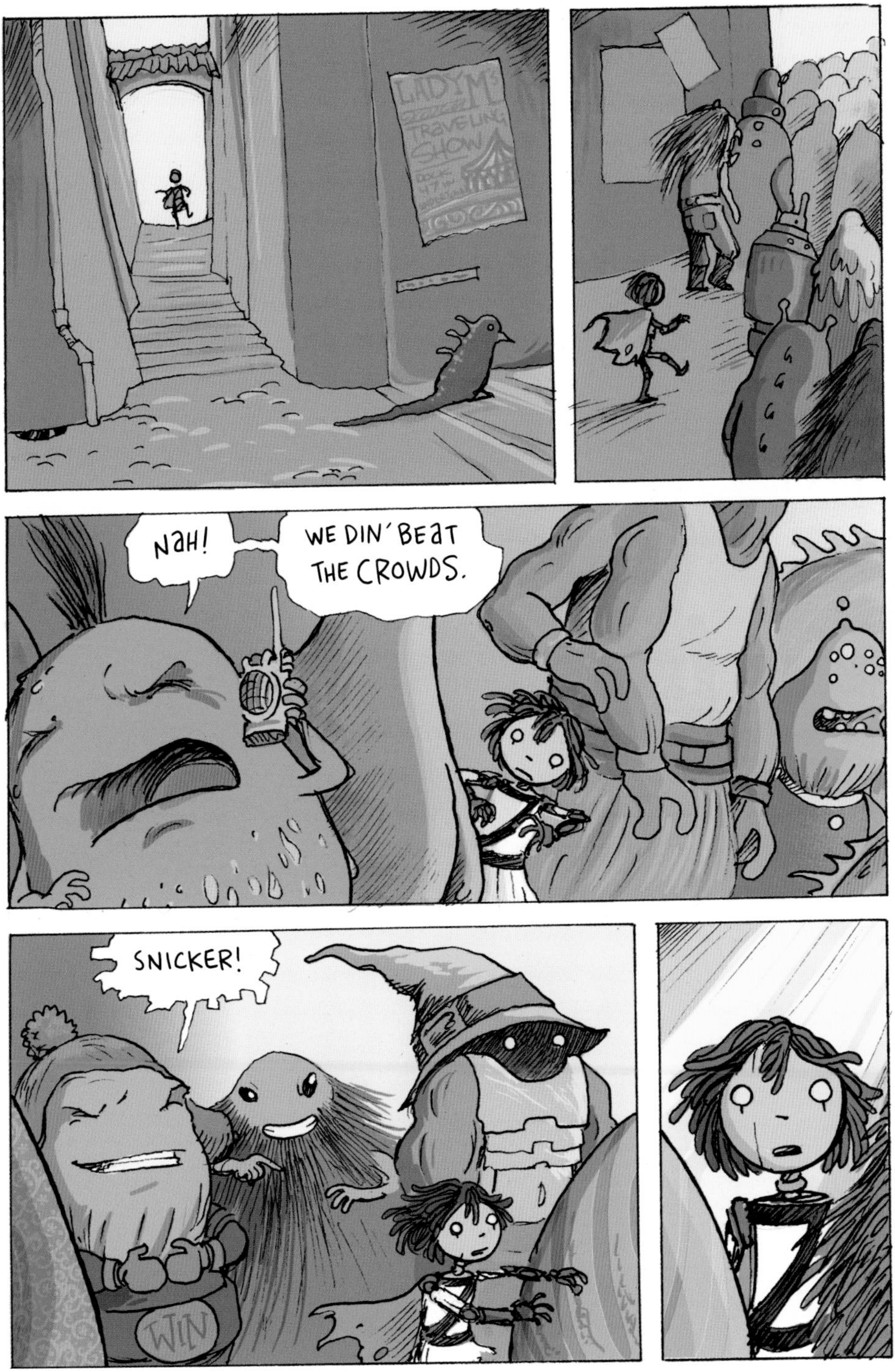
LADY M's
TRAVELING SHOW
NAH!
WE DIN' BEAT THE CROWDS.
SNICKER!
WIN

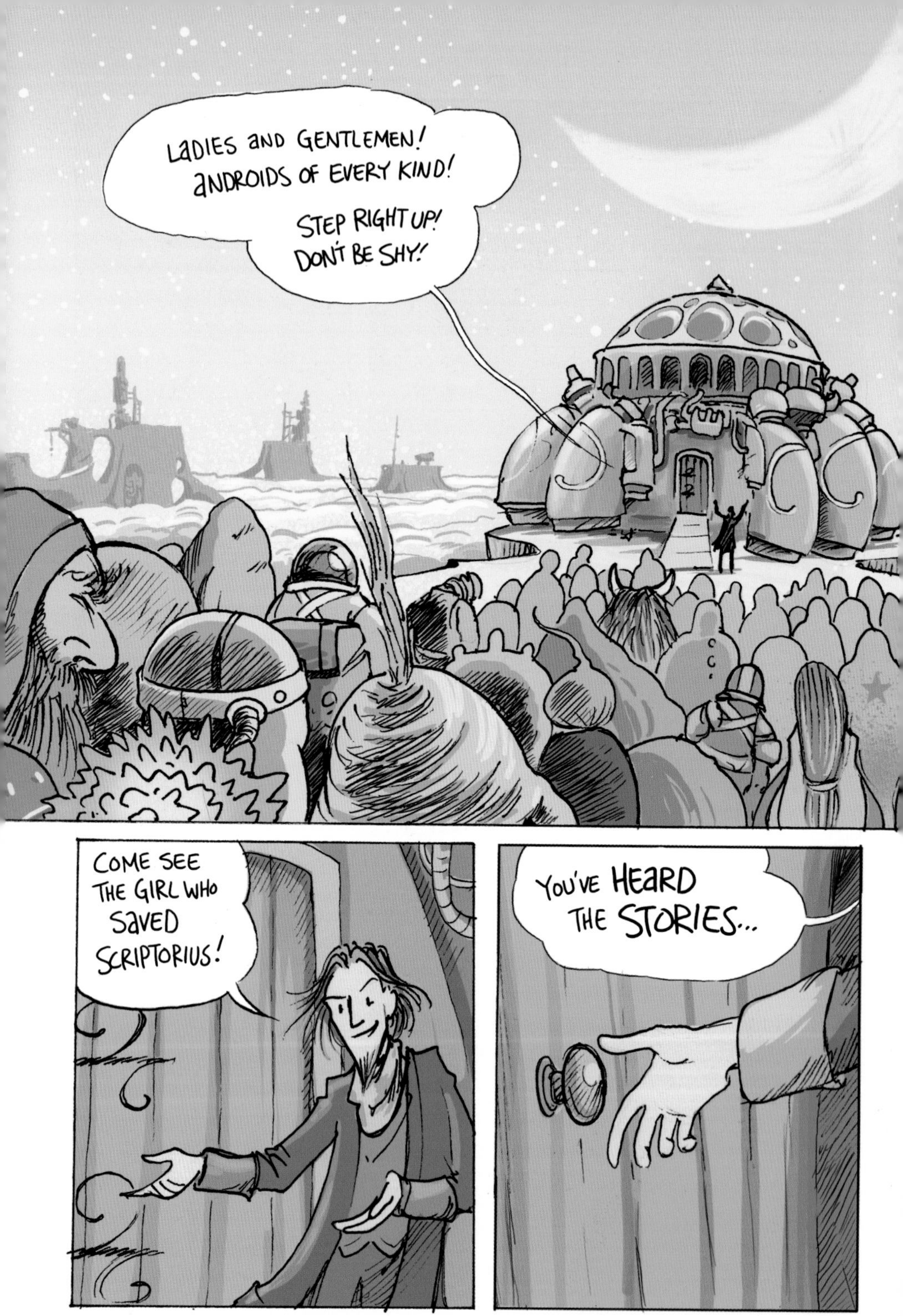
LADIES AND GENTLEMEN! ANDROIDS OF EVERY KIND!
STEP RIGHT UP! DON'T BE SHY!
COME SEE THE GIRL WHO SAVED SCRIPTORIUS!
YOU'VE HEARD THE STORIES...

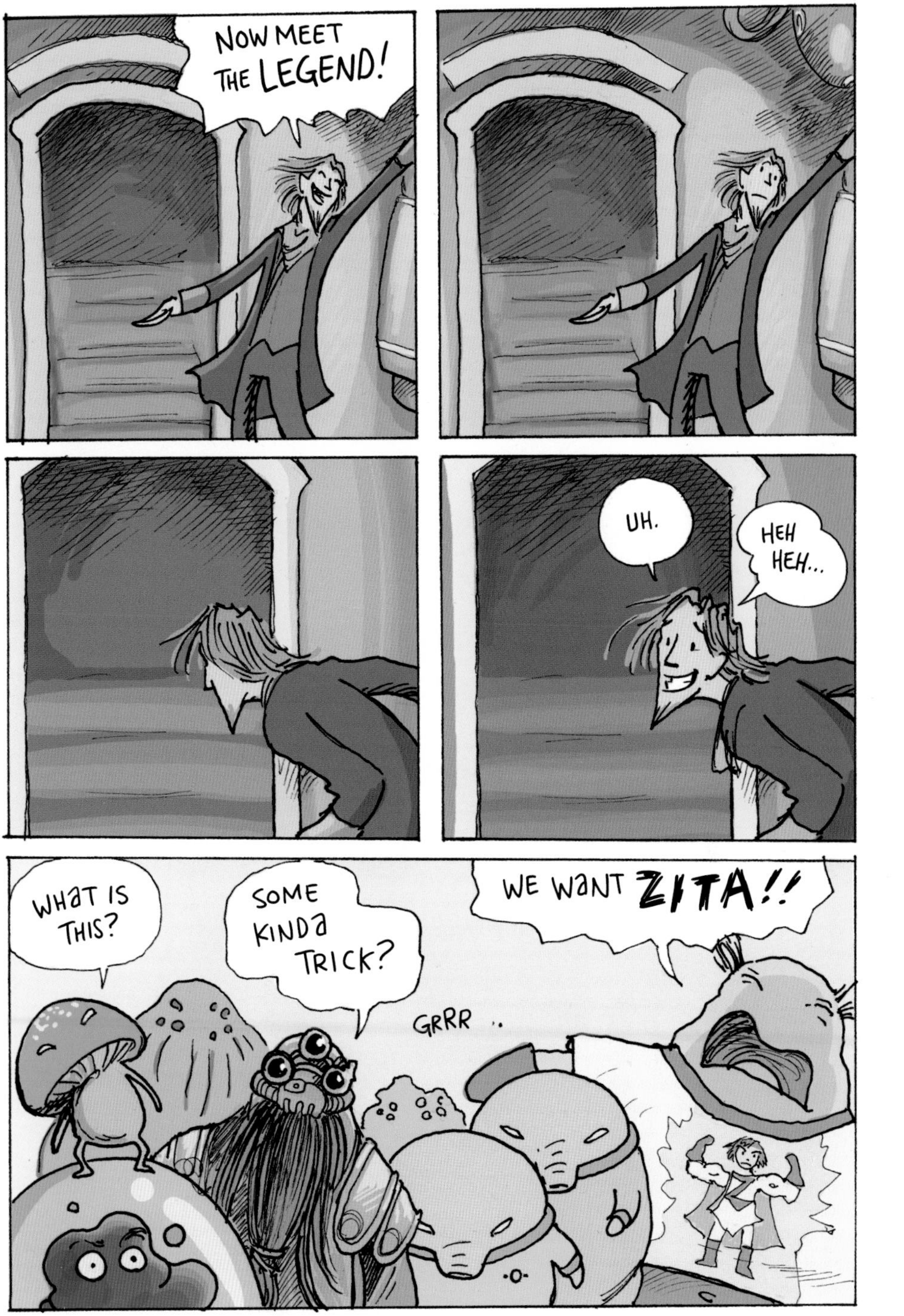
NOW MEET THE LEGEND!
UH.
HEH HEH...
WHAT IS THIS?
SOME KINDA TRICK?
WE WANT ZITA!!
GRRR ..

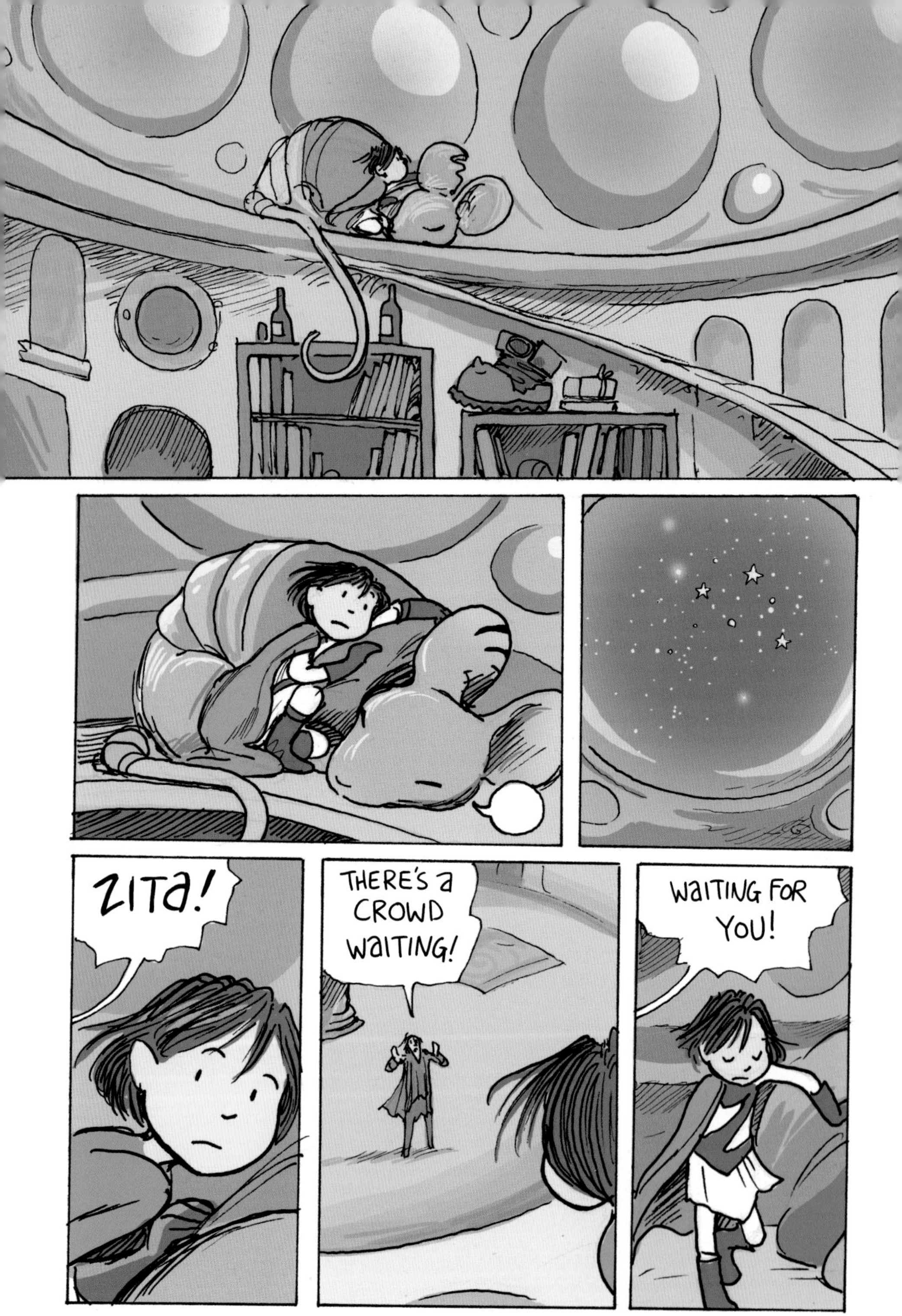
ZITA!
THERE'S A CROWD WAITING!
WAITING FOR YOU!

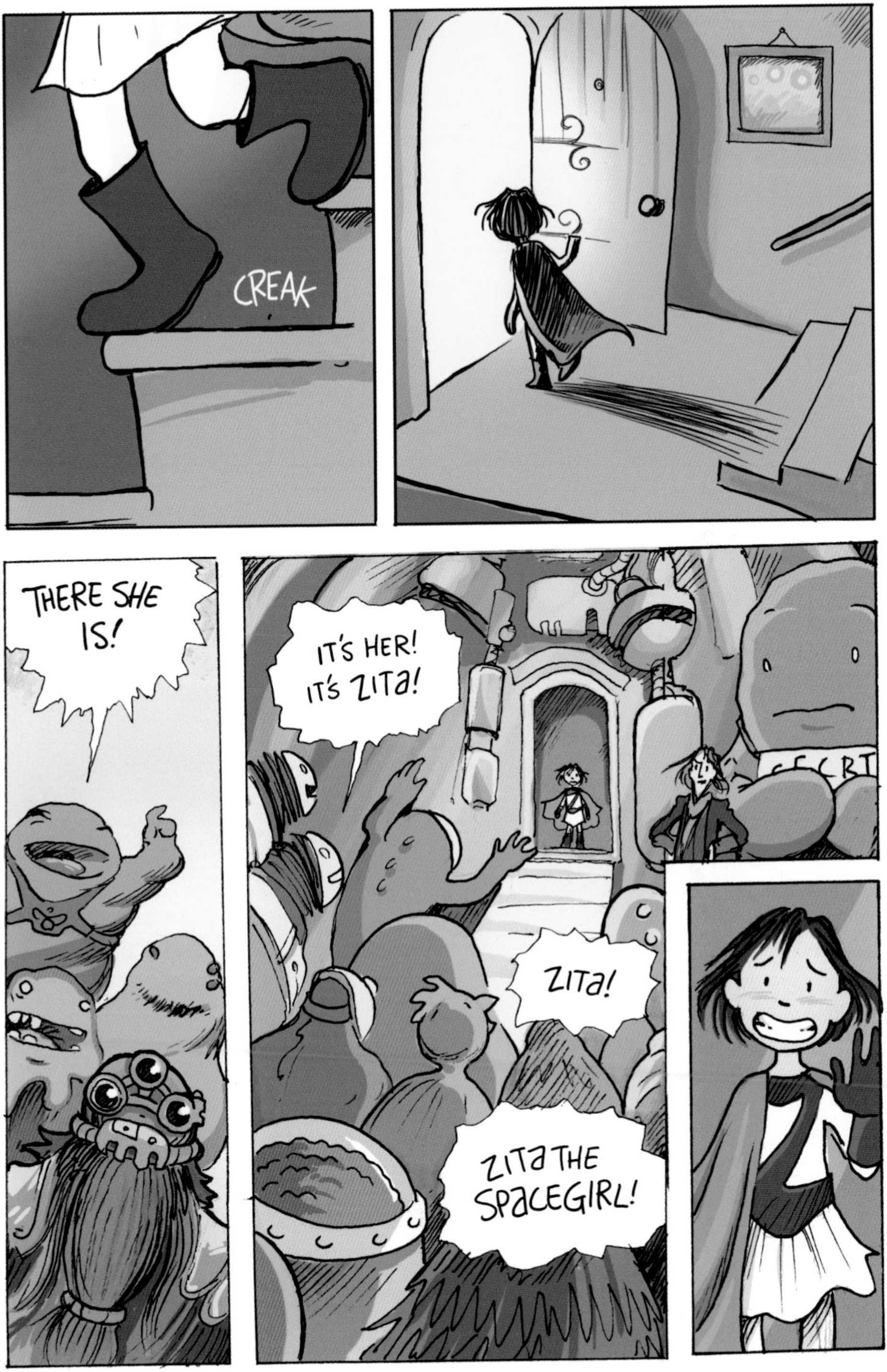
CREAK
THERE SHE IS!
IT'S HER! IT'S ZITA!
ZITA!
ZITA THE SPACEGIRL!

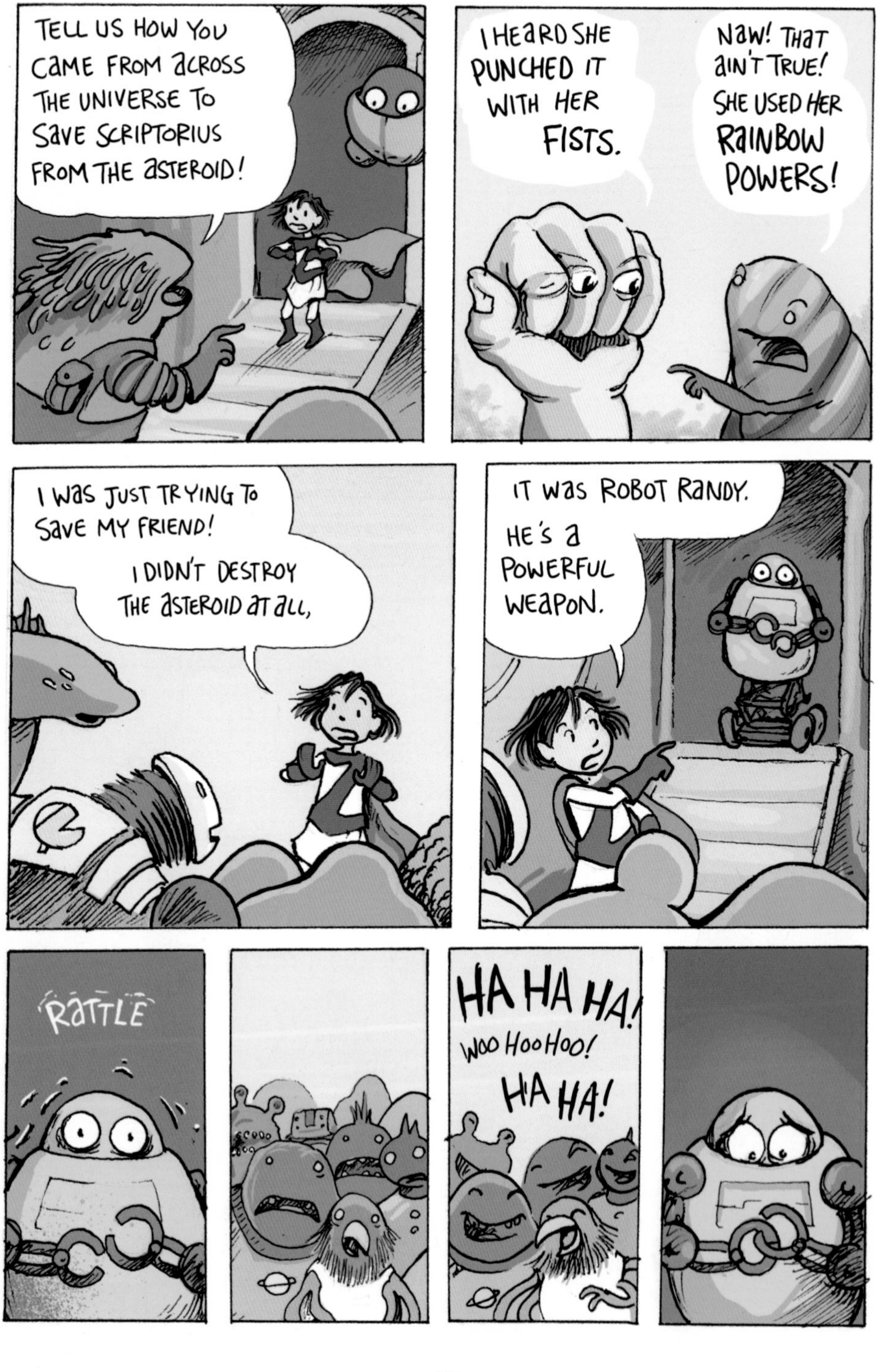
TELL US HOW YOU CAME FROM ACROSS THE UNIVERSE TO SAVE SCRIPTORIUS FROM THE ASTEROID!
I HEARD SHE PUNCHED IT WITH HER FISTS.
NAW! THAT AIN'T TRUE! SHE USED HER RAINBOW POWERS!
I WAS JUST TRYING TO SAVE MY FRIEND!
I DIDN'T DESTROY THE ASTEROID AT ALL,
IT WAS ROBOT RANDY.
HE'S A POWERFUL WEAPON.
RATTLE
HA HA HA!
WOO HOO HOO!
HA HA!

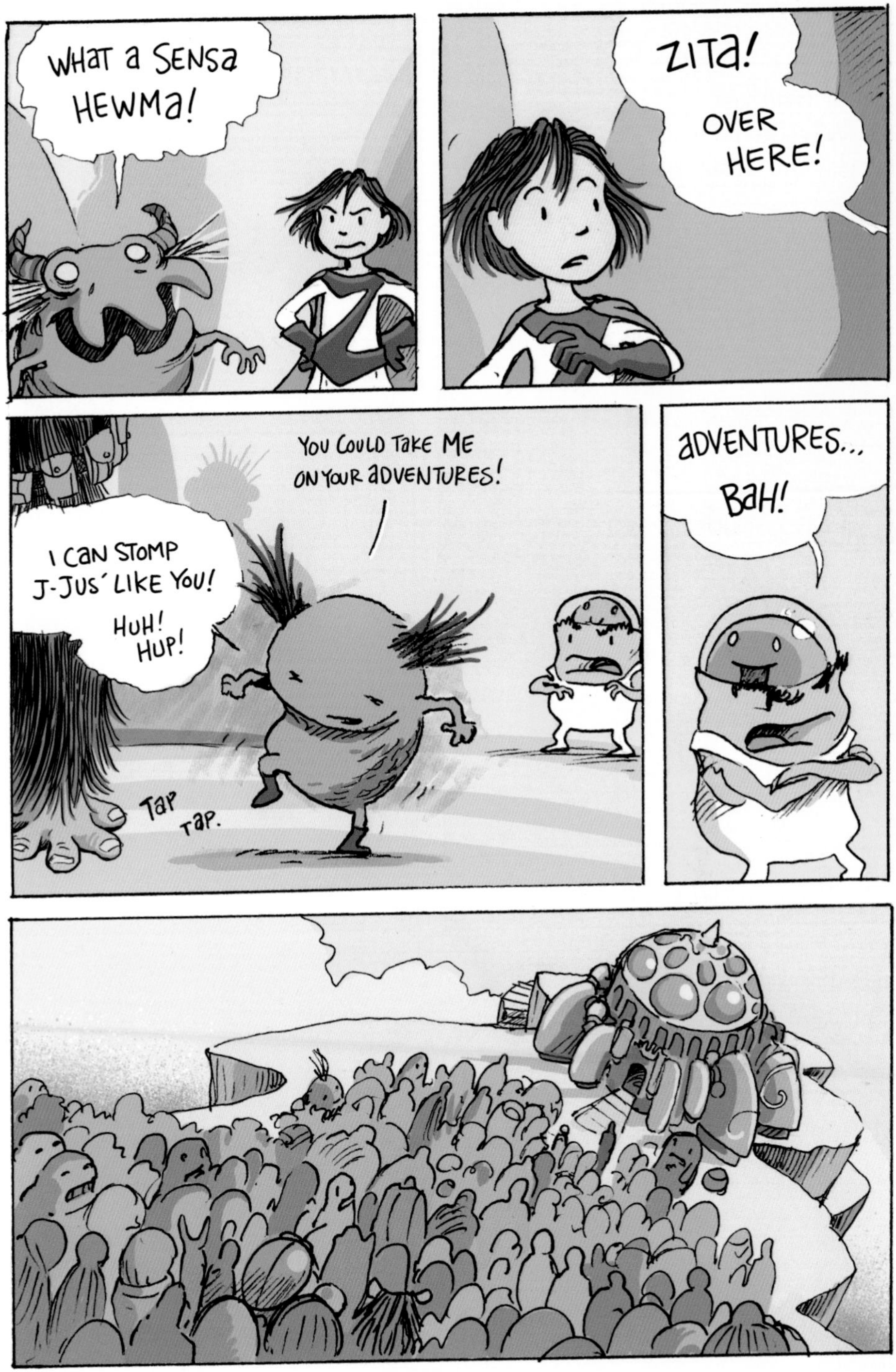
WHAT a SENSa HEWMa!
ZITa!
OVER HERE!
YOU COULD TAKE ME ON YOUR aDVENTURES!
I CaN STOMP J-JUS' LIKE YOU!
HUH! HUP!
TaP TaP.
aDVENTURES... BaH!

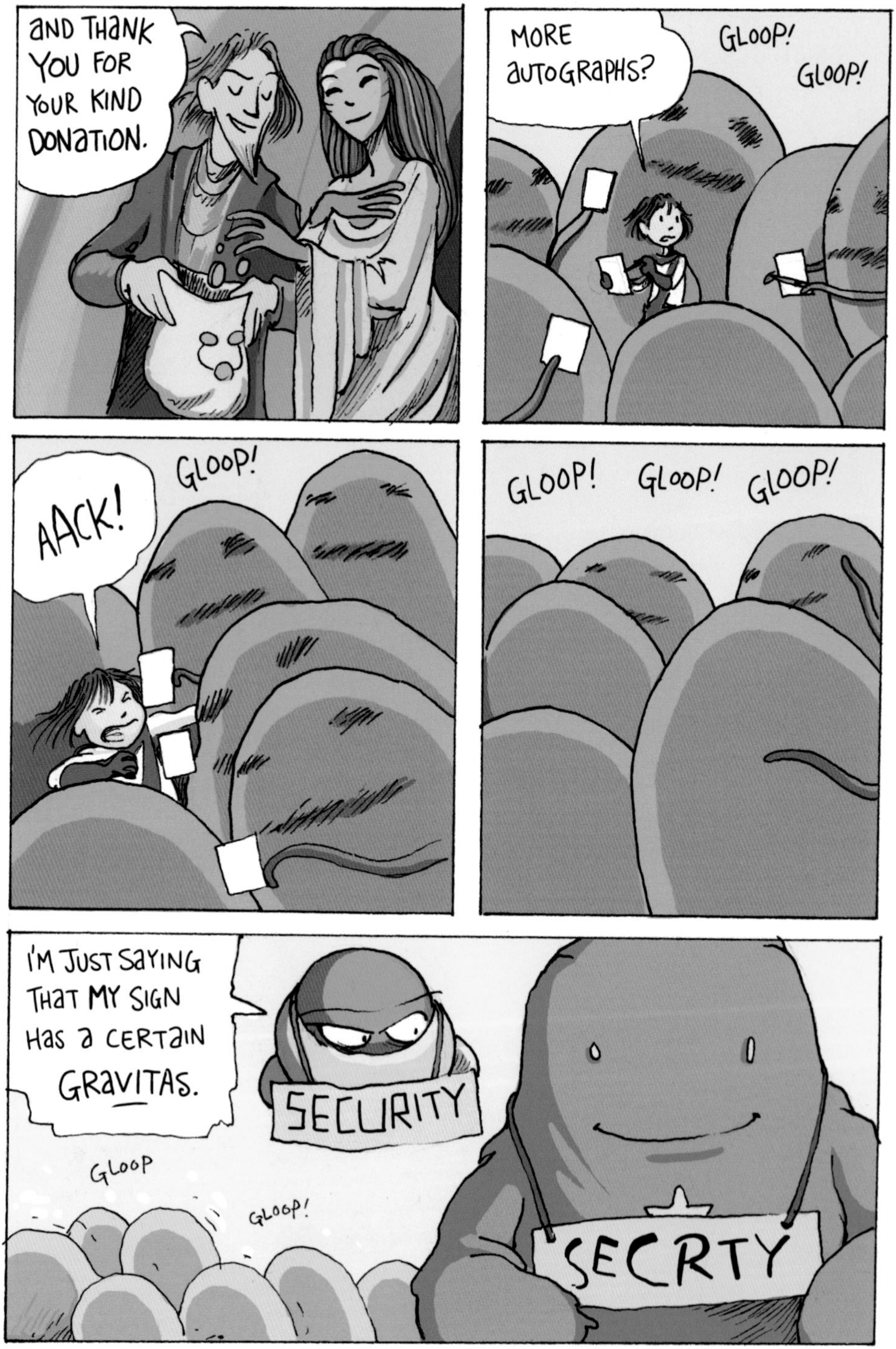
AND THANK YOU FOR YOUR KIND DONATION.
MORE AUTOGRAPHS?
GLOOP!
GLOOP!
AACK!
GLOOP!
GLOOP!
GLOOP!
GLOOP!
I'M JUST SAYING THAT MY SIGN HAS A CERTAIN GRAVITAS.
SECURITY
SECRTY
GLOOP
GLOOP!

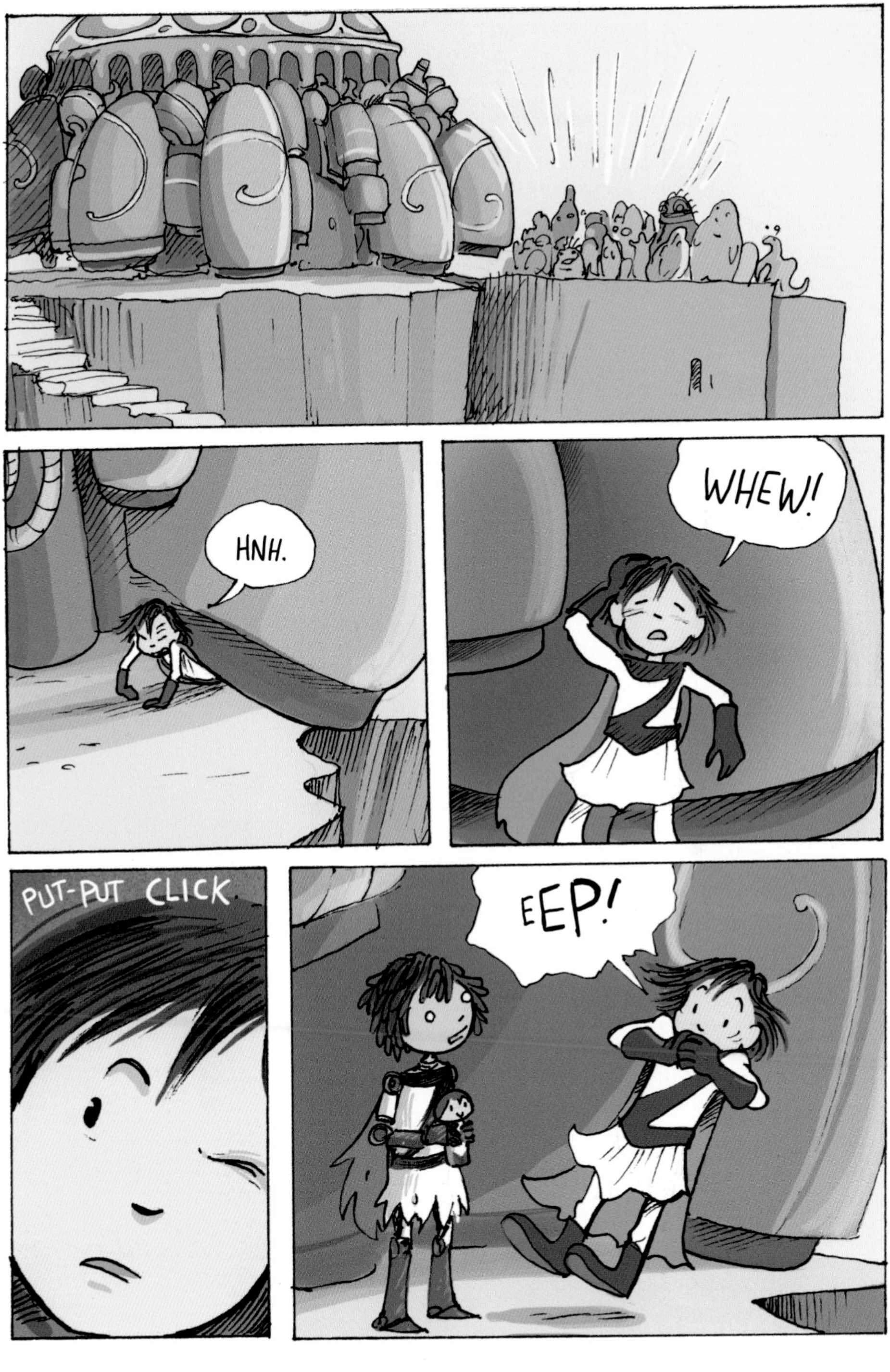
HNH.
WHEW!
PUT-PUT CLICK
EEP!

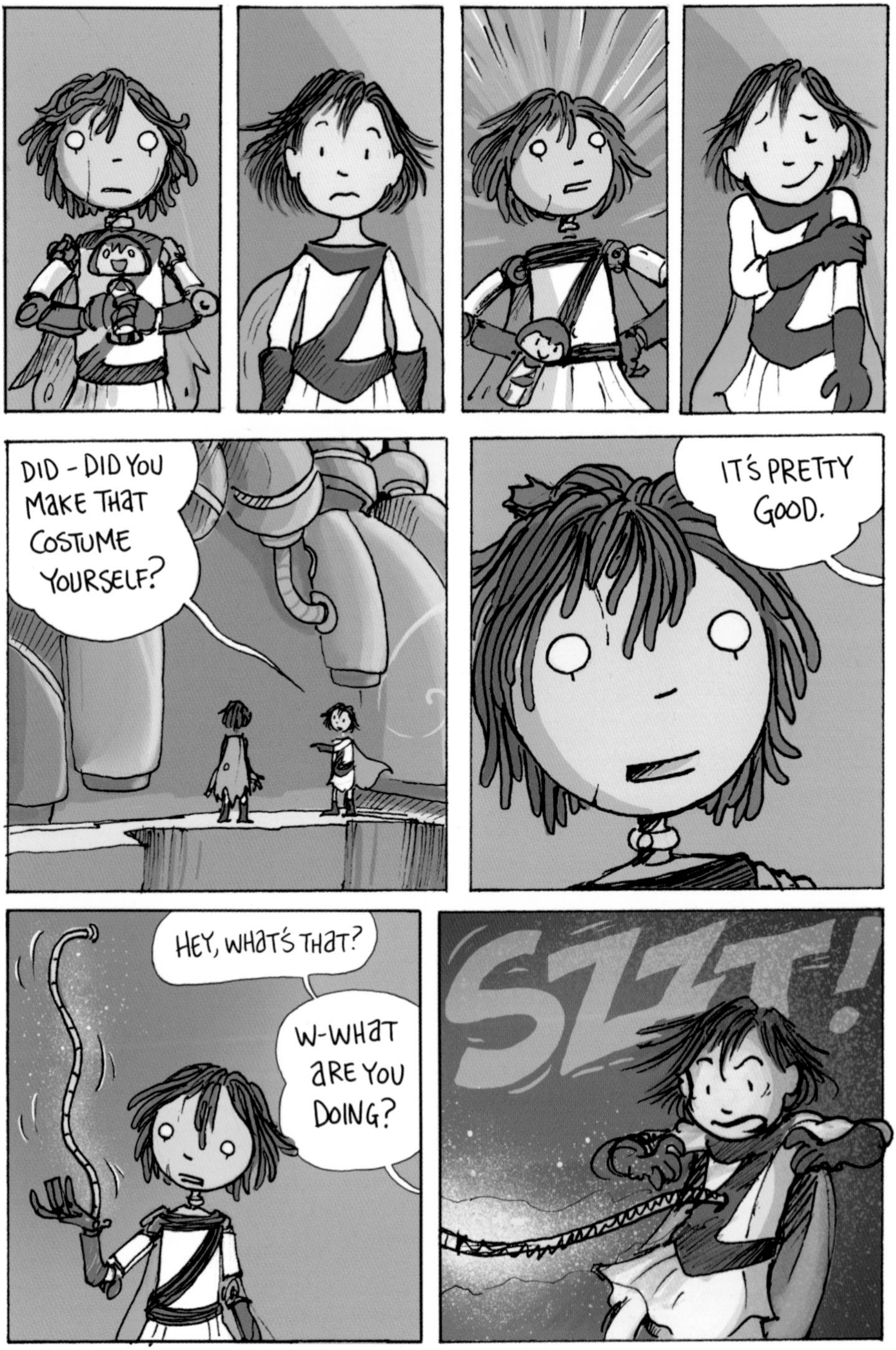
DID - DID YOU MAKE THAT COSTUME YOURSELF?
IT'S PRETTY GOOD.
HEY, WHAT'S THAT?
W-WHAT ARE YOU DOING?
SZZT!

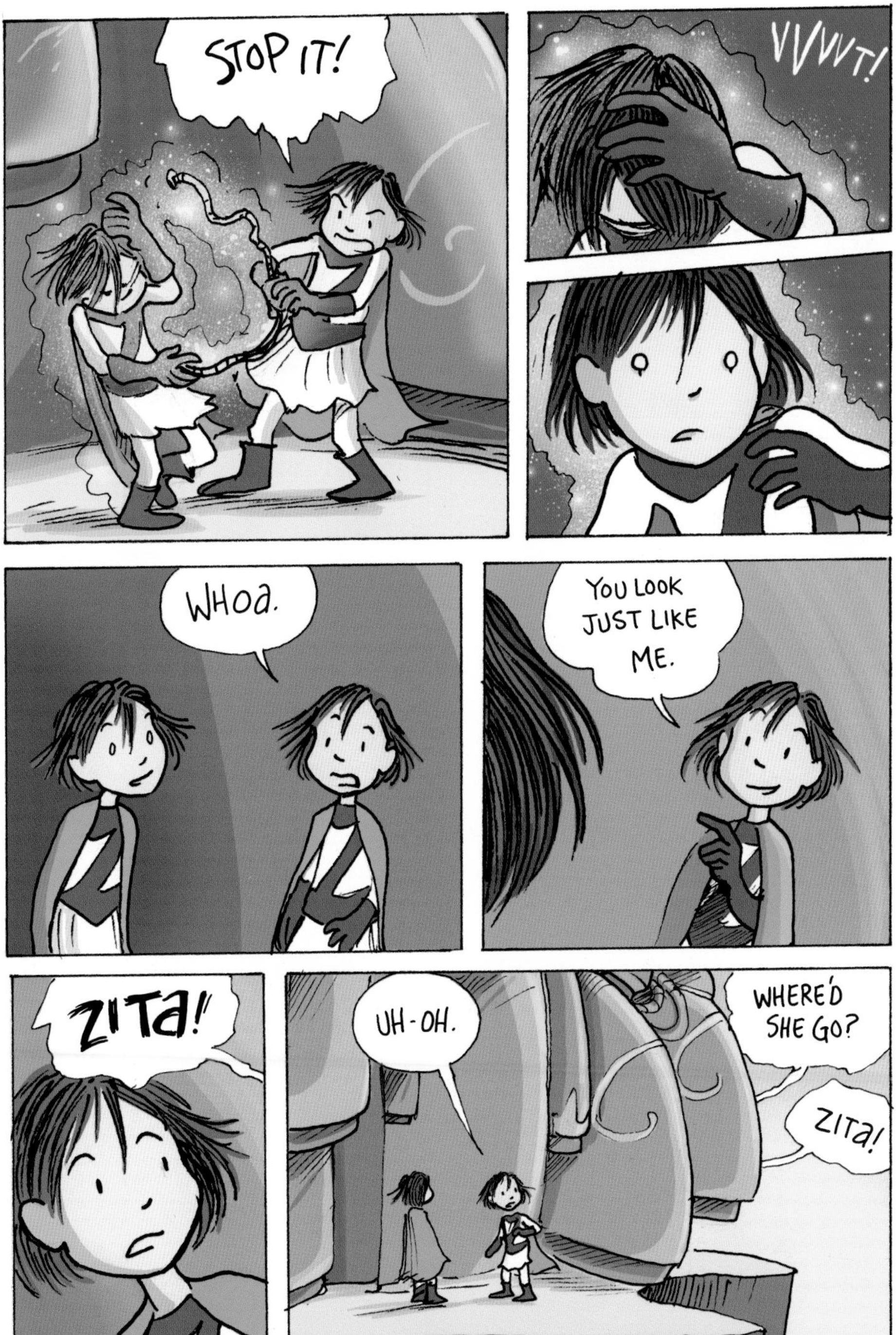
STOP IT!
VVVVT!
WHOa.
YOU LOOK JUST LIKE ME.
ZITa!
UH-OH.
WHERE'D SHE GO?
ZITa!

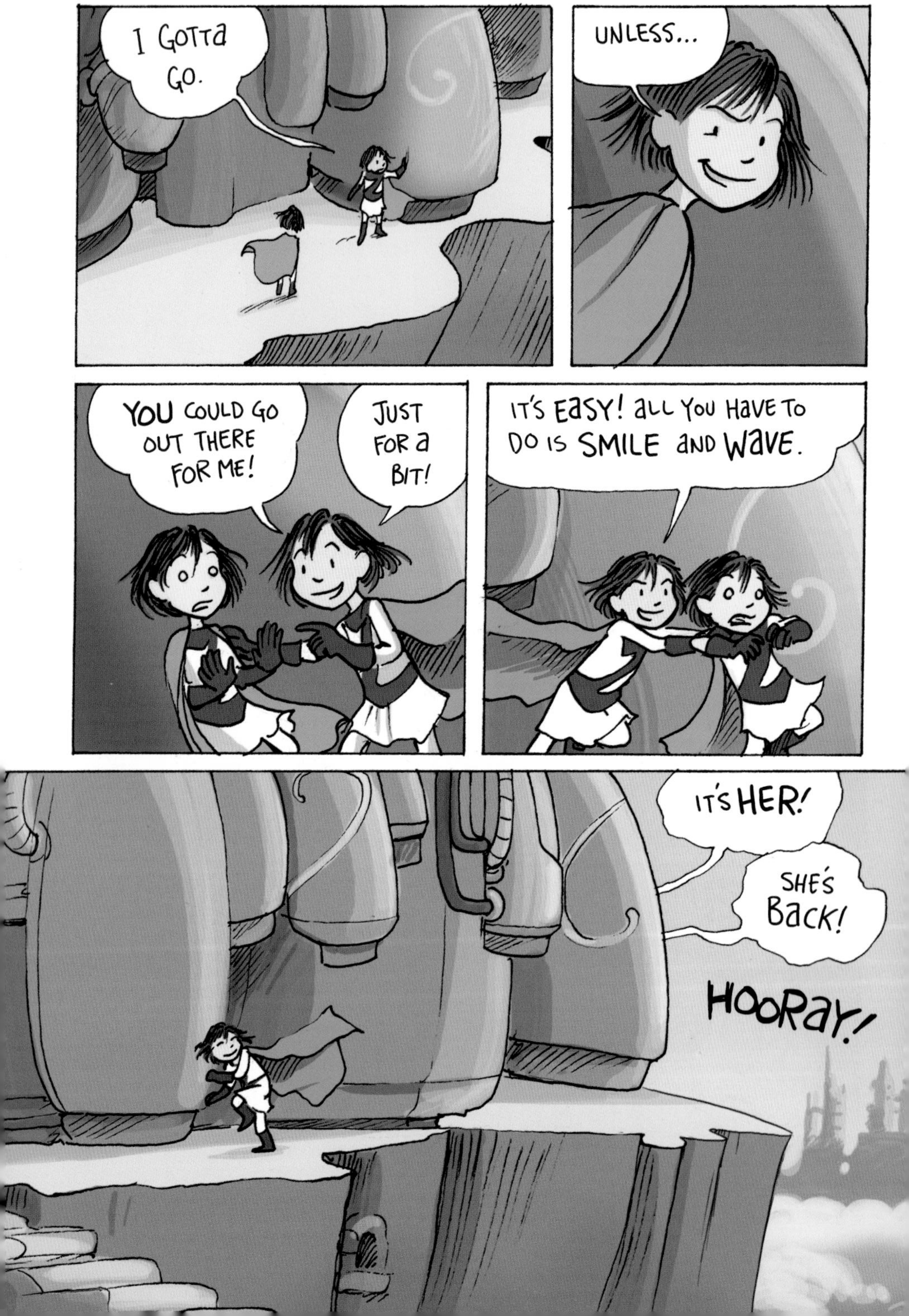
I GOTTA GO.
UNLESS...
YOU COULD GO OUT THERE FOR ME!
JUST FOR A BIT!
IT'S EASY! ALL YOU HAVE TO DO IS SMILE AND WAVE.
IT'S HER!
SHE'S BACK!
HOORAY!

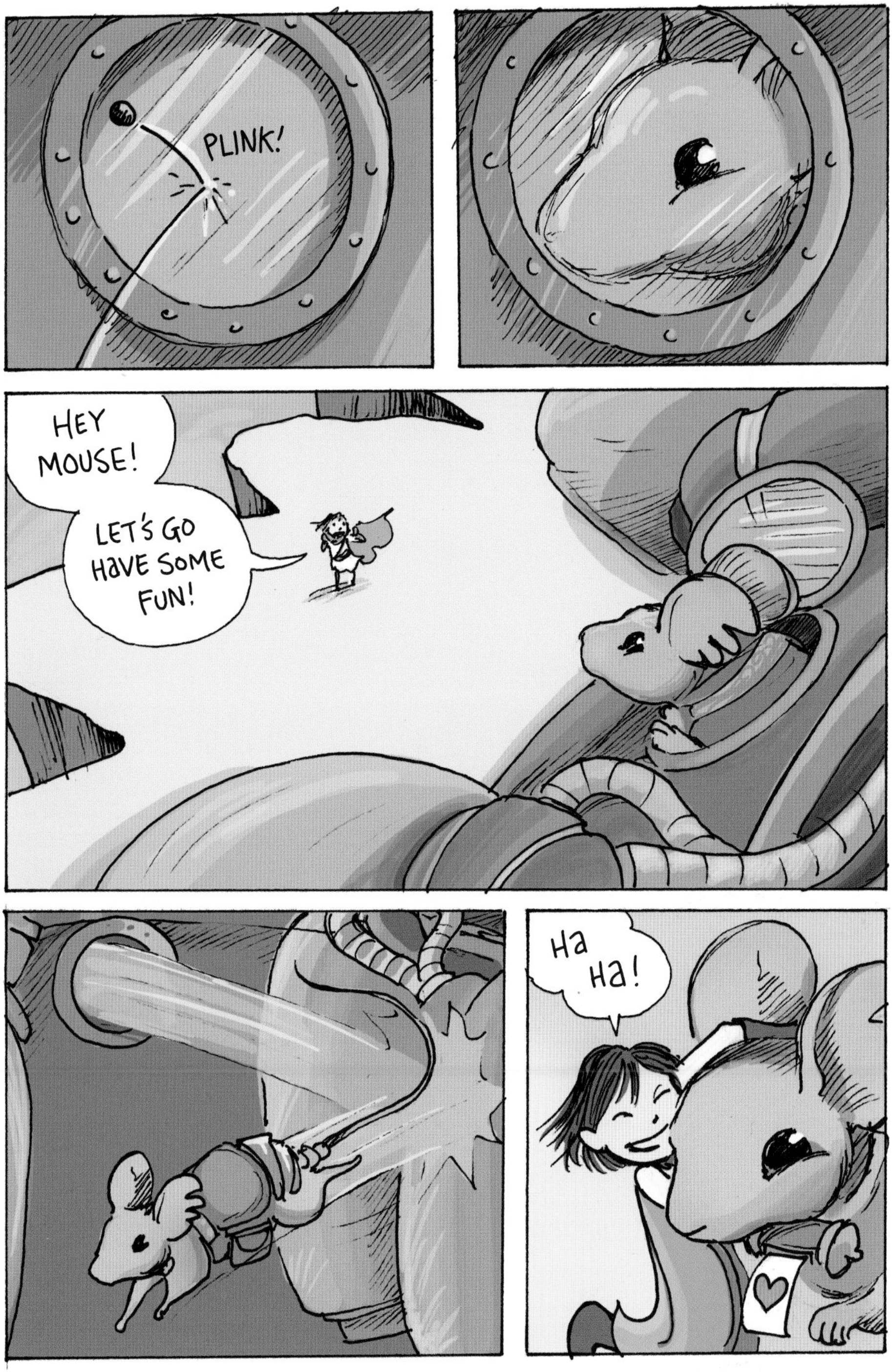
PLINK!
HEY MOUSE!
LET'S GO HAVE SOME FUN!
HA HA!

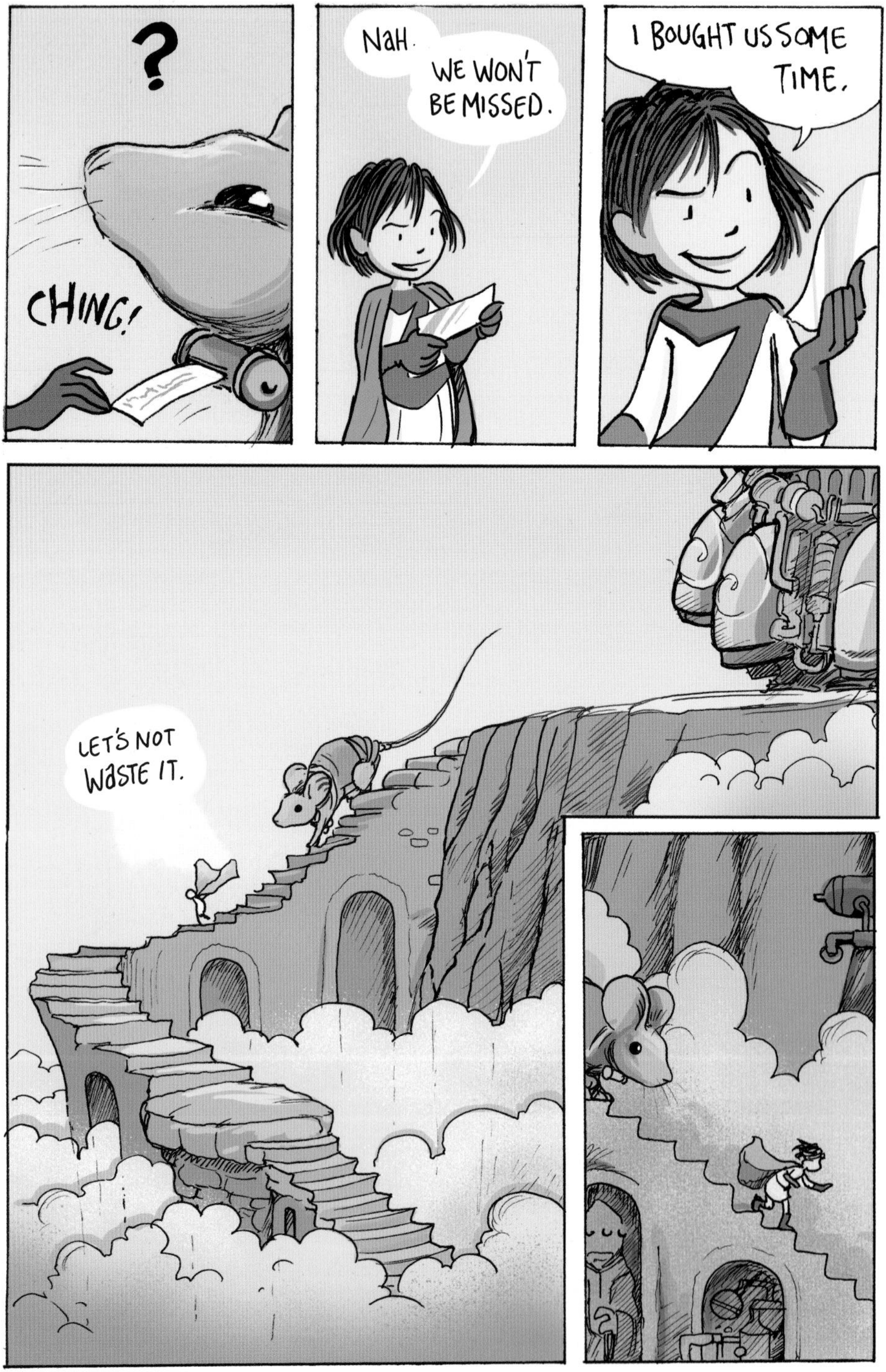
?
CHING!
NaH.
WE WON'T BE MISSED.
I BOUGHT US SOME TIME.
LET'S NOT WASTE IT.

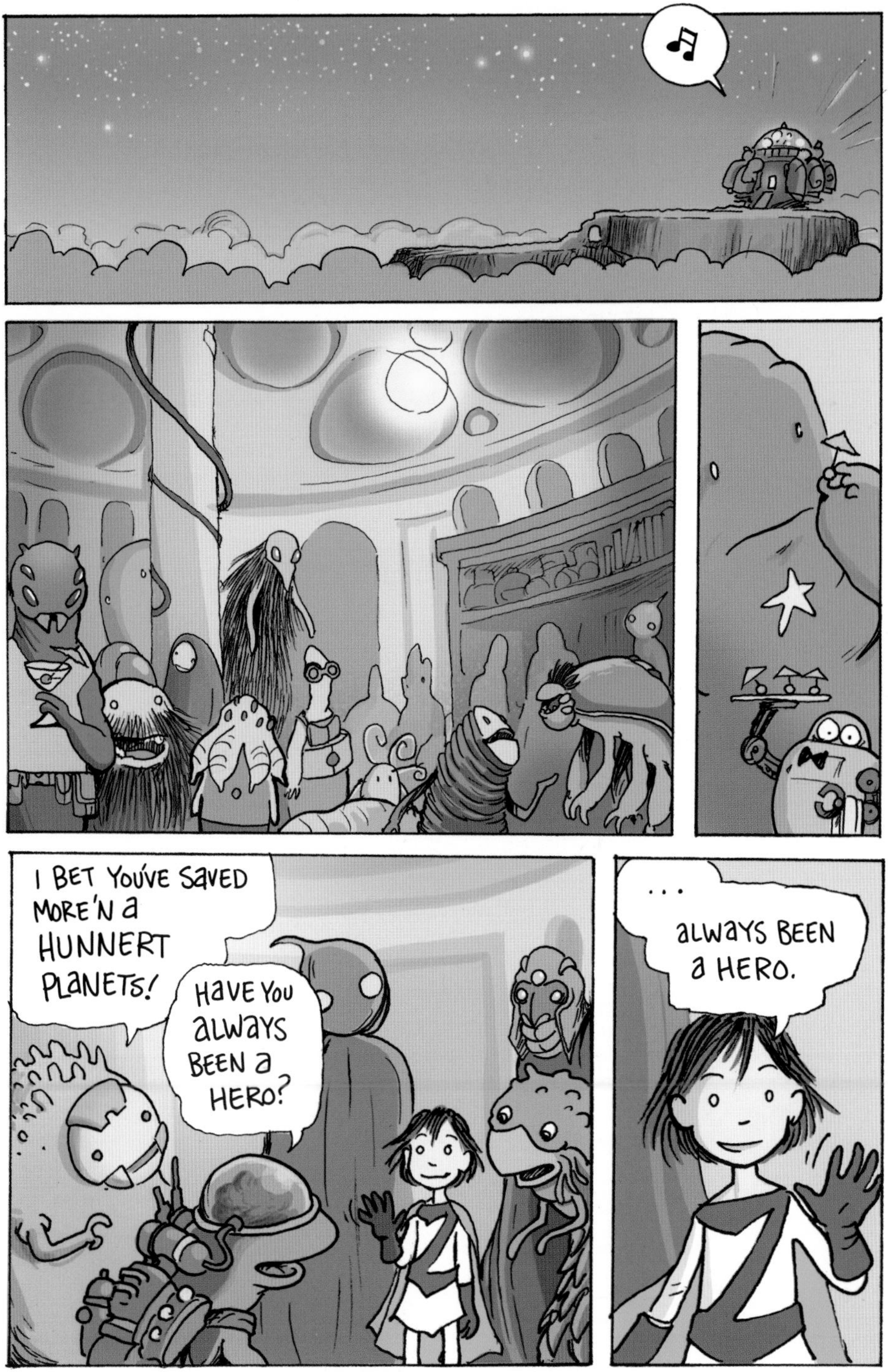
♫
I BET YOU'VE SAVED MORE'N A HUNNERT PLANETS!
HAVE YOU ALWAYS BEEN A HERO?
. . .
ALWAYS BEEN A HERO.

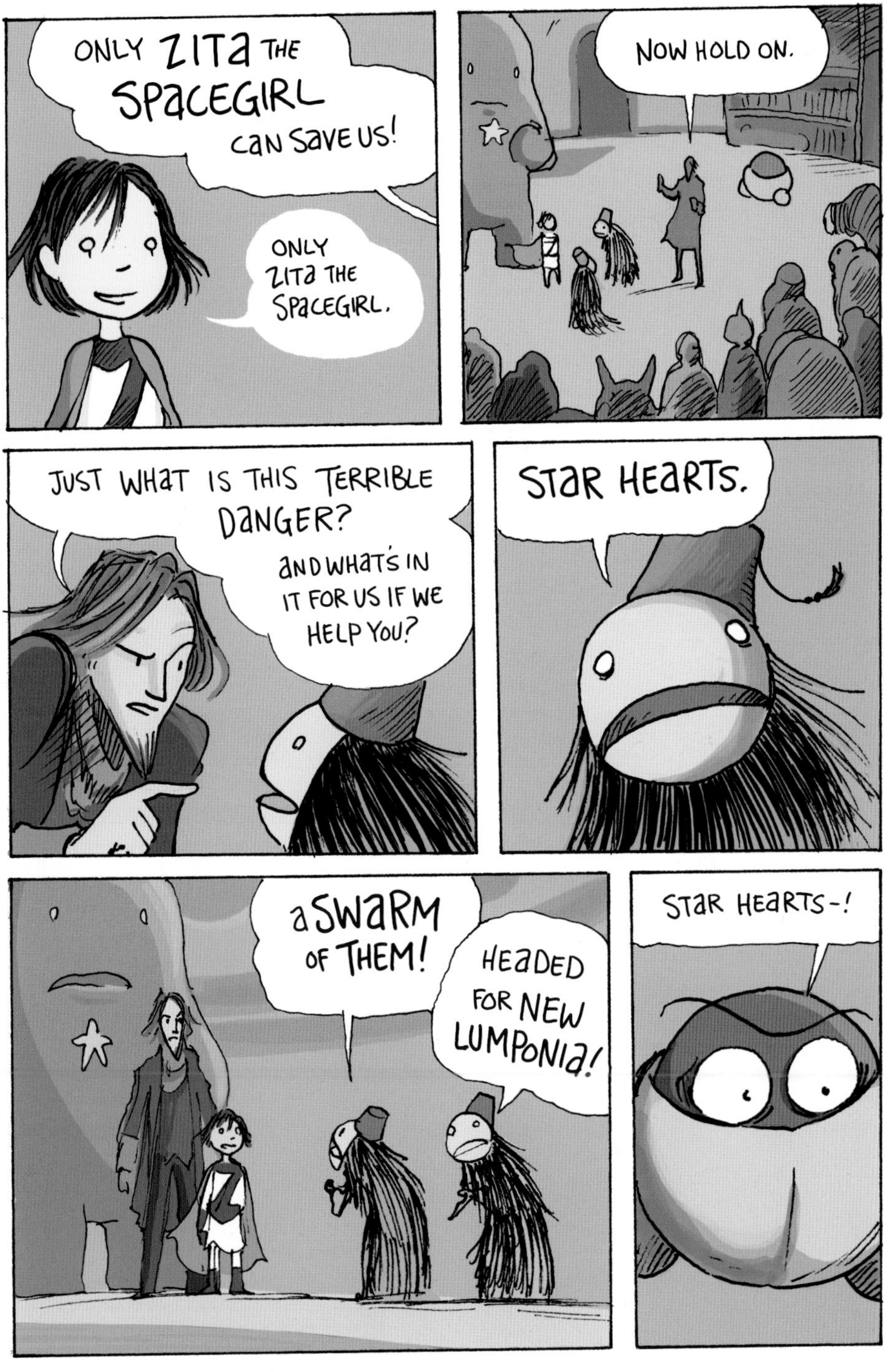
ONLY ZITA THE SPACEGIRL CAN SAVE US!
ONLY ZITA THE SPACEGIRL.
NOW HOLD ON.
JUST WHAT IS THIS TERRIBLE DANGER?
AND WHAT'S IN IT FOR US IF WE HELP YOU?
STAR HEARTS.
A SWARM OF THEM!
HEADED FOR NEW LUMPONIA!
STAR HEARTS-!

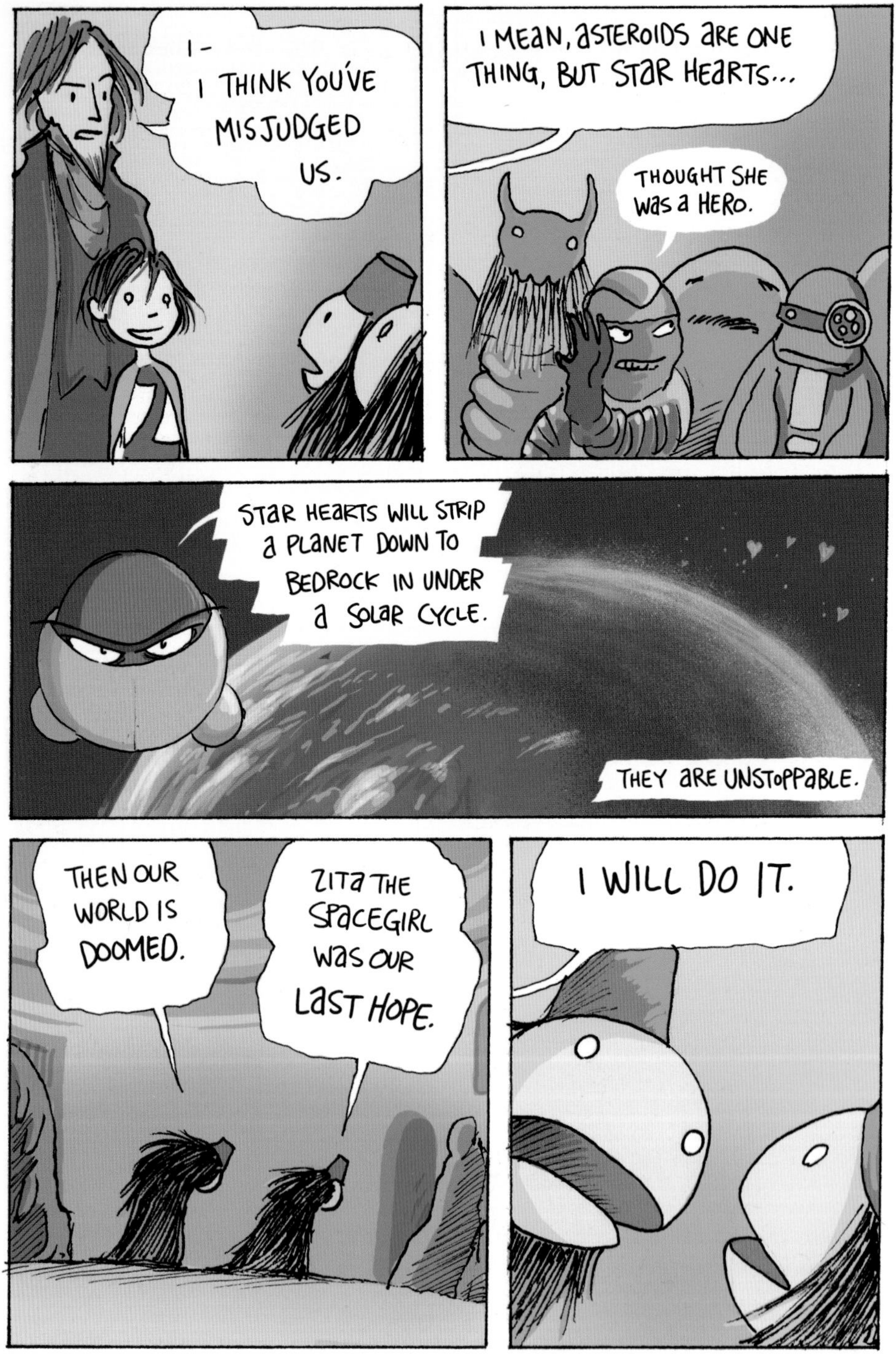
I-
I THINK YOU'VE MISJUDGED US.
I MEAN, ASTEROIDS ARE ONE THING, BUT STAR HEARTS...
THOUGHT SHE WAS A HERO.
STAR HEARTS WILL STRIP A PLANET DOWN TO BEDROCK IN UNDER A SOLAR CYCLE.
THEY ARE UNSTOPPABLE.
THEN OUR WORLD IS DOOMED.
ZITA THE SPACEGIRL WAS OUR LAST HOPE.
I WILL DO IT.

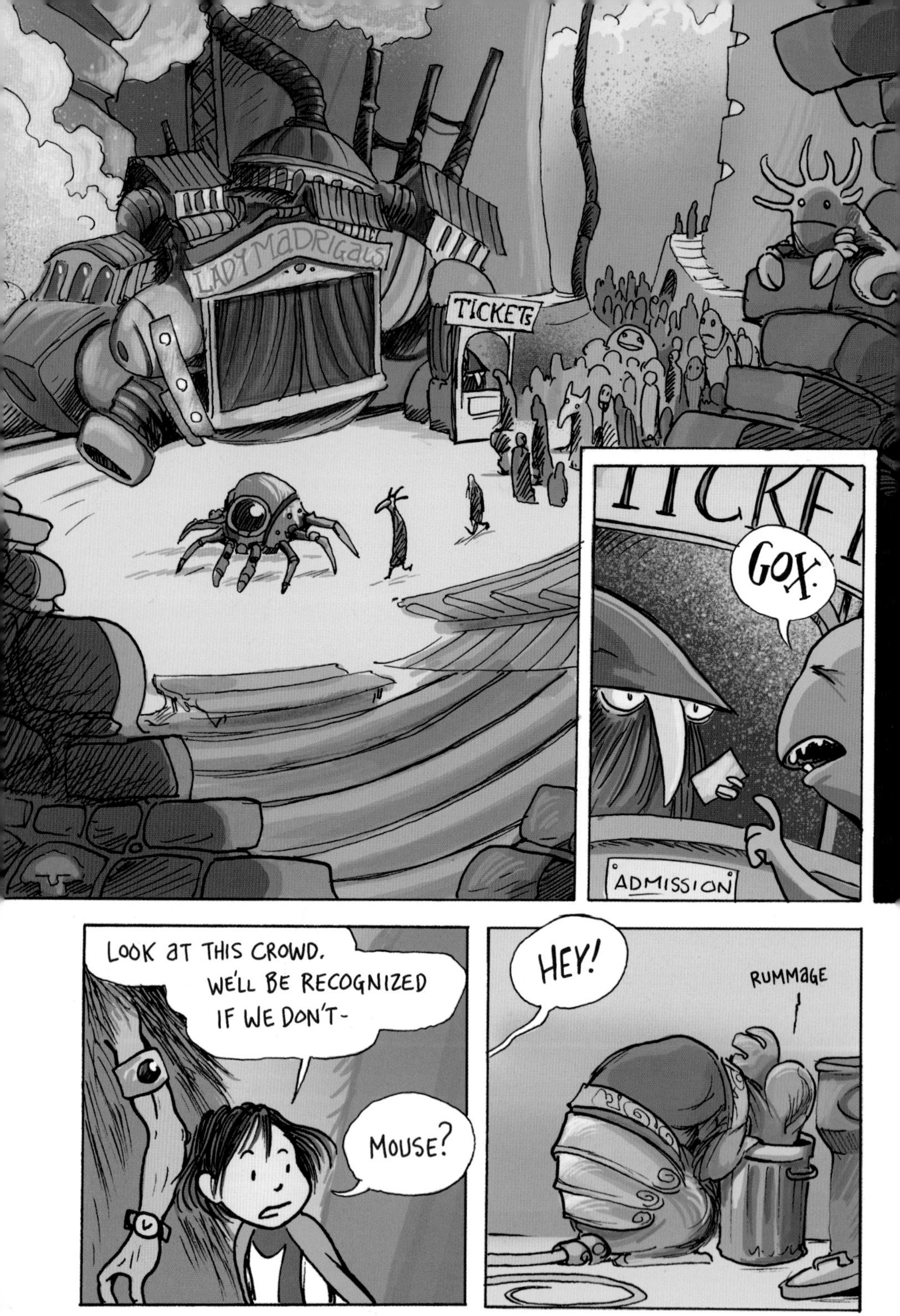
LADY MADRIGALS
TICKETS
TICKET
GOX.
ADMISSION
LOOK AT THIS CROWD. WE'LL BE RECOGNIZED IF WE DON'T-
MOUSE?
HEY!
RUMMAGE

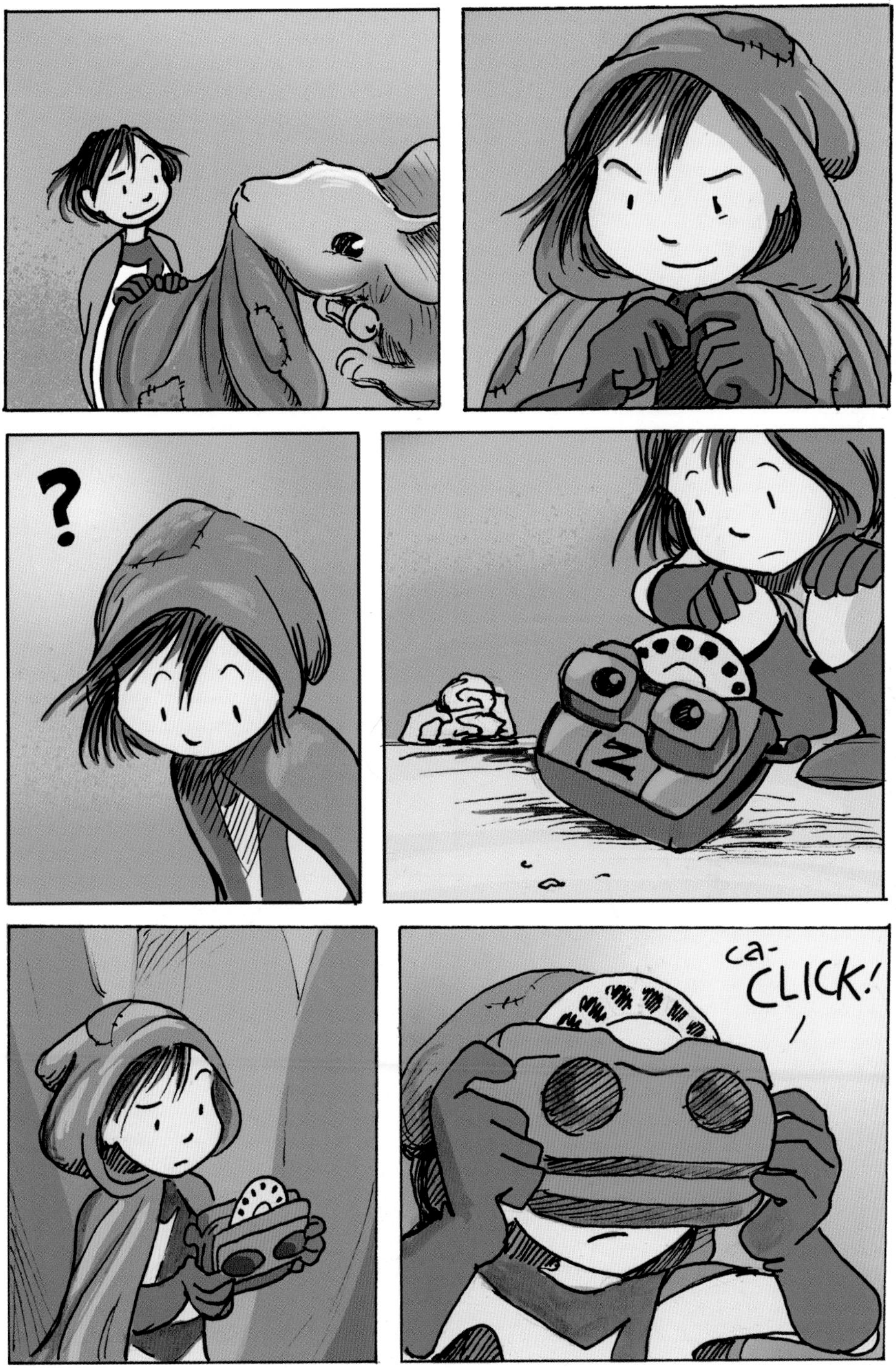
?
ca-
CLICK!

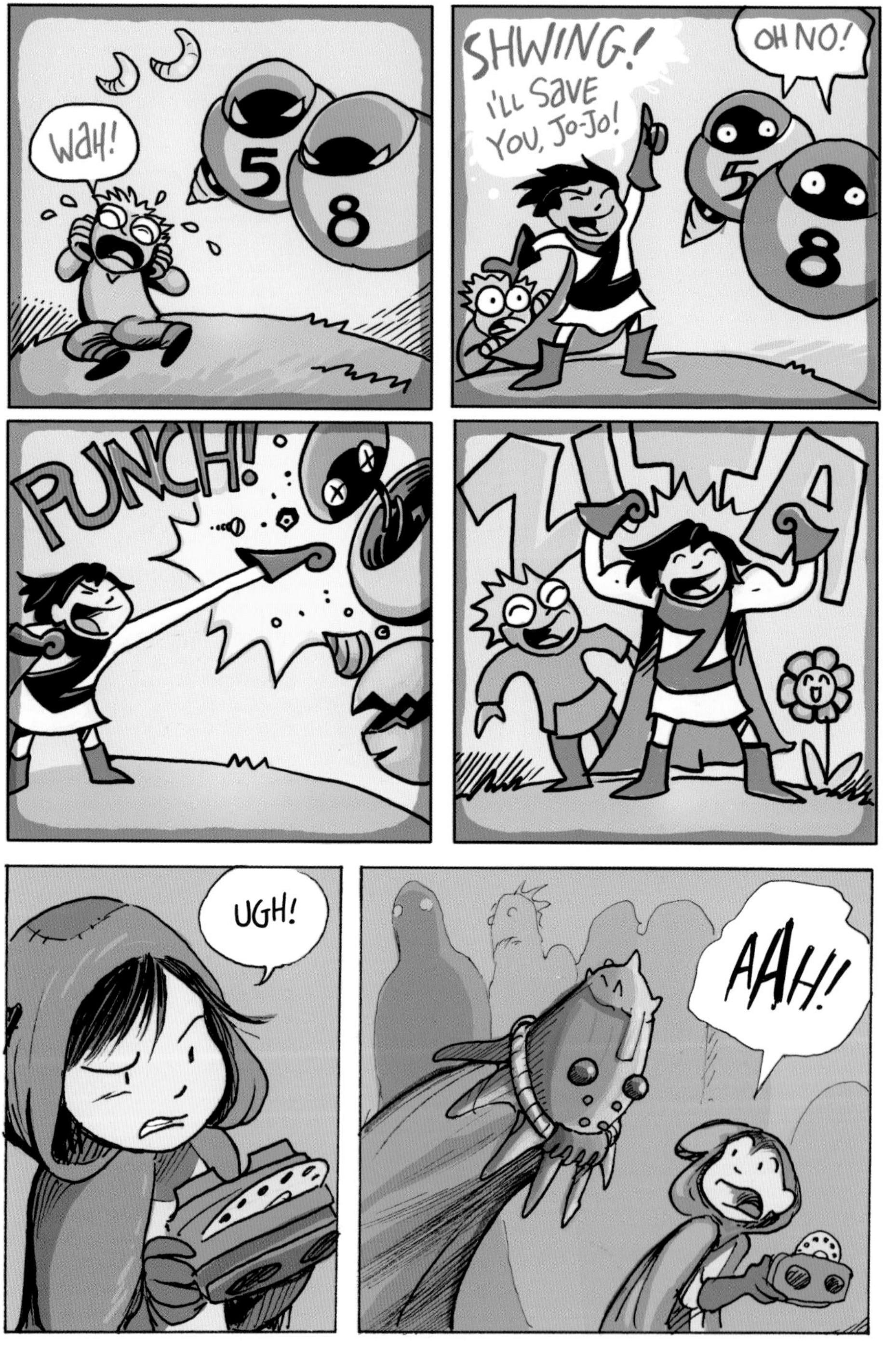
WAH!
SHWING!
I'LL SAVE YOU, JO-JO!
OH NO!
PUNCH!
UGH!
AAH!

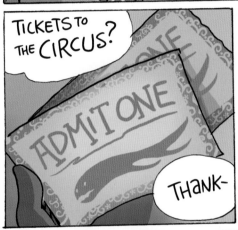

31

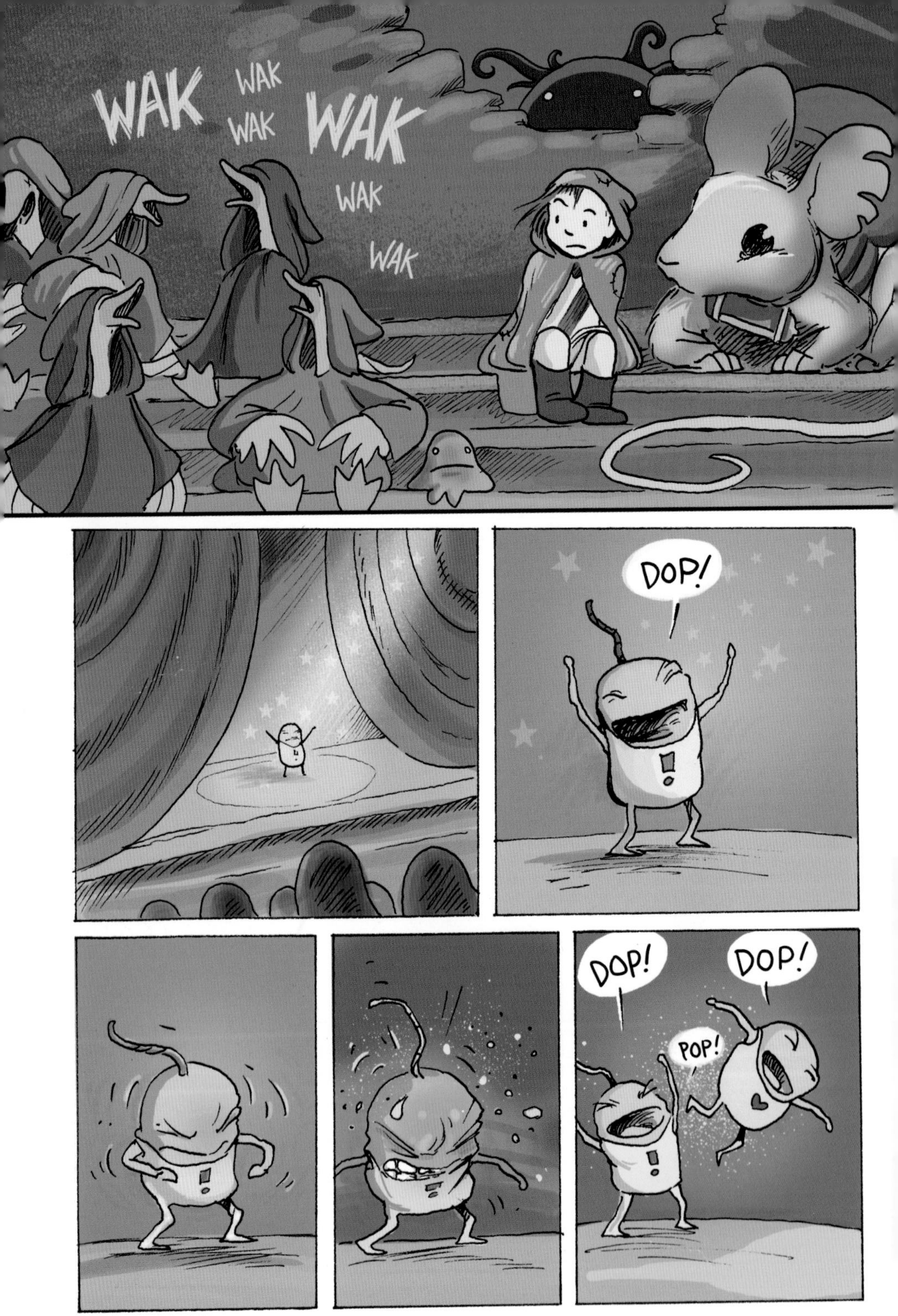
WAK
WAK
WAK
WAK
WAK
WAK
DOP!
DOP!
POP!
DOP!

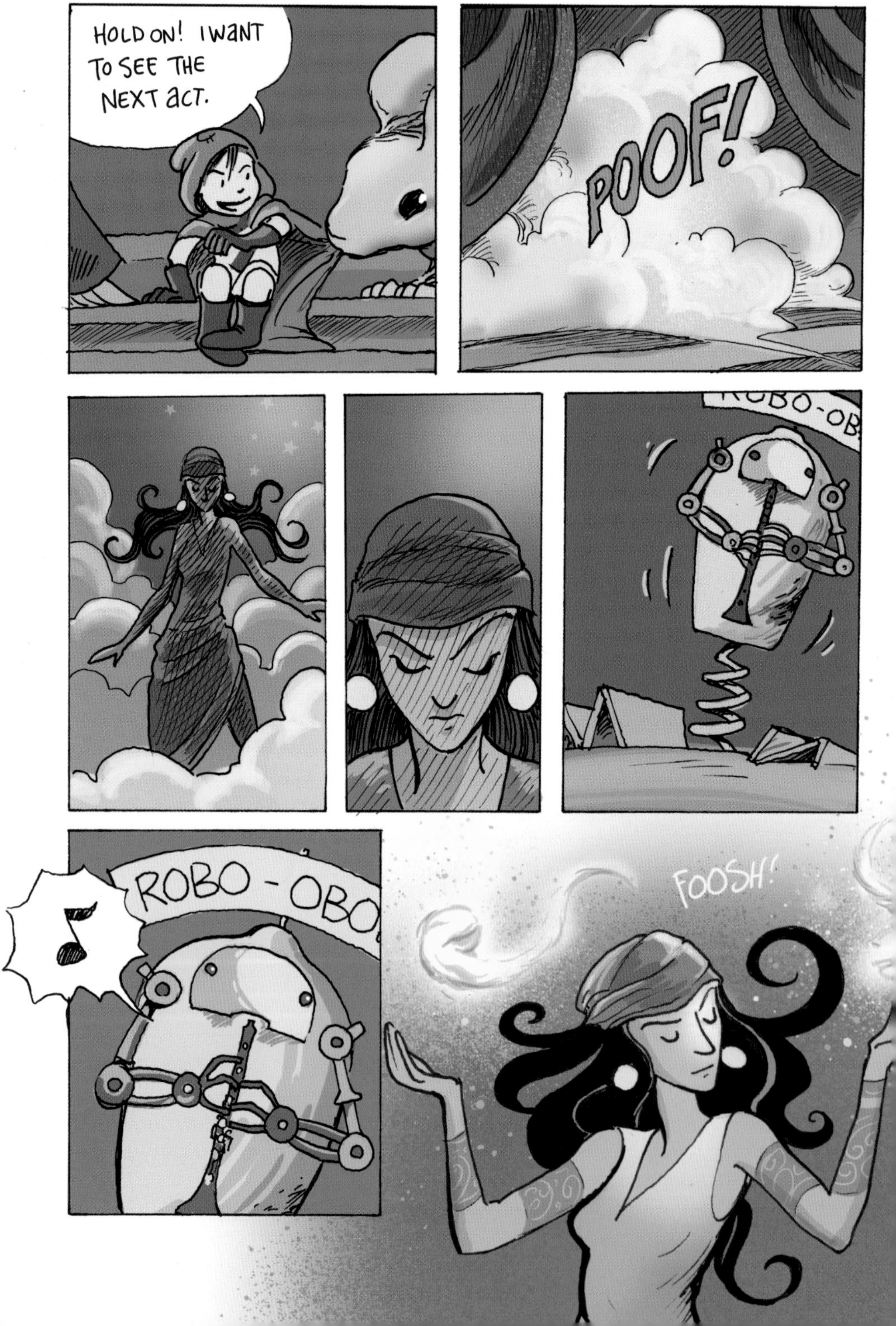
HOLD ON! I WANT TO SEE THE NEXT ACT.
POOF!
ROBO-OB
ROBO-OBO
FOOSH!

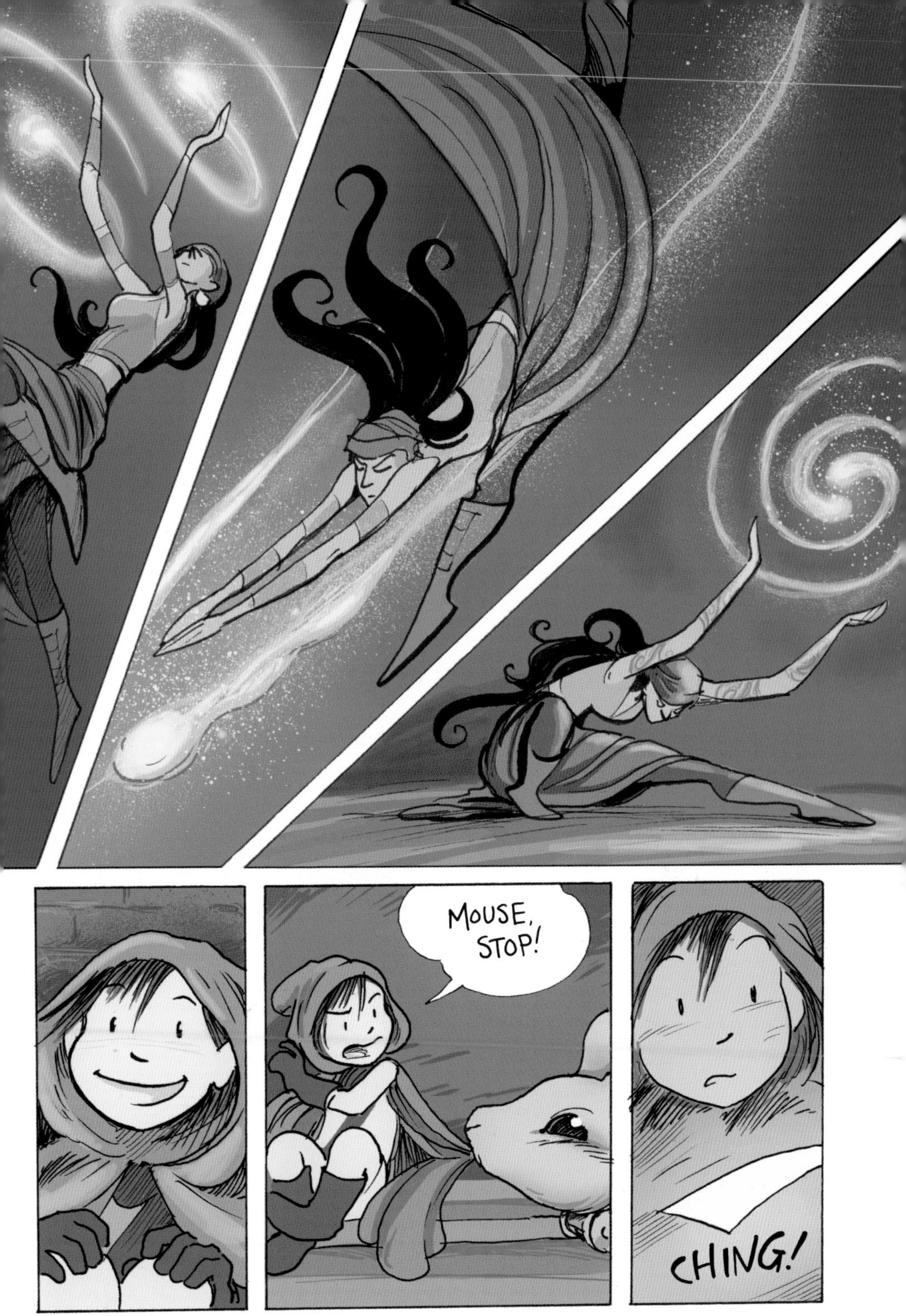
MOUSE, STOP!
CHING!

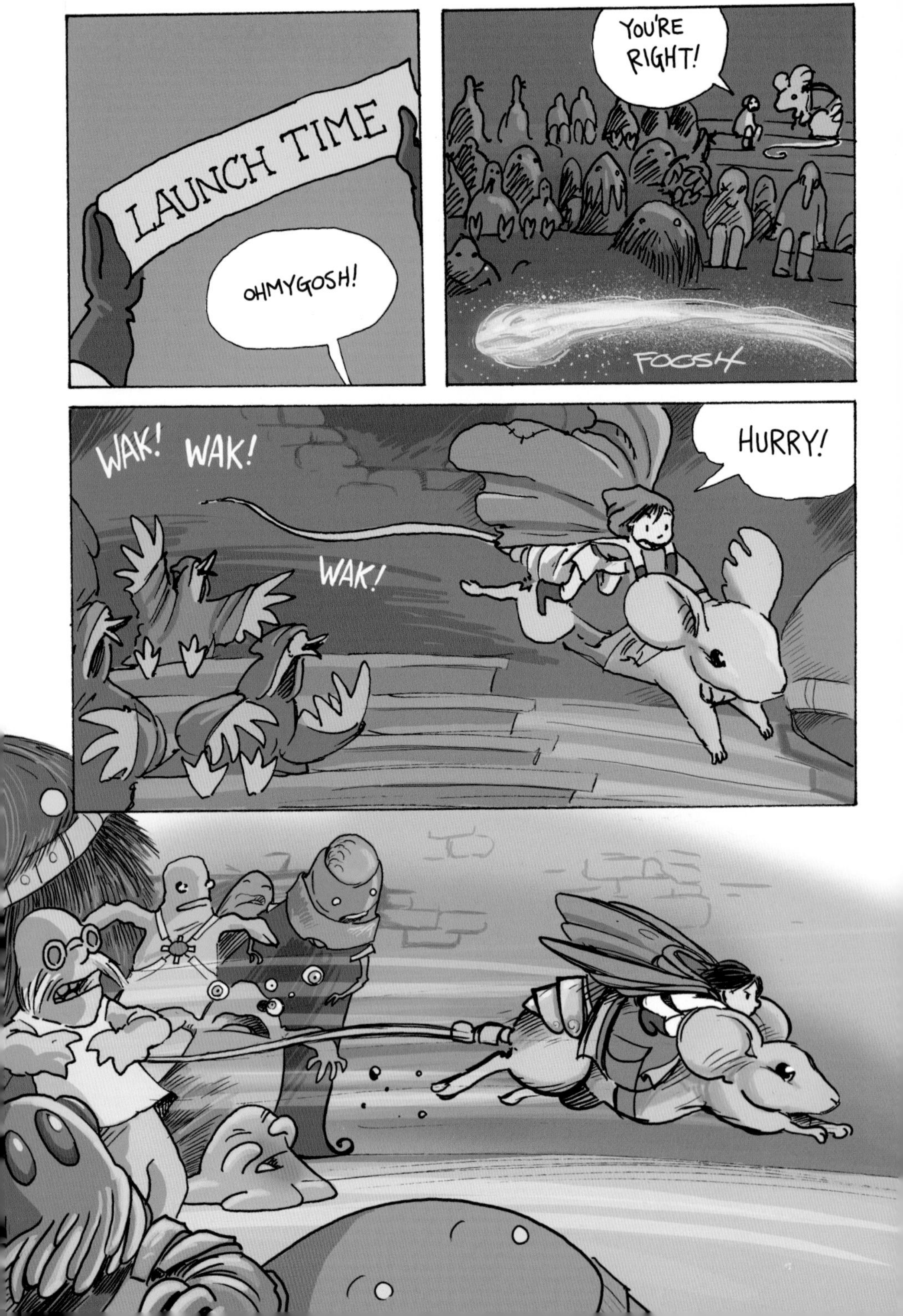
LAUNCH TIME
OHMYGOSH!
YOU'RE RIGHT!
FOOSH
WAK! WAK!
WAK!
HURRY!

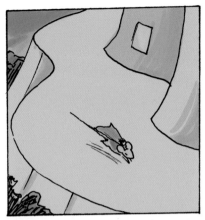

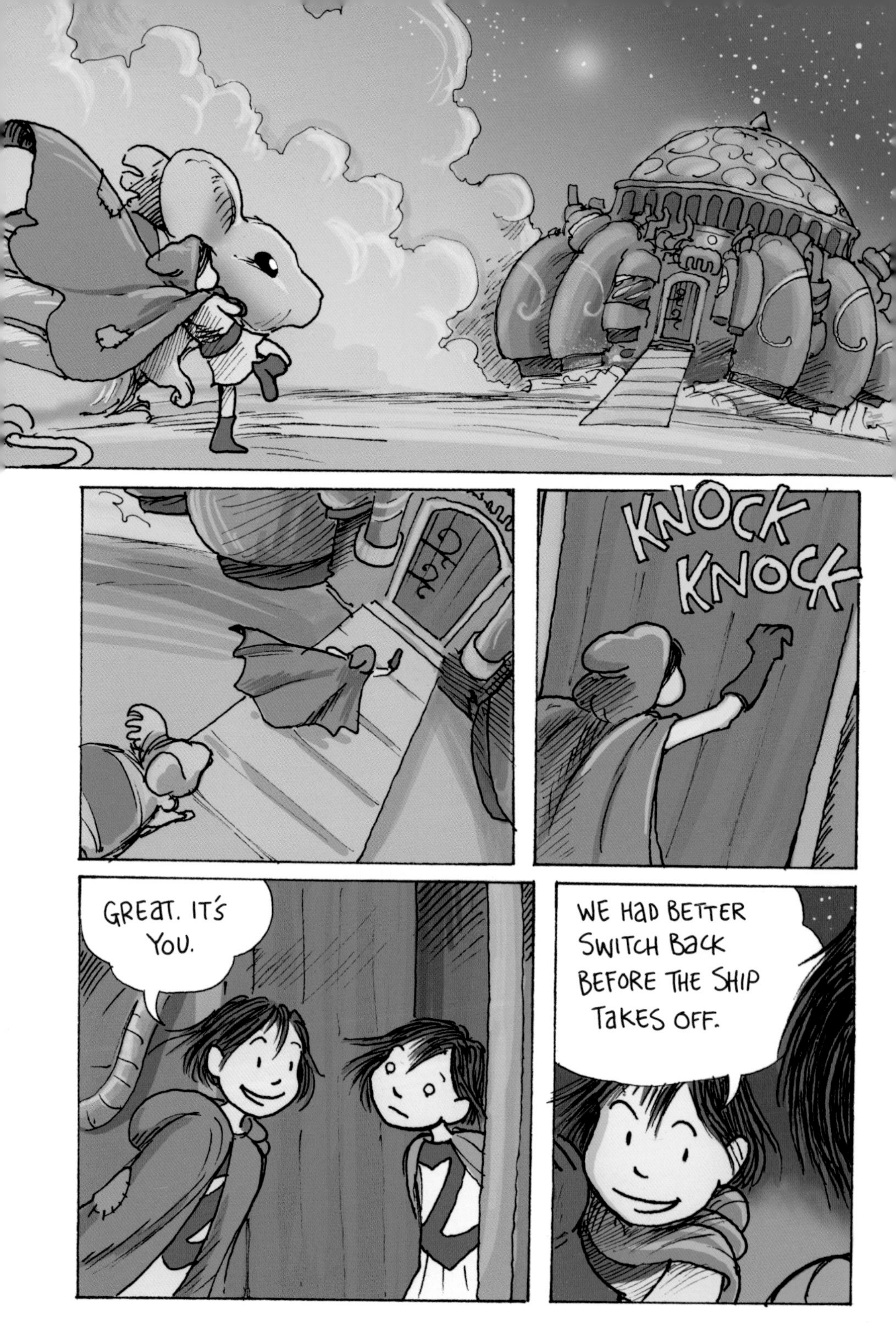
KNOCK KNOCK
GREAT. IT'S YOU.
WE HAD BETTER SWITCH BACK BEFORE THE SHIP TAKES OFF.

39

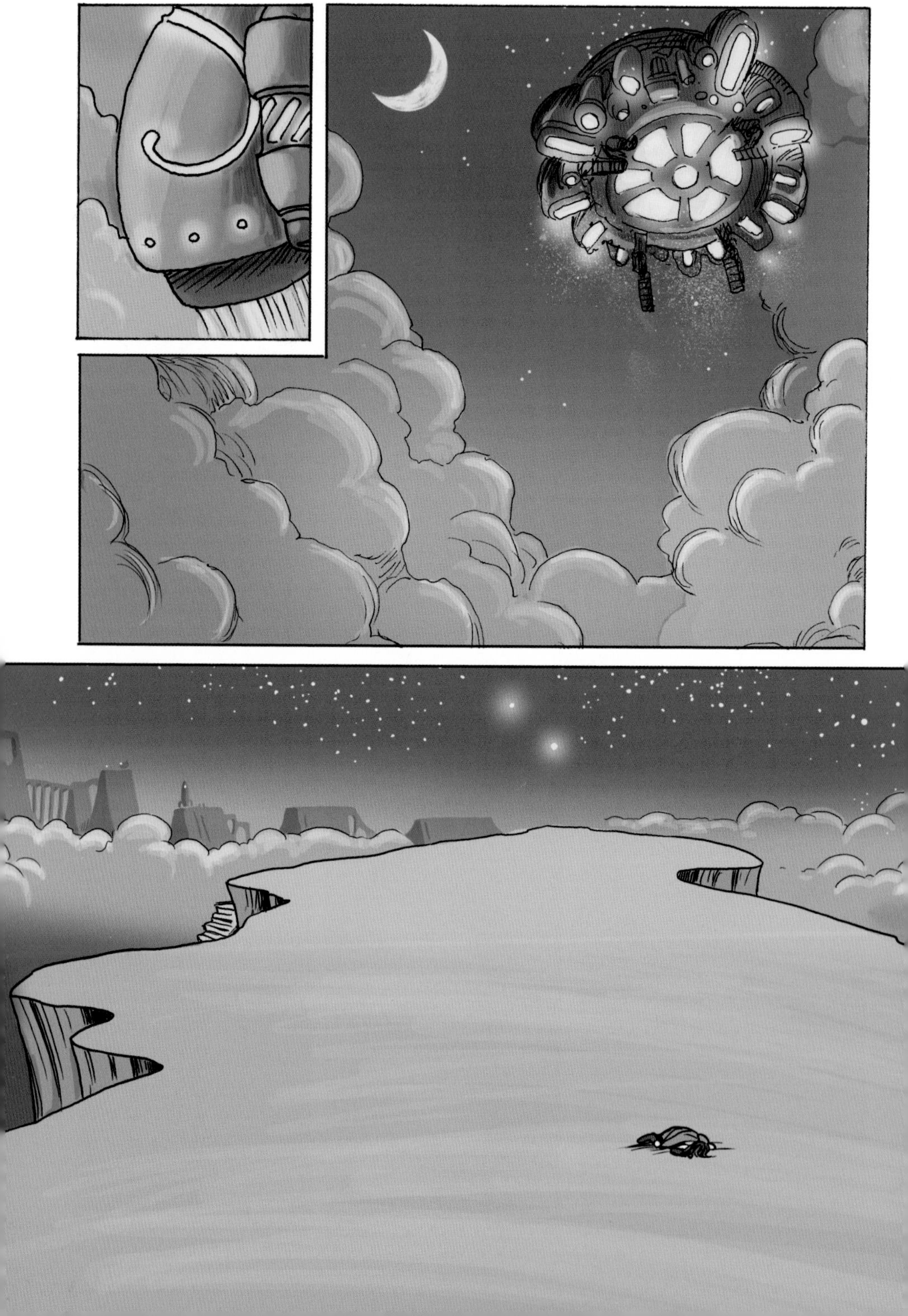

Chapter
Two

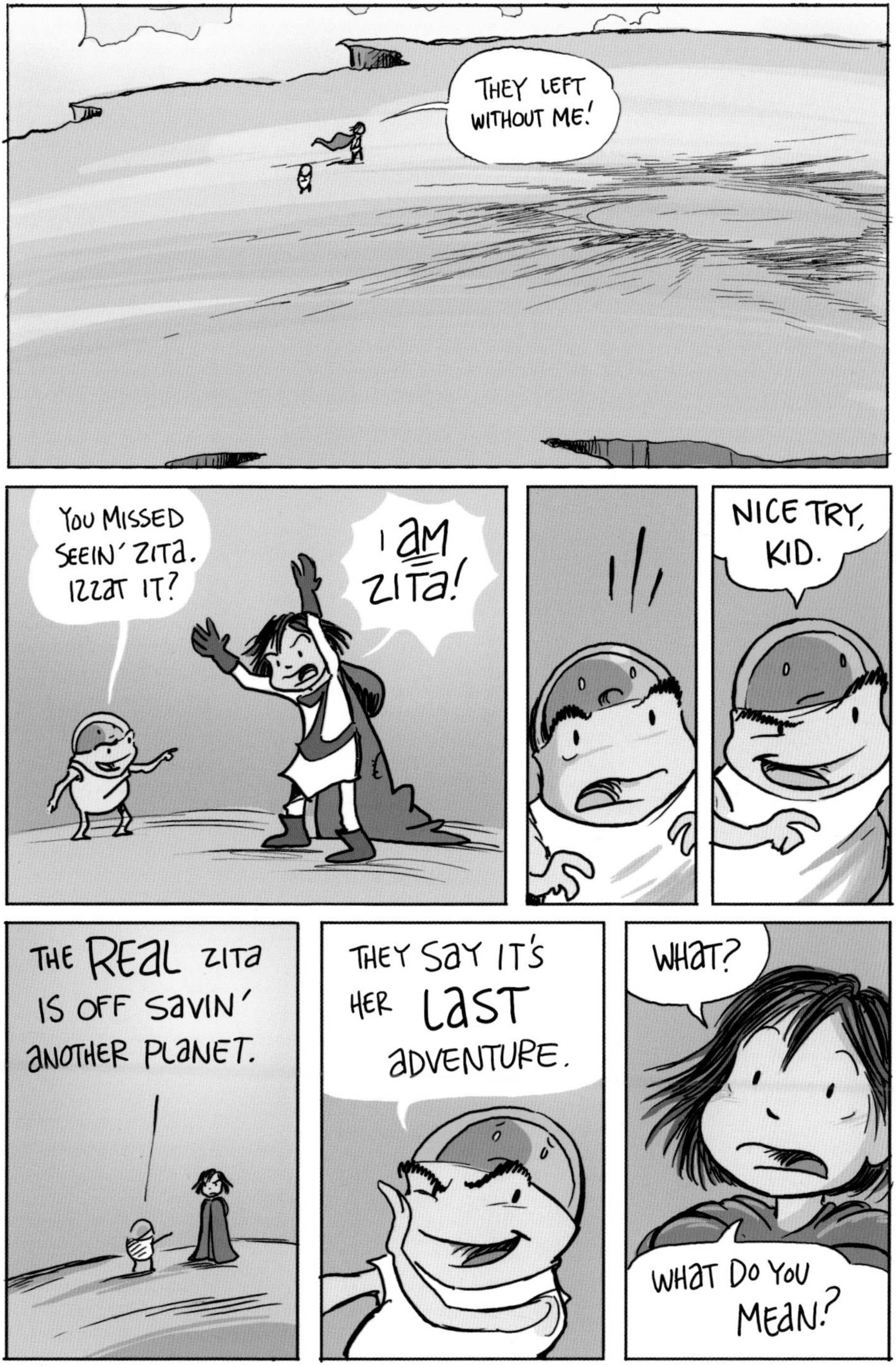
THEY LEFT WITHOUT ME!
YOU MISSED SEEIN' ZITA. IZZAT IT?
I AM ZITA!
NICE TRY, KID.
THE REAL ZITA IS OFF SAVIN' ANOTHER PLANET.
THEY SAY IT'S HER LAST ADVENTURE.
WHAT?
WHAT DO YOU MEAN?

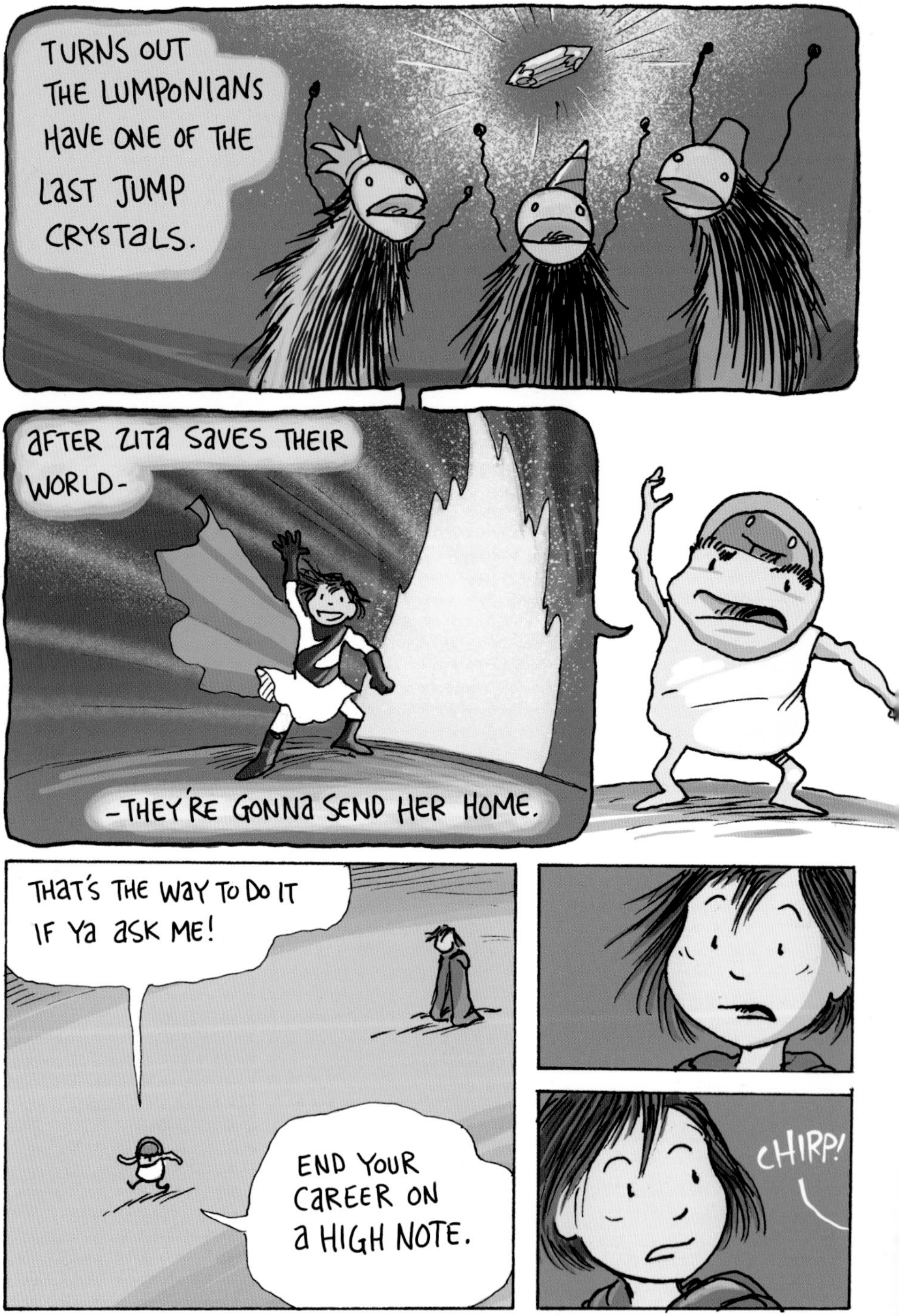
TURNS OUT THE LUMPONIANS HAVE ONE OF THE LAST JUMP CRYSTALS.
AFTER ZITA SAVES THEIR WORLD-
-THEY'RE GONNA SEND HER HOME.
THAT'S THE WAY TO DO IT IF YA ASK ME!
END YOUR CAREER ON A HIGH NOTE.
CHIRP!

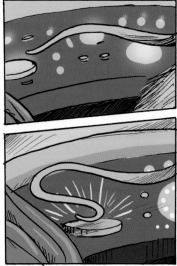

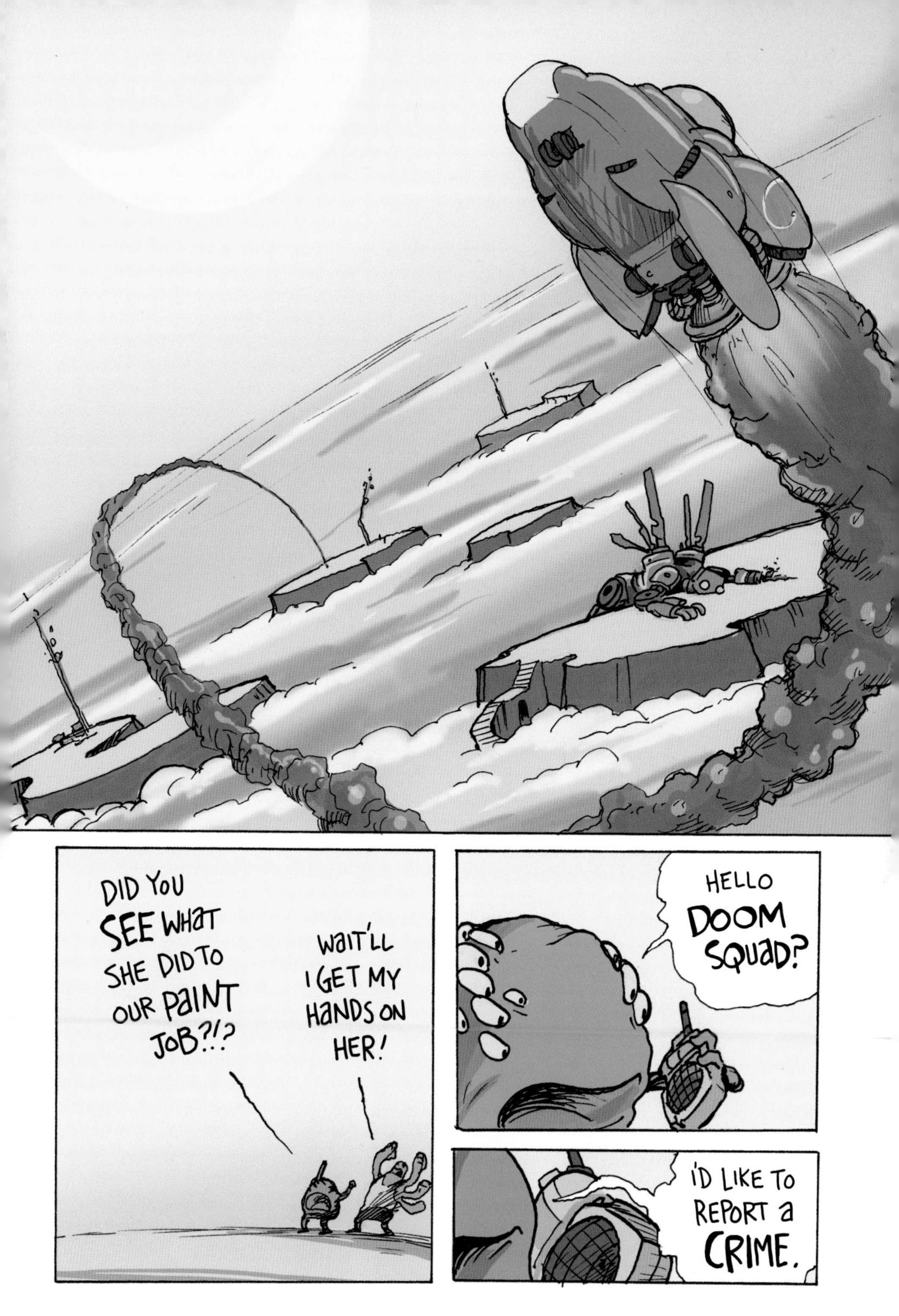

DID YOU SEE WHAT SHE DID TO OUR PAINT JOB?!?
WAIT'LL I GET MY HANDS ON HER!
HELLO DOOM SQUAD?
I'D LIKE TO REPORT a CRIME.

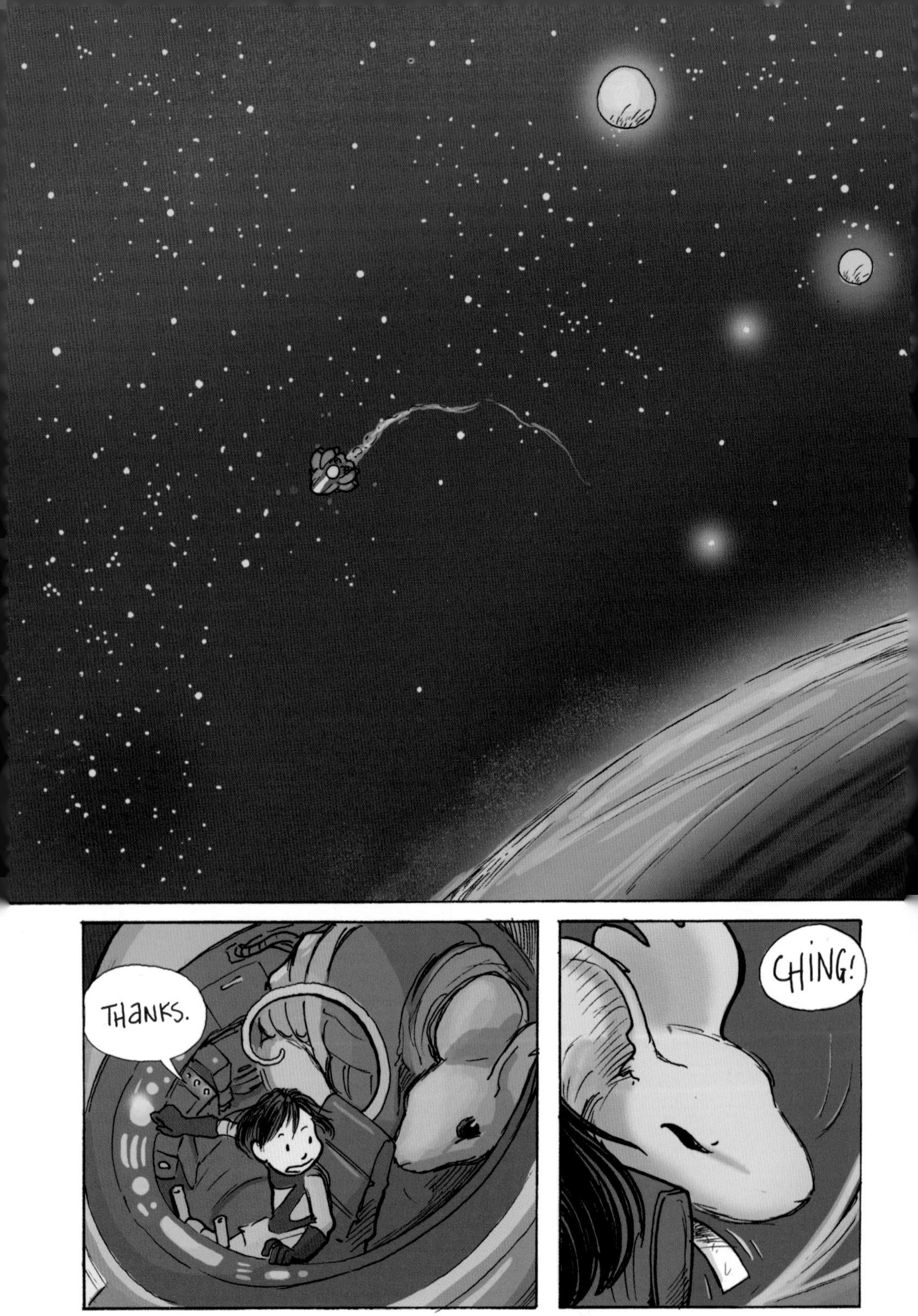
THANKS.
CHING!

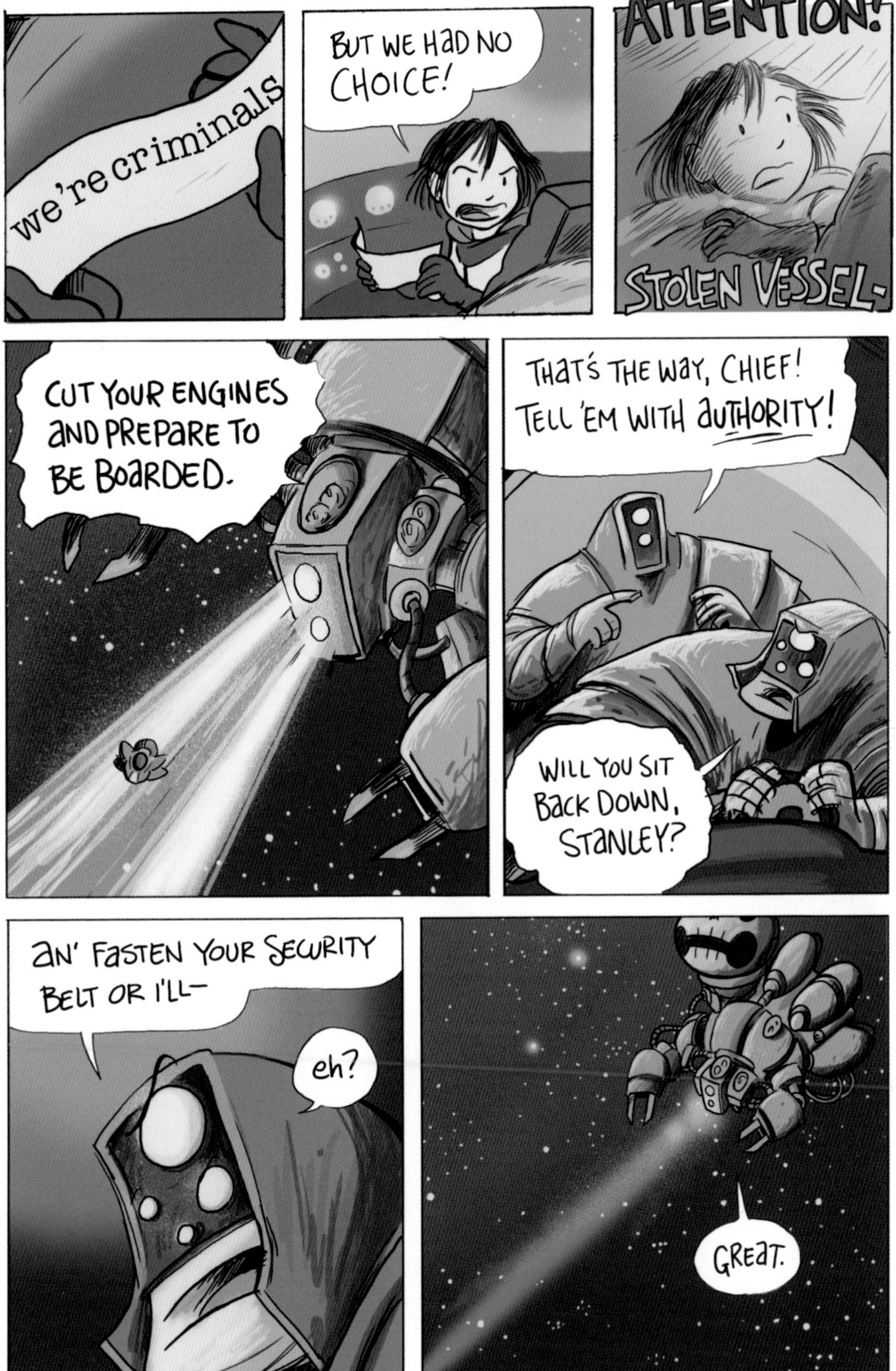
we're criminals
BUT WE HAD NO CHOICE!
ATTENTION!
STOLEN VESSEL-
CUT YOUR ENGINES AND PREPARE TO BE BOARDED.
THAT'S THE WAY, CHIEF! TELL 'EM WITH AUTHORITY!
WILL YOU SIT BACK DOWN, STANLEY?
AN' FASTEN YOUR SECURITY BELT OR I'LL—
eh?
GREAT.

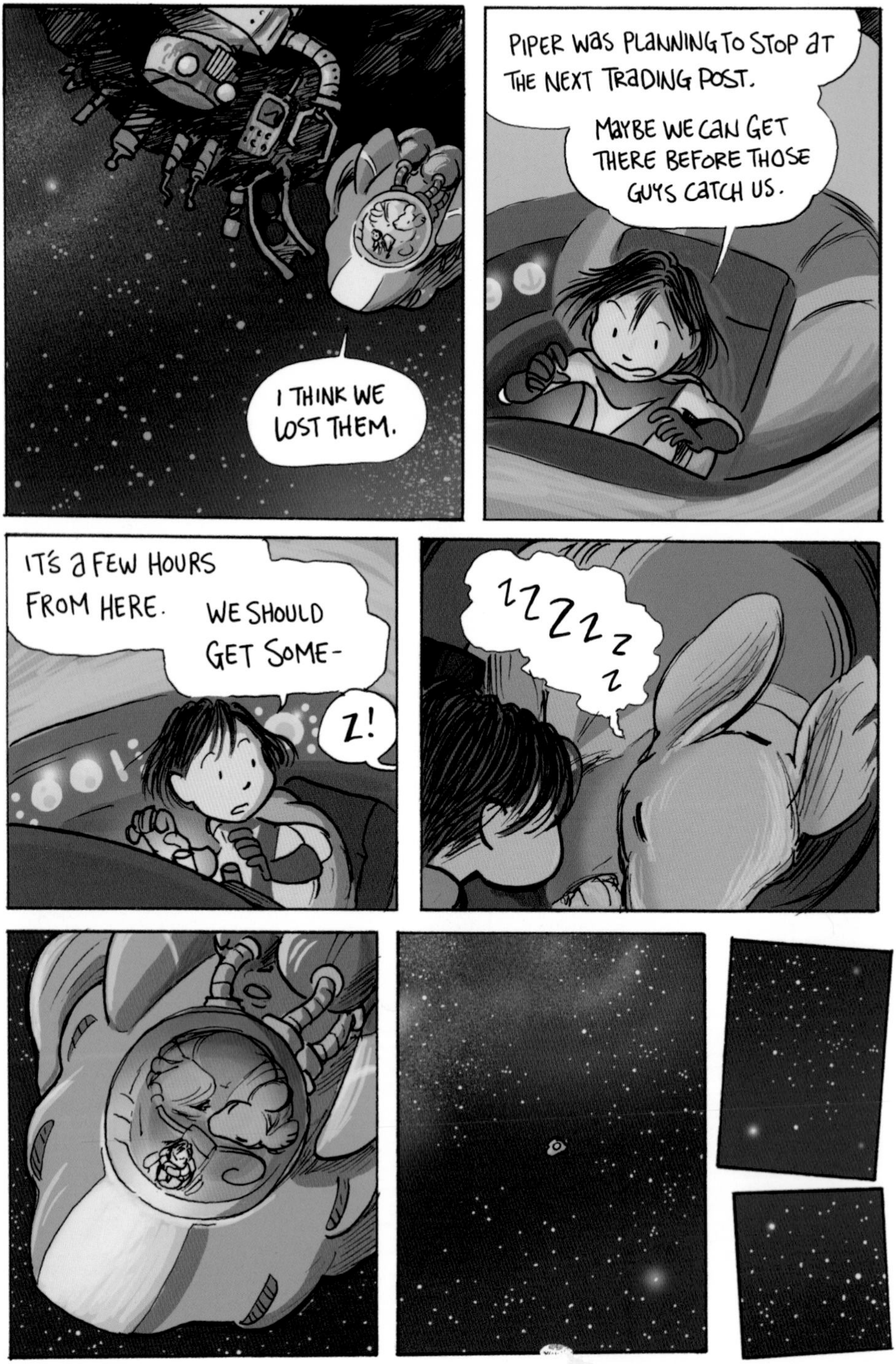
I THINK WE LOST THEM.
PIPER WAS PLANNING TO STOP AT THE NEXT TRADING POST.
MAYBE WE CAN GET THERE BEFORE THOSE GUYS CATCH US.
IT'S A FEW HOURS FROM HERE.
WE SHOULD GET SOME-
Z!
ZZZZZZ

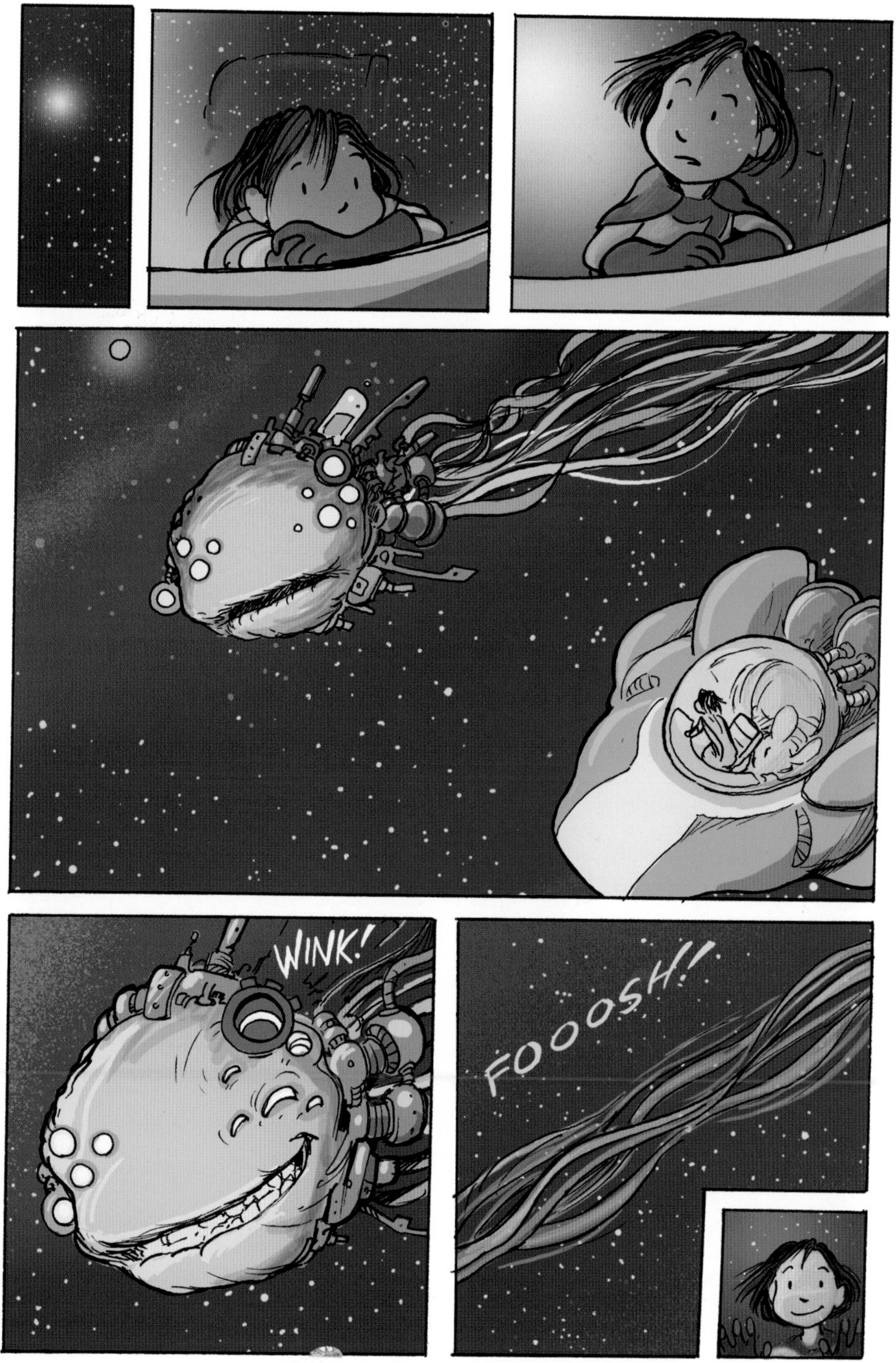
WINK!
FOOOSH!

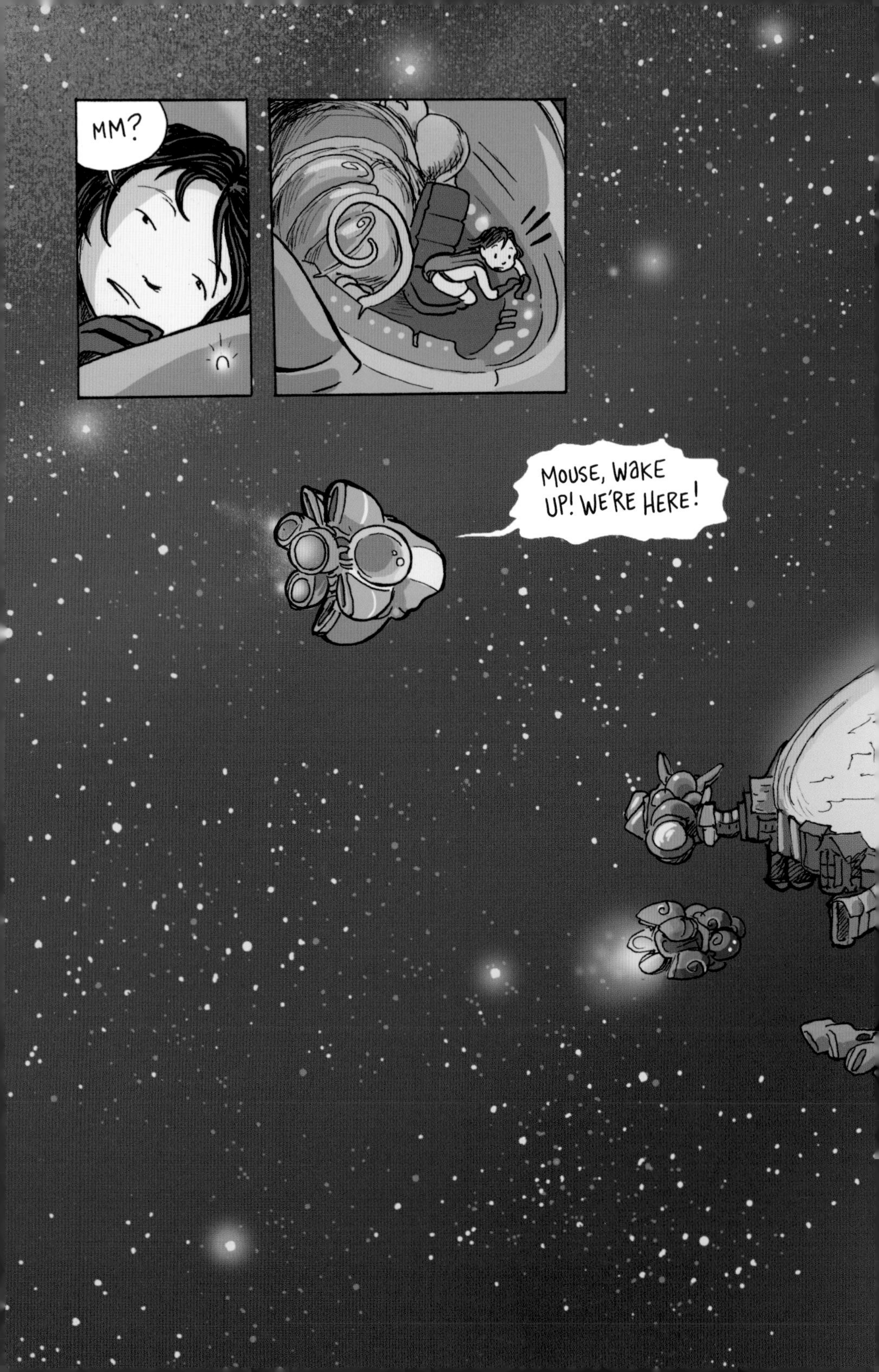
MM?
MOUSE, WAKE UP! WE'RE HERE!

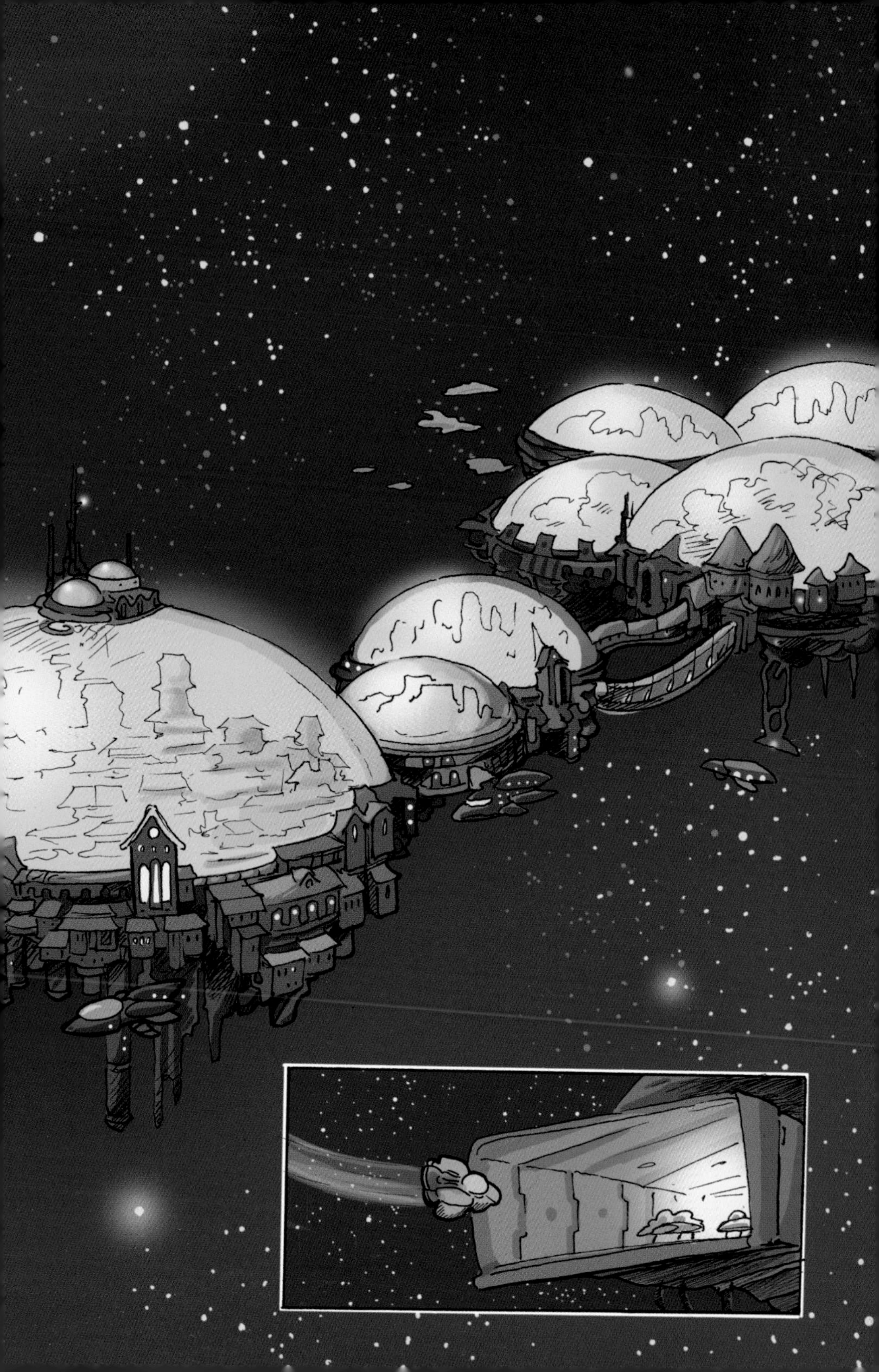

PSSH

HEY!

WADDLE IT BE, LADY?
REFUEL?
REPAIR?
TOP OFF THE FLUIDS?

TOUCH UP THE PAINT JOB?

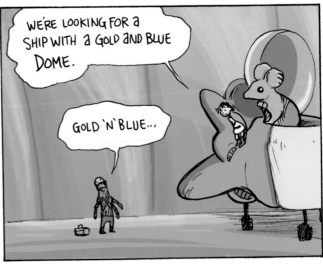
WE'RE LOOKING FOR A SHIP WITH A GOLD AND BLUE DOME.

GOLD 'N' BLUE...

YOU MEAN PIPER'S SHIP!

YOU KNOW IT?

WELL SHOR 'IN I DO! HE TRAVELS WITH ZITA THE SPACEGIRL! SHE'S AWESOME!

SAAAY, YOU KINDA LOOK LIKE HER. SHORTER MAYBE.

I-IS THE SHIP STILL HERE?

SHORE 'TIS! JES' TWO DOCKS OVER! NUMMER FOUR!

THANKS.

HEH HEH. LOOKS JES' LIKE—

BREEP!

UHH.

STOLEN VESSEL

SUSPECTS

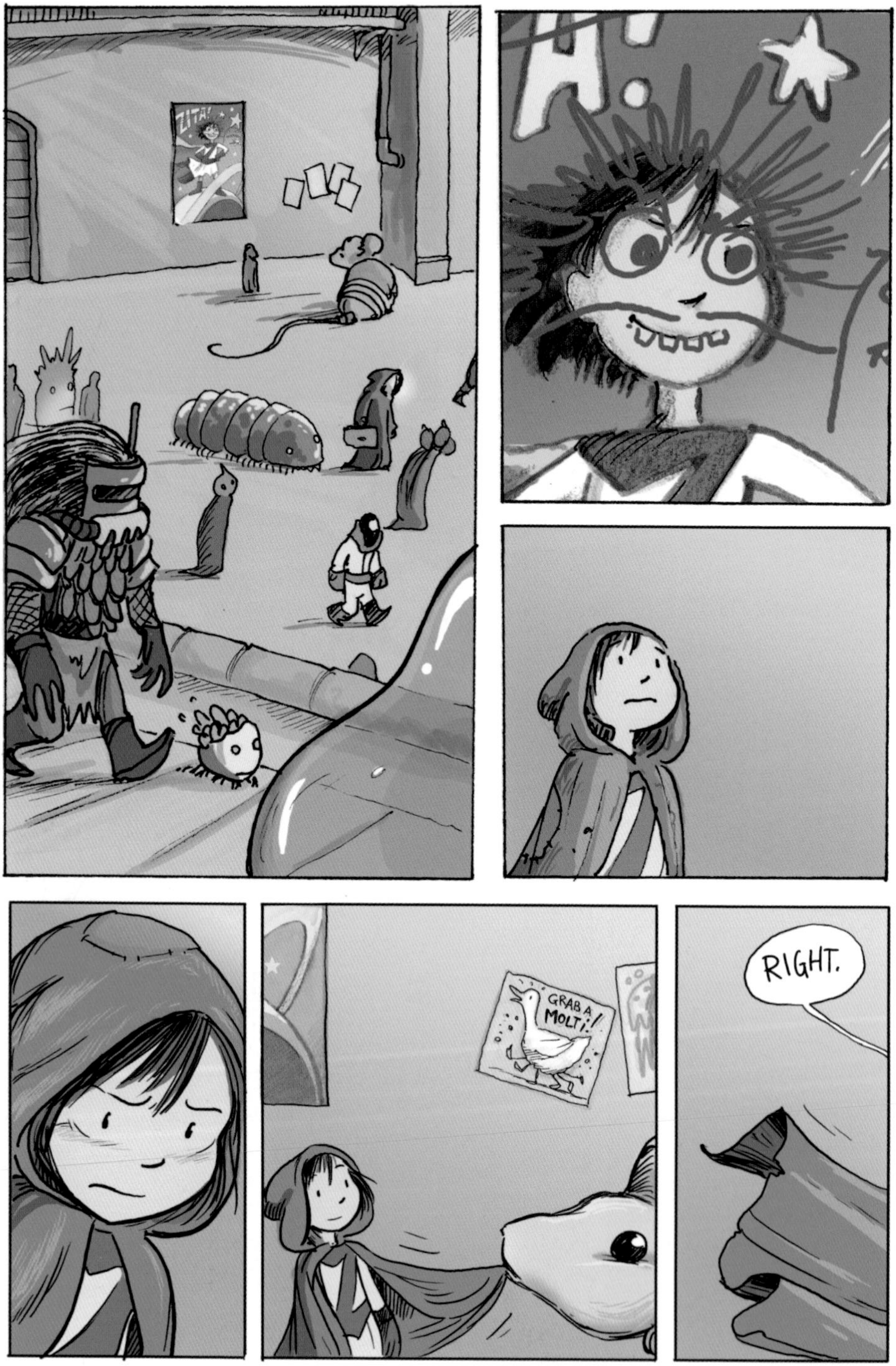
ZITA!
GRAB A MOLTI!
RIGHT.

THERE.

HEY!

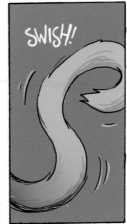

SWISH!

THERE IT IS!

SHE WENT THIS WAY.

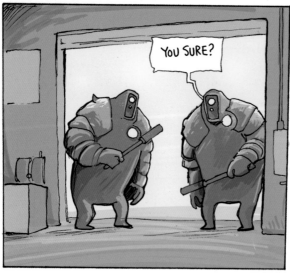

YOU SURE?

FAN OUT.

61

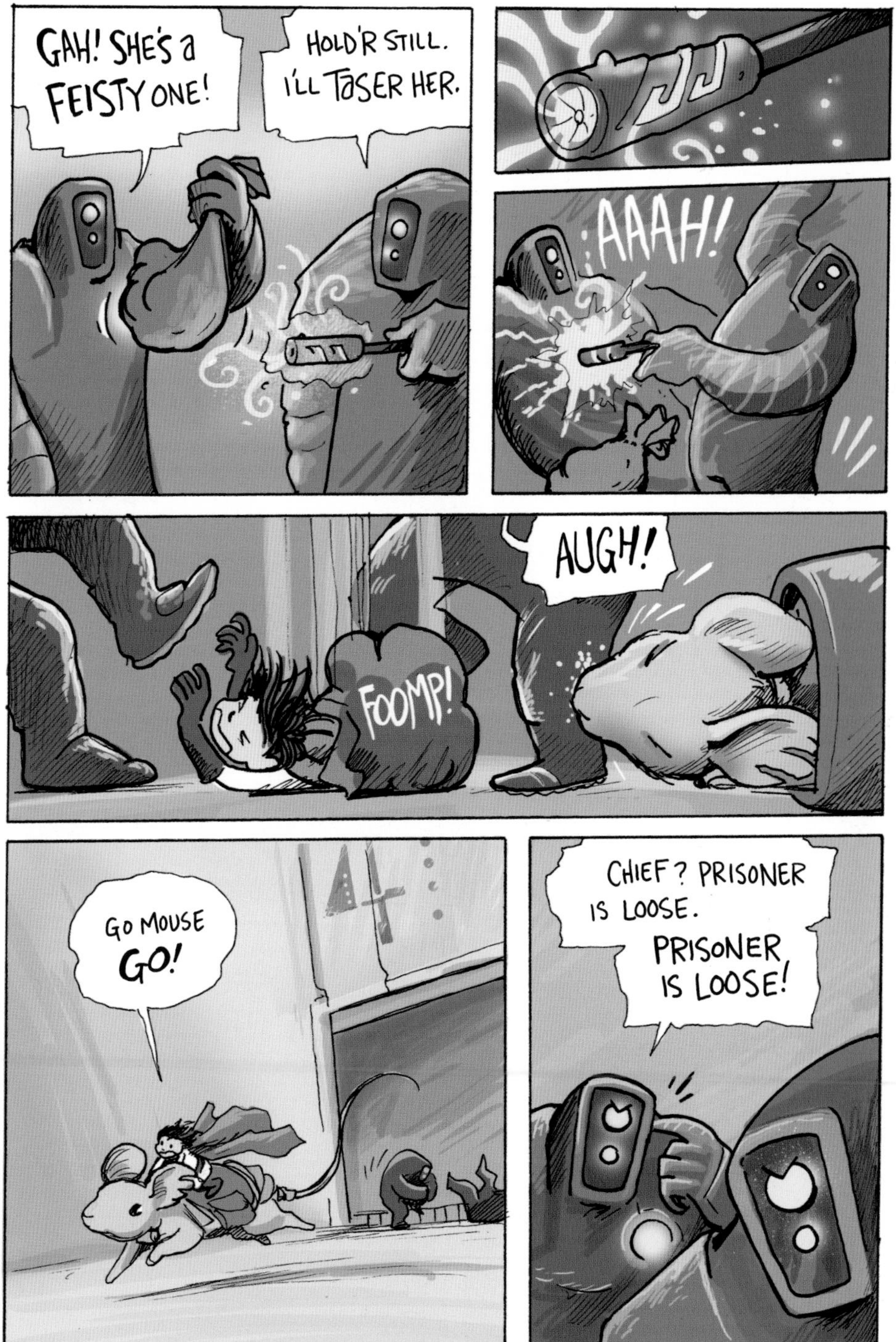
GAH! SHE'S a FEISTY ONE!
HOLD'R STILL. I'LL TASER HER.
AAAH!
AUGH!
FOOMP!
GO MOUSE GO!
CHIEF? PRISONER IS LOOSE.
PRISONER IS LOOSE!

WHOO.

ZITA THE SPACEGIRL-

HERO OR MENACE?

THE GIRL FROM PARTS UNKNOWN WHO ROCKETED TO FAME AFTER SHE SAVED PLANET SCRIPTORIUS FROM AN ASTEROID.

SEEN IN THIS SECURITY FEED HIJACKING A SPACECRAFT!

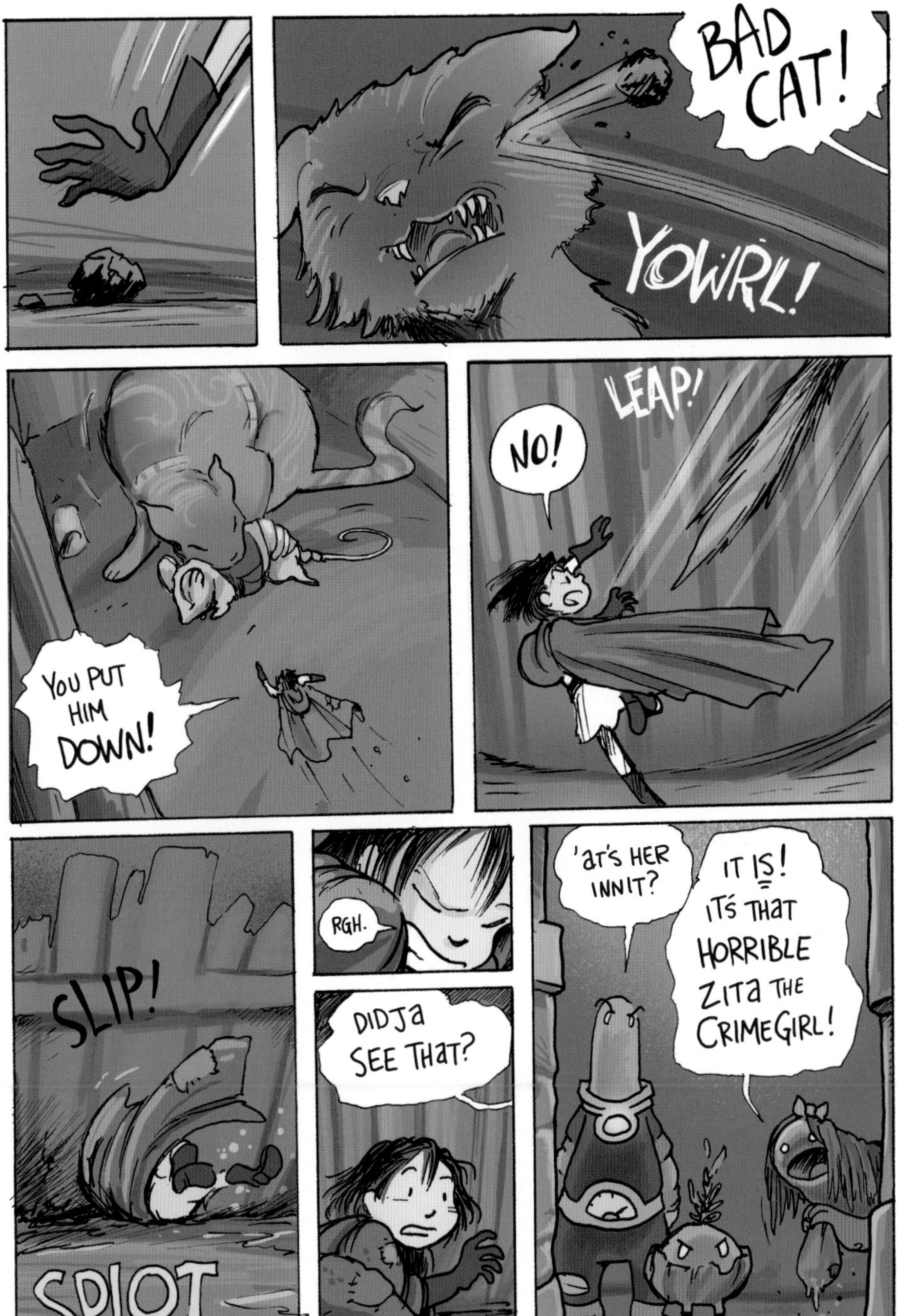
BAD CAT!
YOWRL!
YOU PUT HIM DOWN!
LEAP!
NO!
SLIP!
SPLOT
RGH.
DIDJA SEE THAT?
'AT'S HER INNIT?
IT IS! IT'S THAT HORRIBLE ZITA THE CRIMEGIRL!

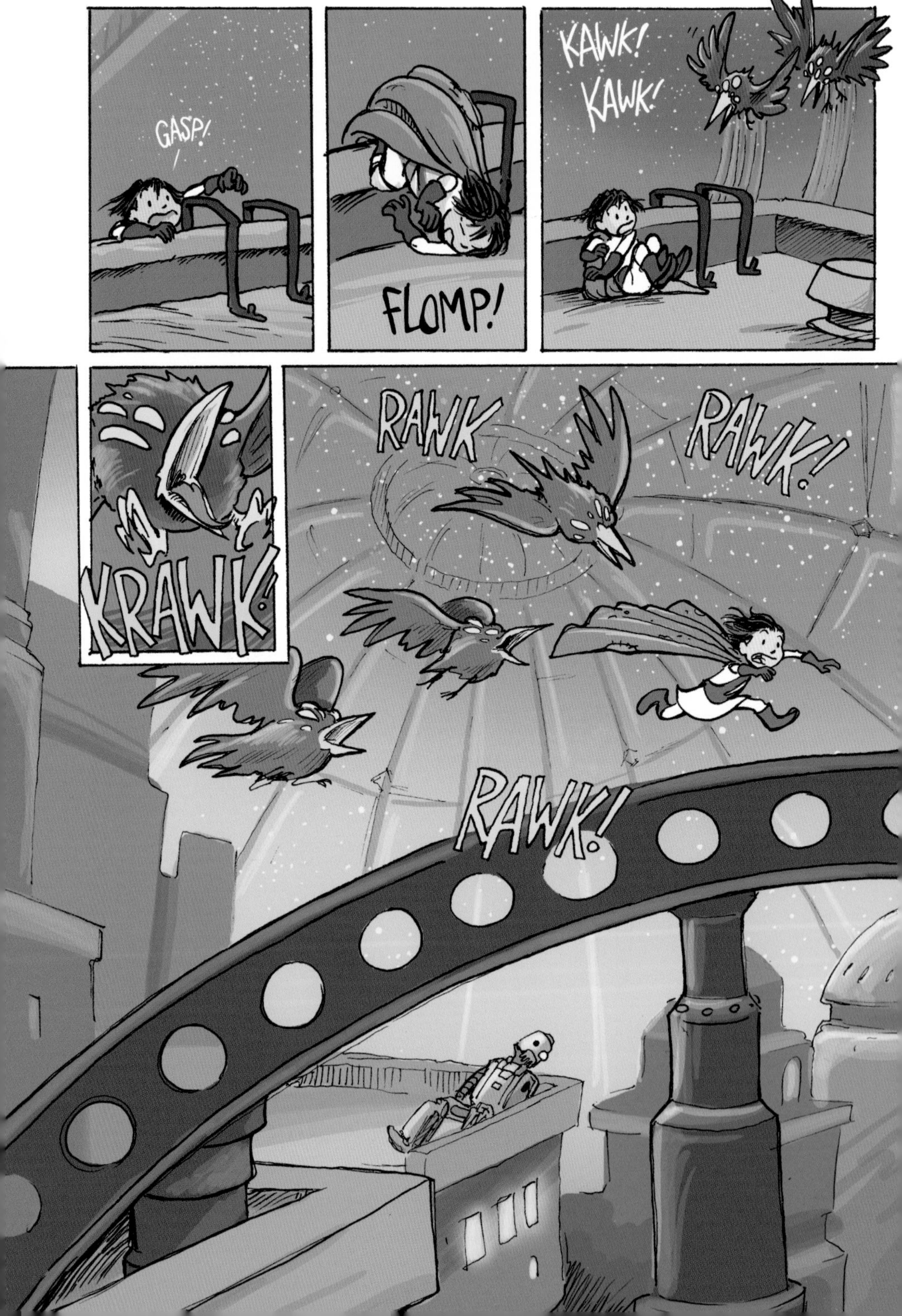
GASP!
FLOMP!
KAWK!
KAWK!
KRAWK!
RAWK
RAWK!
RAWK!

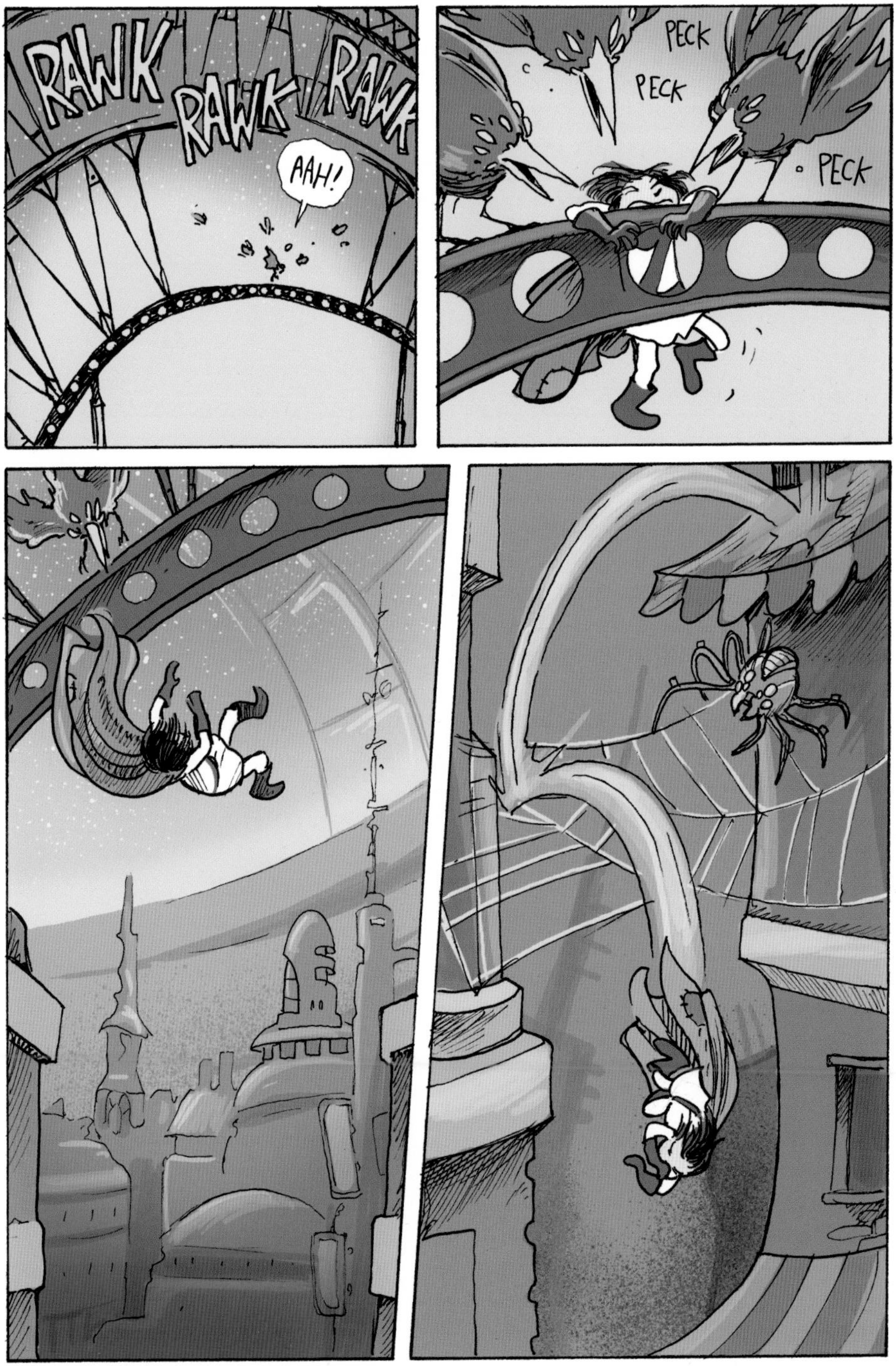
RAWK
RAWK
RAWK
AAH!
PECK
PECK
PECK

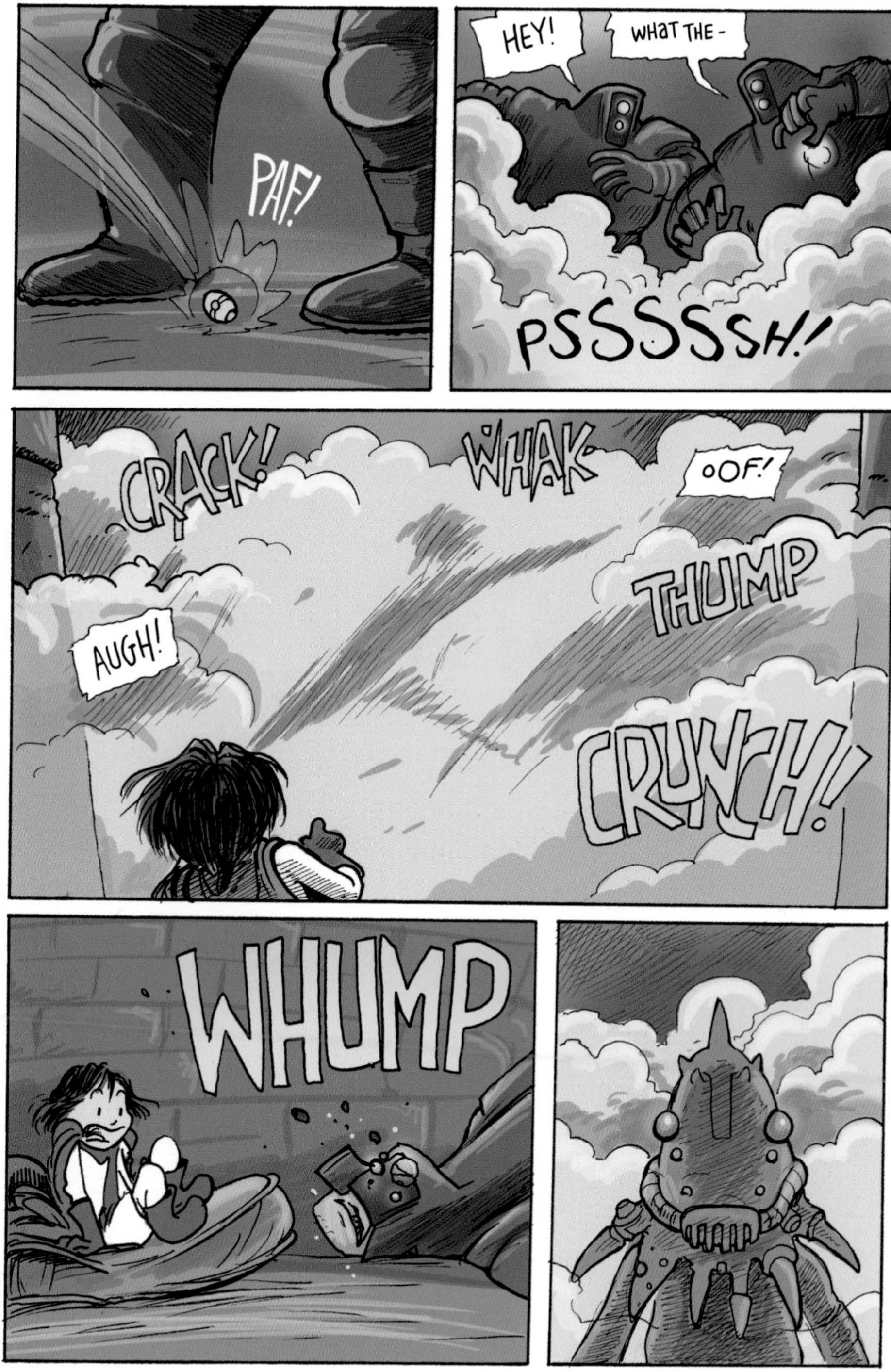
PAF!
HEY!
WHAT THE -
PSSSSSH!
CRACK!
WHAK
OOF!
THUMP
AUGH!
CRUNCH!
WHUMP

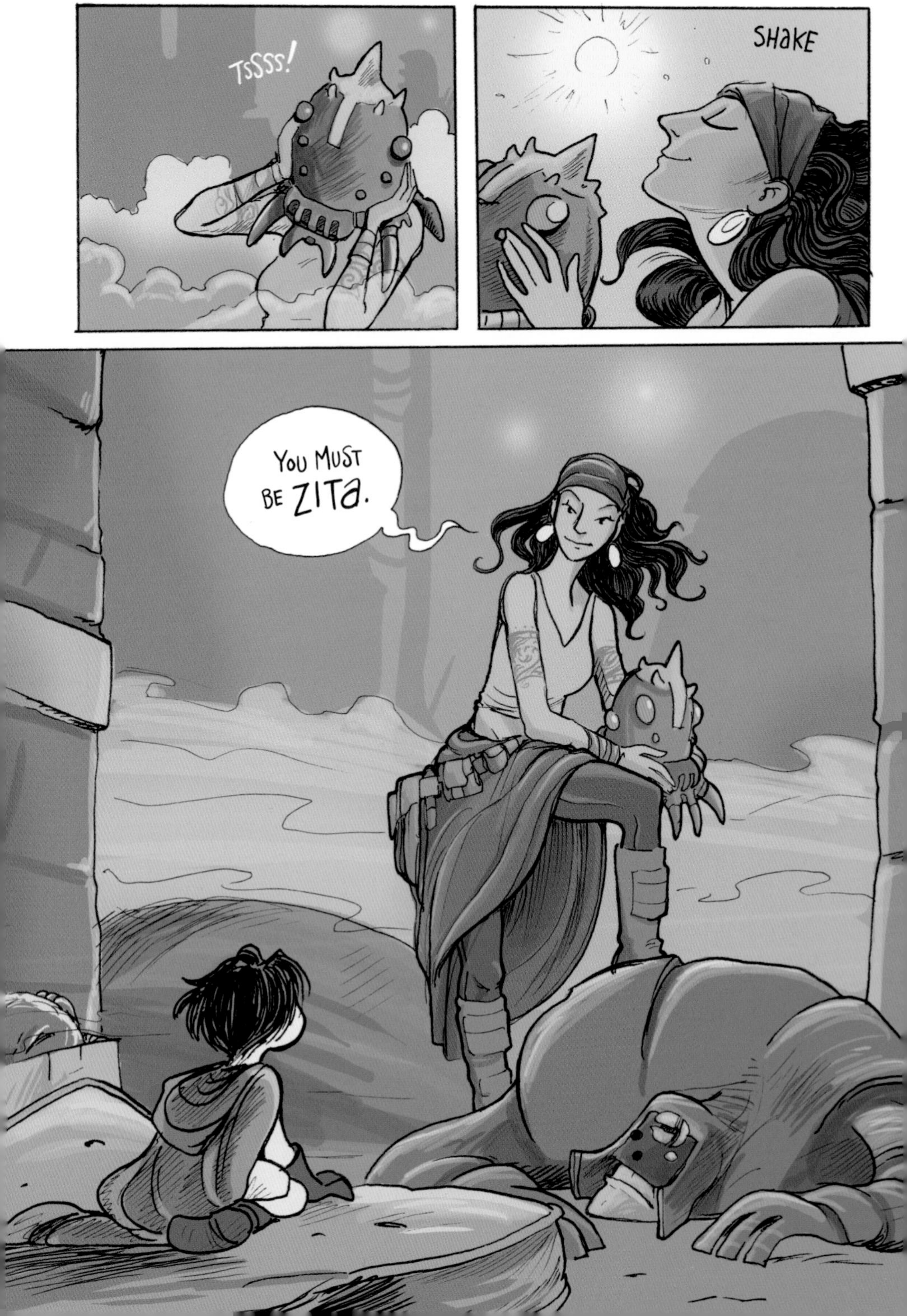
TSSSS!
SHAKE
YOU MUST BE ZITA.

Chapter
Three

 YOU!

 KAWK KAWK

 YOU NEED TO COME WITH ME.

 HOW DO I KNOW I CAN TRUST YOU?

DON' TRUST'ER!

 YOU DON'T. BUT I'M YOUR BEST CHANCE AT ESCAPING THIS PLACE.

WE HAVE TO HURRY.

 I CAN'T. MY FRIEND WAS— WAS—

YOU MEAN YOUR "MOUSE"?

 HE'S SAFE.

CHAK

BOOM

I DINNAE SEE NUFFIN!

KAWK!

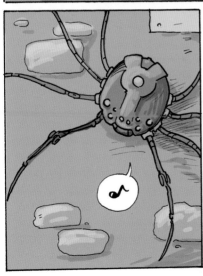

♪

KEEP RUNNING! I'LL SLOW THEM DOWN!

?

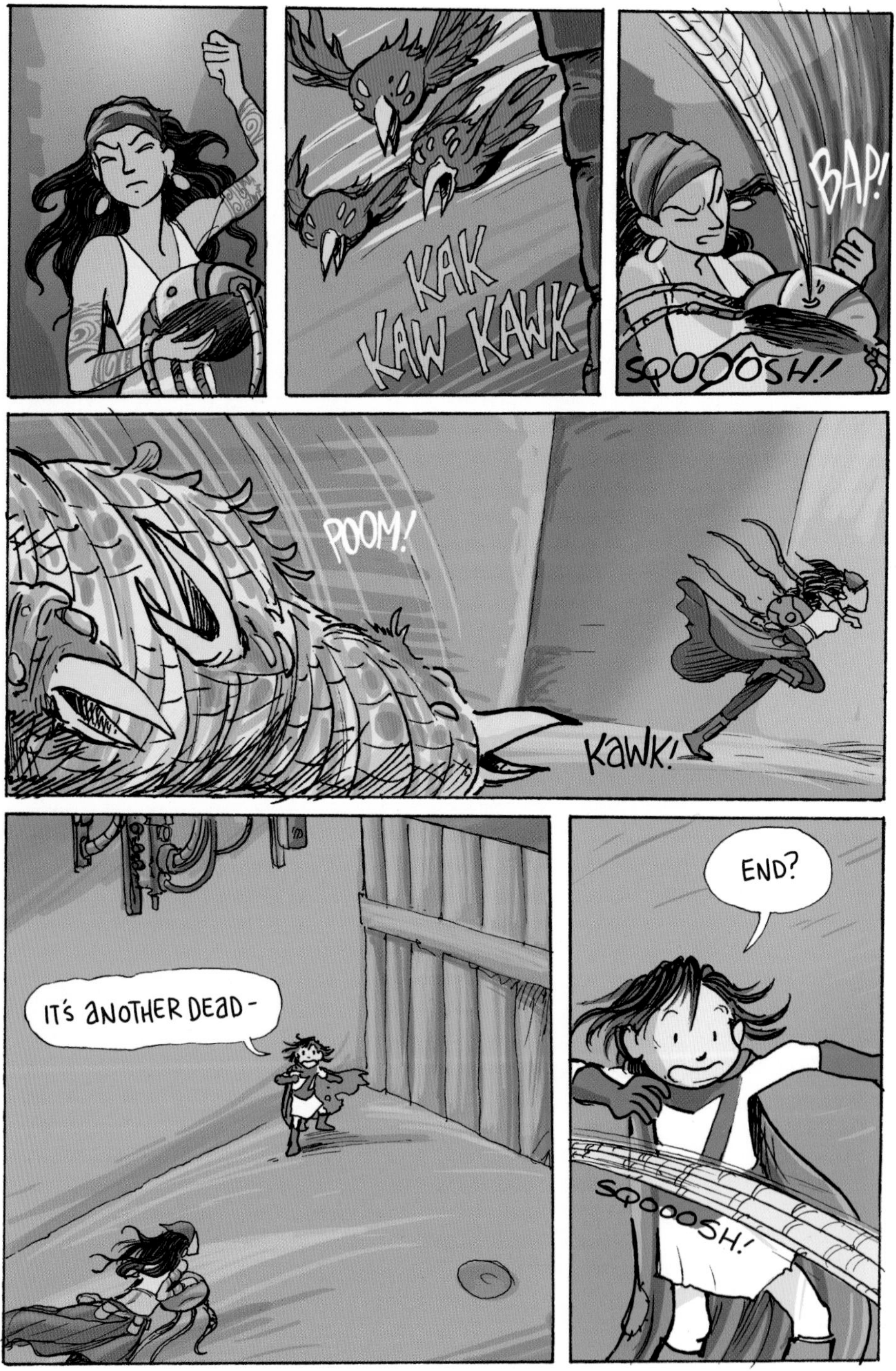
KAK
KAW KAWK
BAP!
SPOOOOSH!
POOM!
KAWK!
IT'S ANOTHER DEAD-
END?
SPOOOOSH!

SPROING

ZITA! MOVE!

GULP.

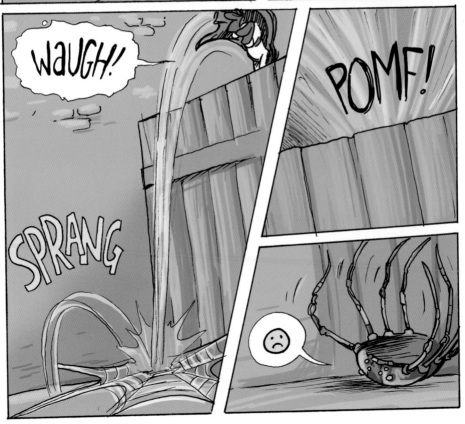

WAUGH!

SPRANG

POMF!

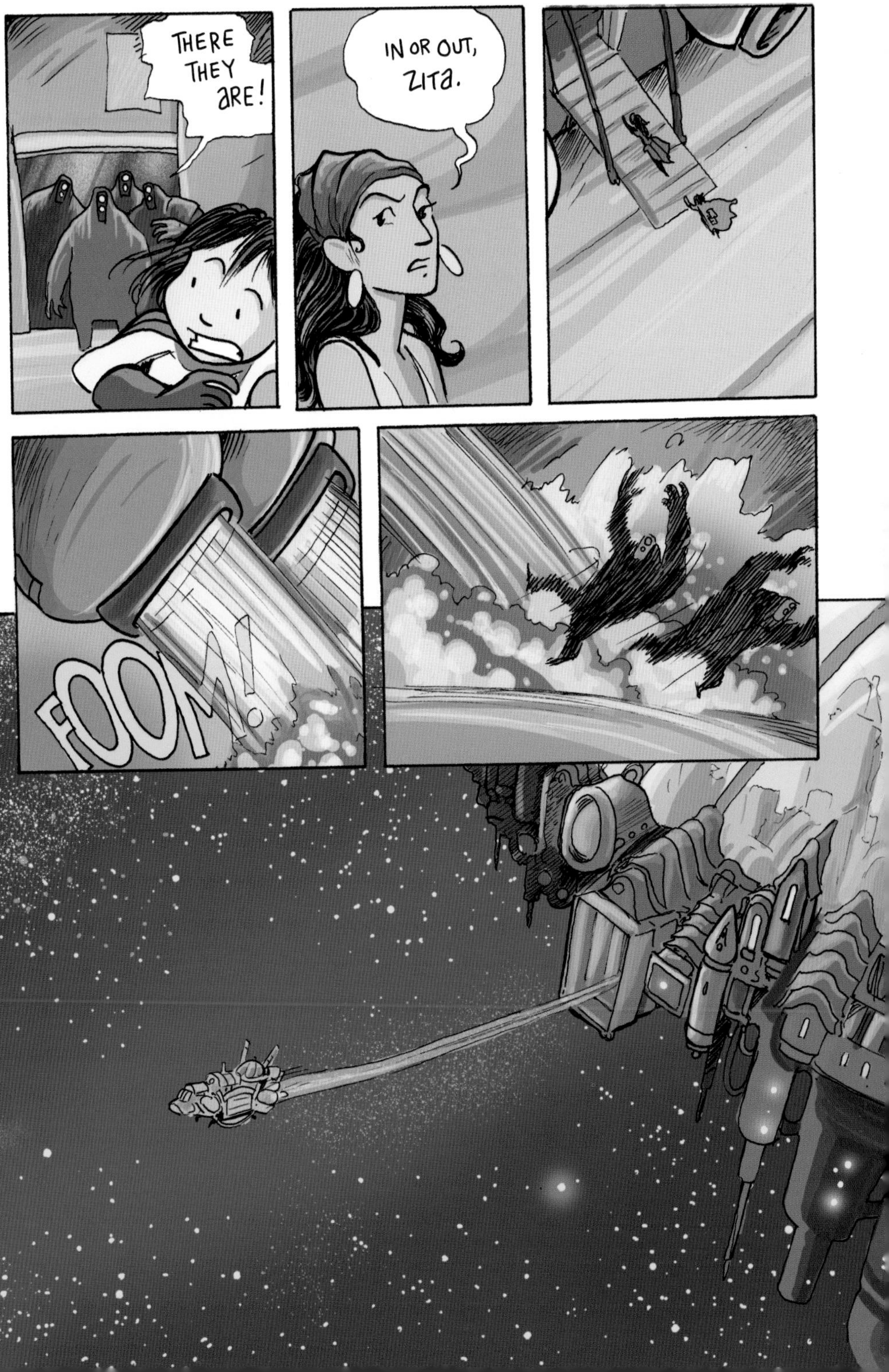
THERE THEY ARE!
IN OR OUT, ZITA.
FOOM!

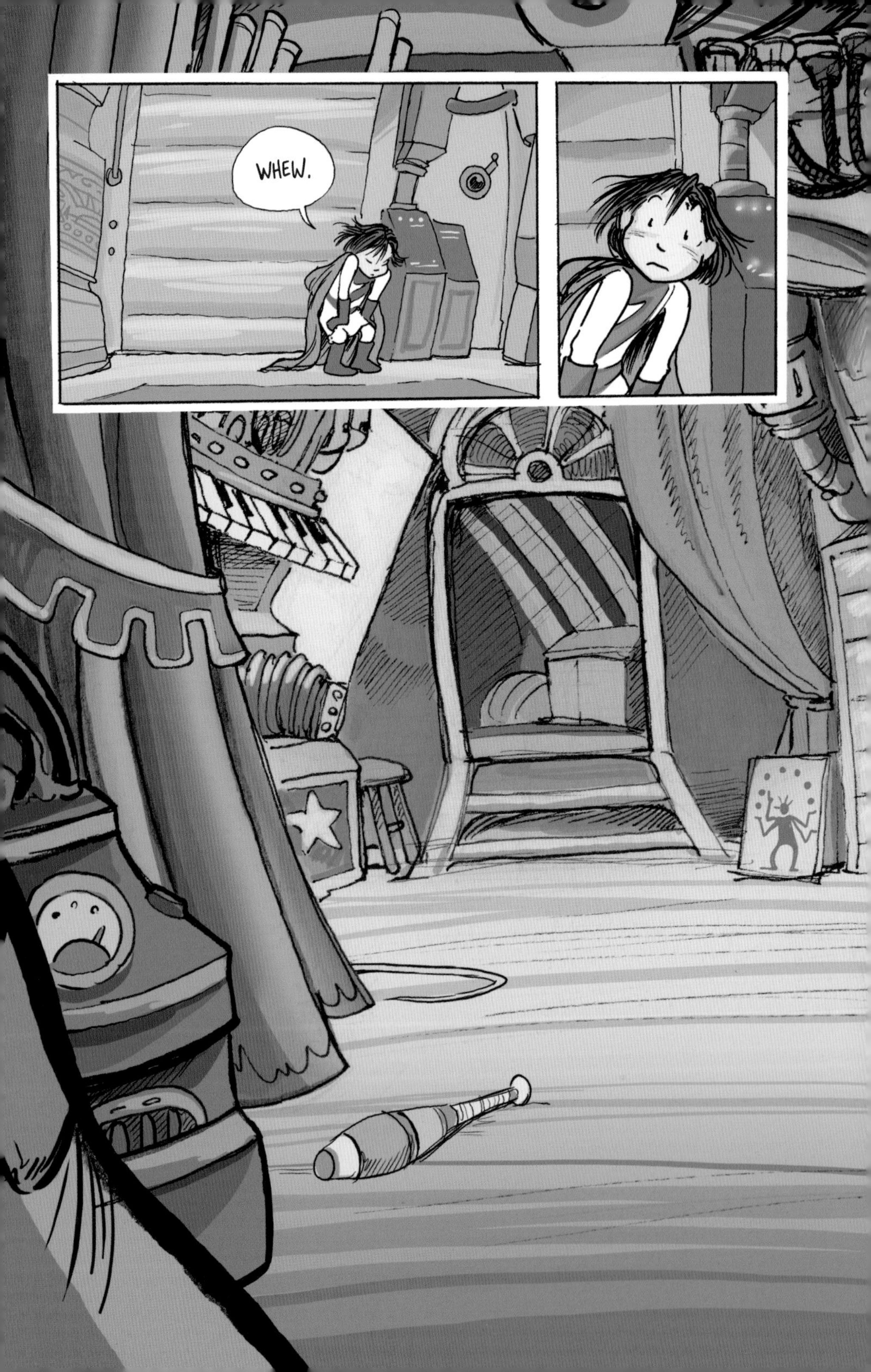
WHEW.

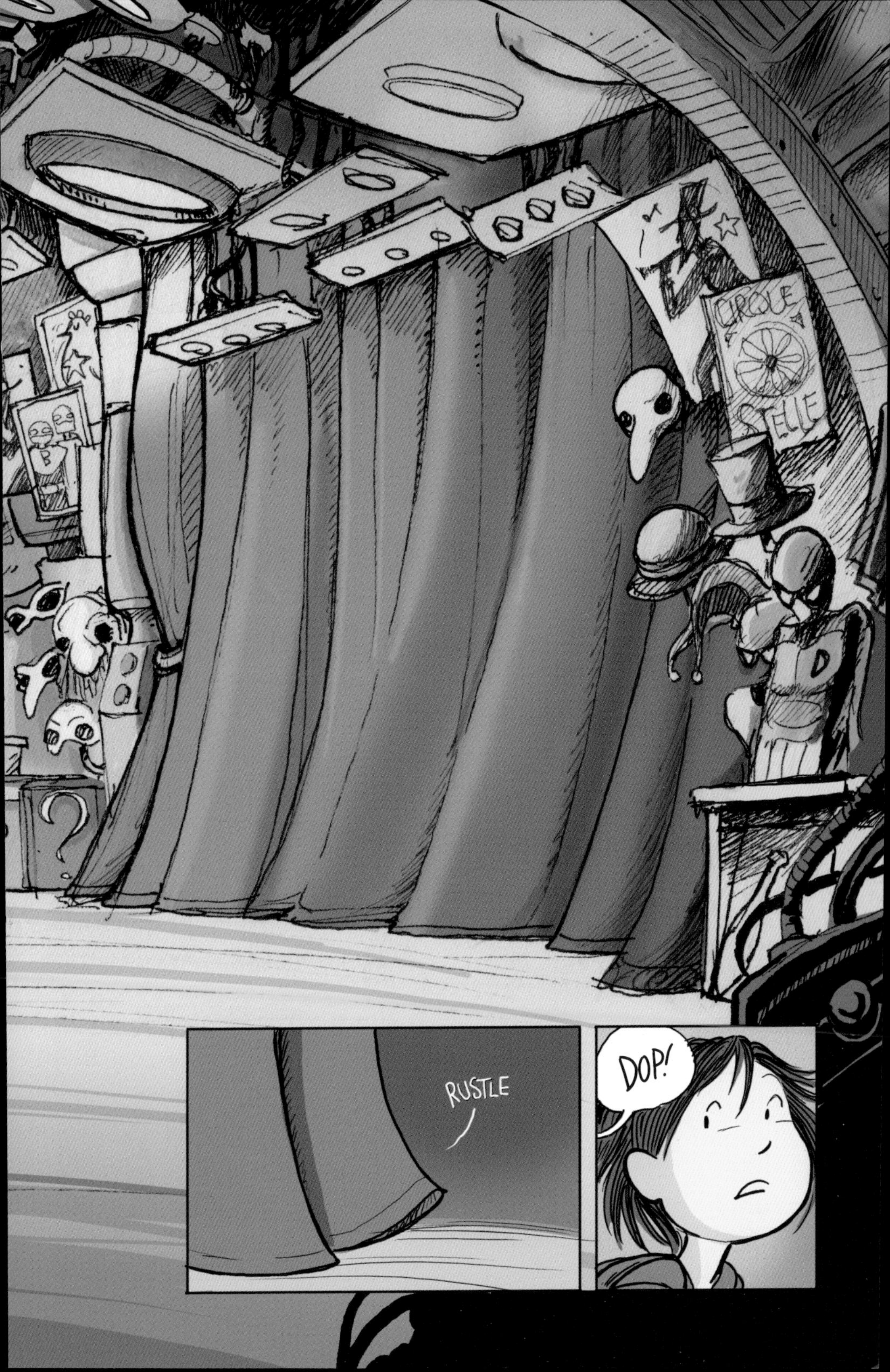
RUSTLE
DOP!

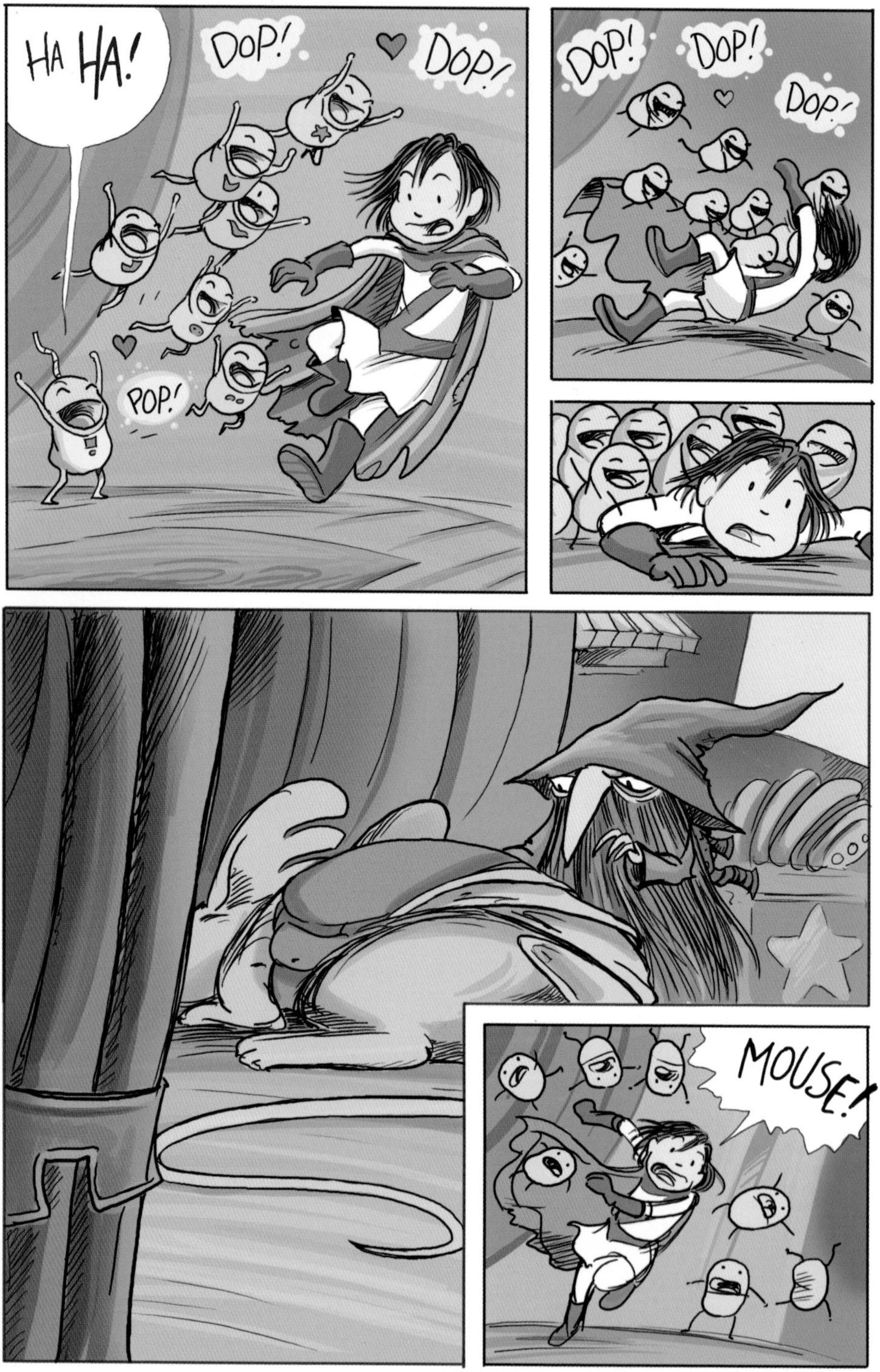
HA HA!
DOP!
DOP!
POP!
DOP!
DOP!
DOP!
MOUSE!

85

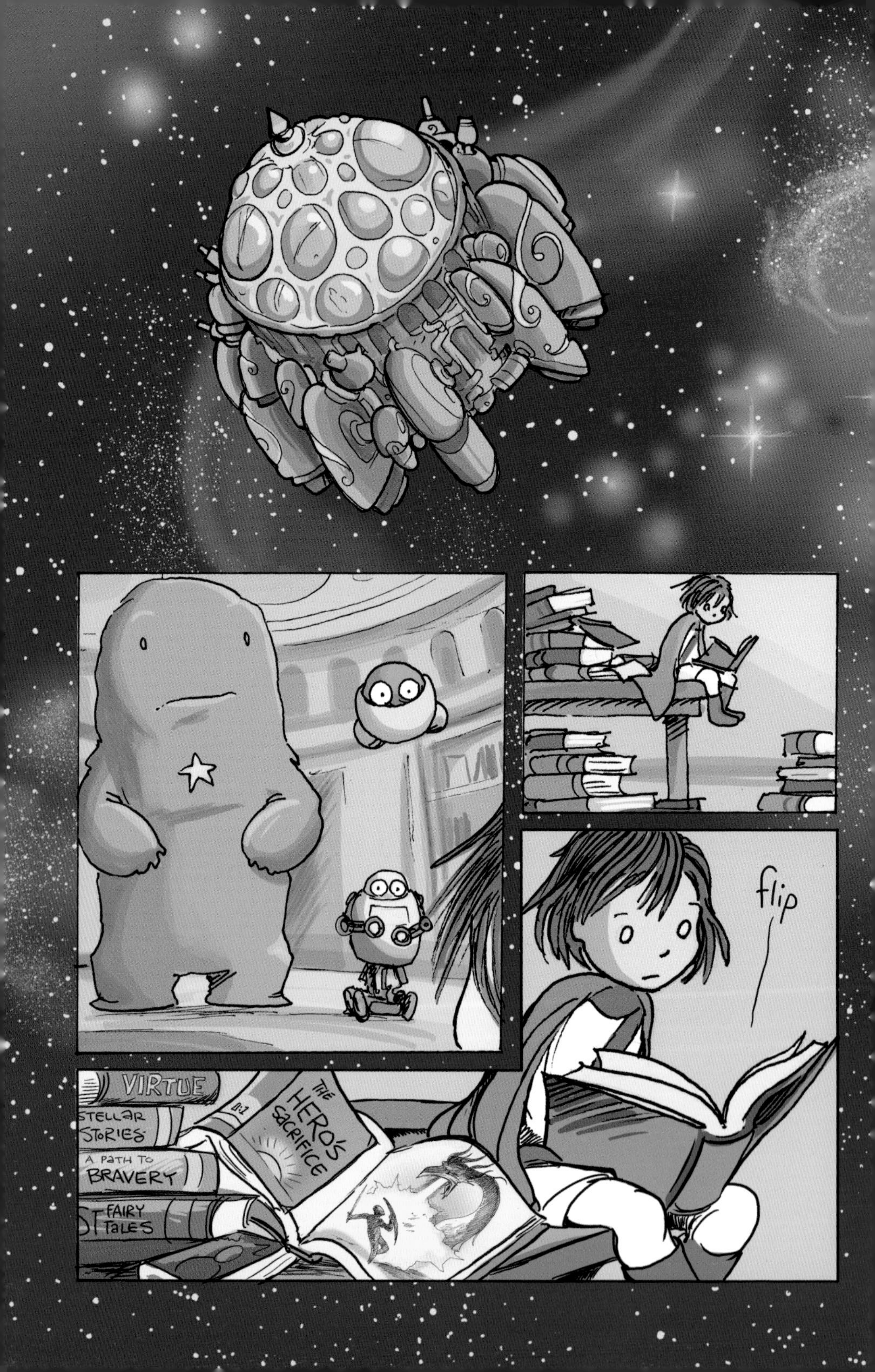
flip
VIRTUE
STELLAR STORIES
A PATH TO BRAVERY
FAIRY TALES
THE HERO'S SACRIFICE

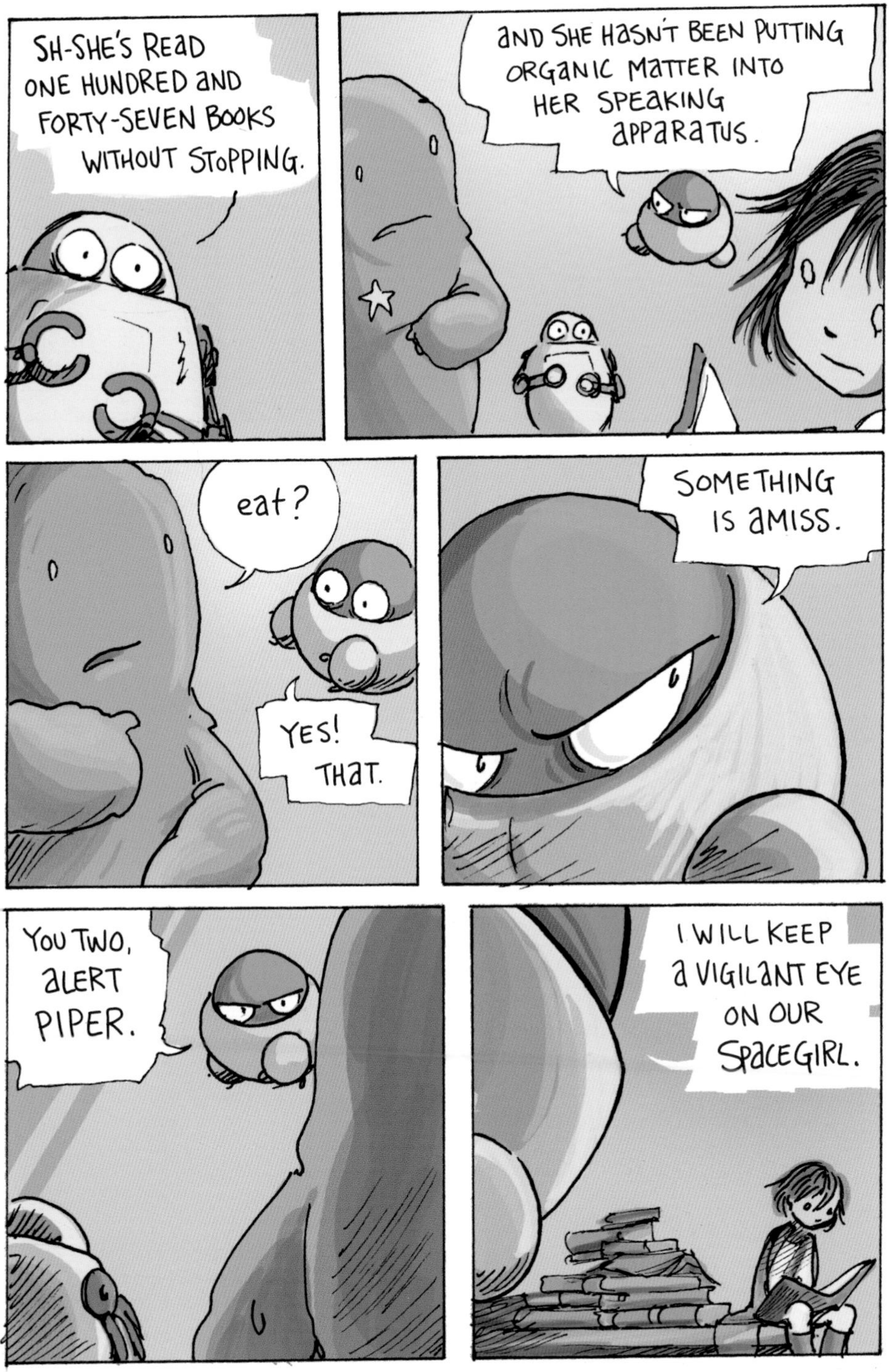
SH-SHE'S READ ONE HUNDRED AND FORTY-SEVEN BOOKS WITHOUT STOPPING.
AND SHE HASN'T BEEN PUTTING ORGANIC MATTER INTO HER SPEAKING APPARATUS.
eat?
YES! THAT.
SOMETHING IS AMISS.
YOU TWO, ALERT PIPER.
I WILL KEEP A VIGILANT EYE ON OUR SPACEGIRL.

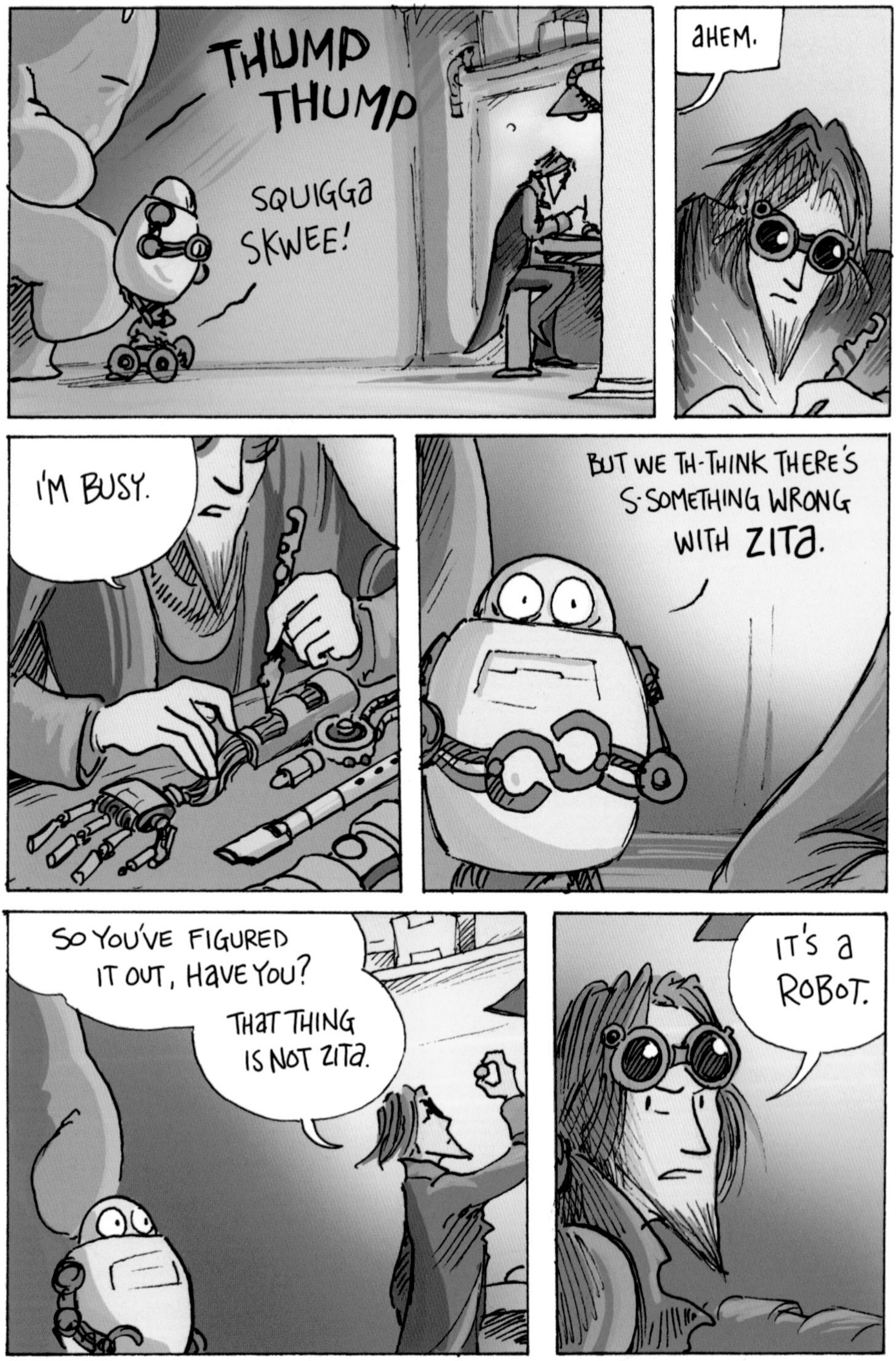
THUMP
THUMP
SQUIGGA SKWEE!
AHEM.
I'M BUSY.
BUT WE TH-THINK THERE'S S-SOMETHING WRONG WITH ZITA.
SO YOU'VE FIGURED IT OUT, HAVE YOU?
THAT THING IS NOT ZITA.
IT'S A ROBOT.

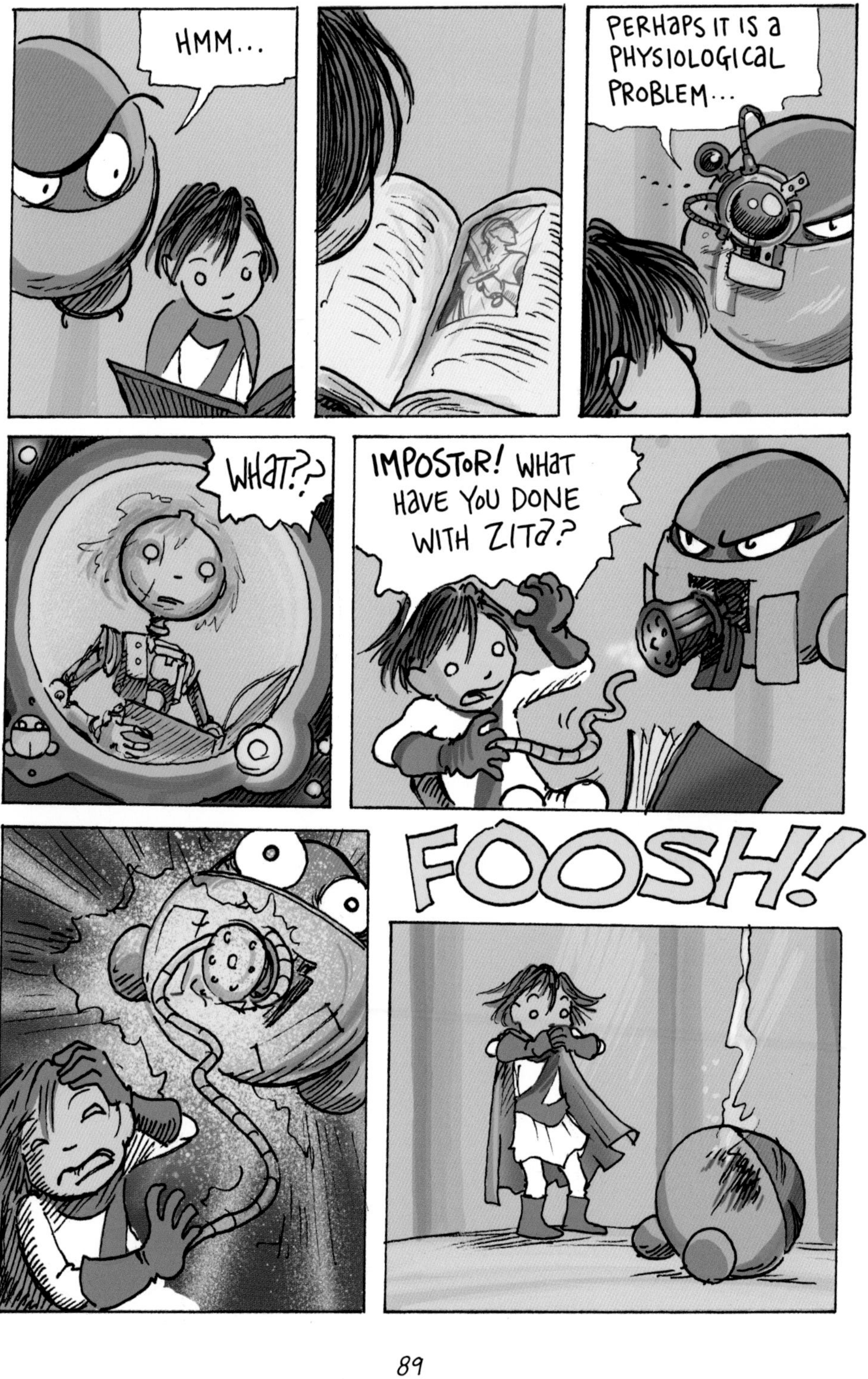
HMM...
PERHAPS IT IS A PHYSIOLOGICAL PROBLEM...
WHAT??
IMPOSTOR! WHAT HAVE YOU DONE WITH ZITA??
FOOSH!

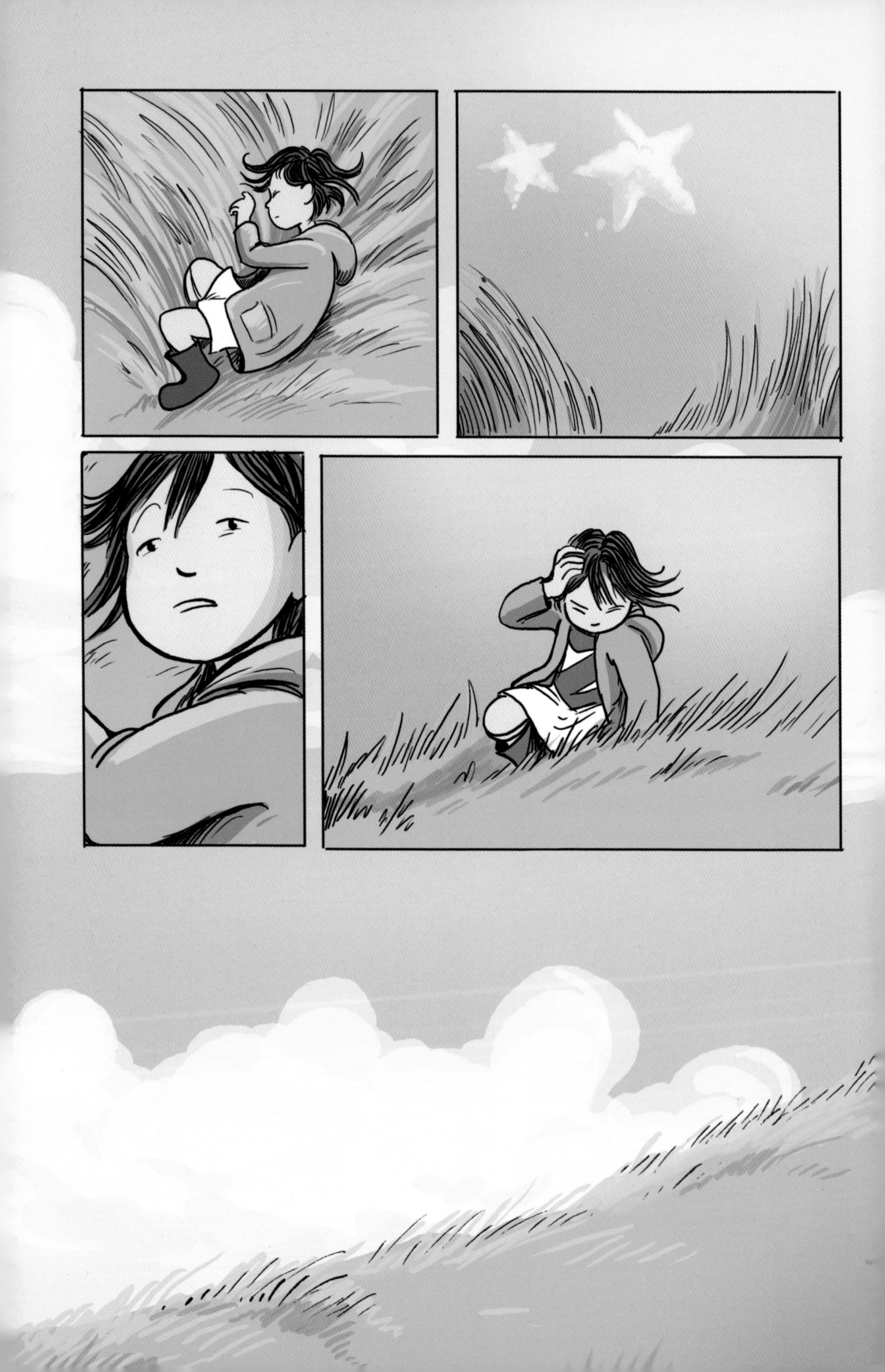

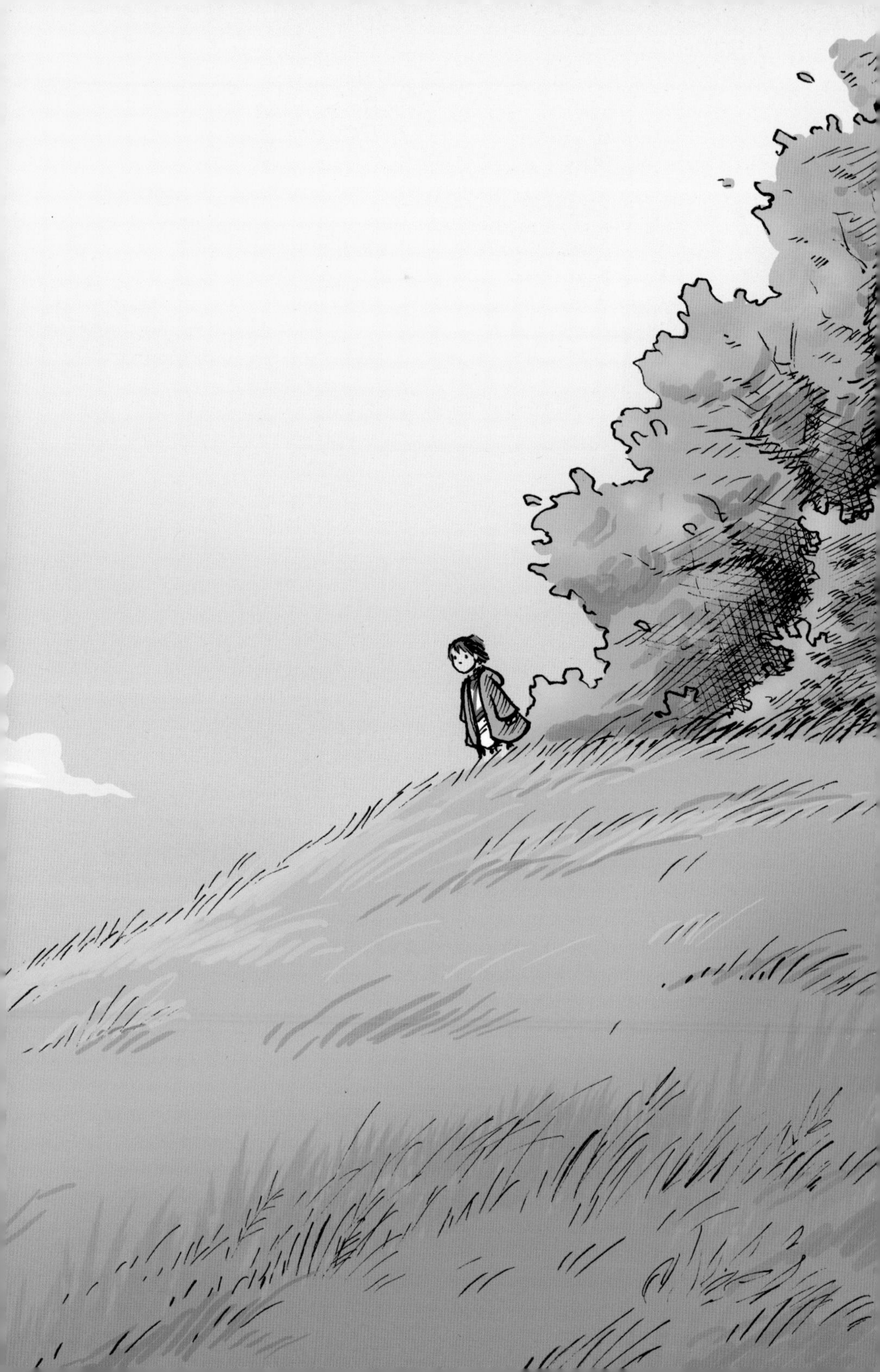

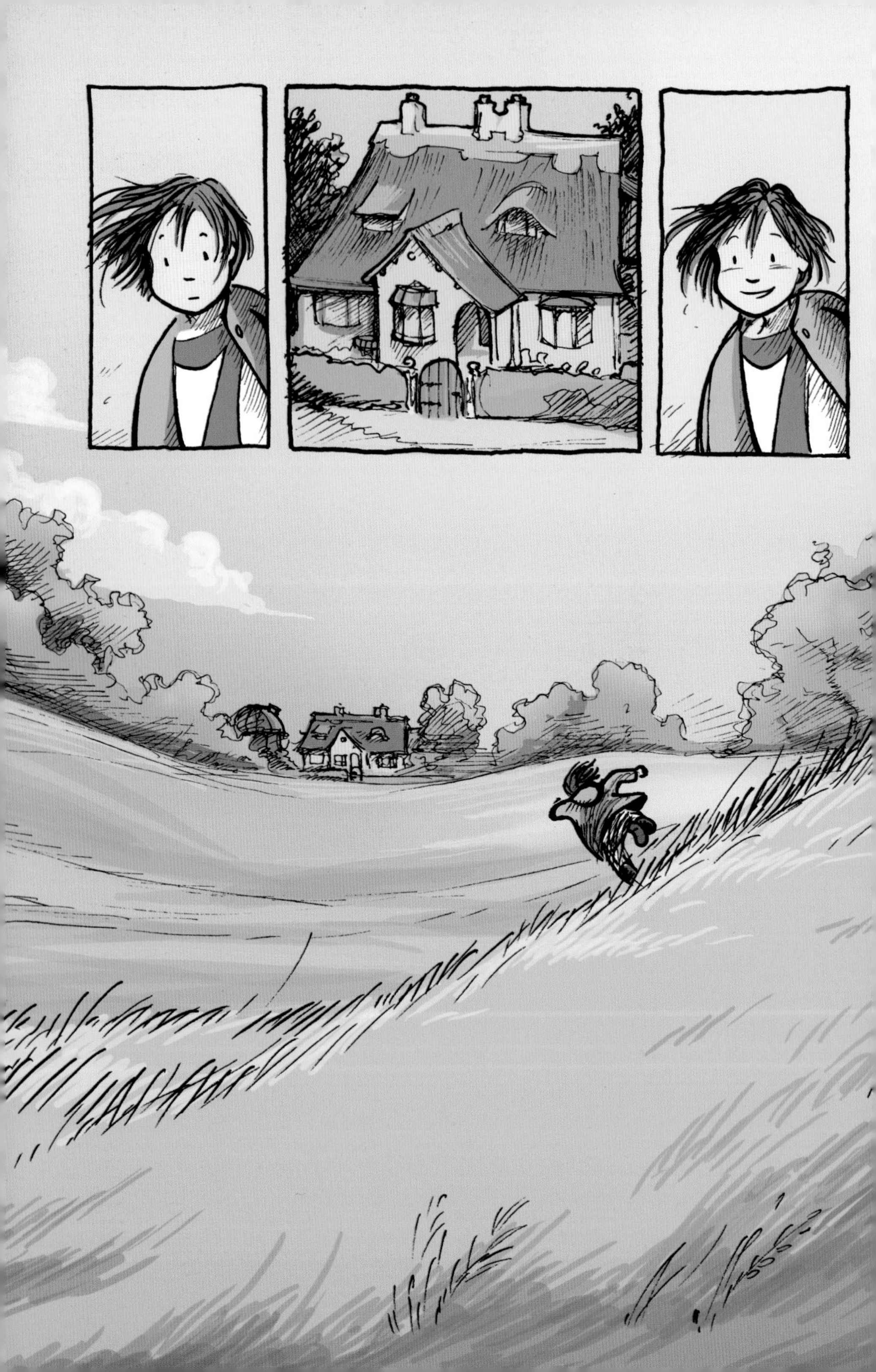

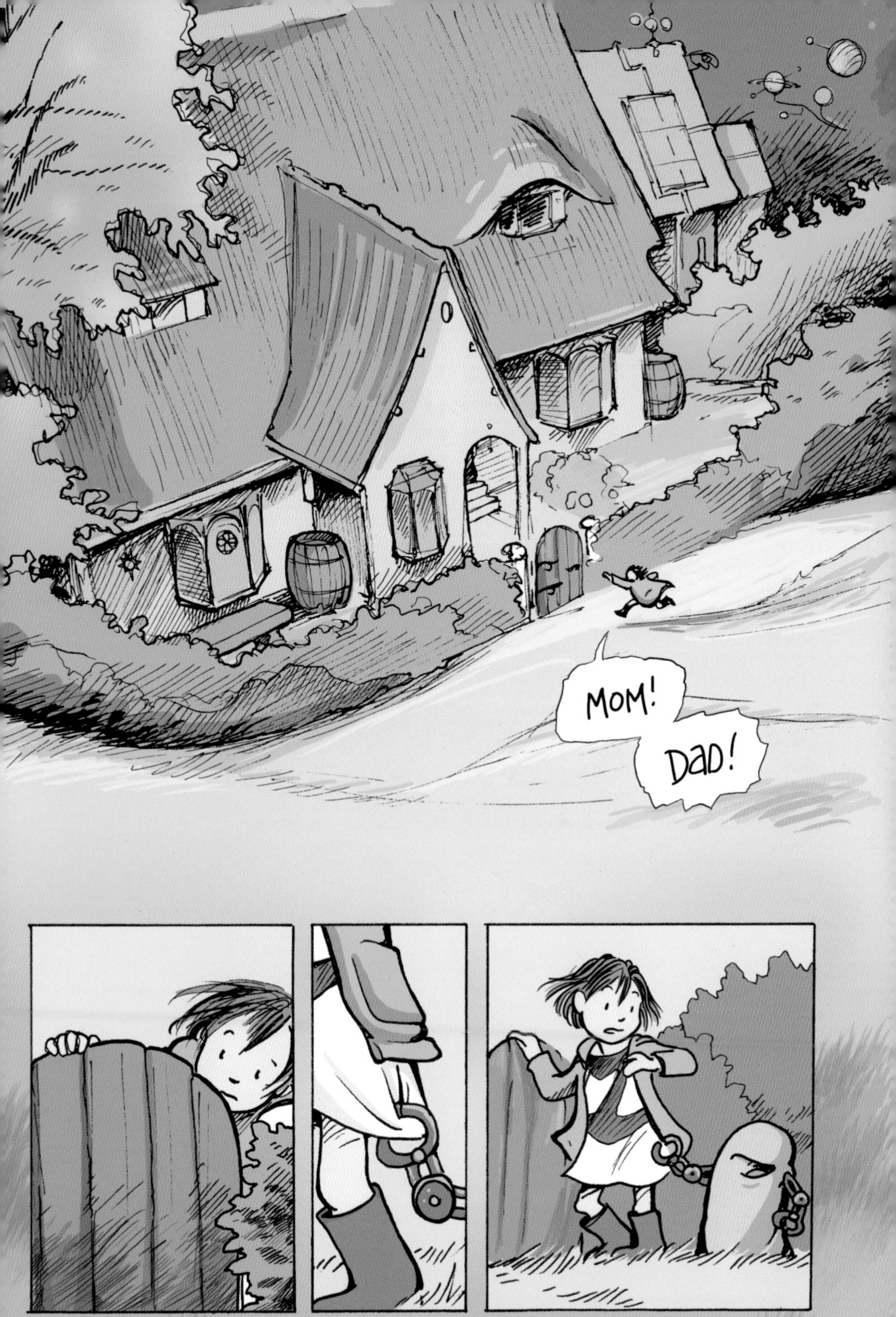
MOM!
DAD!

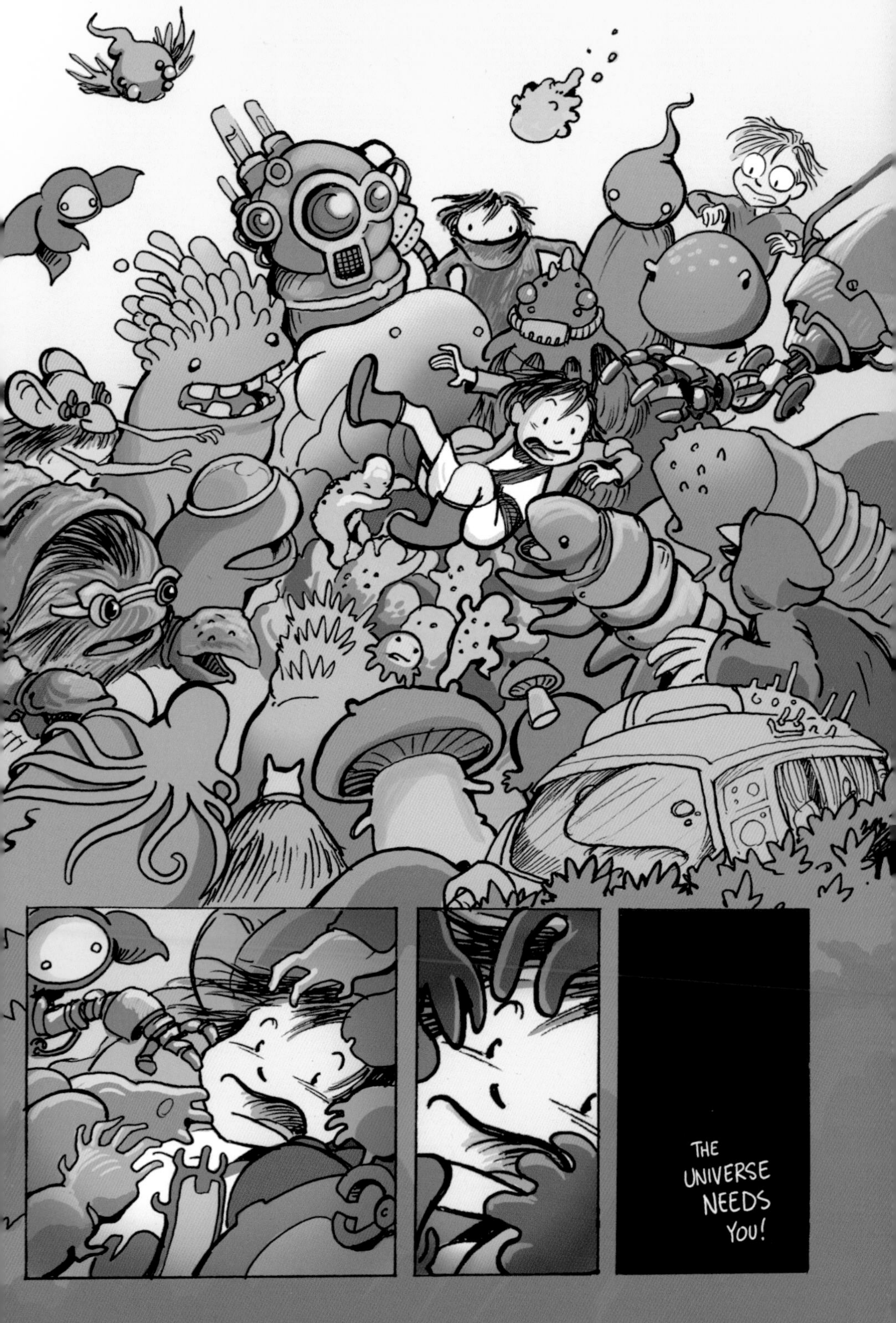
THE UNIVERSE NEEDS YOU!

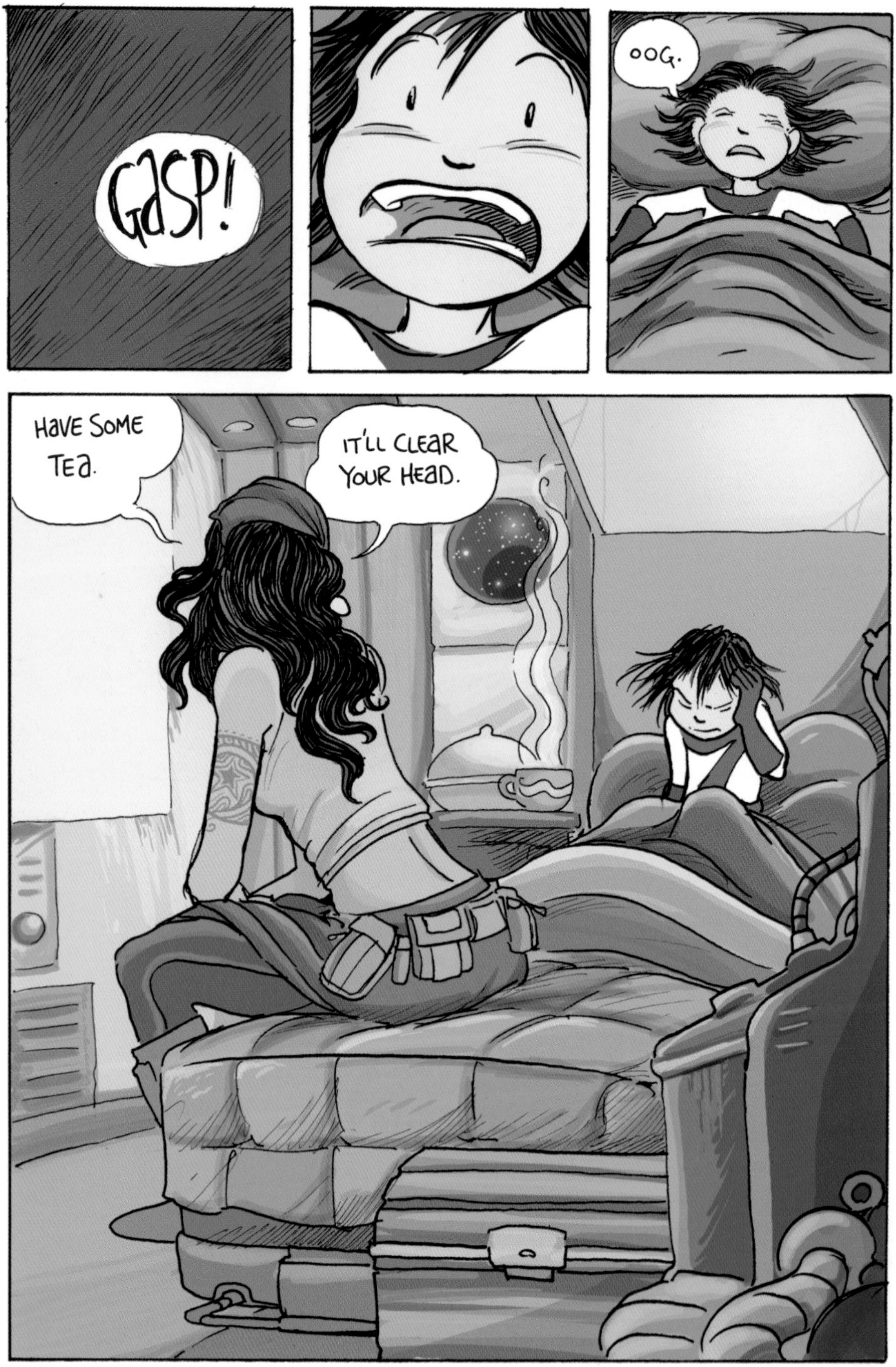
GASP!
OOG.
HAVE SOME TEA.
IT'LL CLEAR YOUR HEAD.

97

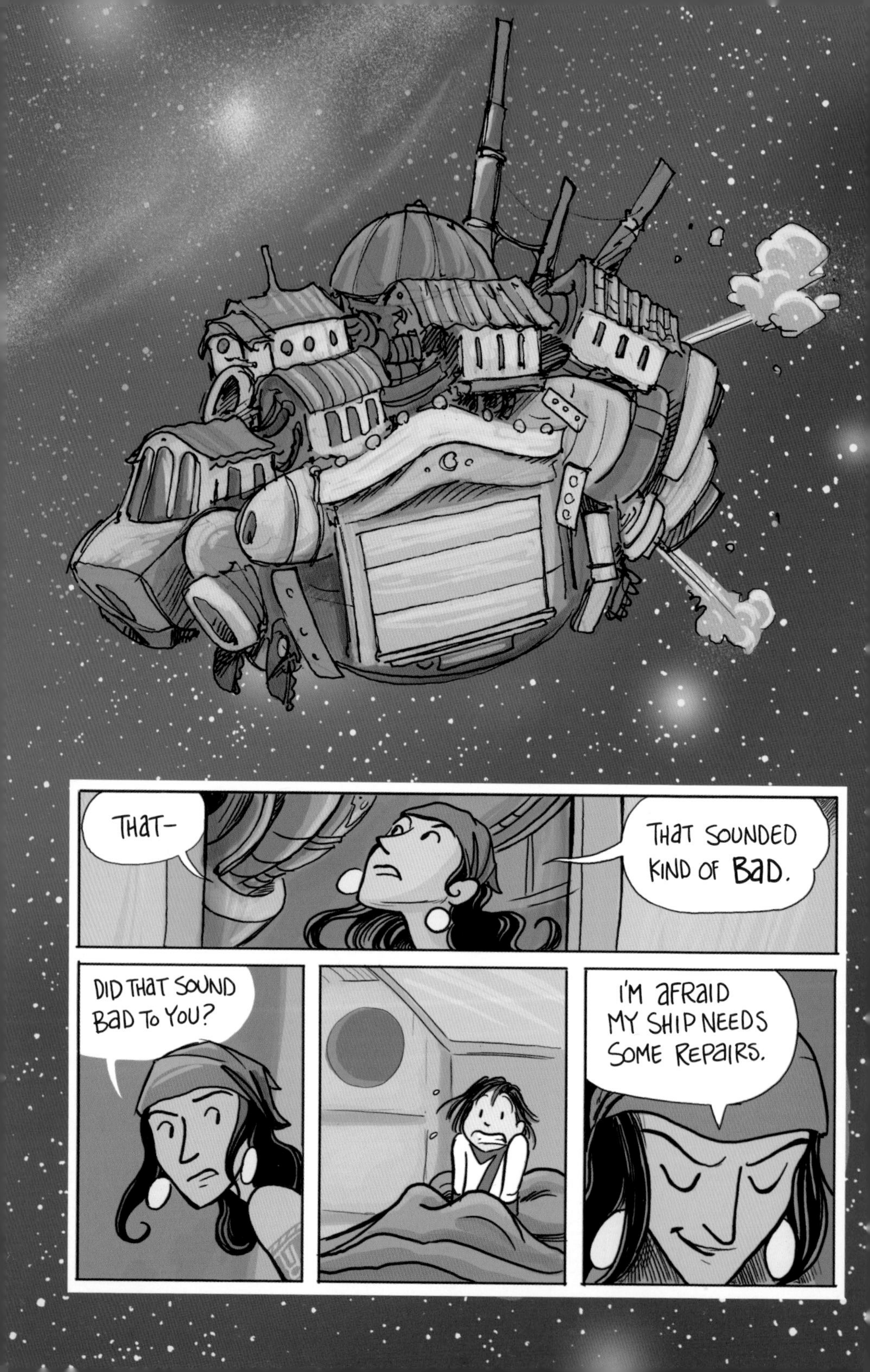
THAT-
THAT SOUNDED KIND OF BAD.
DID THAT SOUND BAD TO YOU?
I'M AFRAID MY SHIP NEEDS SOME REPAIRS.

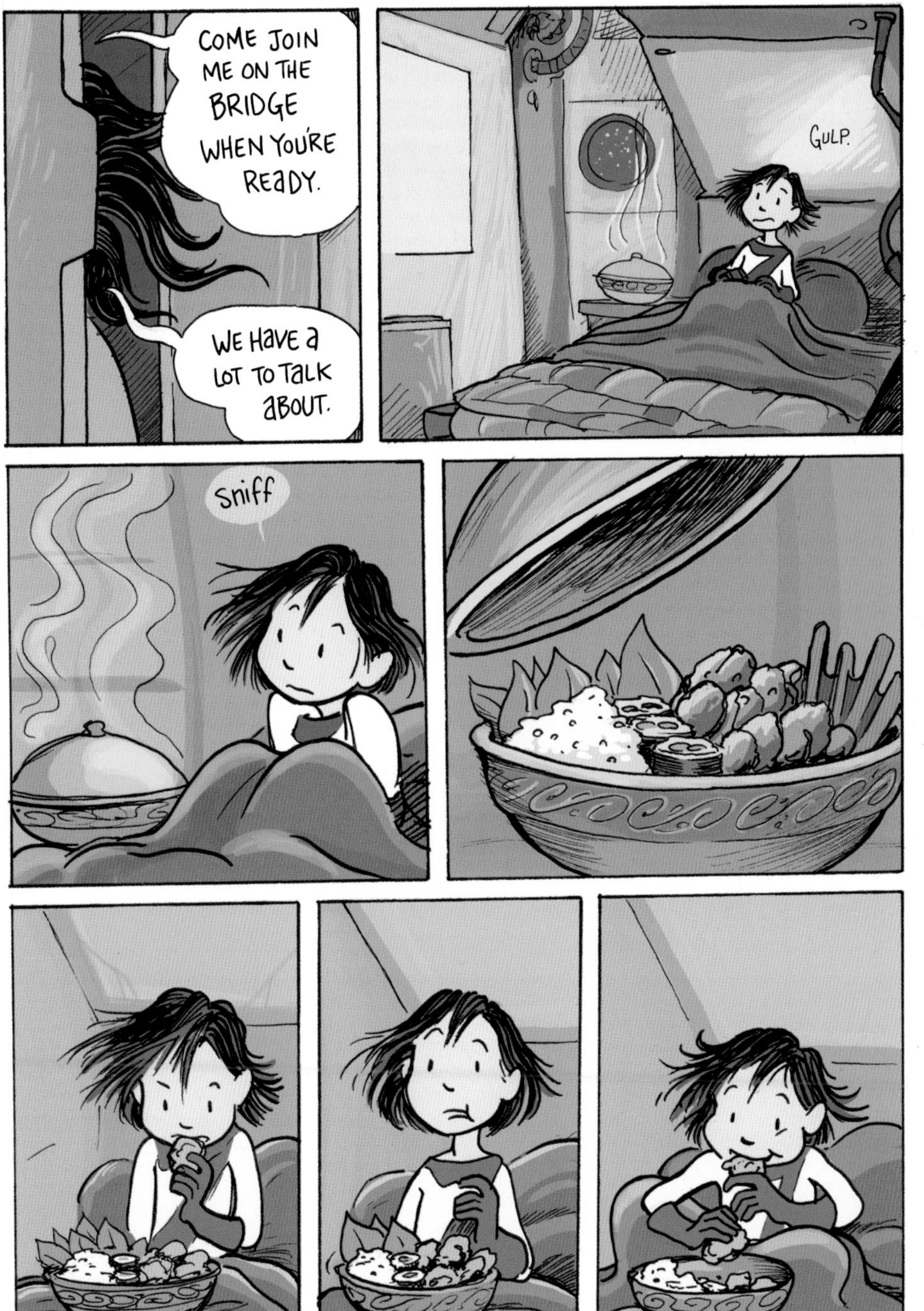
COME JOIN ME ON THE BRIDGE WHEN YOU'RE READY.
WE HAVE A LOT TO TALK ABOUT.
GULP.
SNIFF

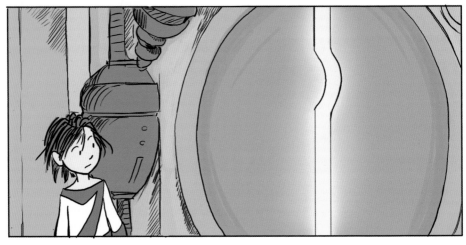

SCOOTCH

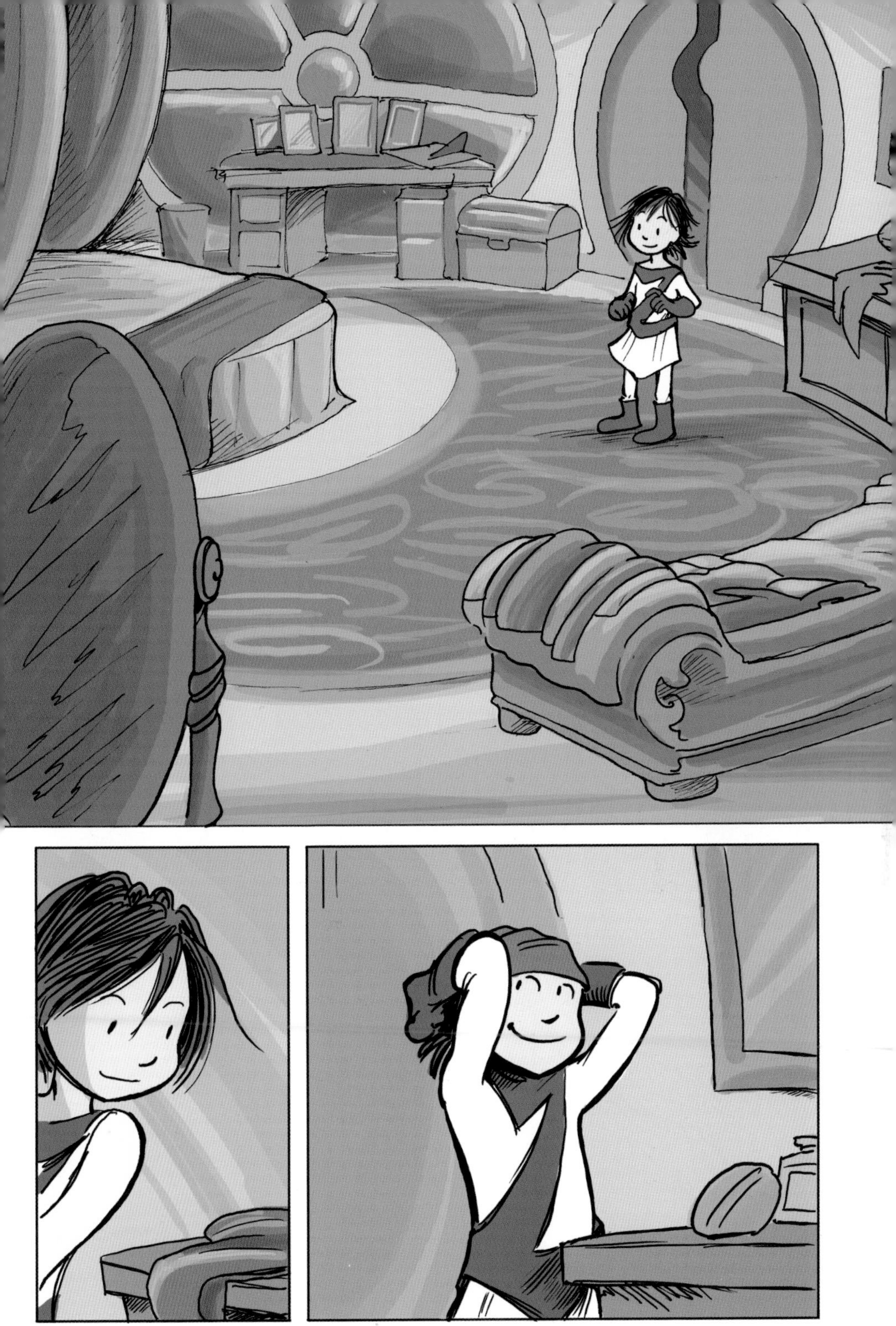

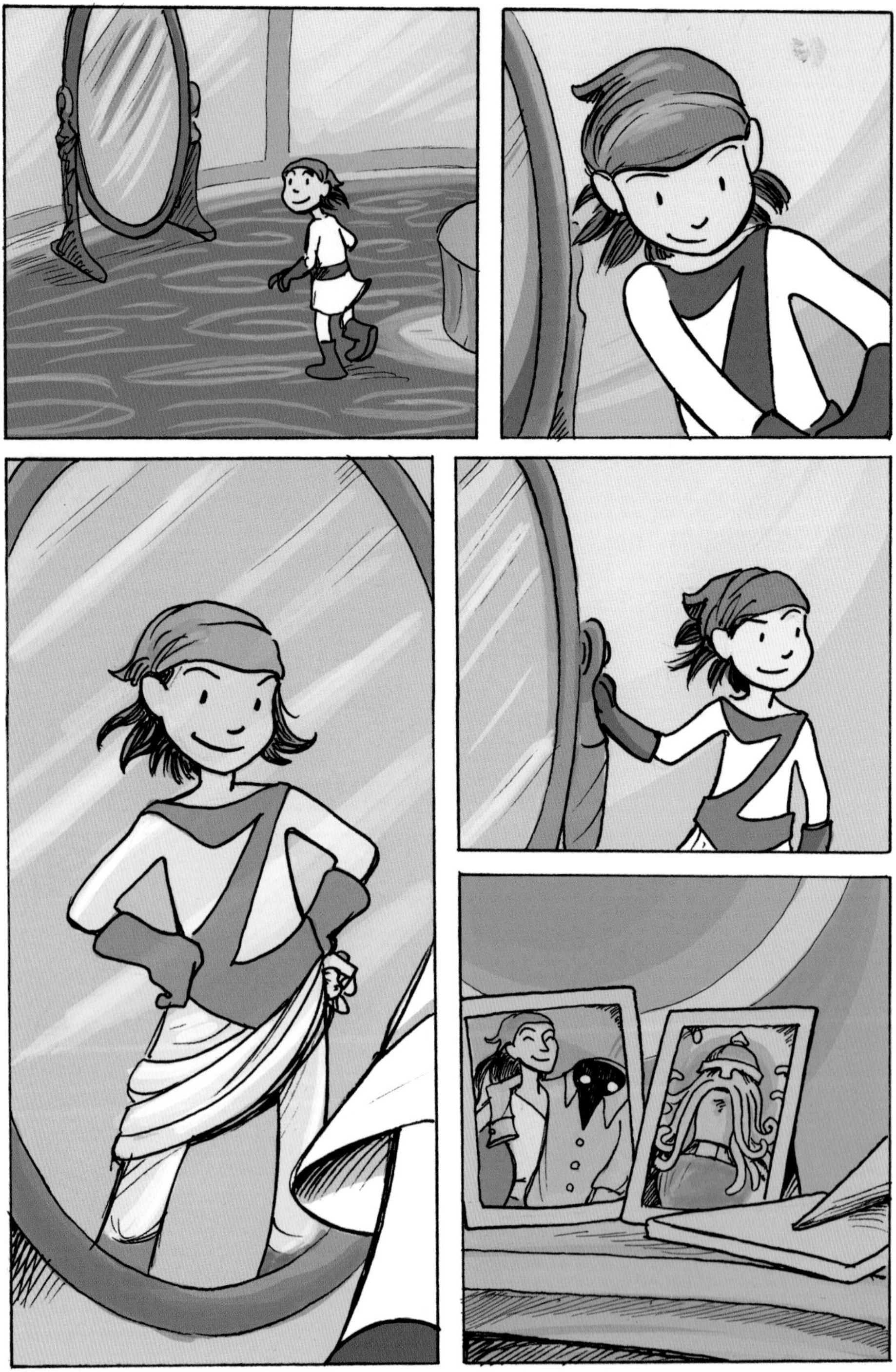

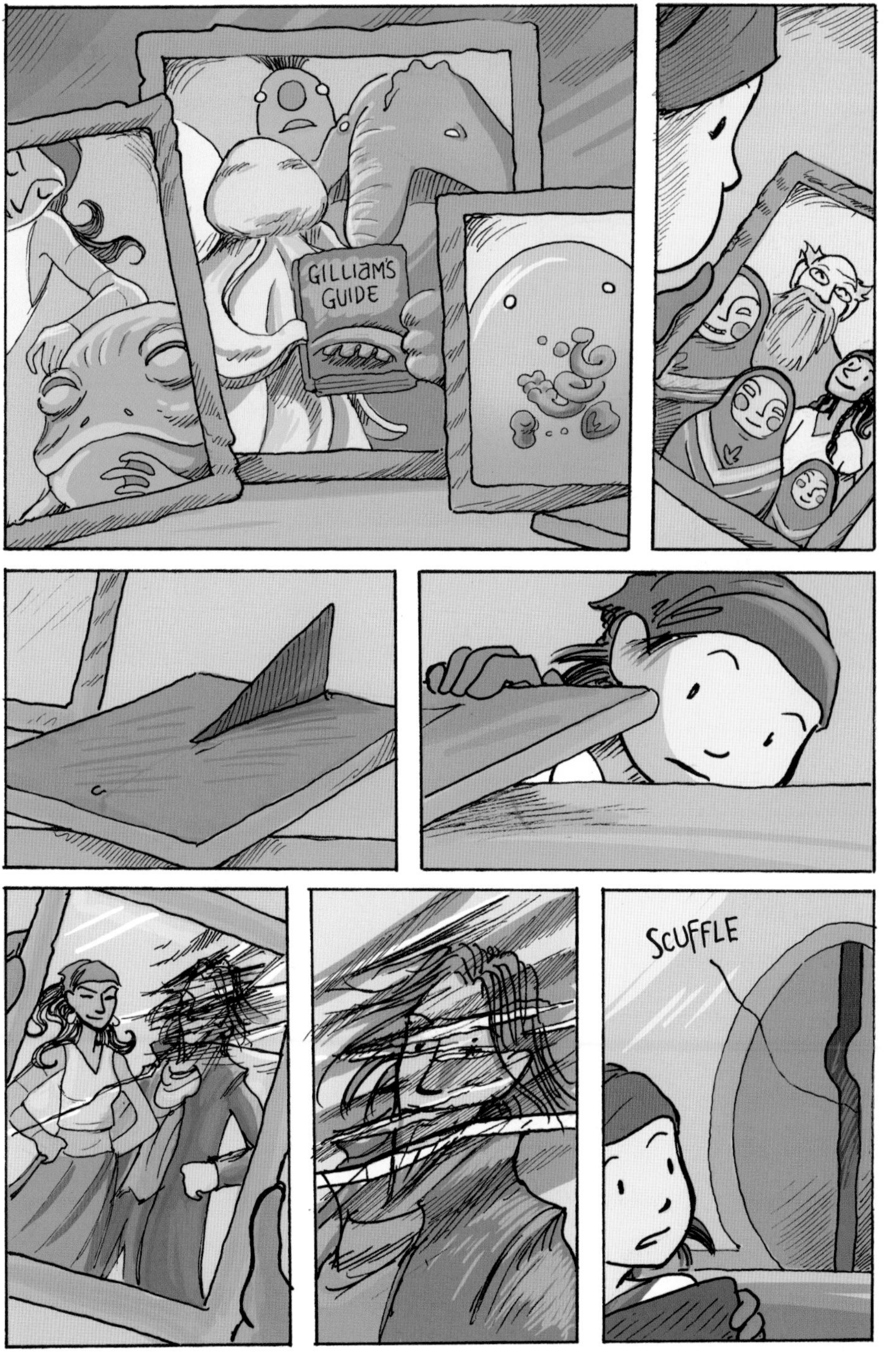
GILLIAM'S GUIDE
SCUFFLE

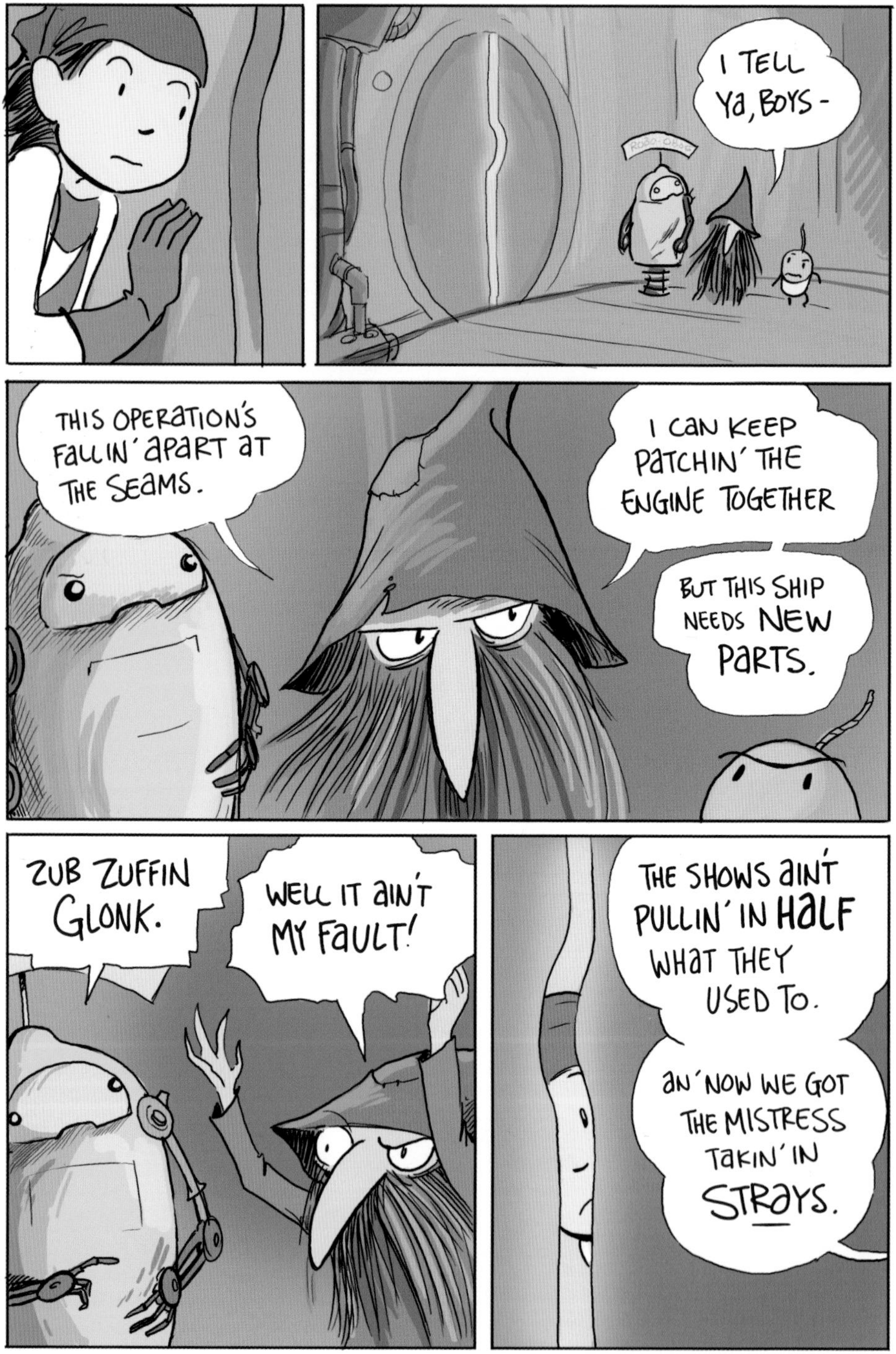

ROBO-OBOE
I TELL Ya, BOYS -
THIS OPERaTION'S FaLLIN' aPaRT aT THE SEaMS.
I CaN KEEP PaTCHIN' THE ENGINE TOGETHER
BUT THIS SHIP NEEDS NEW PaRTS.
ZUB ZUFFIN GLONK.
WELL IT aIN'T MY FaULT!
THE SHOWS aIN'T PULLIN' IN HaLF WHaT THEY USED TO.
aN' NOW WE GOT THE MISTRESS TaKIN' IN STRaYS.

MARK MY WORDS: THAT GIRL AN' HER RODENT ARE TROUBLE.

WE OUGHTA TOSS 'EM OUT THE AIRLOCK.

DOP!

POP!

DOP, DOP DOPPLE DOP!

NOW DON'T YOU START MORALIZIN' AT ME, DOPPELGANGER!

BAH! YOU TWO GOT NO IMAGINATION.

BUT THINGS ARE DUE FOR A CHANGE AROUND HERE.

105

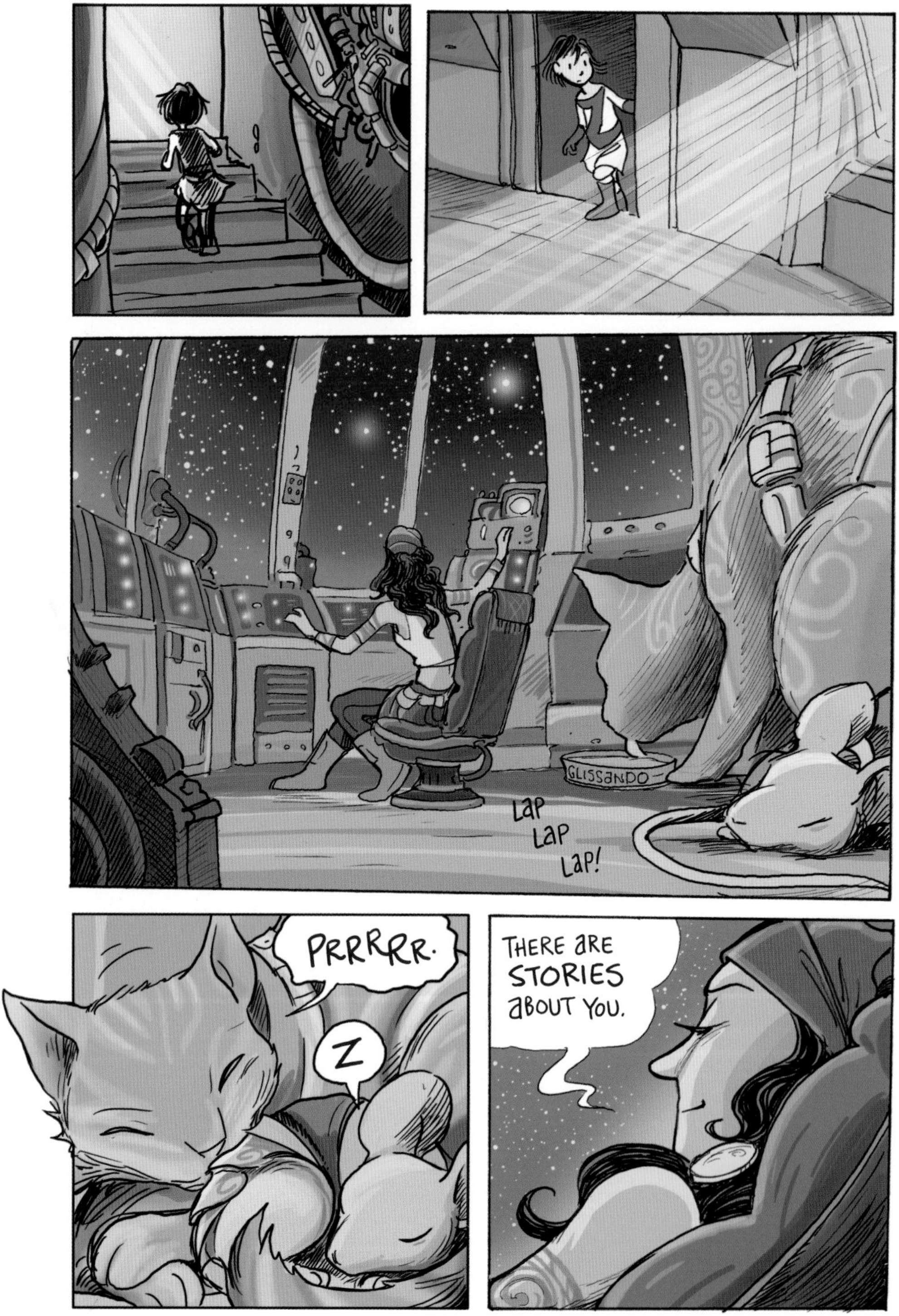
GLISSANDO
LAP
LAP
LAP!
PRRRRR.
Z
THERE ARE STORIES ABOUT YOU.

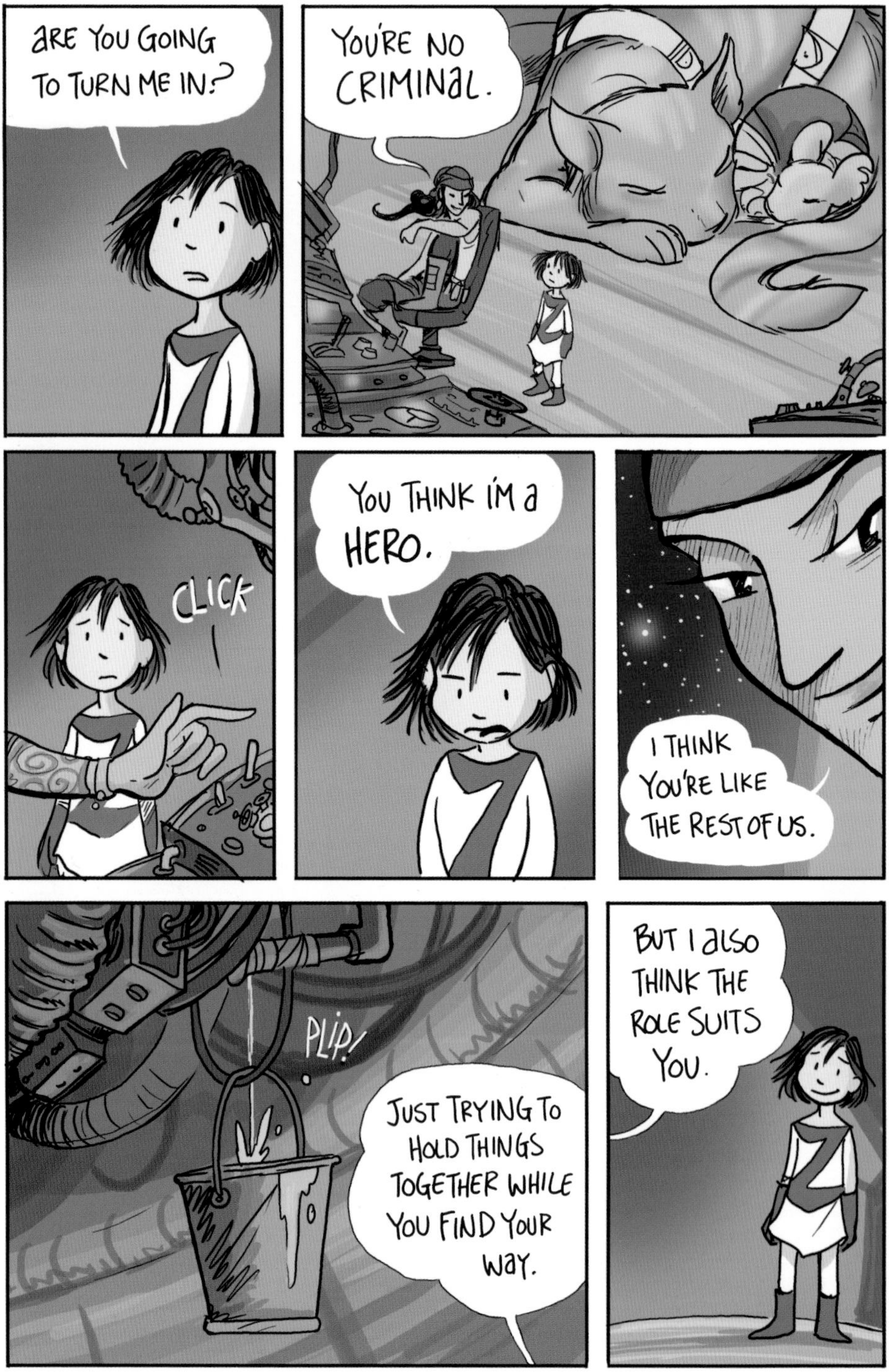
ARE YOU GOING TO TURN ME IN?
YOU'RE NO CRIMINAL.
CLICK
YOU THINK I'M A HERO.
I THINK YOU'RE LIKE THE REST OF US.
PLIP!
JUST TRYING TO HOLD THINGS TOGETHER WHILE YOU FIND YOUR WAY.
BUT I ALSO THINK THE ROLE SUITS YOU.

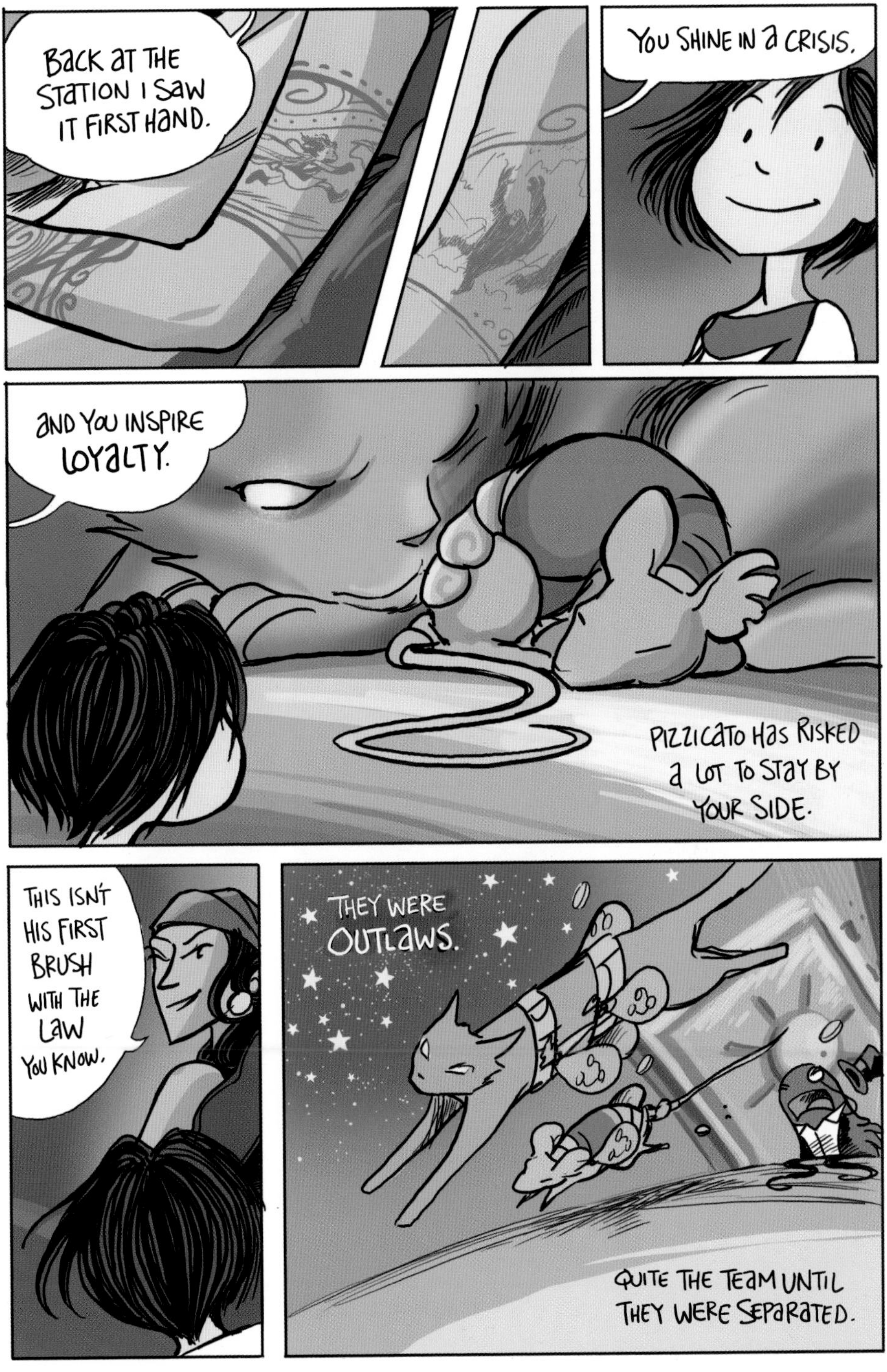
BACK AT THE STATION I SAW IT FIRST HAND.
YOU SHINE IN A CRISIS.
AND YOU INSPIRE LOYALTY.
PIZZICATO HAS RISKED A LOT TO STAY BY YOUR SIDE.
THIS ISN'T HIS FIRST BRUSH WITH THE LAW YOU KNOW.
THEY WERE OUTLAWS.
QUITE THE TEAM UNTIL THEY WERE SEPARATED.

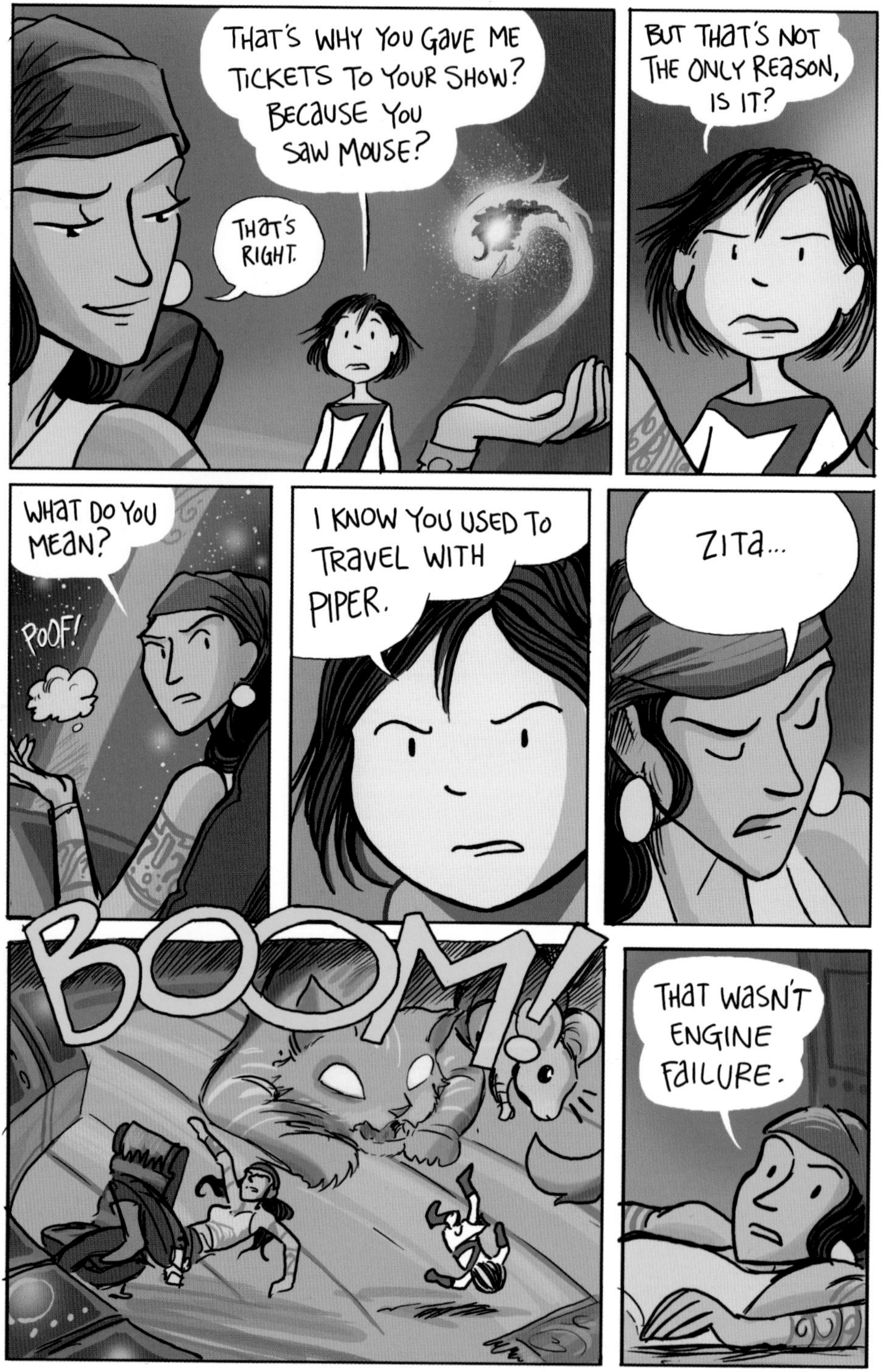

THAT'S WHY YOU GAVE ME TICKETS TO YOUR SHOW? BECAUSE YOU SAW MOUSE?
THAT'S RIGHT.
BUT THAT'S NOT THE ONLY REASON, IS IT?
WHAT DO YOU MEAN?
POOF!
I KNOW YOU USED TO TRAVEL WITH PIPER.
ZITA...
BOOM!
THAT WASN'T ENGINE FAILURE.

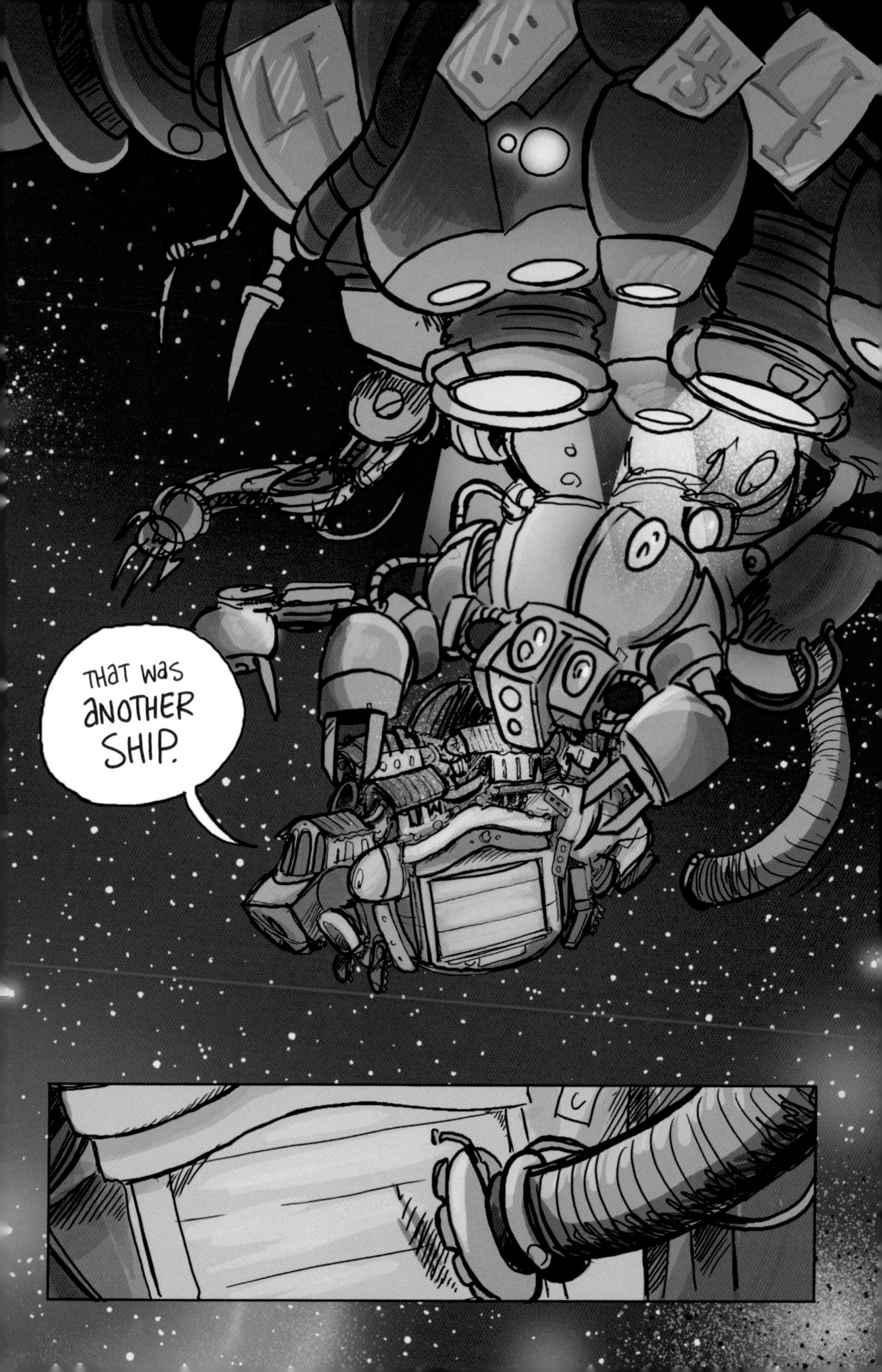
THAT WAS ANOTHER SHIP.

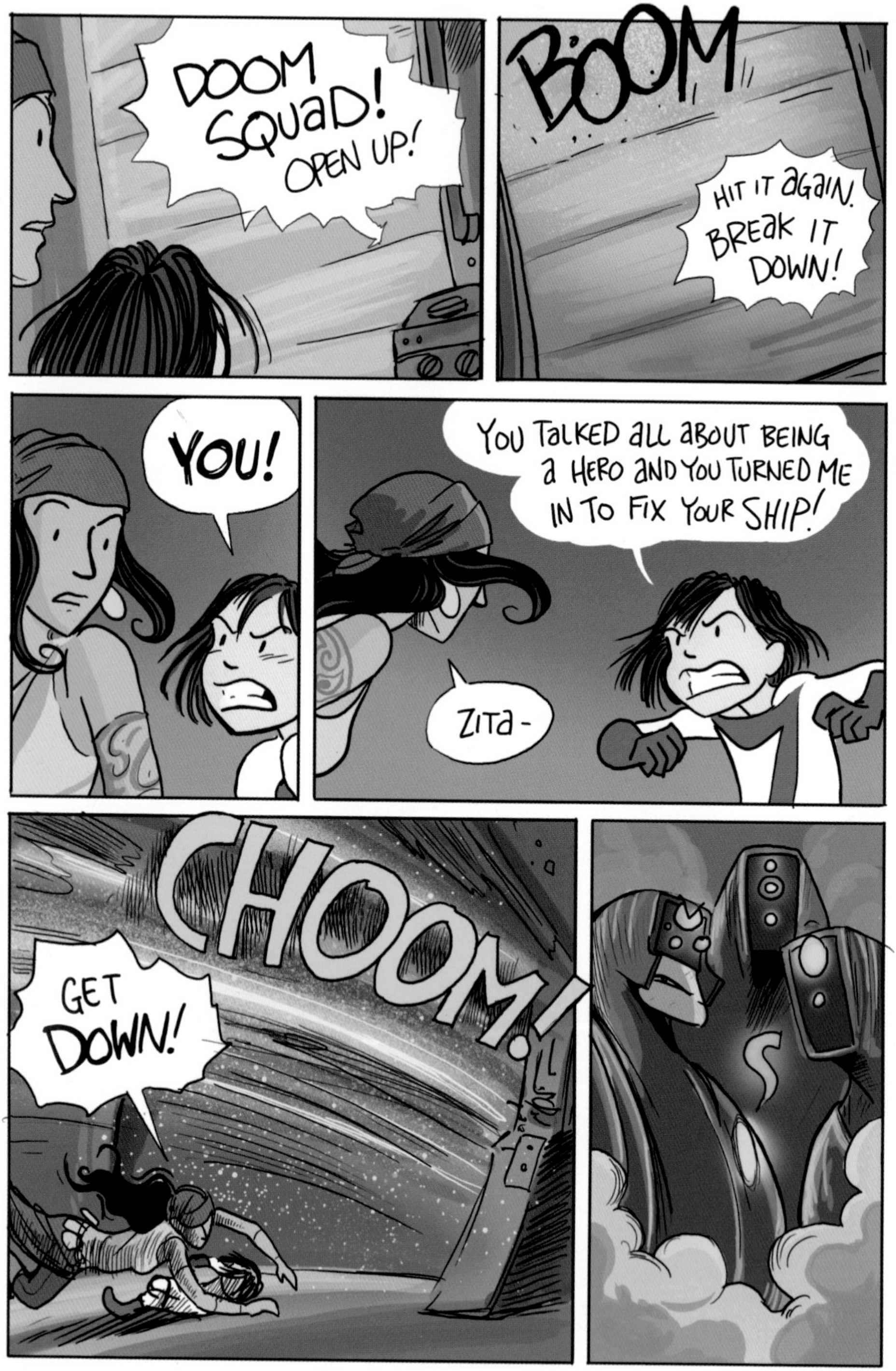
DOOM SQUAD! OPEN UP!
BOOM
HIT IT AGAIN. BREAK IT DOWN!
YOU!
YOU TALKED ALL ABOUT BEING A HERO AND YOU TURNED ME IN TO FIX YOUR SHIP!
ZITA-
CHOOM!
GET DOWN!

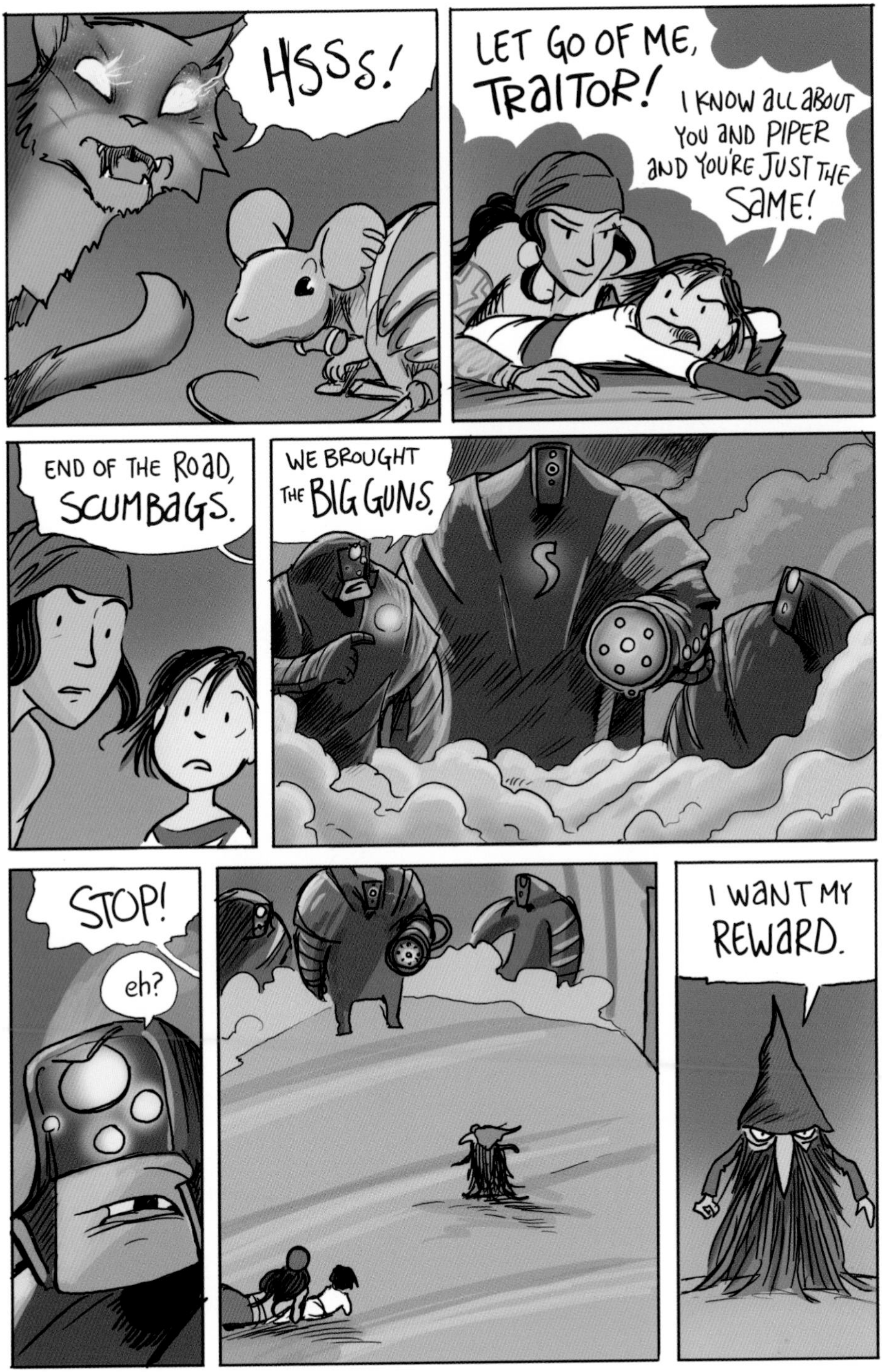
HSSs!
LET GO OF ME, TRAITOR!
I KNOW ALL ABOUT YOU AND PIPER AND YOU'RE JUST THE SAME!
END OF THE ROAD, SCUMBAGS.
WE BROUGHT THE BIG GUNS.
STOP!
eh?
I WANT MY REWARD.

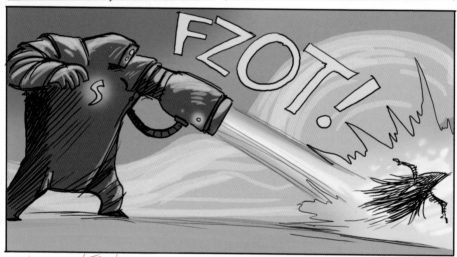

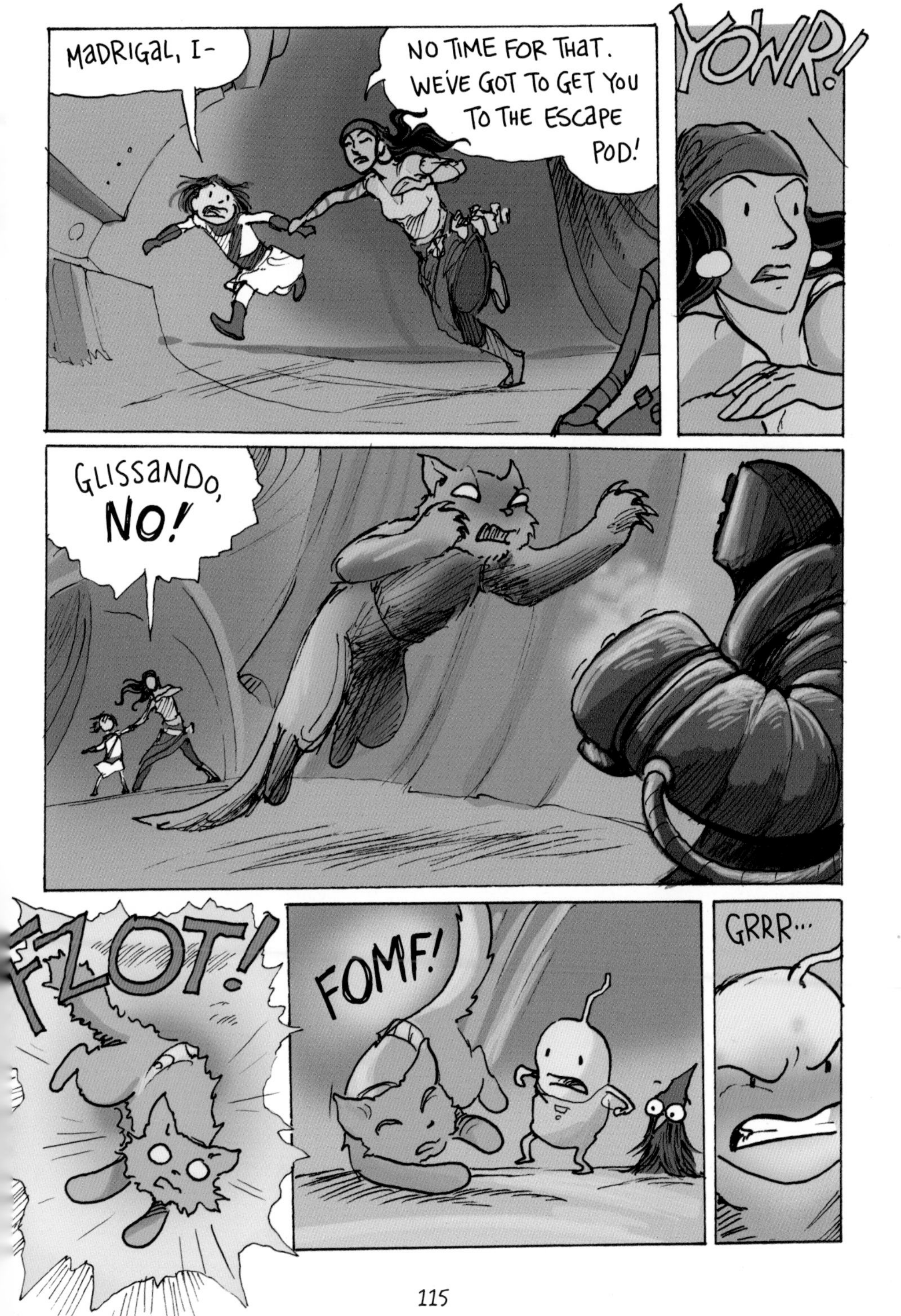
MADRIGAL, I-
NO TIME FOR THAT. WE'VE GOT TO GET YOU TO THE ESCAPE POD!
YOWR!
GLISSANDO, NO!
FZOT!
FOMF!
GRRR...

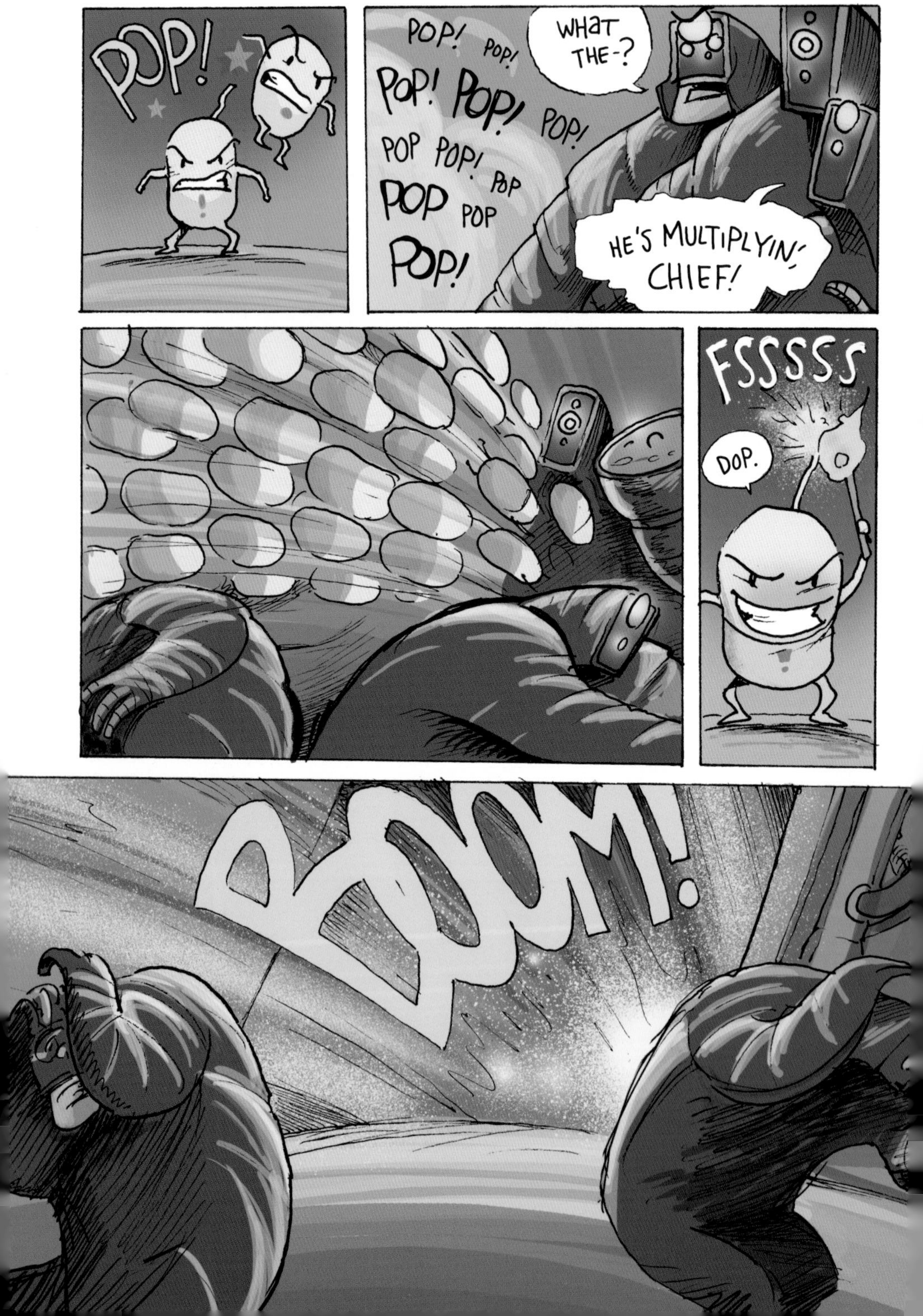
POP!
POP! POP!
POP! POP! POP!
POP POP! POP
POP POP
POP!
WHAT THE-?
HE'S MULTIPLYIN', CHIEF!
FSSSSS
DOP.
BOOM!

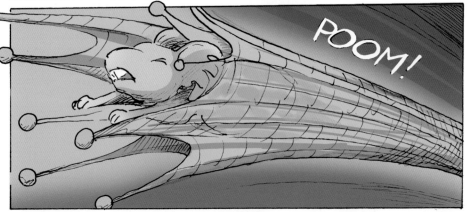

THEY'VE GOT MOUSE!

AND IF THEY CATCH YOU TOO THEN YOUR JOURNEY IS OVER!

LET GO!

CHING!

GO!

I'LL COME FIND YOU, MOUSE!

CLOMP CLOMP CLOMP!

I PROMISE

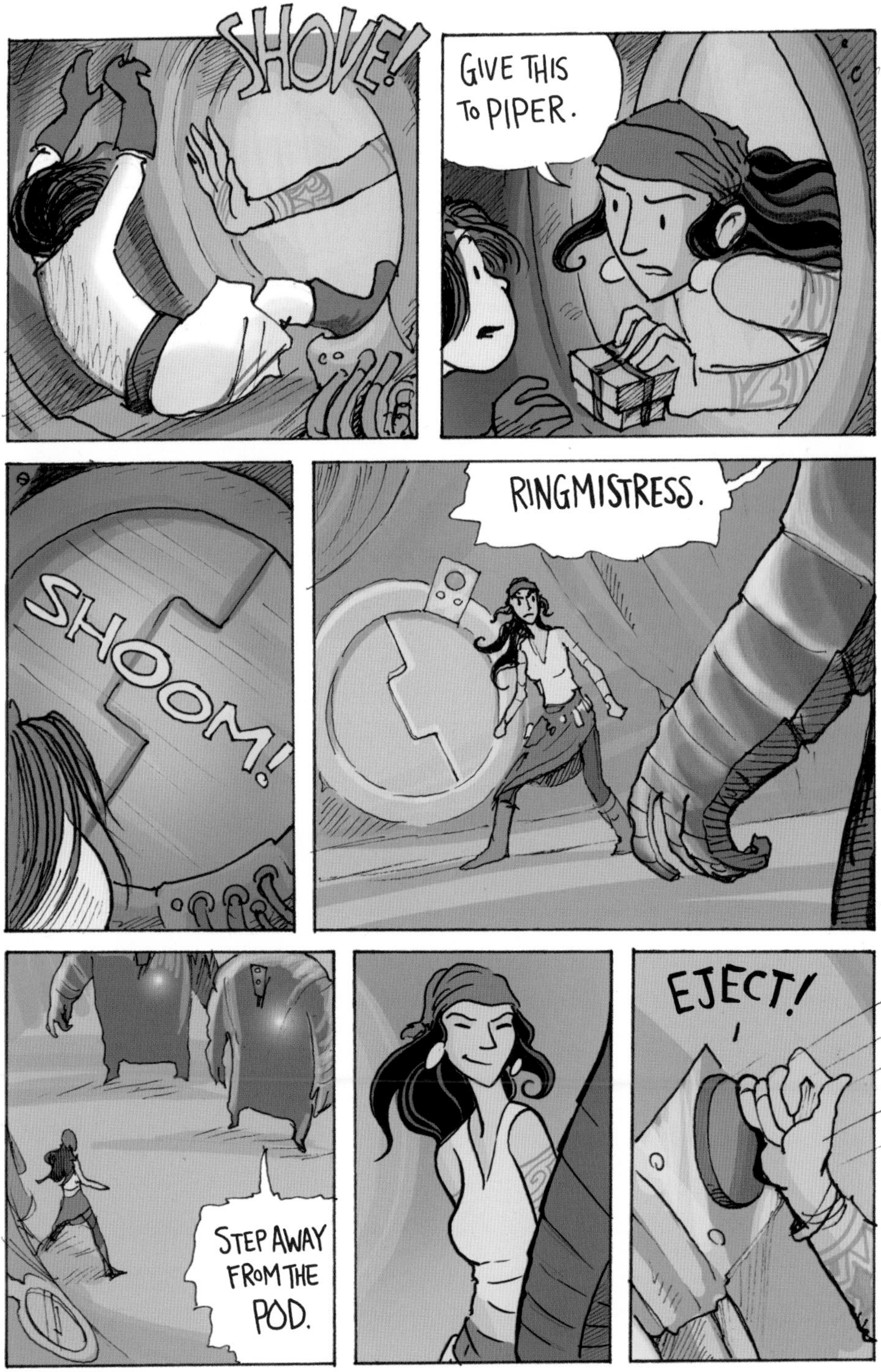
SHOVE!
GIVE THIS
TO PIPER.
SHOOM!
RINGMISTRESS.
STEP AWAY
FROM THE
POD.
EJECT!

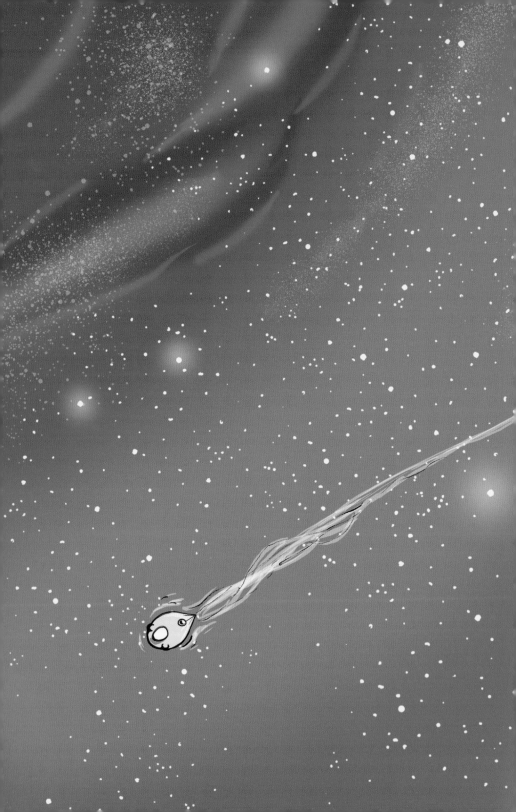

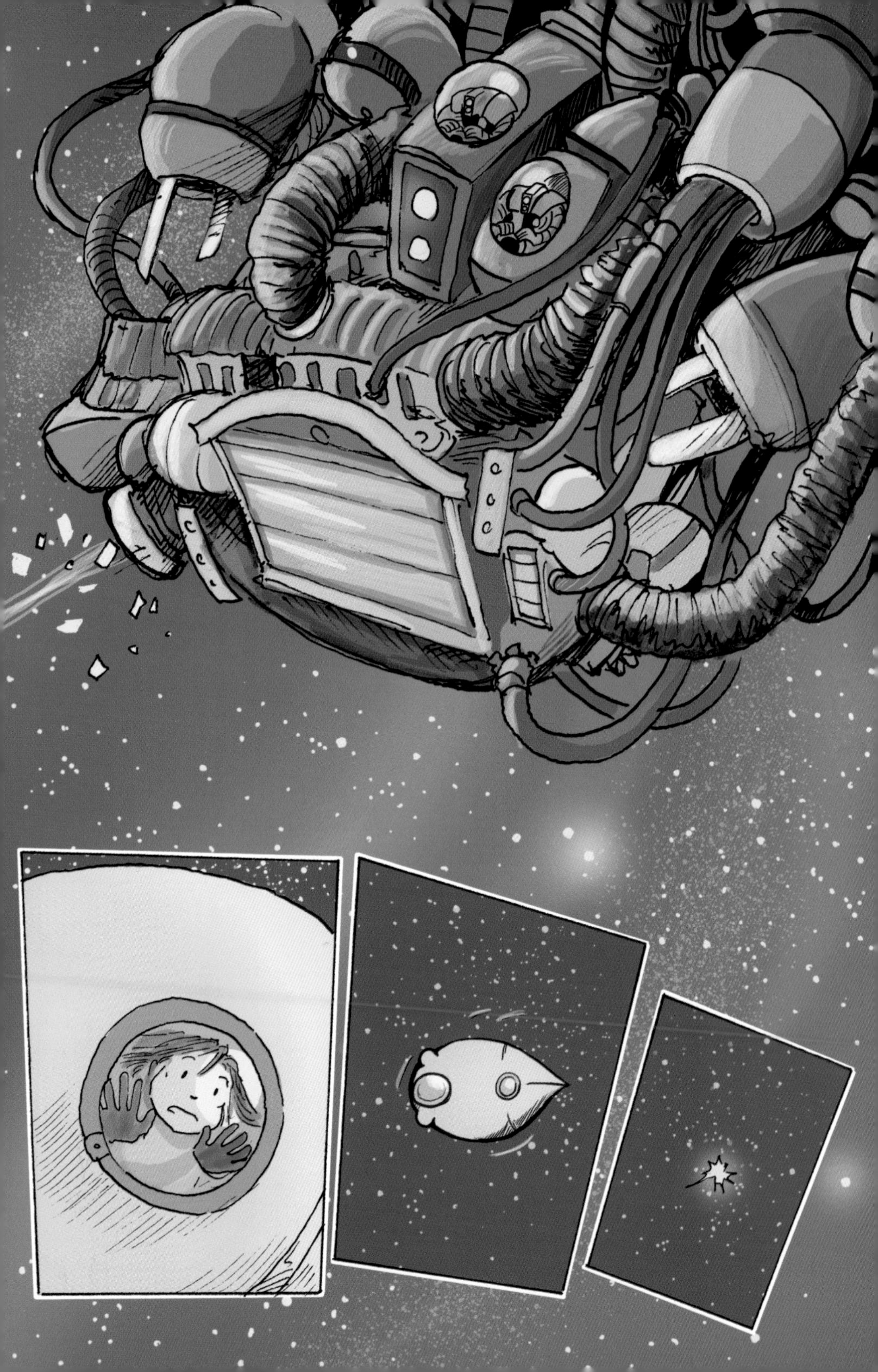

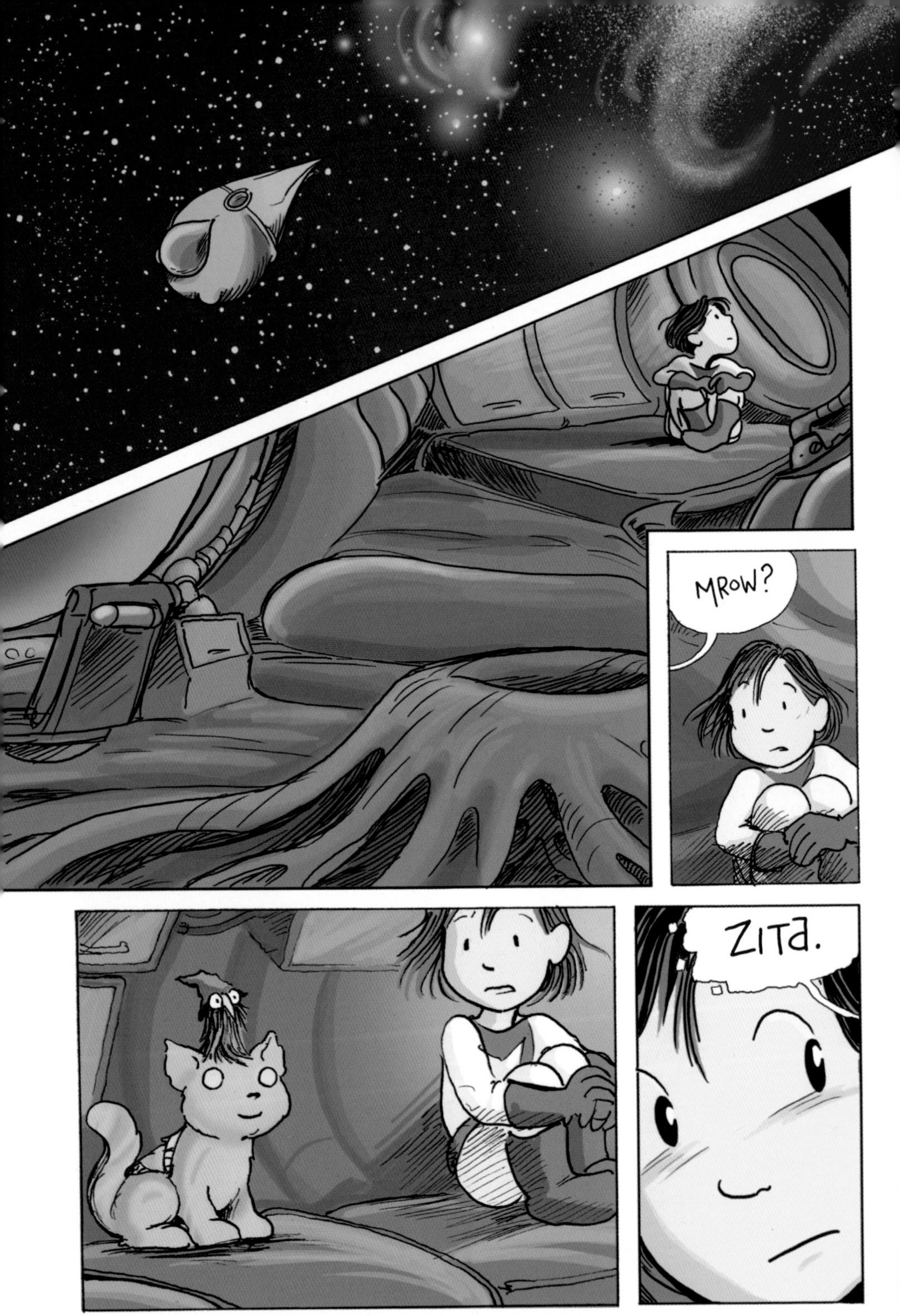
MROW?
ZITA.

LISTEN CLOSELY.

IF YOU ARE RECEIVING THIS, THEN I'VE GIVEN YOU THE POD AHEAD OF SCHEDULE.

THERE ARE THINGS YOU SHOULD KNOW.

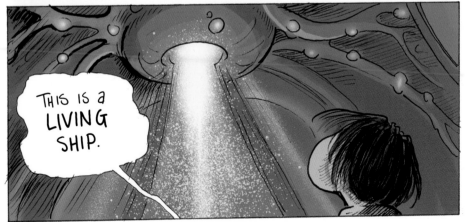

THIS IS A LIVING SHIP.

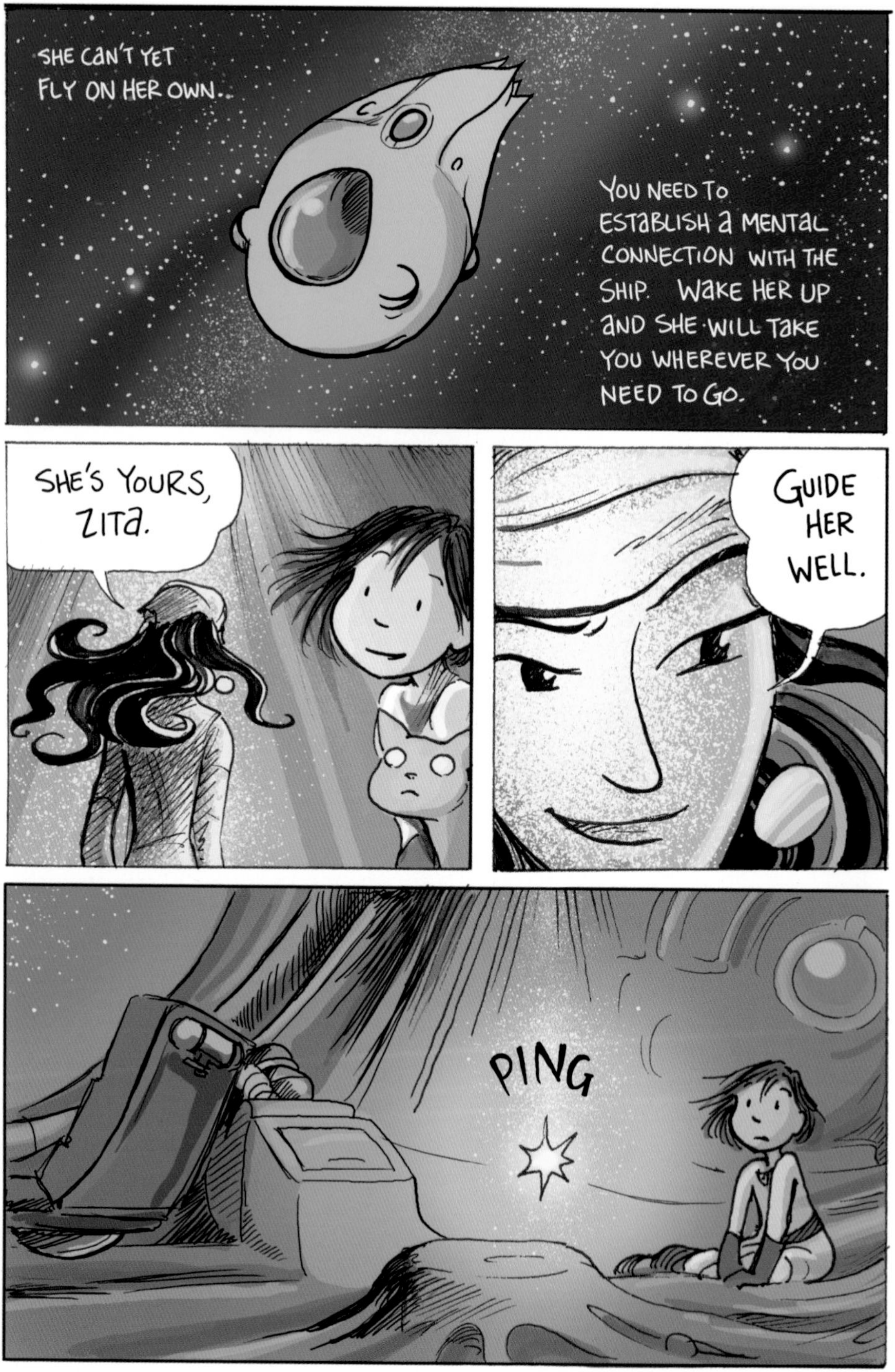
SHE CAN'T YET FLY ON HER OWN...
YOU NEED TO ESTABLISH A MENTAL CONNECTION WITH THE SHIP. WAKE HER UP AND SHE WILL TAKE YOU WHEREVER YOU NEED TO GO.
SHE'S YOURS, ZITA.
GUIDE HER WELL.
PING

Chapter
Four

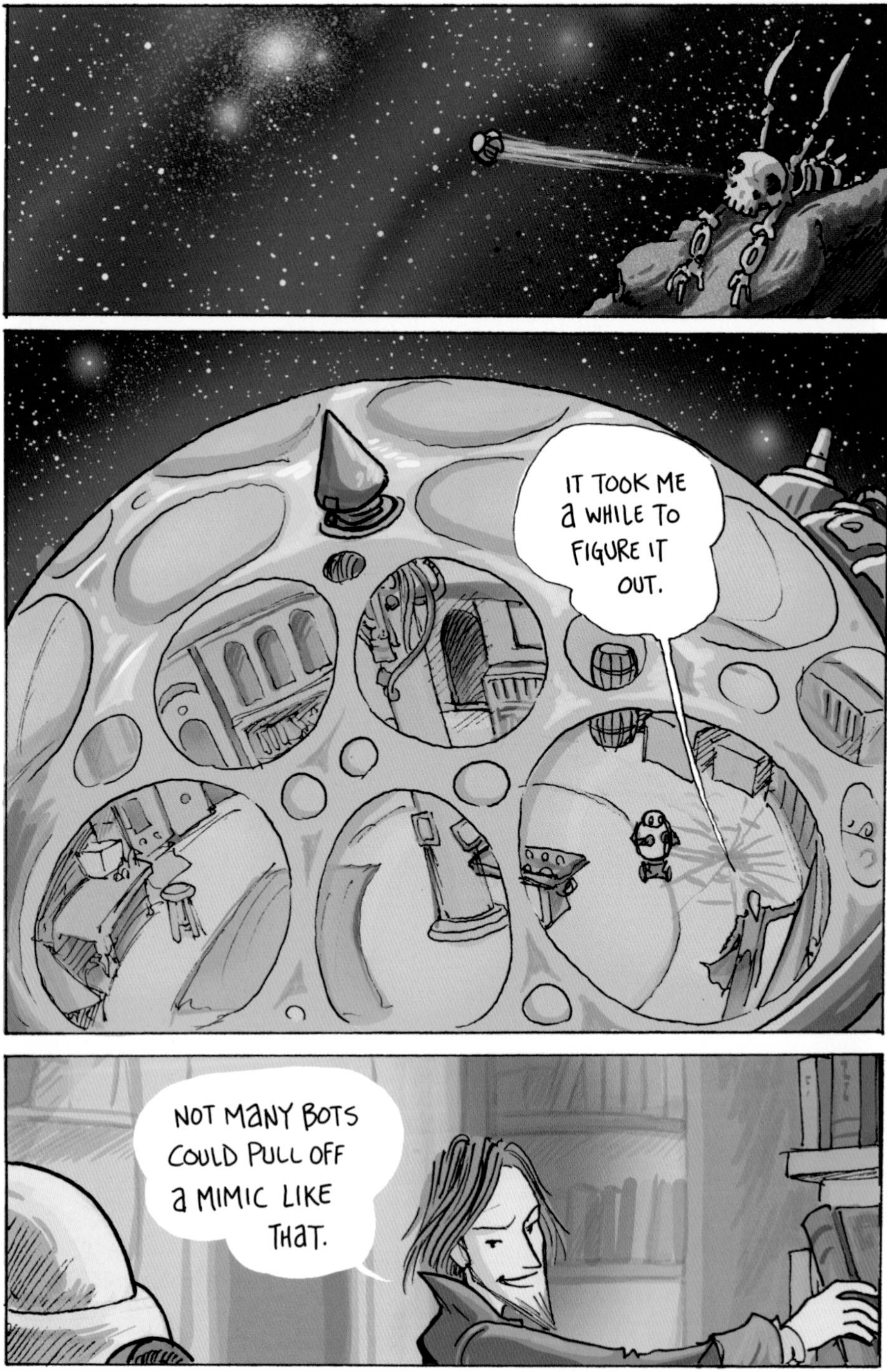
IT TOOK ME a WHILE TO FIGURE IT OUT.
NOT MaNY BOTS COULD PULL OFF a MIMIC LIKE THaT.

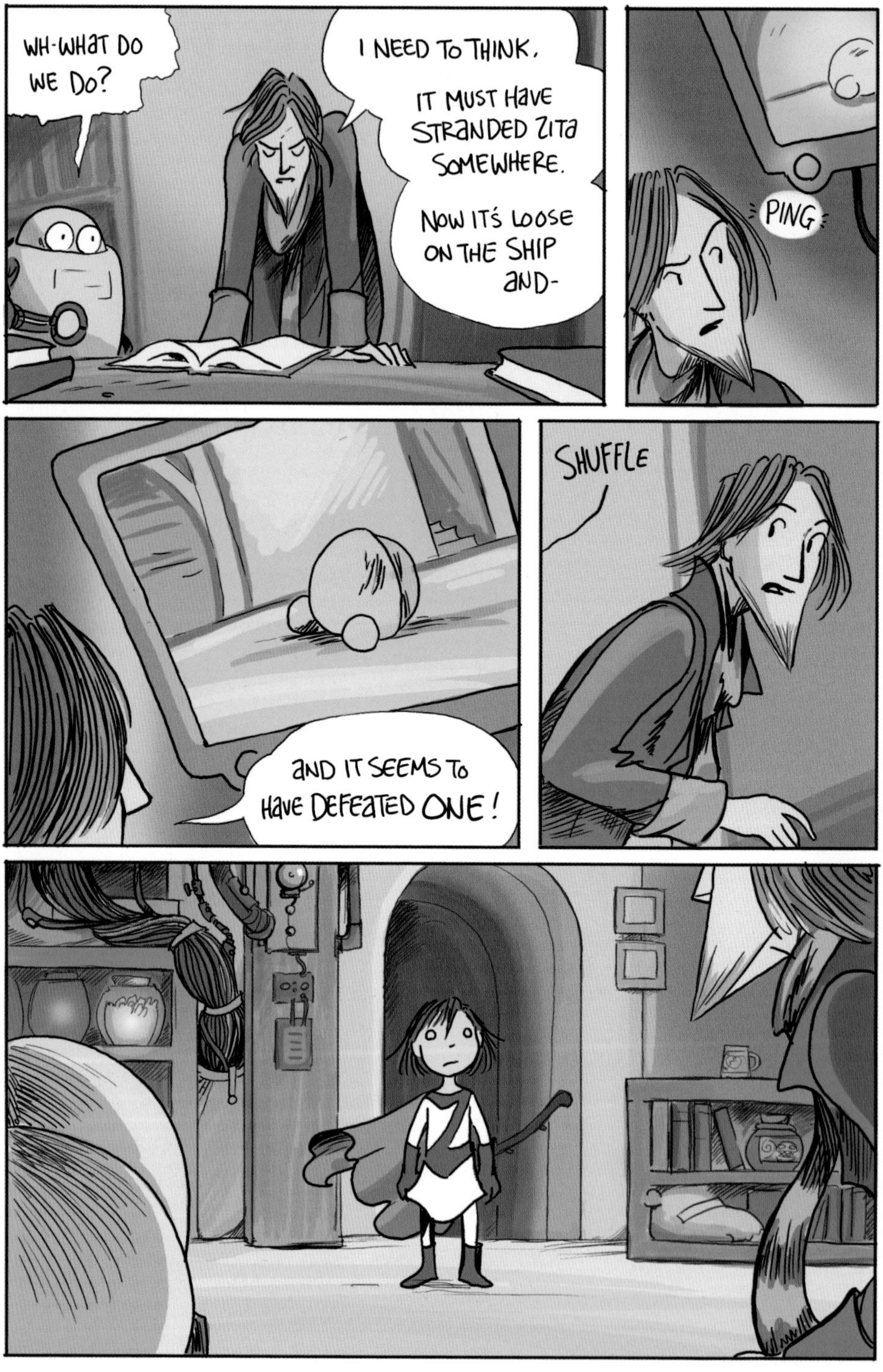
WH-WHAT DO WE DO?
I NEED TO THINK.
IT MUST HAVE STRANDED ZITA SOMEWHERE.
NOW IT'S LOOSE ON THE SHIP AND-
PING
AND IT SEEMS TO HAVE DEFEATED ONE!
SHUFFLE

C-CAN YOU M-MAKE HER DANCE?

IT'S STILL A ROBOT. MY MUSIC WON'T AFFECT IT.

STEP

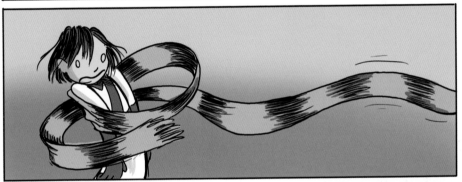

CAREFUL. IT ONLY GETS TIGHTER IF YOU STRUGGLE.

SO GLAD I LEARNED TO KNIT.

NOW DON'T MAKE TROUBLE.

WHISTLE MAN?

"PIPER!" MY NAME IS "PIPER."

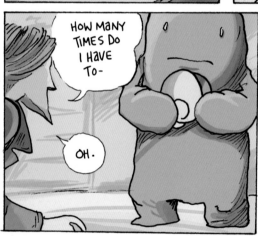

HOW MANY TIMES DO I HAVE TO—

OH.

HIS INITIALIZER IS FRIED BUT HIS SYSTEM SHOULD REBOOT.

NO PERMANENT DAMAGE.

P-P-PIPER?

WE'RE APPROACHING A P-PLANET.

BLING!

YOU MADE IT!

WE KNEW YOU'D SAVE US!

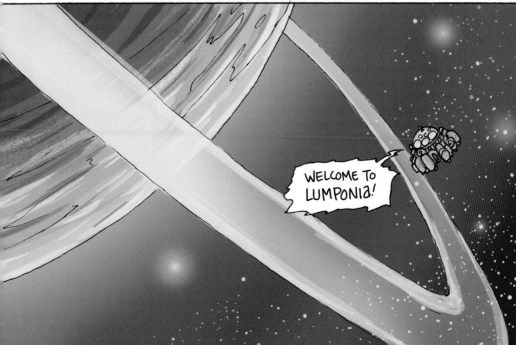

WELCOME TO LUMPONIA!

LOOK, I'M SORRY BUT WE CAN'T HELP YOU.

W-WHAT?

BUT ZITA THE SPACEGIRL! SHE-

SHE PROMISED!

THAT'S THE THING, SEE... WE SORT OF...

LOST HER.

GONE? THE HERO OF LUMPONIA IS -MISSING?

AH! AH HA! YOU JOKE WITH US!

YOU BRING THE LIGHT OF HUMOR TO OUR DARKEST HOUR!

WHAT? NO!

I MEAN IT-WE WILL NOT BE LANDING ON YOUR PLANET!

CHZZT!

132

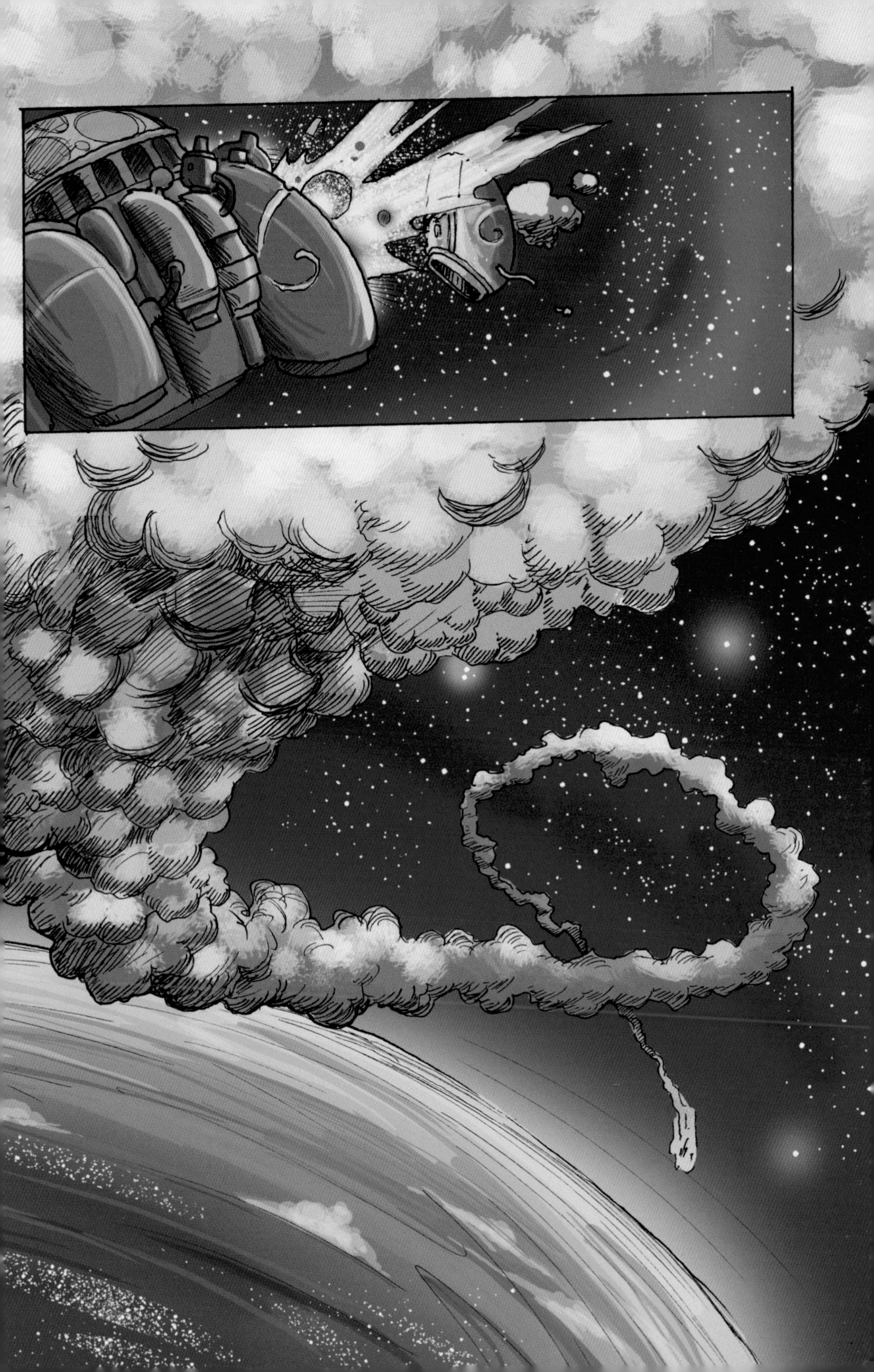

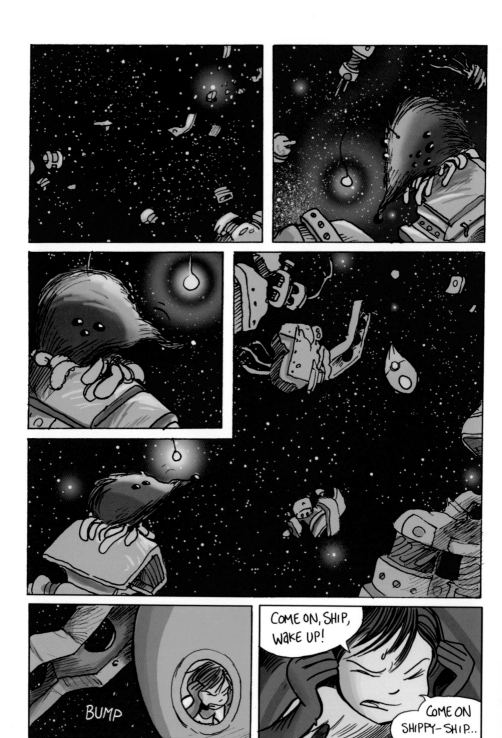

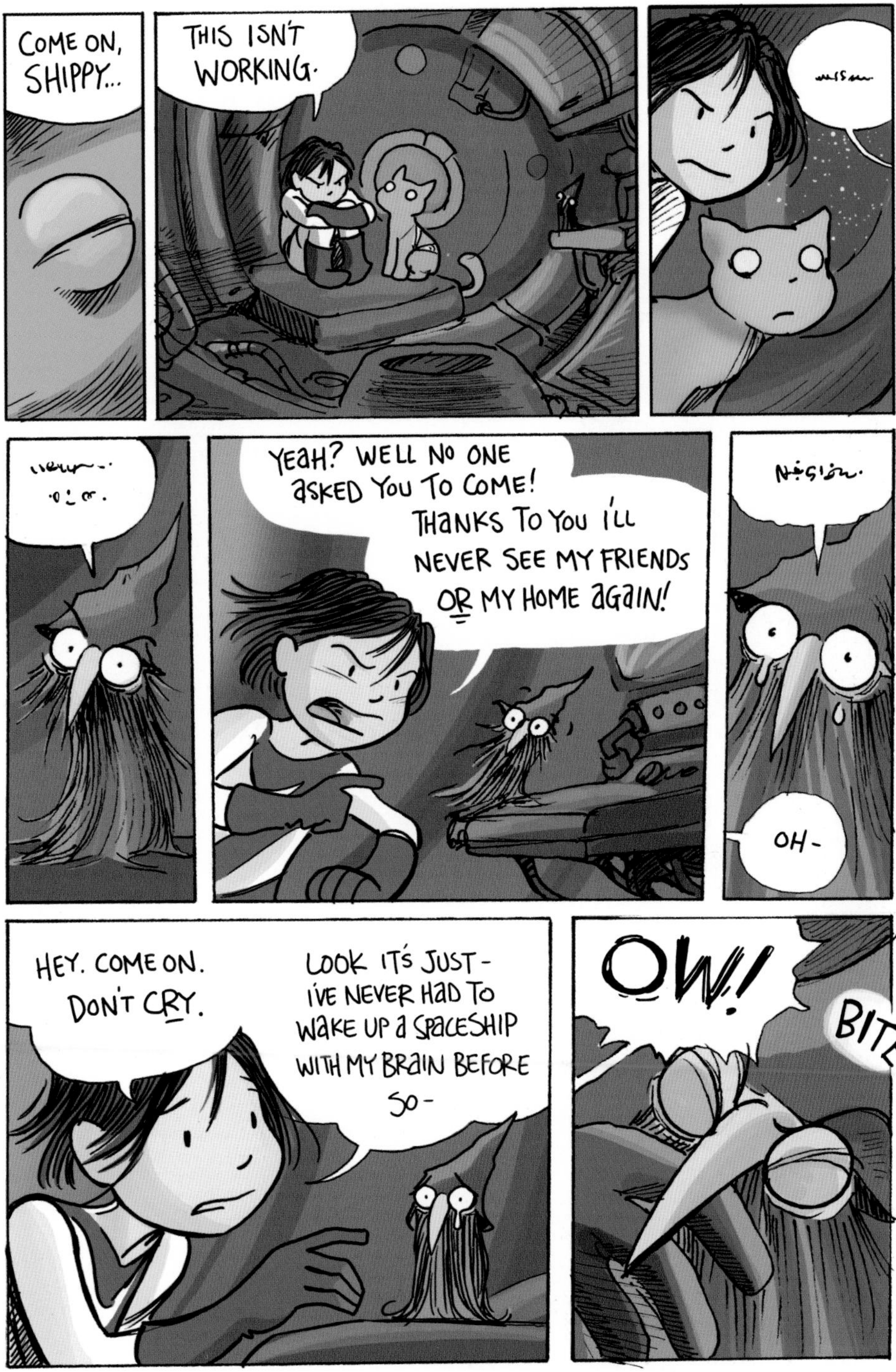
COME ON, SHIPPY...
THIS ISN'T WORKING.
YEAH? WELL NO ONE ASKED YOU TO COME!
THANKS TO YOU I'LL NEVER SEE MY FRIENDS OR MY HOME AGAIN!
OH-
HEY. COME ON. DON'T CRY.
LOOK IT'S JUST- I'VE NEVER HAD TO WAKE UP A SPACESHIP WITH MY BRAIN BEFORE SO-
OW!
BITE!

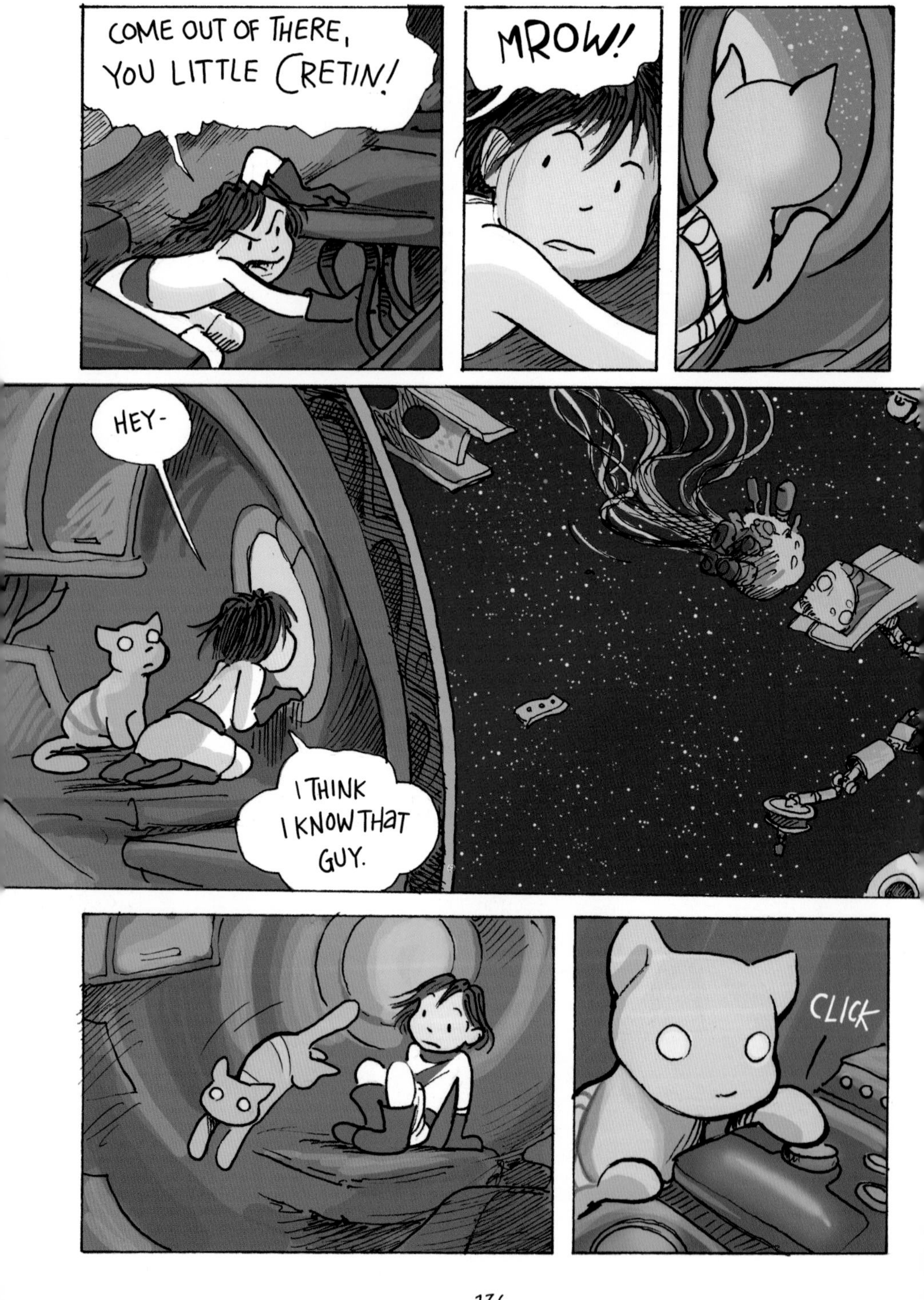
COME OUT OF THERE, YOU LITTLE CRETIN!
MROW!
HEY-
I THINK I KNOW THAT GUY.
CLICK

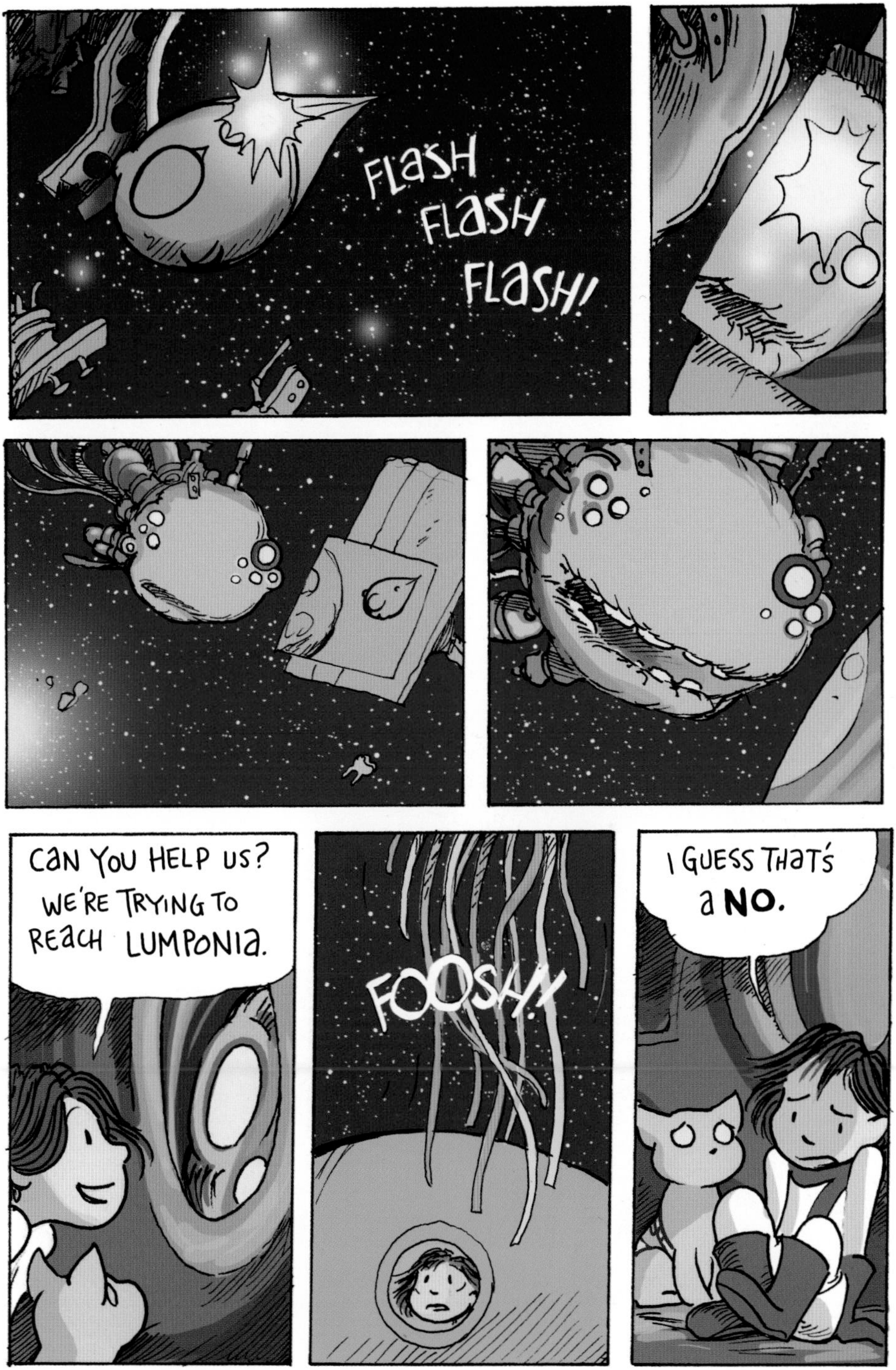
FLASH
FLASH
FLASH!
CAN YOU HELP US? WE'RE TRYING TO REACH LUMPONIA.
FOOSH!
I GUESS THAT'S a NO.

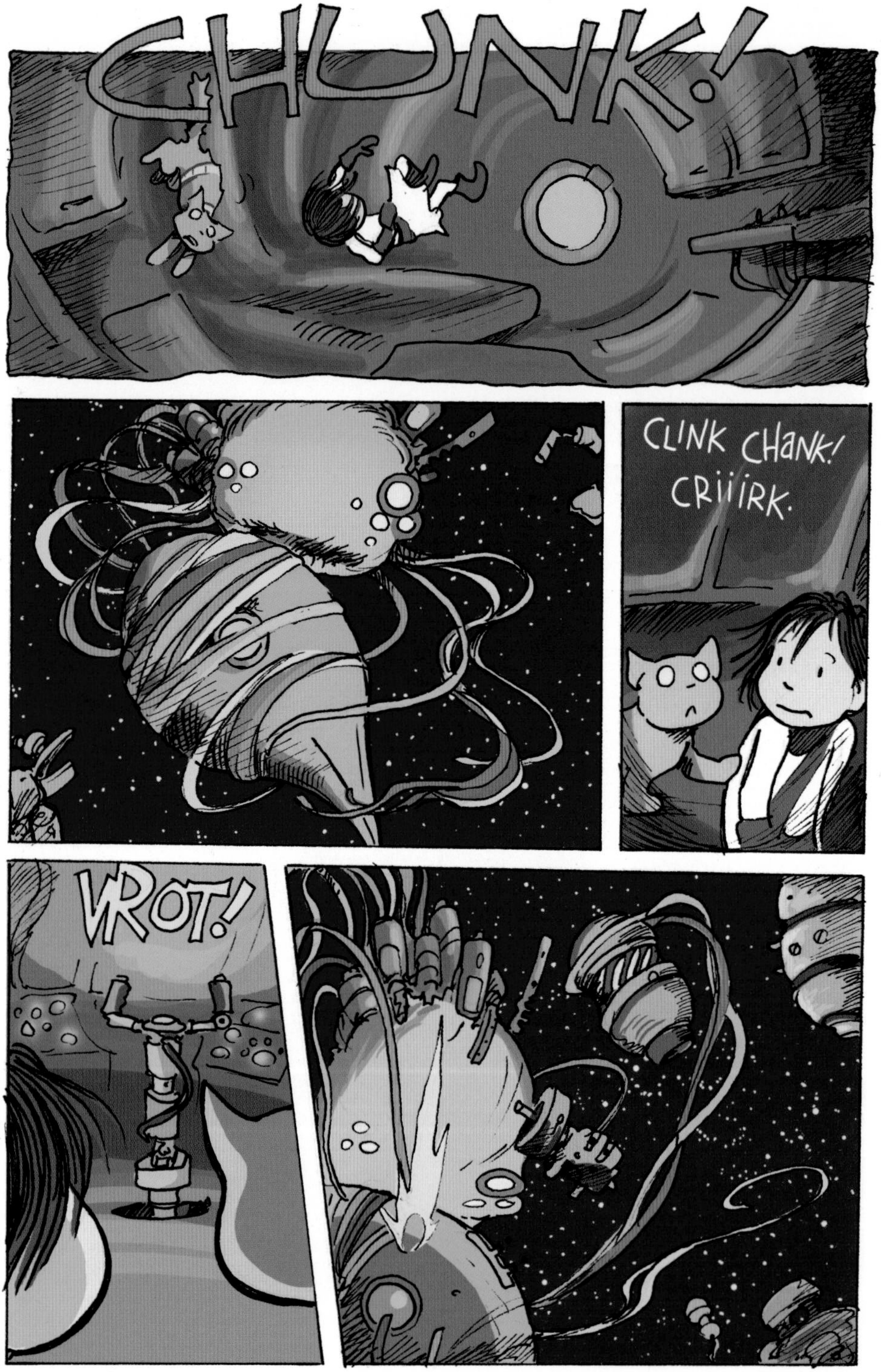
CHUNK!
CLINK CHANK!
CRIIIRK.
VROT!

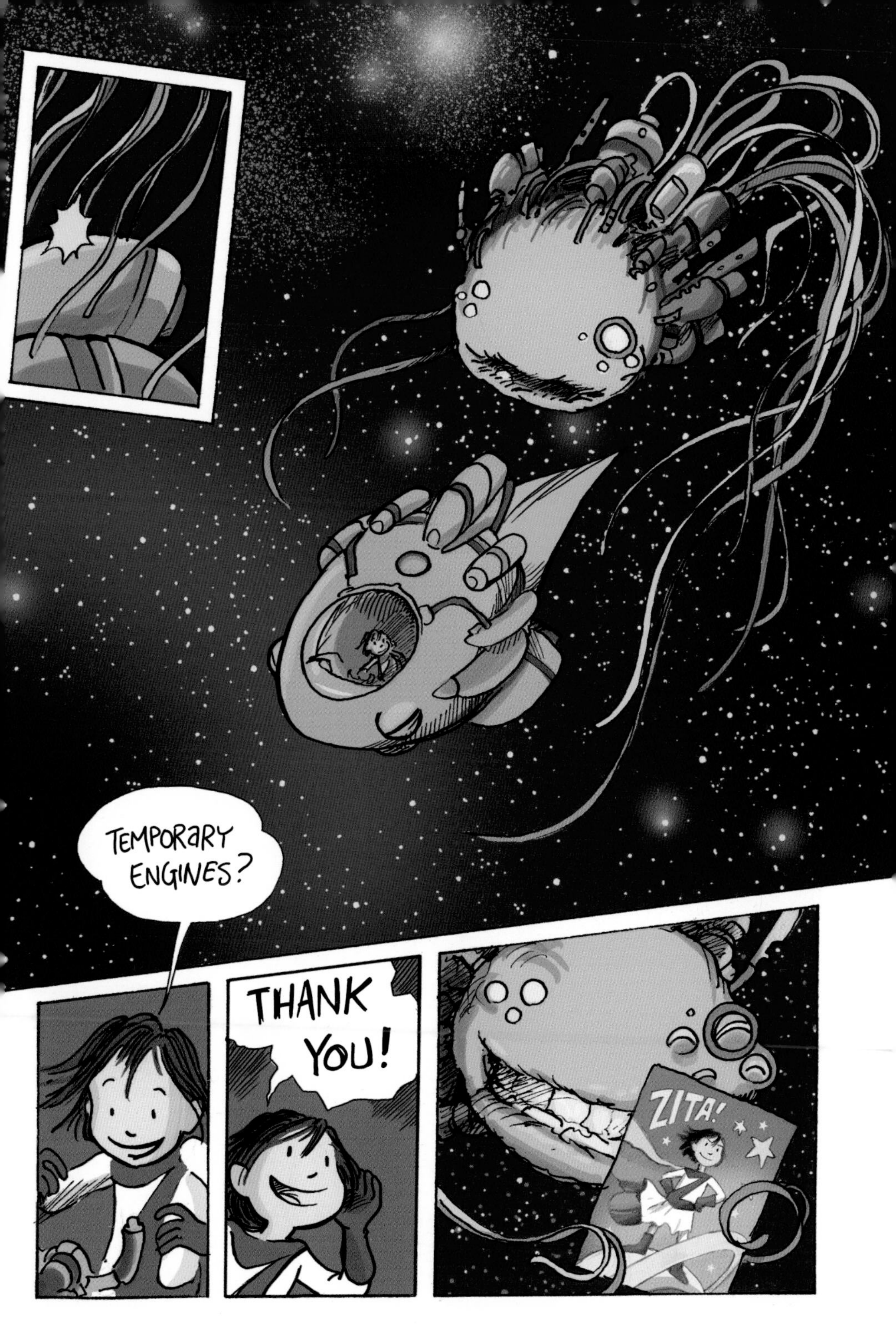
TEMPORARY ENGINES?
THANK YOU!
ZITA!

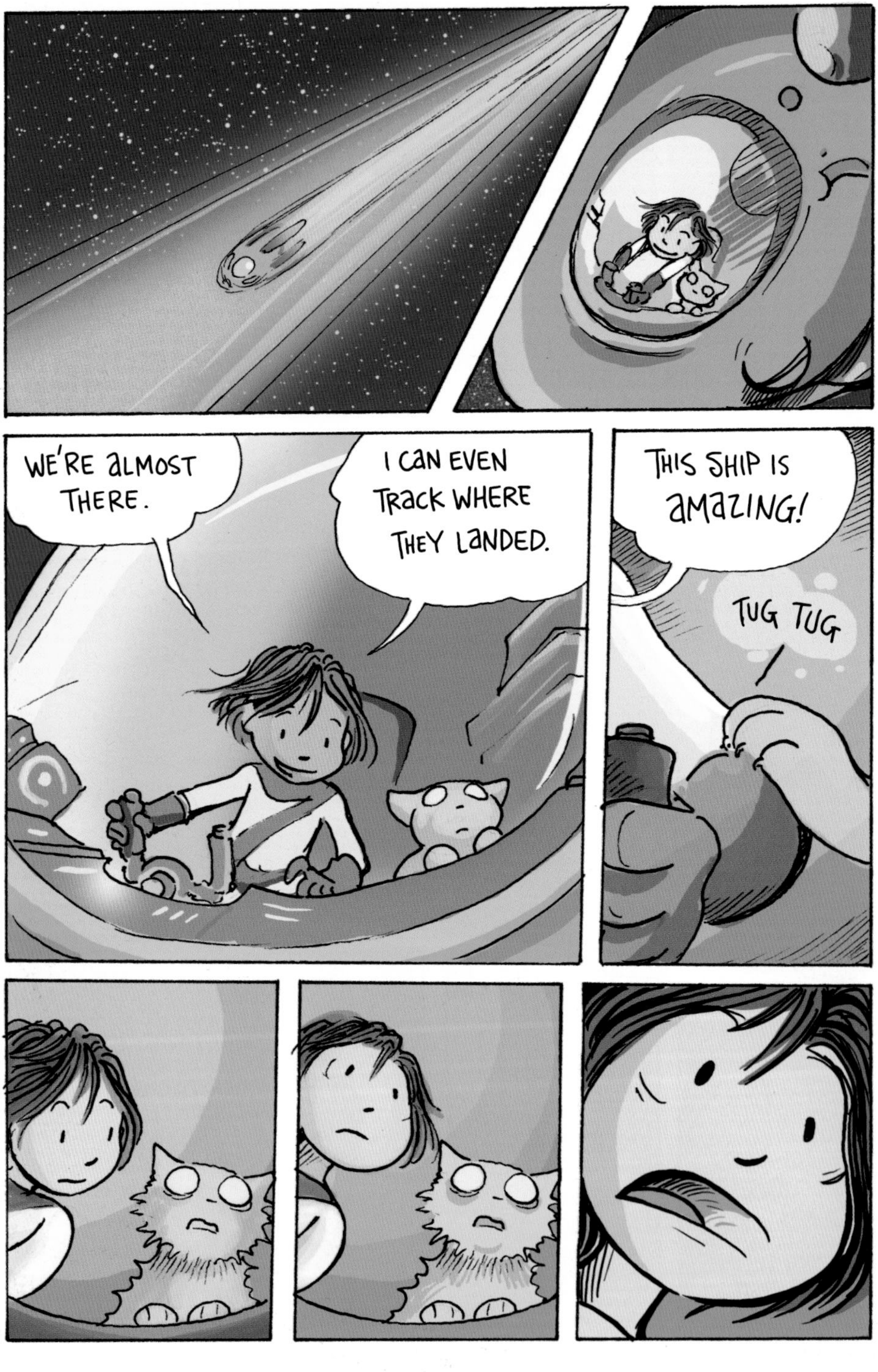
WE'RE ALMOST THERE.
I CAN EVEN TRACK WHERE THEY LANDED.
THIS SHIP IS AMAZING!
TUG TUG

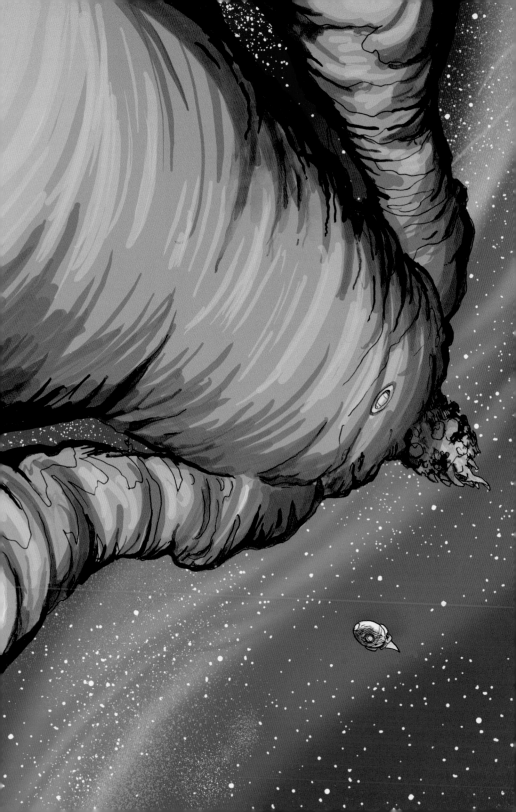

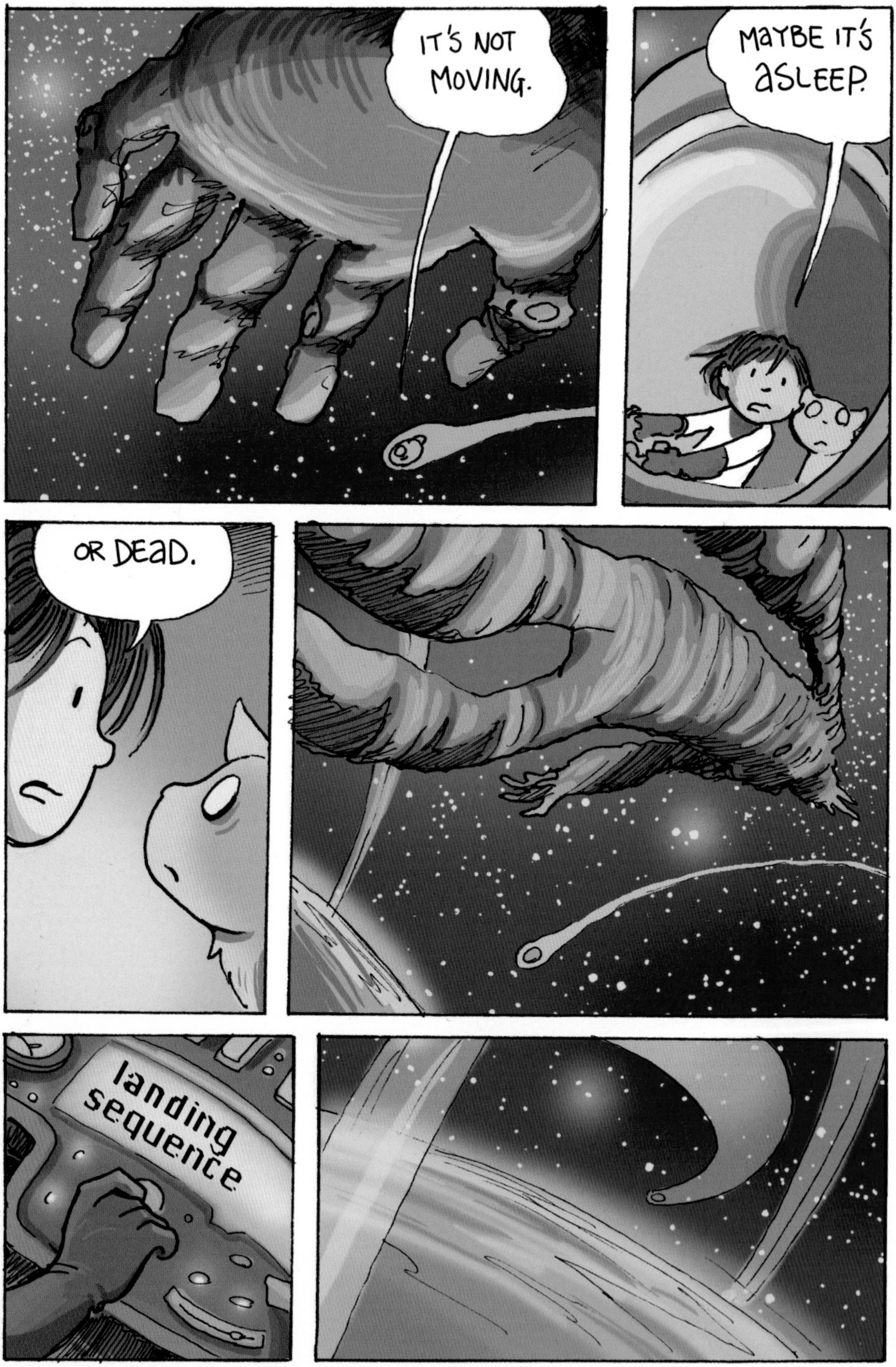
IT'S NOT MOVING.
MAYBE IT'S ASLEEP.
OR DEAD.
landing sequence

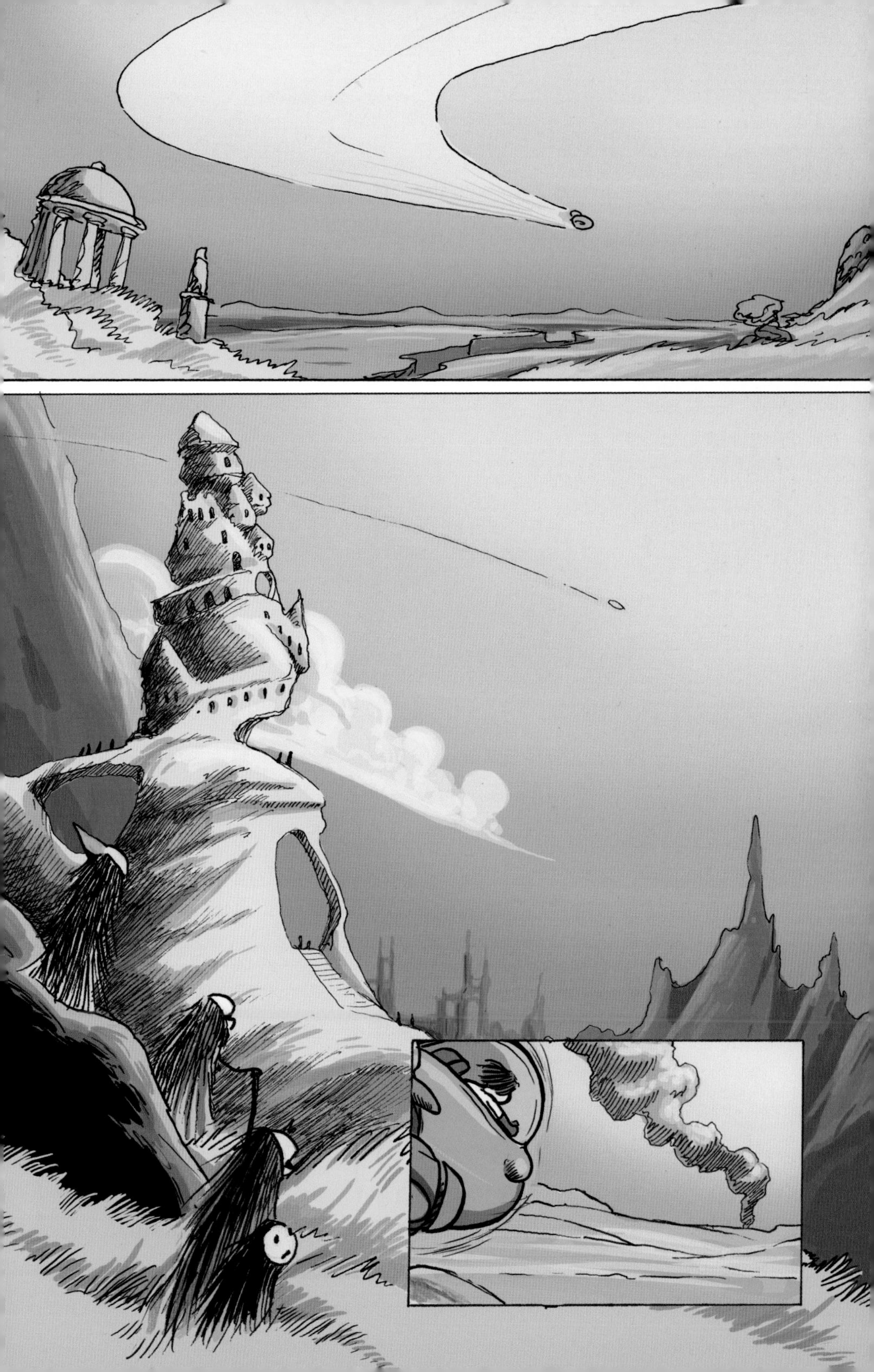

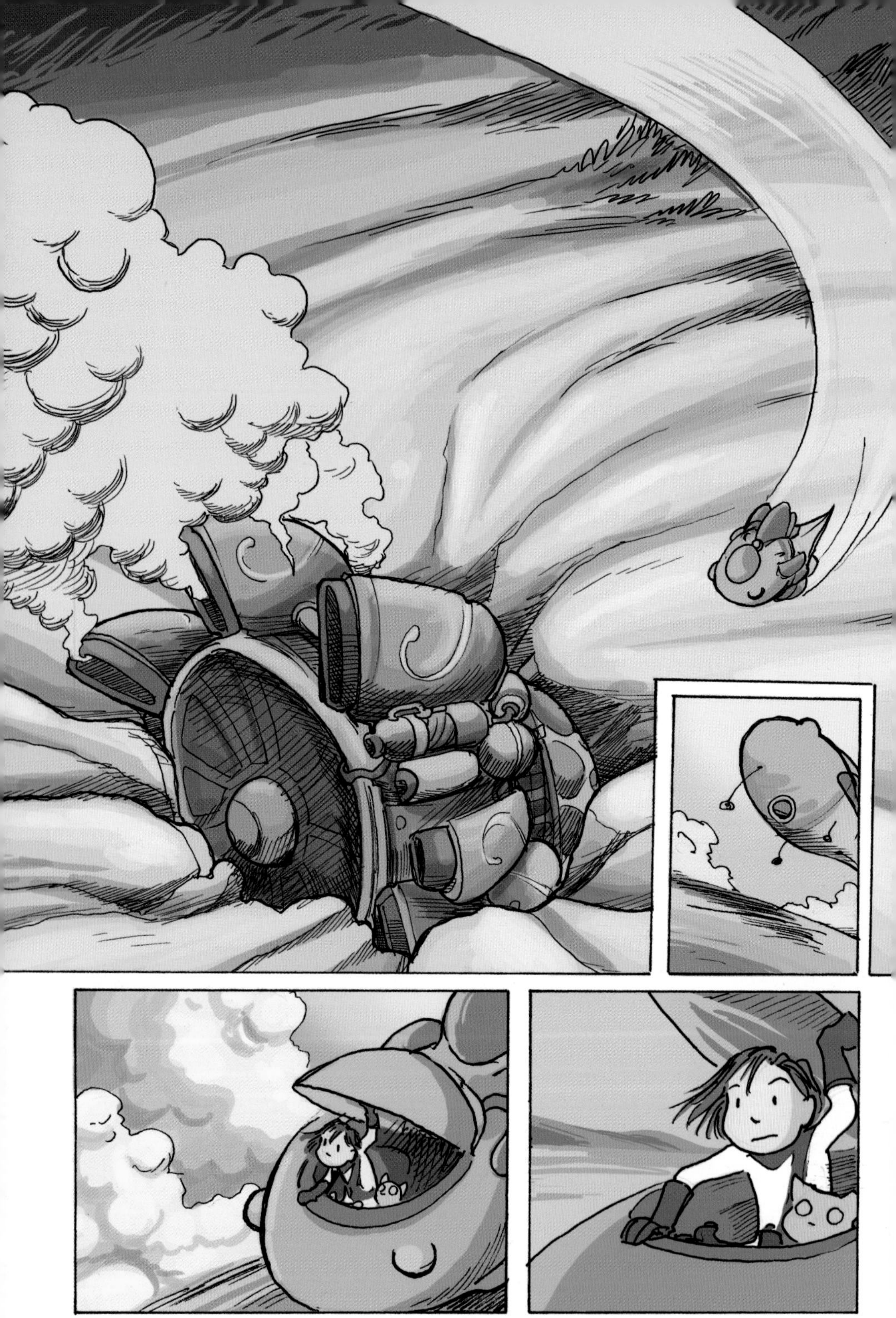

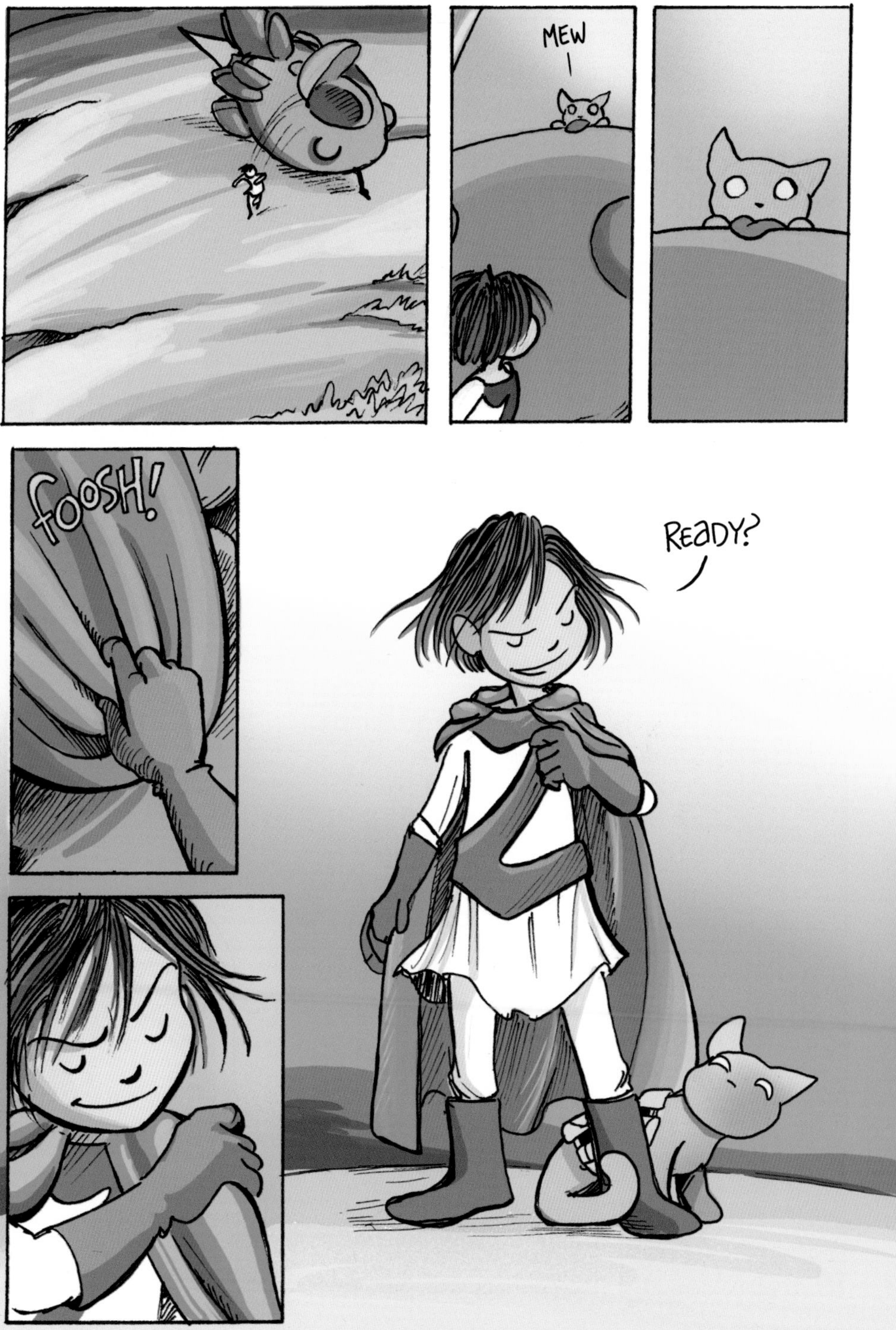
MEW
FOOSH!
READY?

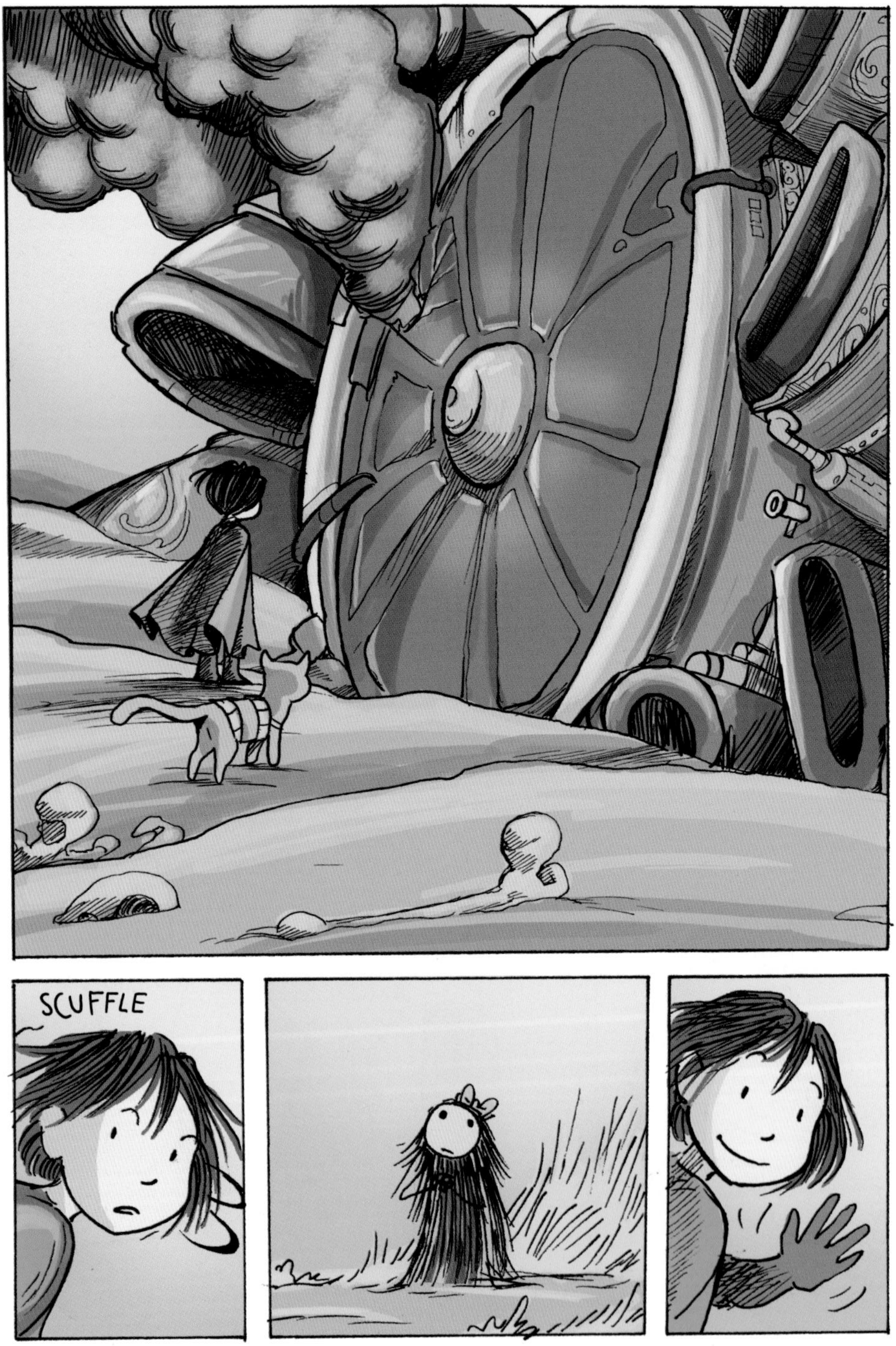
SCUFFLE

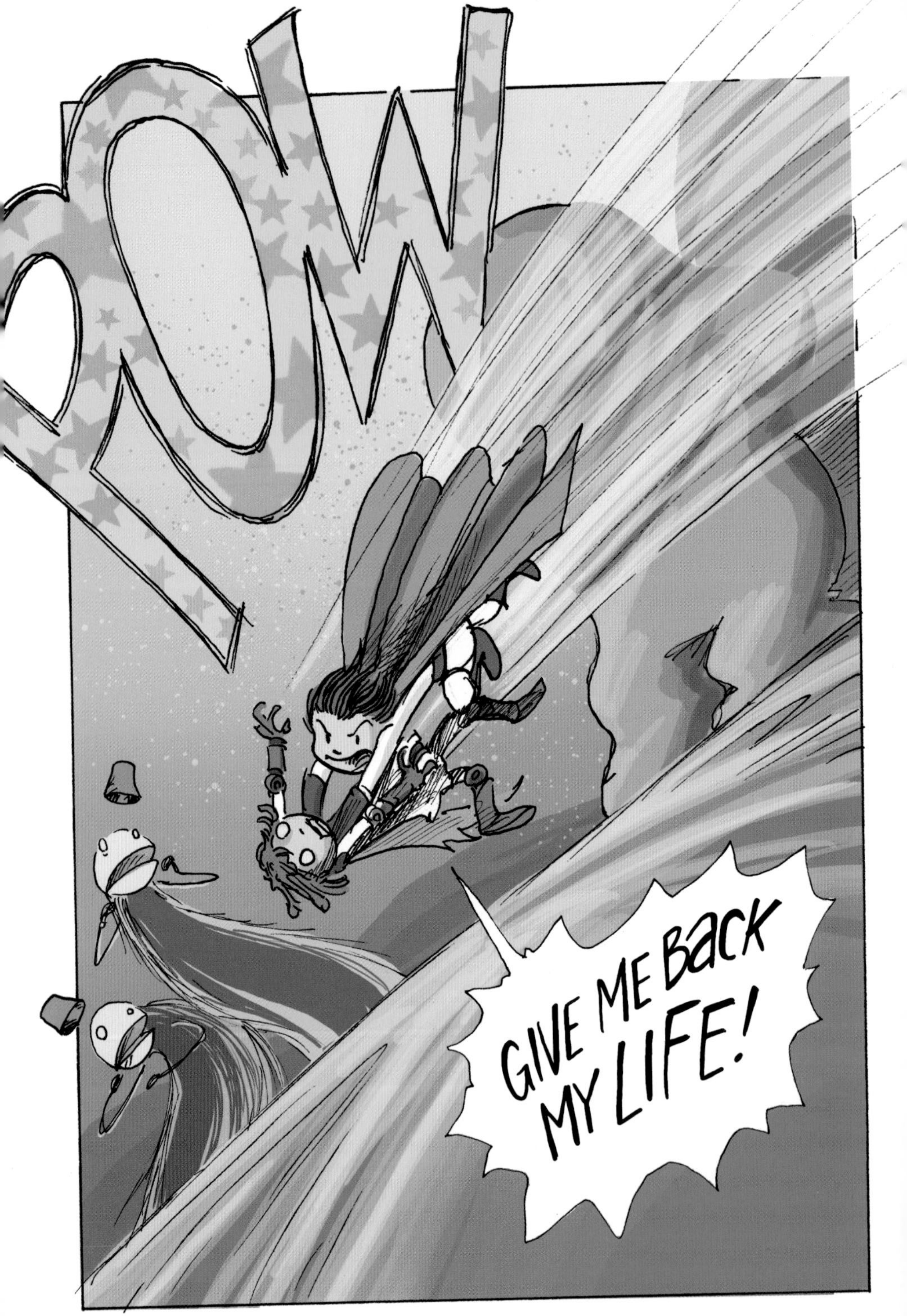
POW!
GIVE ME BACK MY LIFE!

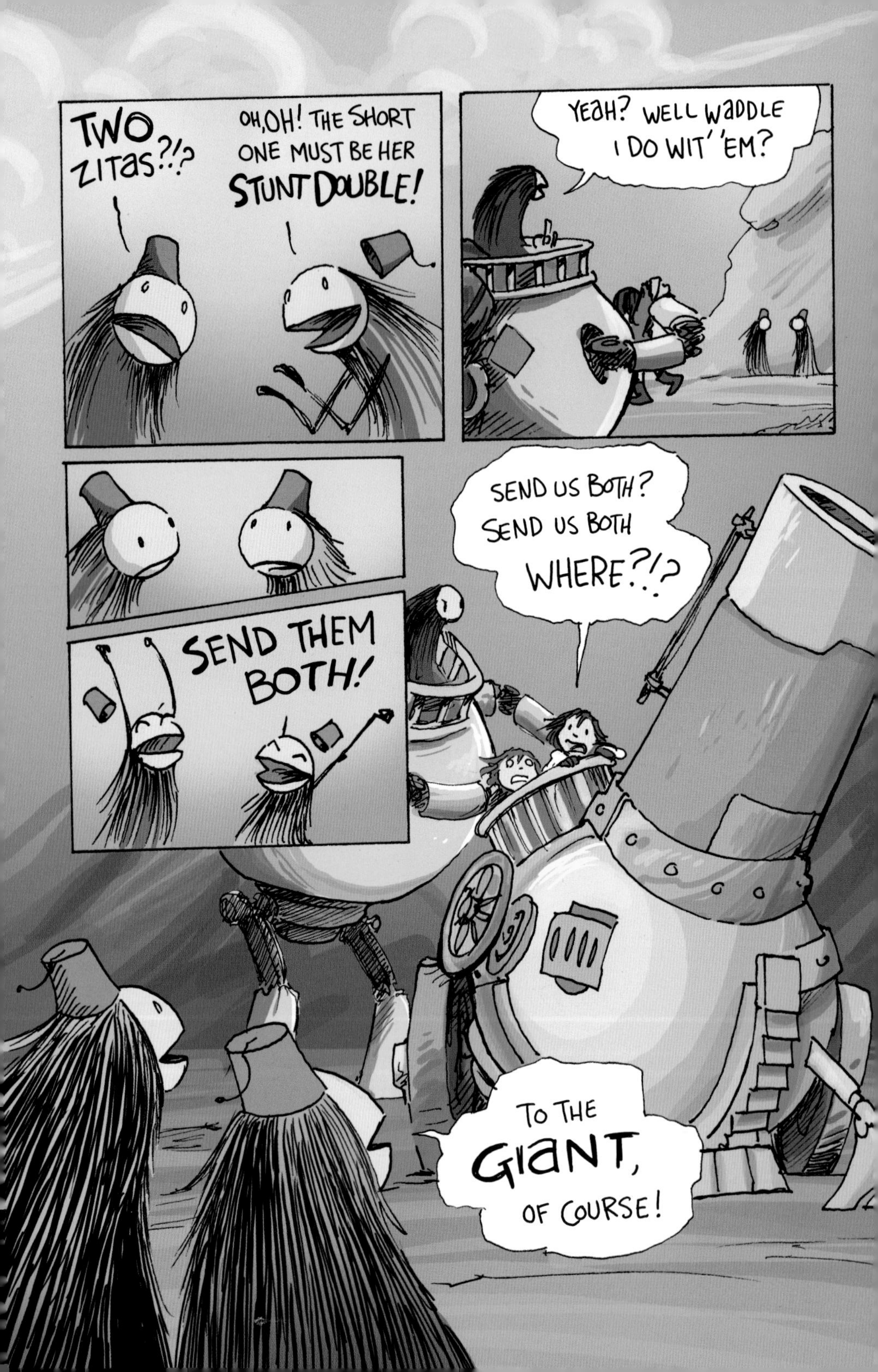
TWO ZITAS?!?
OH, OH! THE SHORT ONE MUST BE HER STUNT DOUBLE!
YEAH? WELL WADDLE I DO WIT' 'EM?
SEND THEM BOTH!
SEND US BOTH? SEND US BOTH WHERE?!?
TO THE GIANT, OF COURSE!

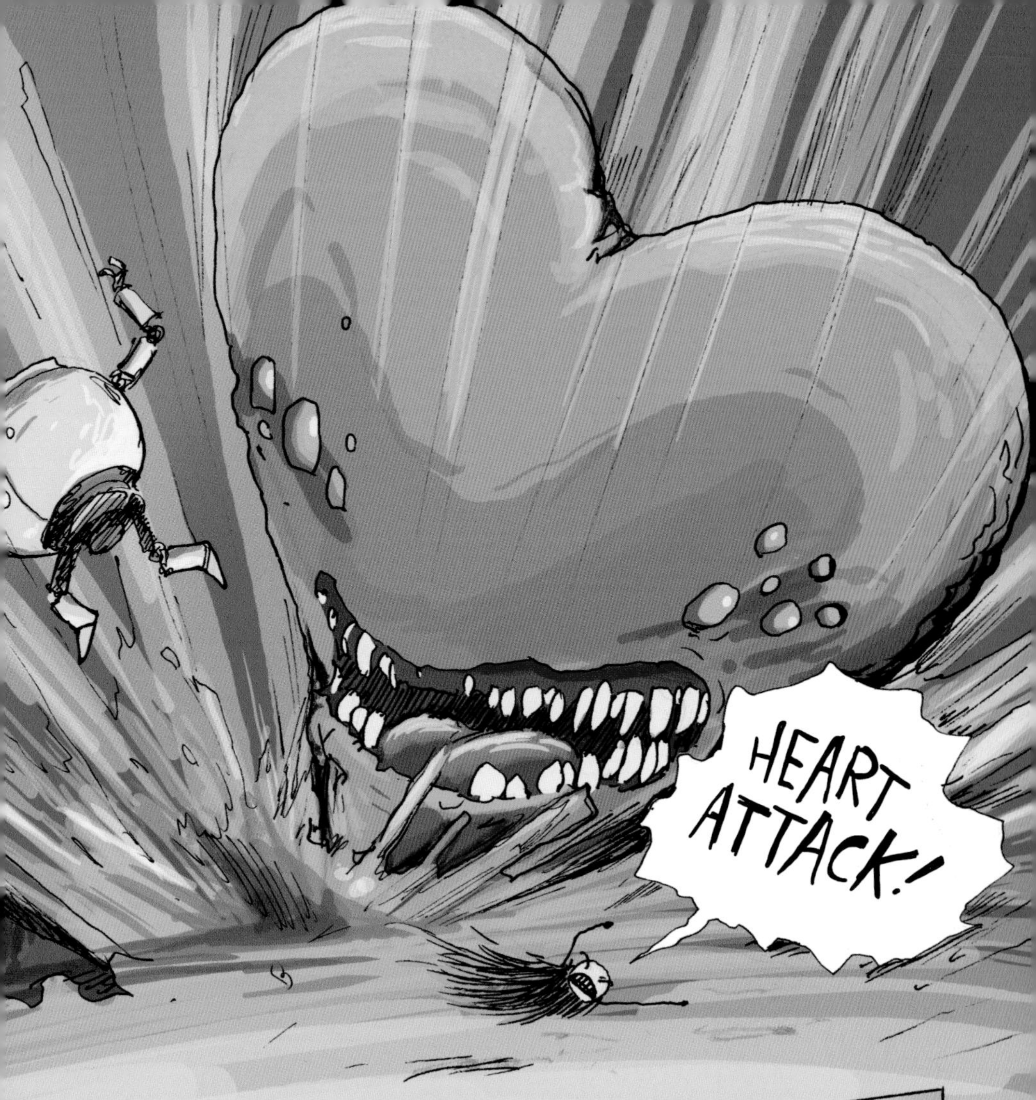
HEART ATTACK!
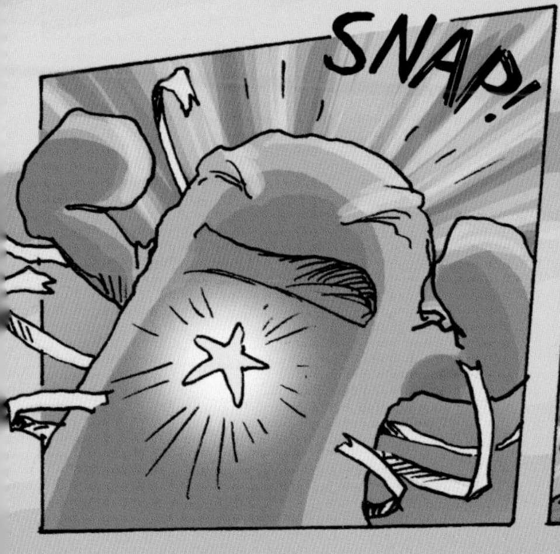
SNAP!
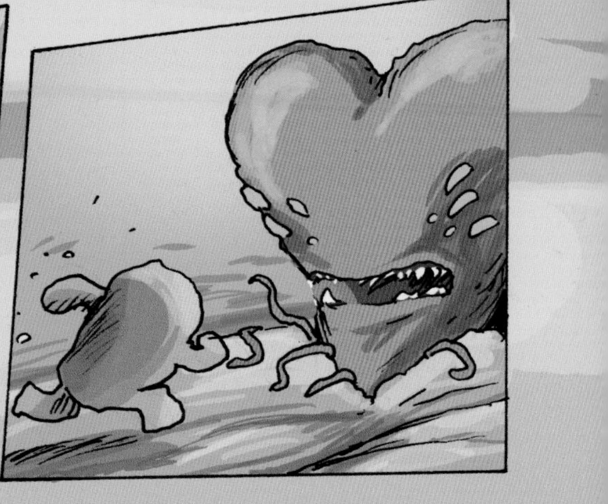

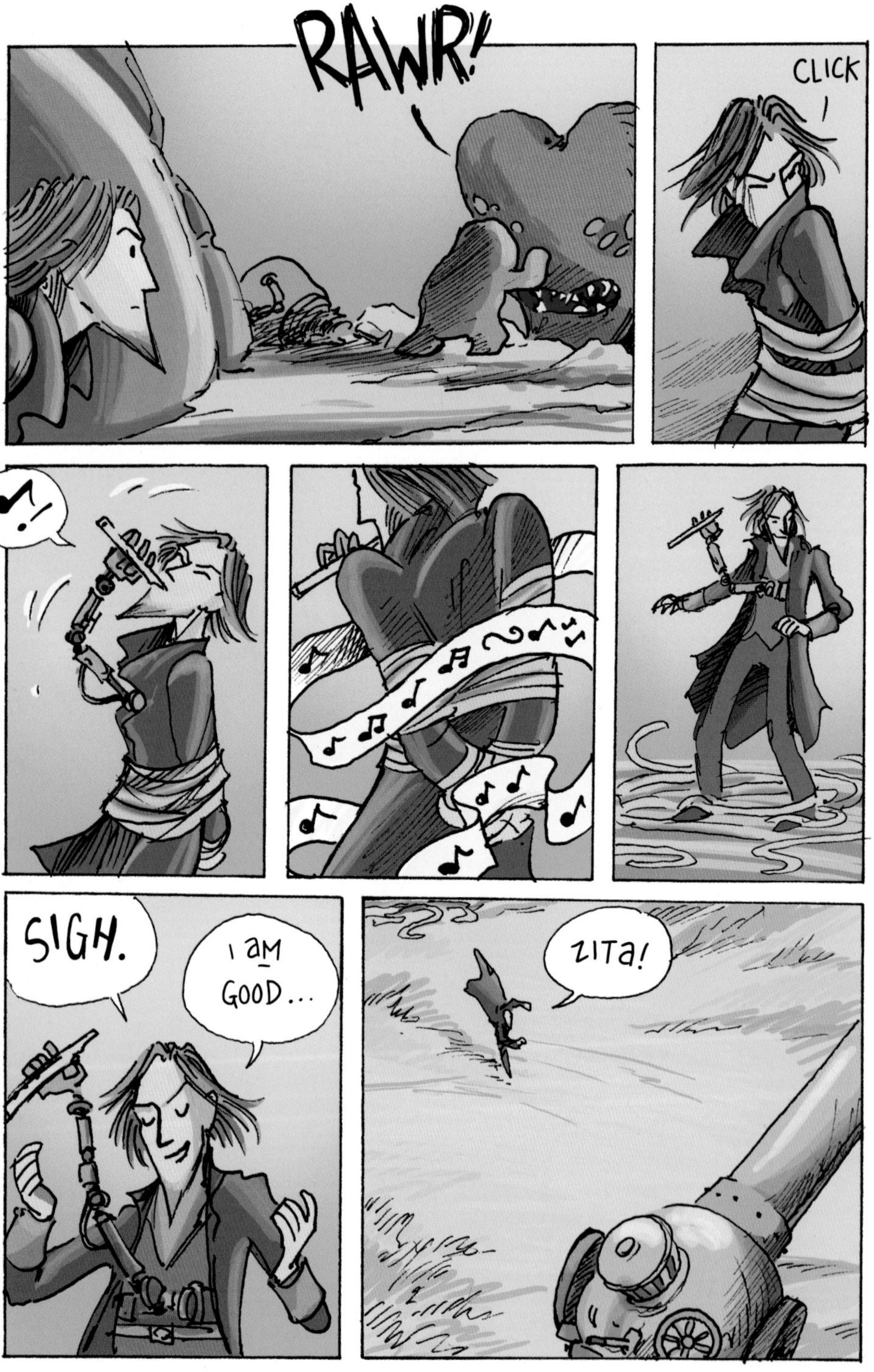
RAWR!
CLICK
SIGH.
I AM GOOD...
ZITA!

157

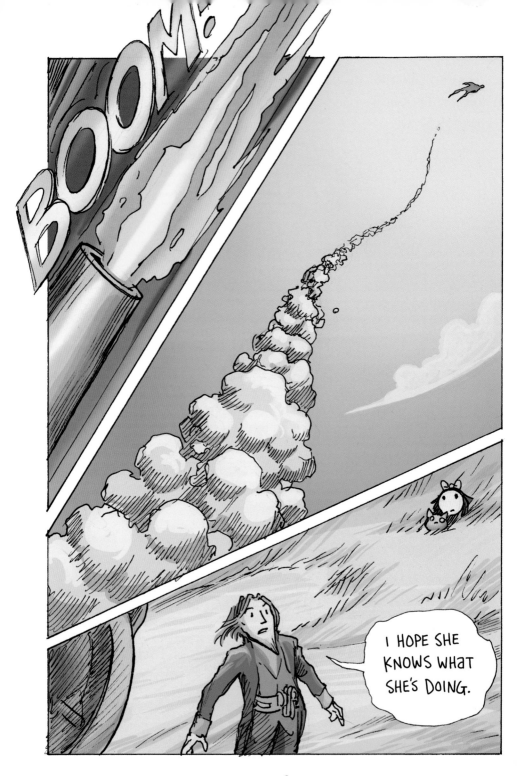

Chapter
Five

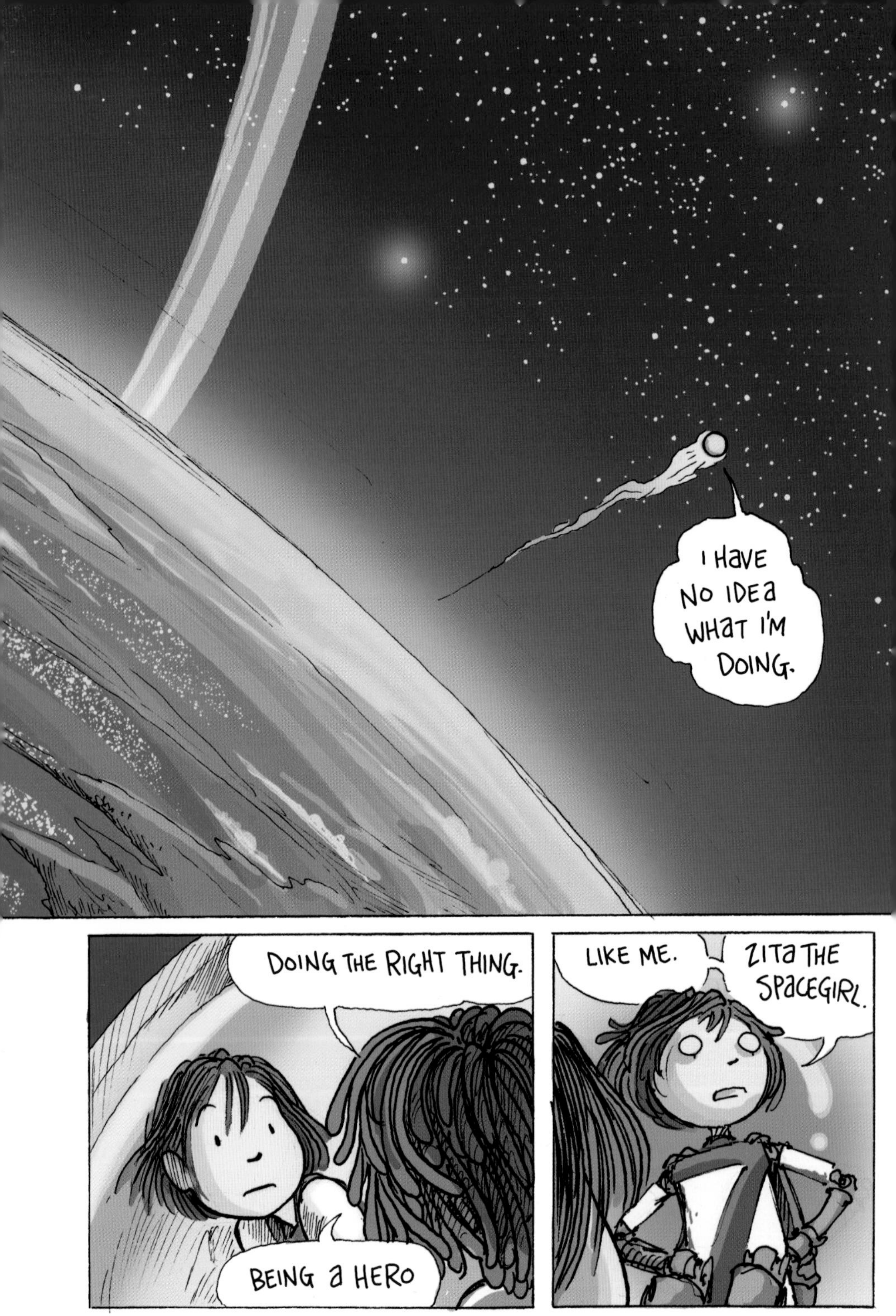
I HAVE NO IDEA WHAT I'M DOING.
DOING THE RIGHT THING.
BEING A HERO
LIKE ME.
ZITA THE SPACEGIRL.

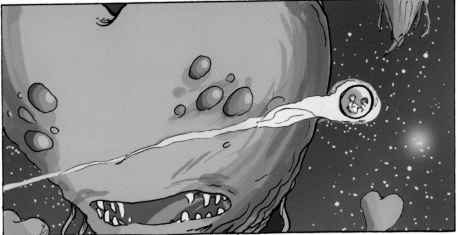

SO MANY OF THEM.

WHY HAVEN'T THEY ATTACKED THE PLANET YET?

THEY WAIT FOR THEIR QUEEN.

THEIR WHAT?

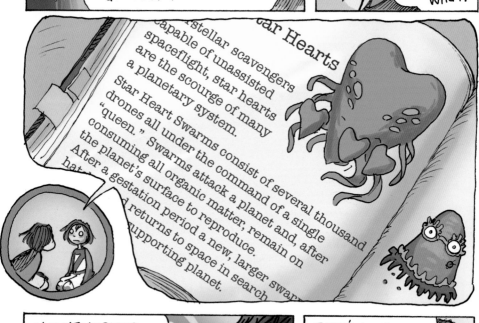

Star Hearts

...stellar scavengers capable of unassisted spaceflight, star hearts are the scourge of many a planetary system.

Star Heart Swarms consist of several thousand drones all under the command of a single "queen." Swarms attack a planet and, after consuming all organic matter, remain on the planet's surface to reproduce. After a gestation period a new, larger swarm... hat... returns to space in search ... supporting planet.

YOU MEMORIZED ALL THAT?

THAT'S—

THAT'S KIND OF AMAZING.

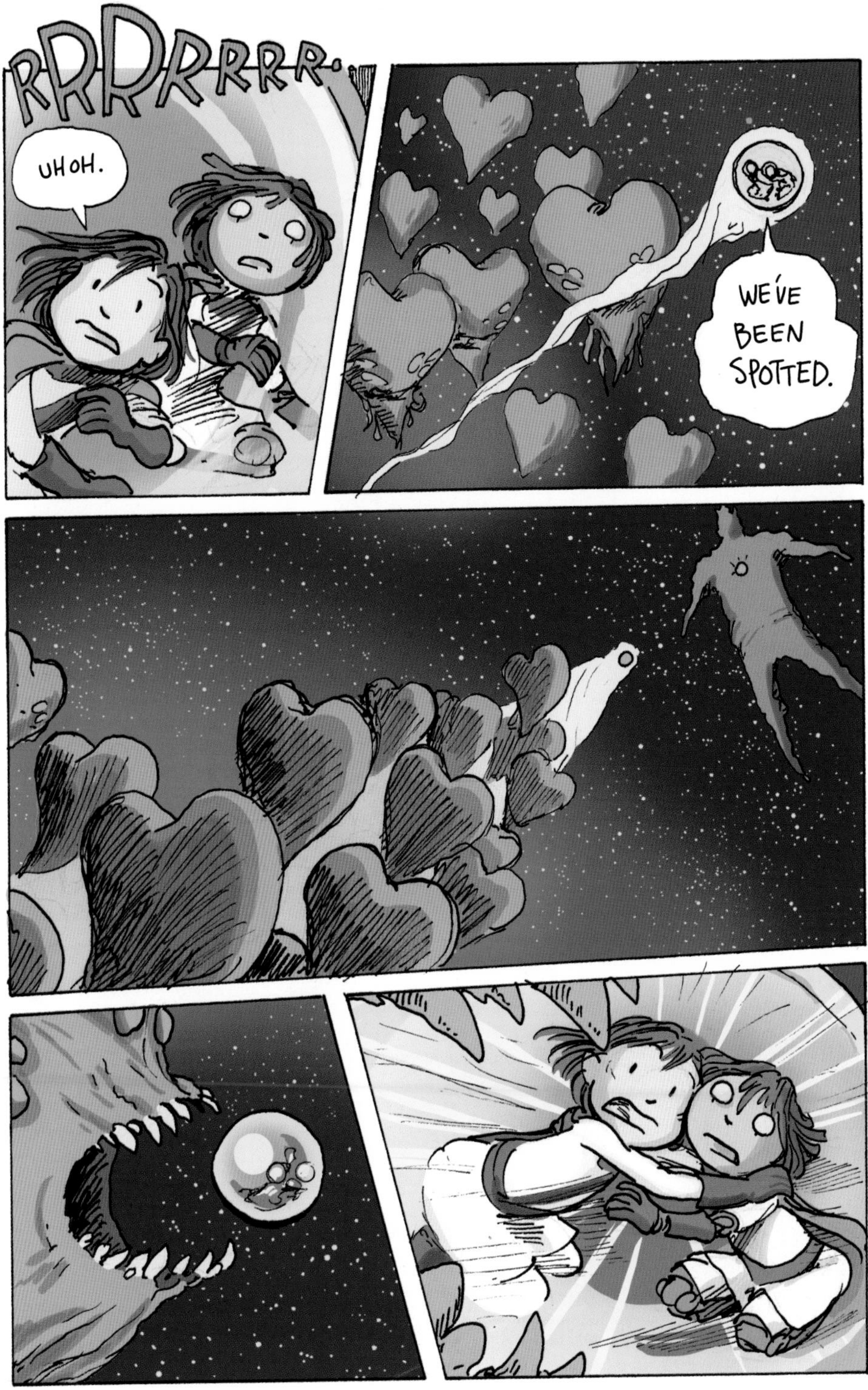
RRRRRRRR
UHOH.
WE'VE BEEN SPOTTED.

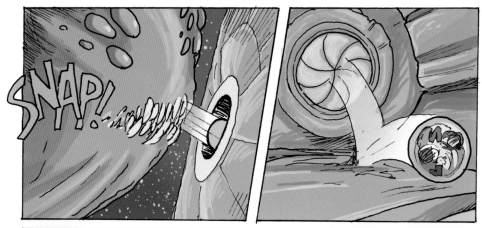

WE MADE IT.

WE MADE IT!! HIGH FIVE!

NOW YOU PUT YOUR HAND UP.

SMEK!

COME ON.

SMEK SMEK

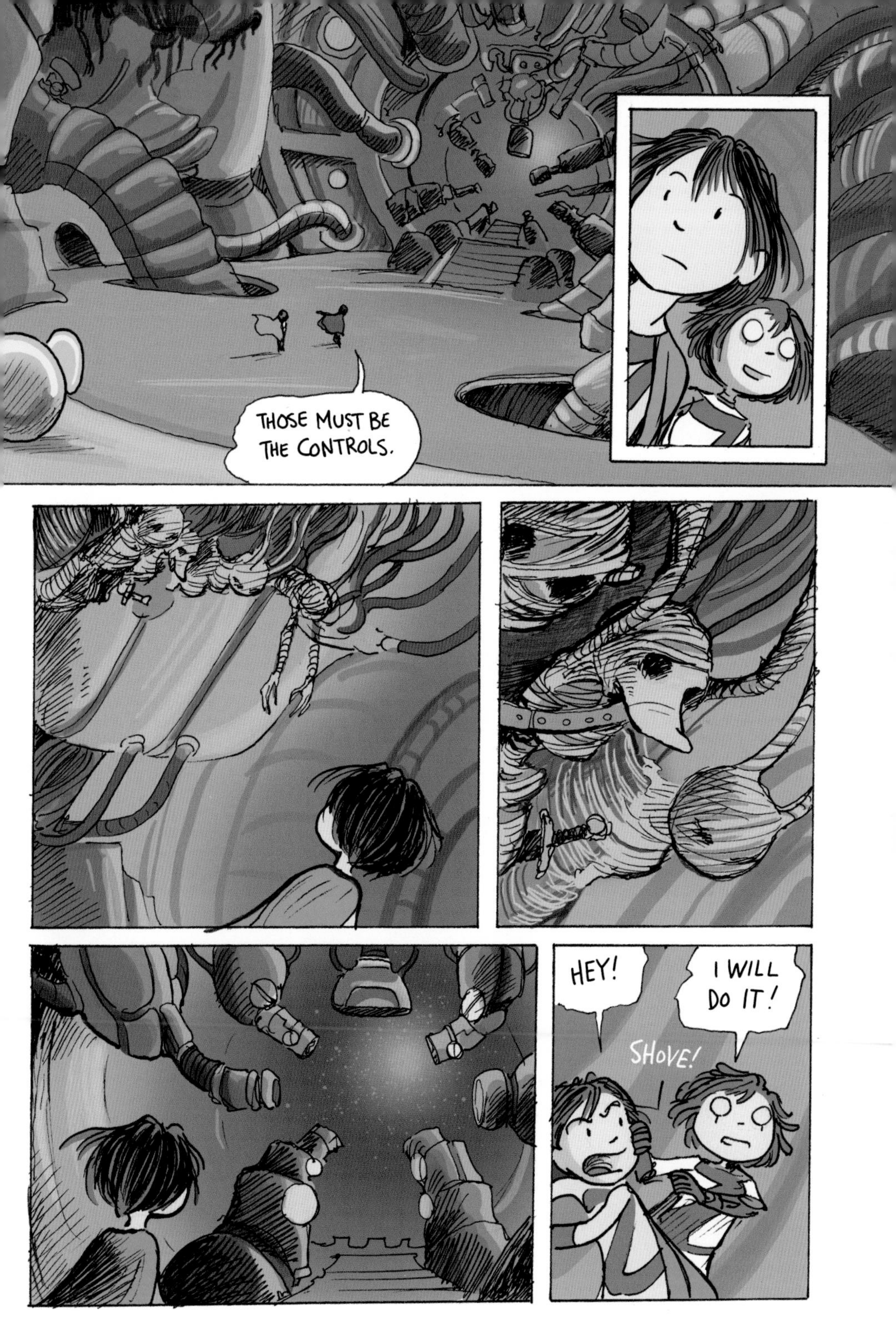
THOSE MUST BE THE CONTROLS.
HEY!
I WILL DO IT!
SHOVE!

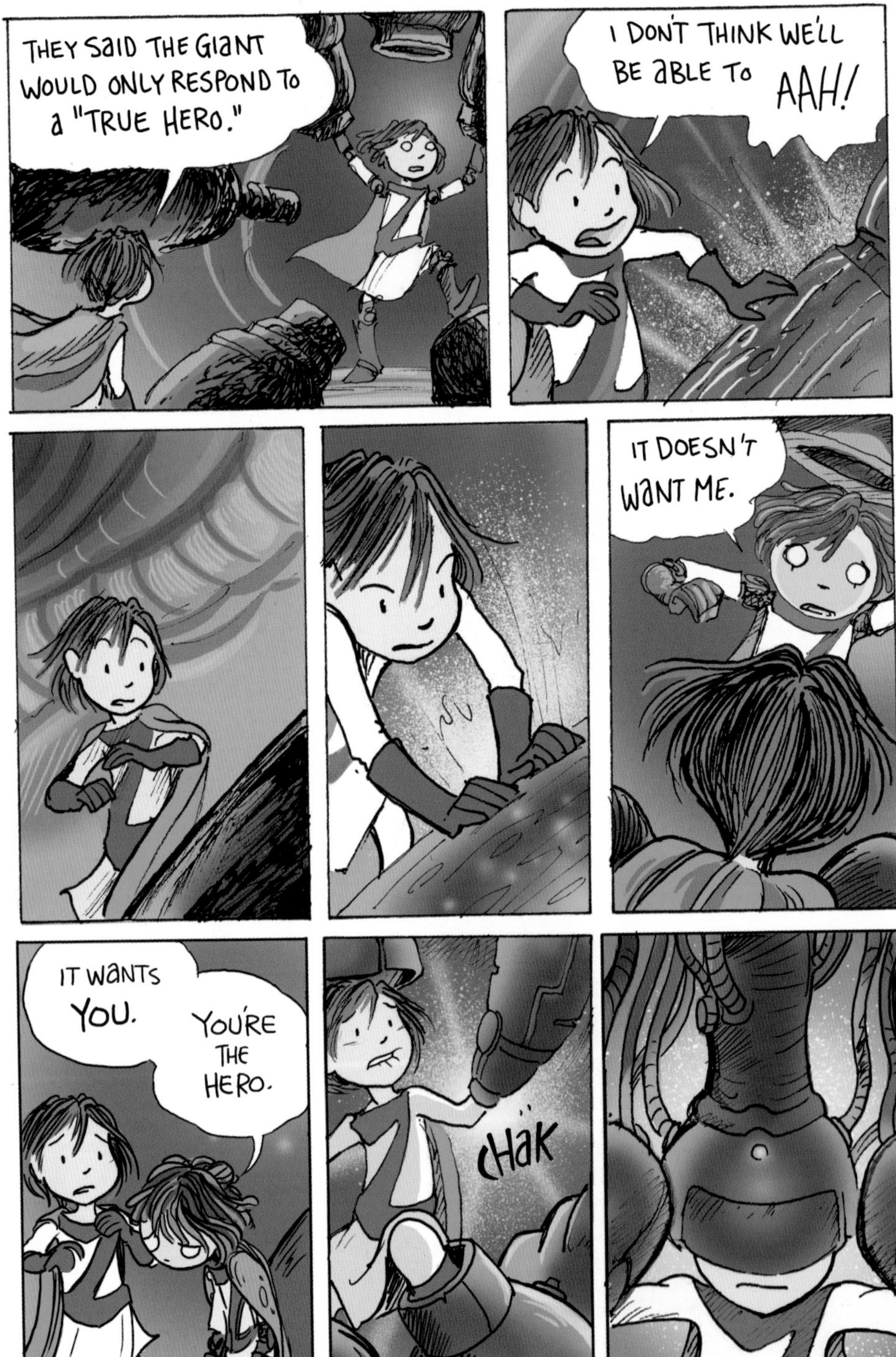
THEY SAID THE GIANT WOULD ONLY RESPOND TO A "TRUE HERO."
I DON'T THINK WE'LL BE ABLE TO
AAH!
IT DOESN'T WANT ME.
IT WANTS YOU.
YOU'RE THE HERO.
CHAK

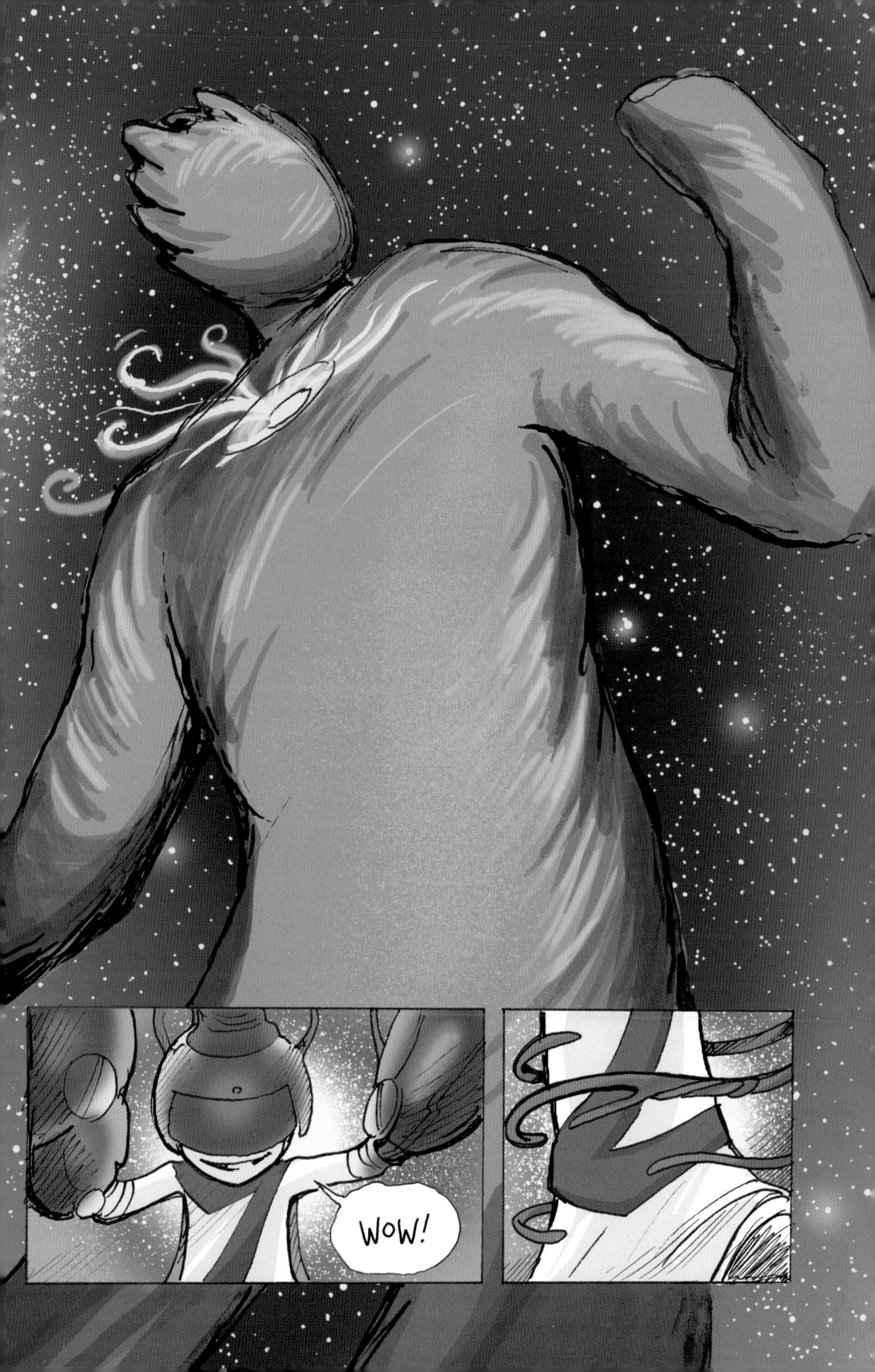
WOW!

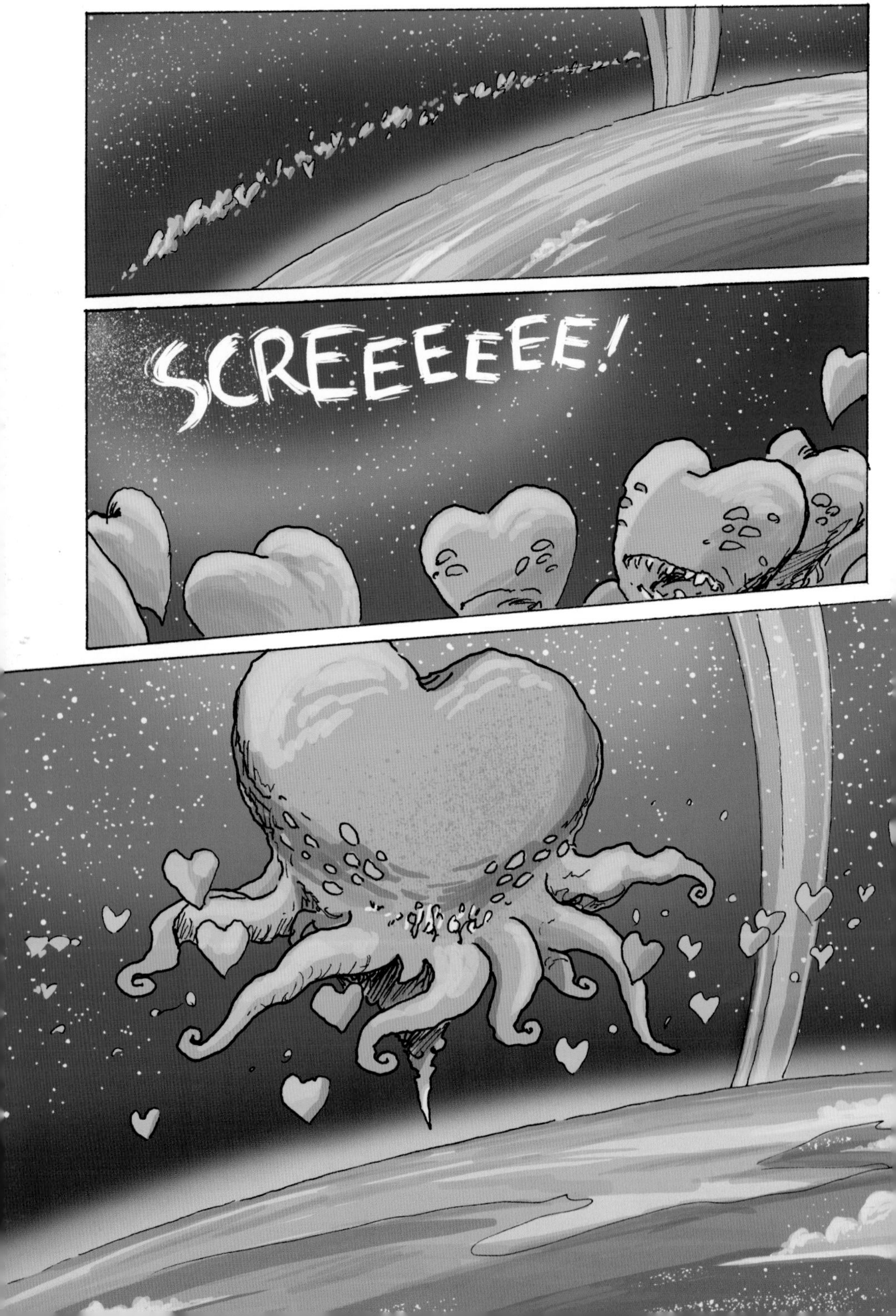
SCREEEEEE!

BLIP
BLIP

PING!

READY FOR BATTLE!

BOOOOM!

OOOH!

KA·BOOM!

aaaHH!

I SEEM TO HAVE MISSED SOMETHING.

ZITA'S USING A GIANT THE SIZE OF A TINY MOON TO BATTLE THE STAR HEARTS

-AND WINNING.

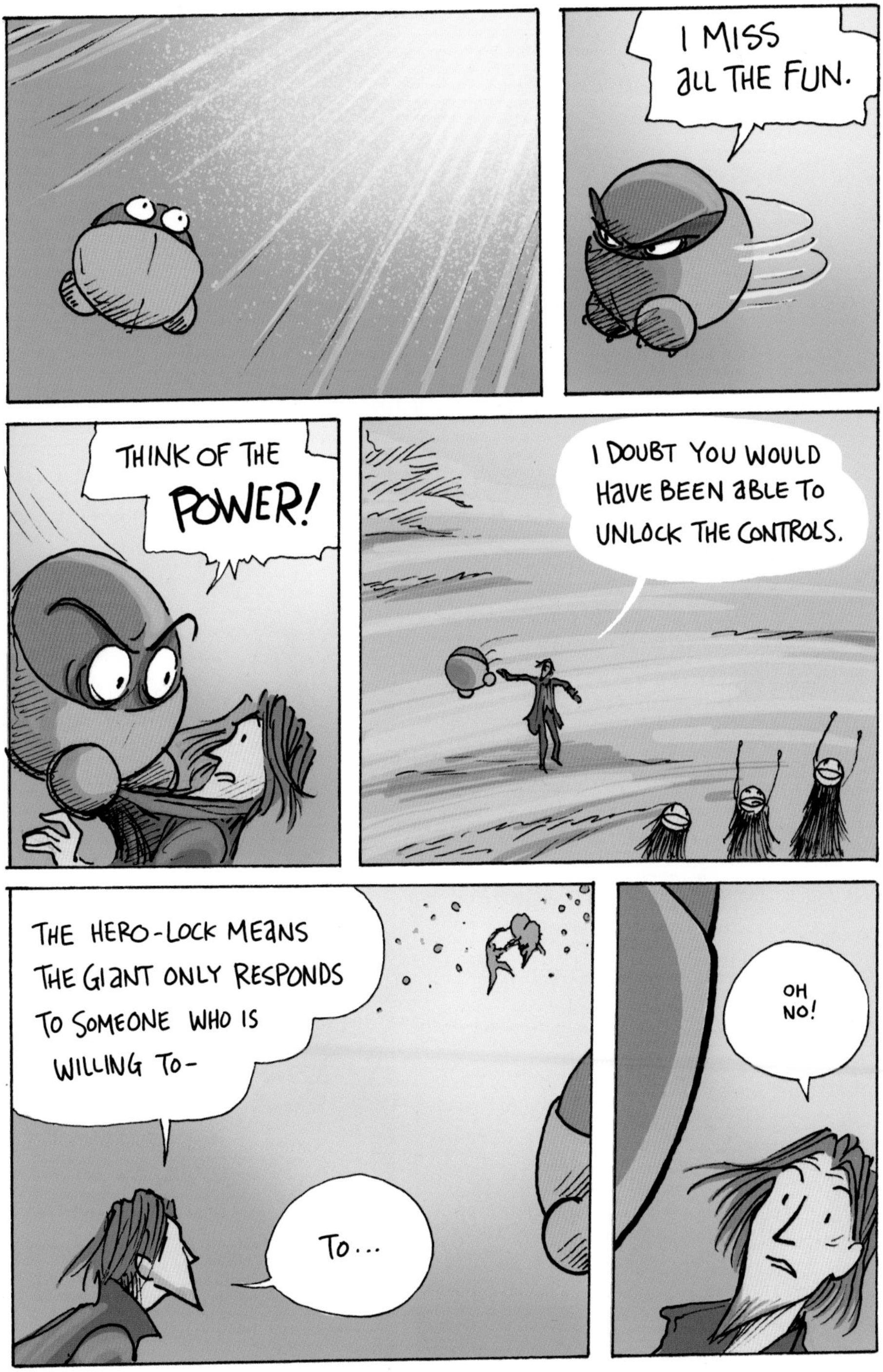
I MISS all THE FUN.
THINK OF THE POWER!
I DOUBT YOU WOULD HaVE BEEN aBLE TO UNLOCK THE CONTROLS.
THE HERO-LOCK MEaNS THE GIaNT ONLY RESPONDS TO SOMEONE WHO IS WILLING TO-
TO...
OH NO!

TELL ME WHAT'S HAPPENING TO HER!

WHOEVER PILOTS THE GIANT IS CONSUMED BY IT!

THEY CONTROL IT UNTIL *DEATH.*

ONE! YOU'VE GOT TO WARN ZITA!

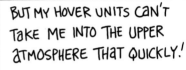
BUT MY HOVER UNITS CAN'T TAKE ME INTO THE UPPER ATMOSPHERE THAT QUICKLY!

NOT WITHOUT SOME KIND OF *BOOST.*

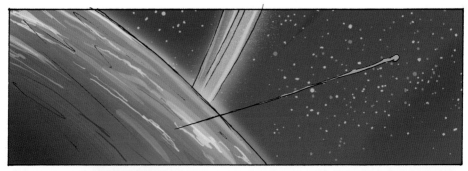

ONE?

ALMOST THERE—

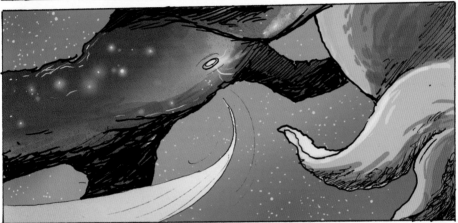

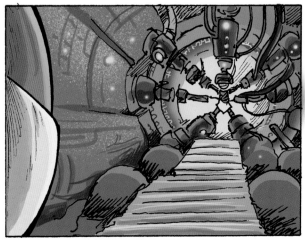

PIPER—

I aM TOO LaTE.

THEN I Was RIGHT.

THE LOCK IS BaSED ON **SELF-SaCRIFICE**

SHE'S MERGING WITH THE GIaNT.

IF YOU PULL HER OUT NOW IT WILL SHUT DOWN aND NOTHING WILL STOP THOSE HEARTS.

BUT IF SHE STaYS CONNECTED—

WE'VE LOST HER.

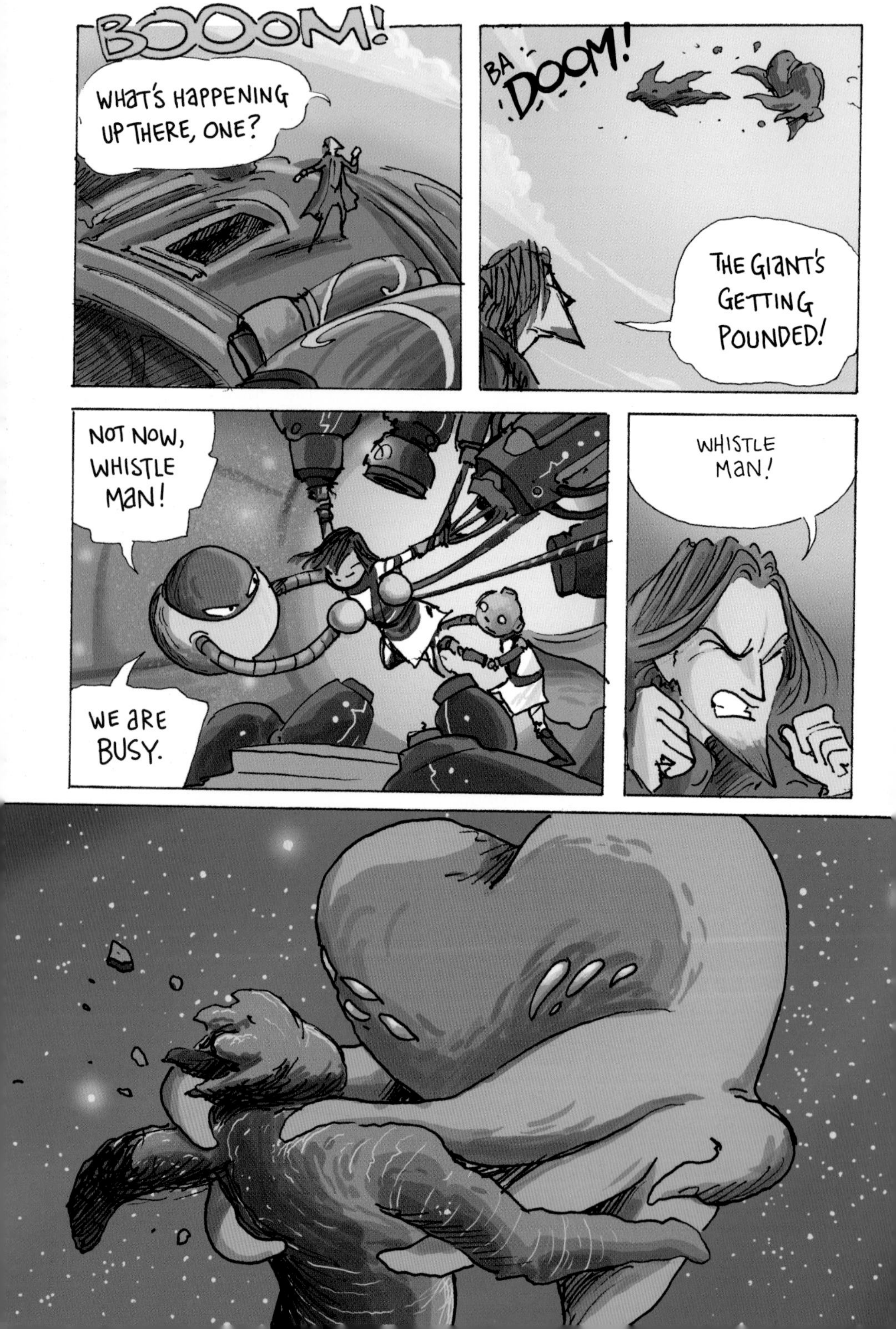
BOOOM!
WHAT'S HAPPENING UP THERE, ONE?
BA DOOM!
THE GIANT'S GETTING POUNDED!
NOT NOW, WHISTLE MAN!
WE ARE BUSY.
WHISTLE MAN!

CRACK

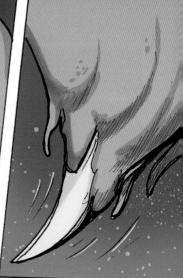

AAH!

STAND ASIDE!

VVT!

VVVT!

SNAP!

SNAP!

SNAP!

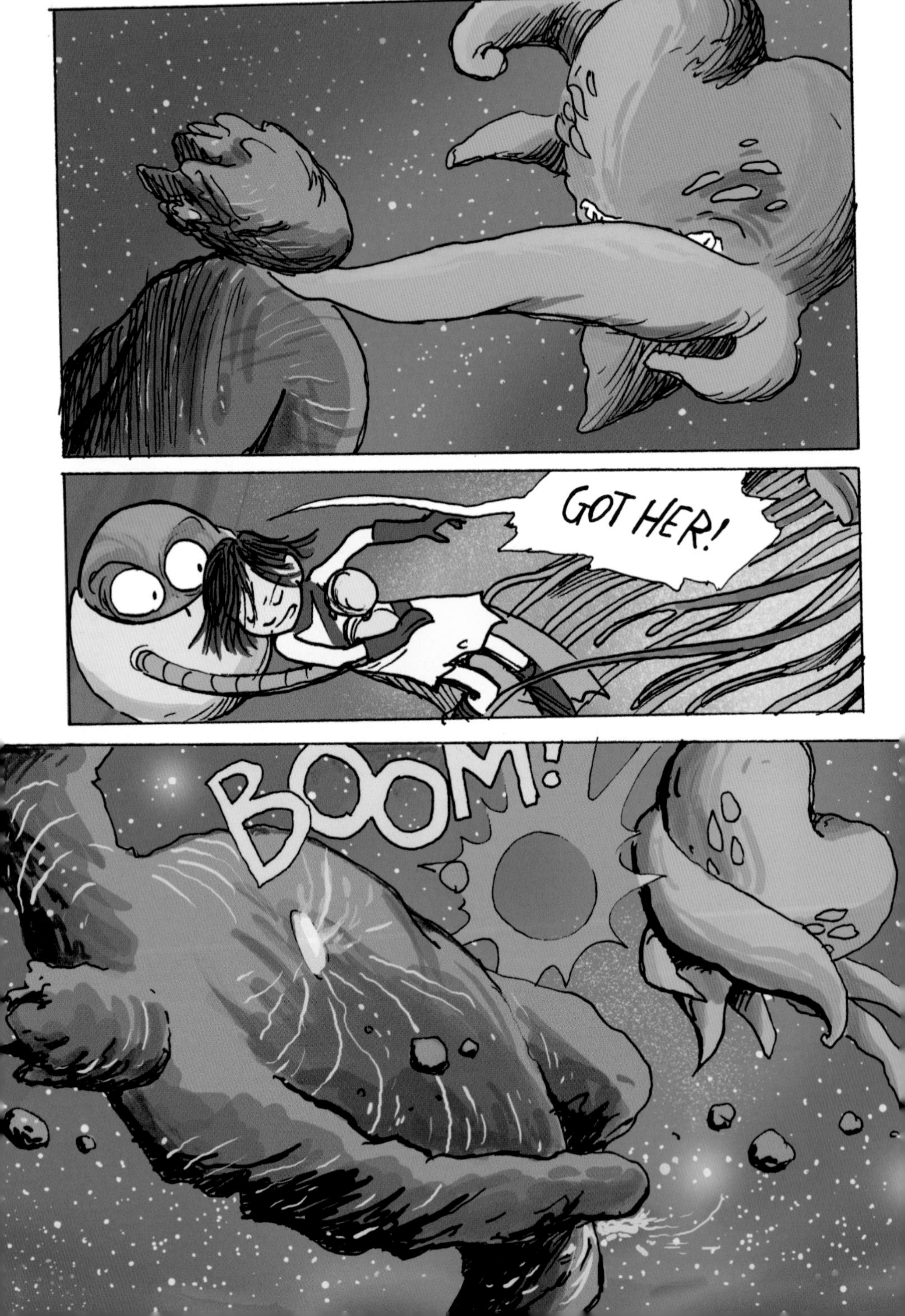
GOT HER!
BOOM!

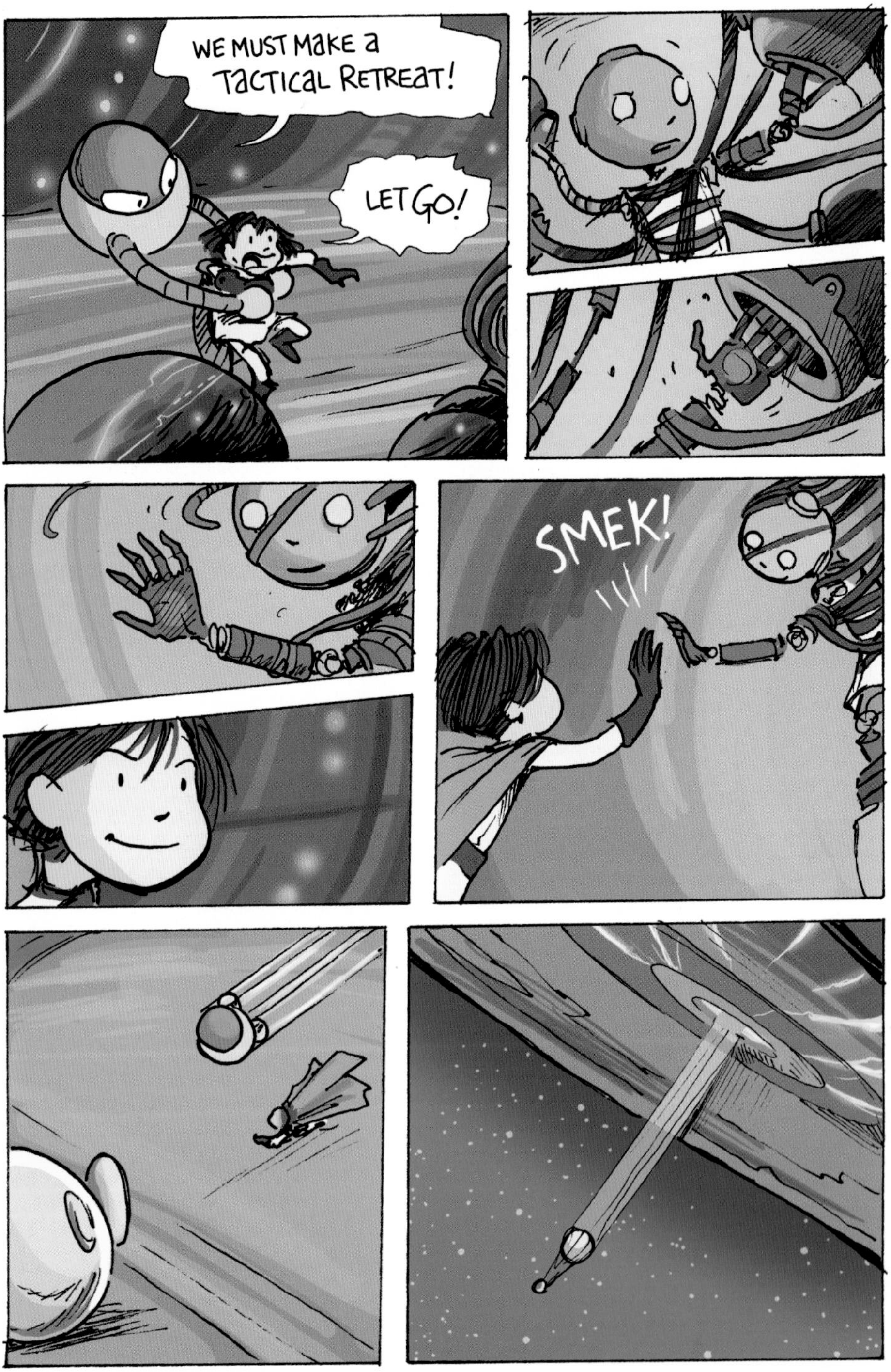
WE MUST MAKE A TACTICAL RETREAT!
LET GO!
SMEK!

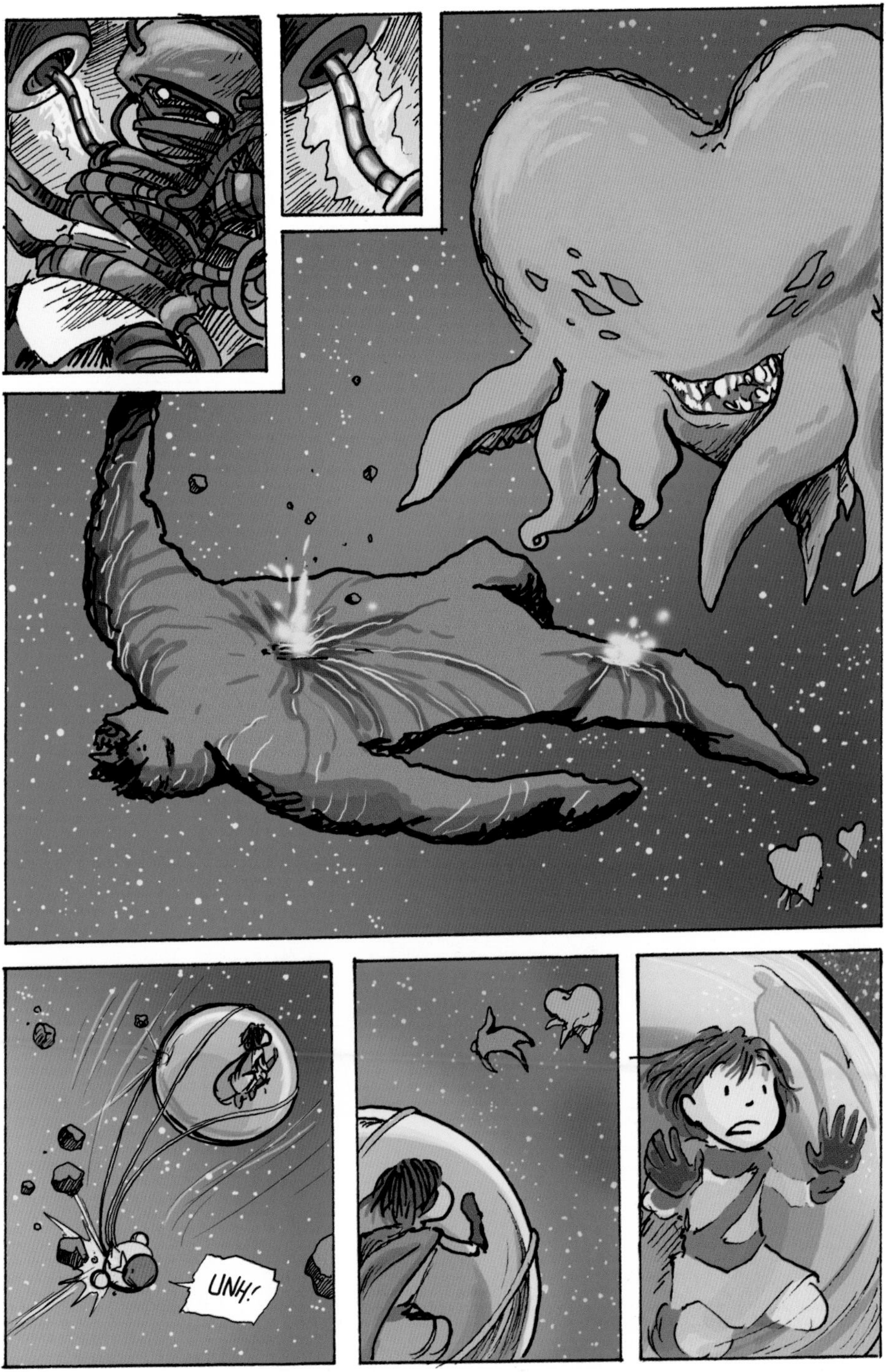
UNH!

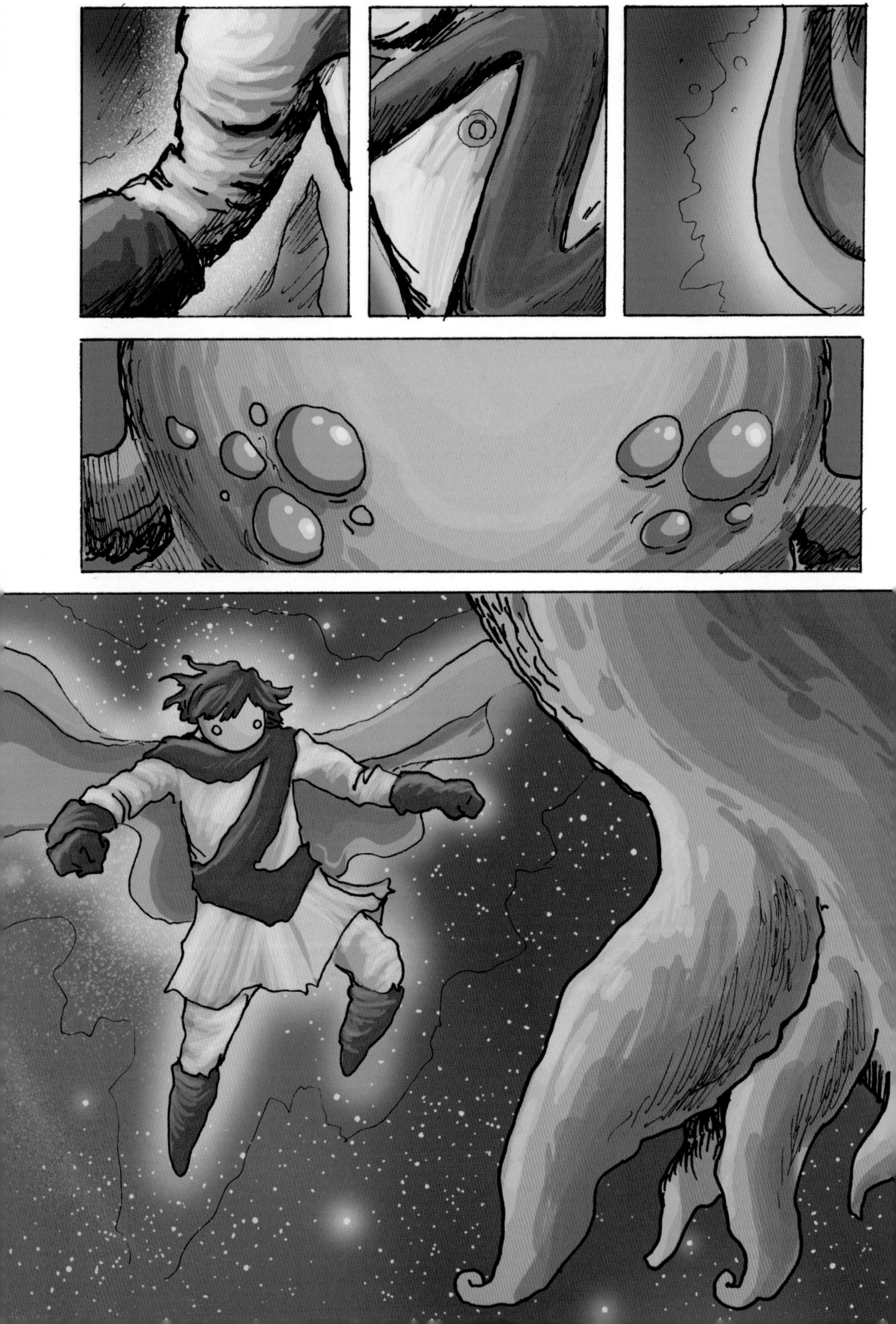

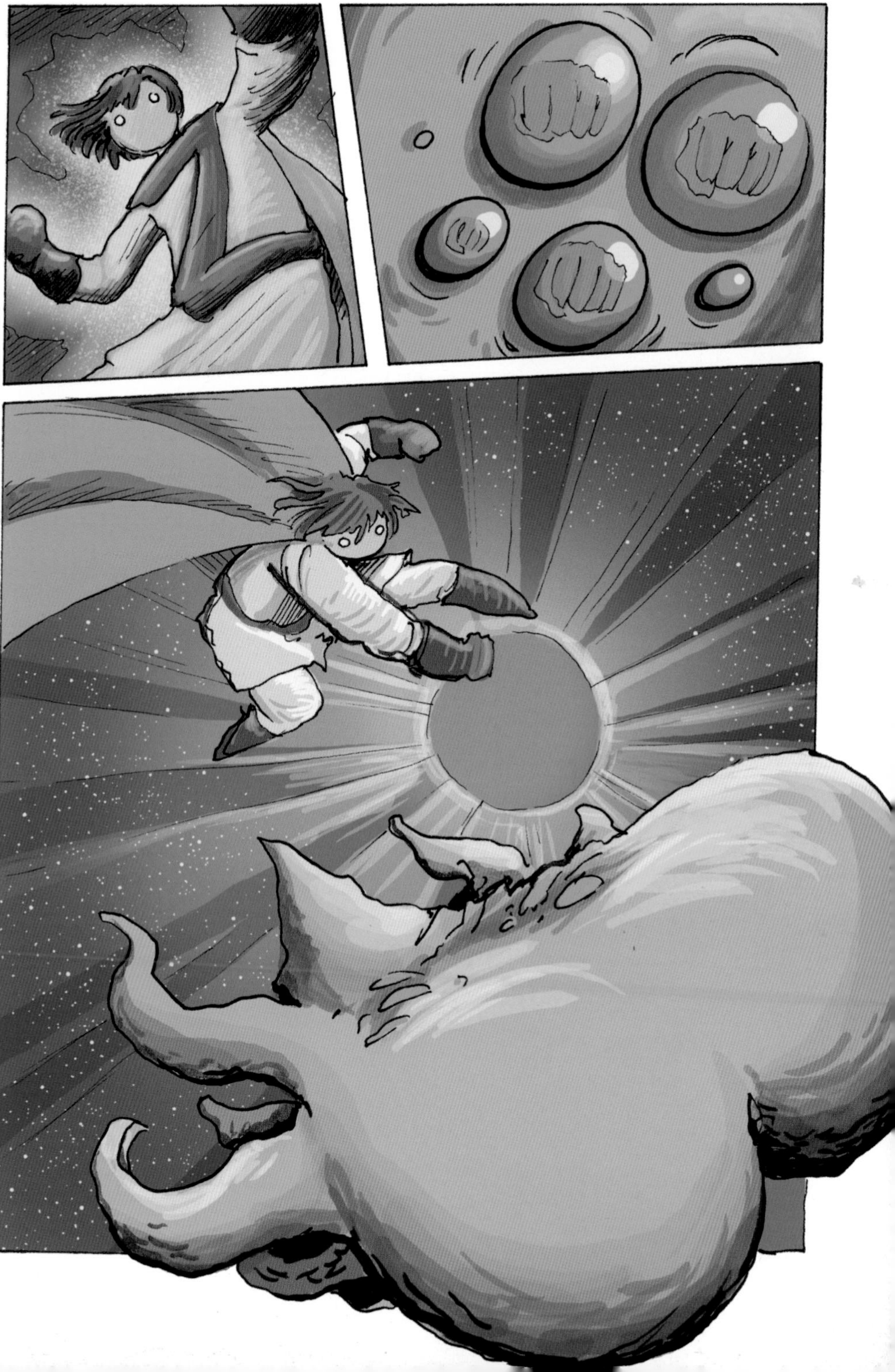

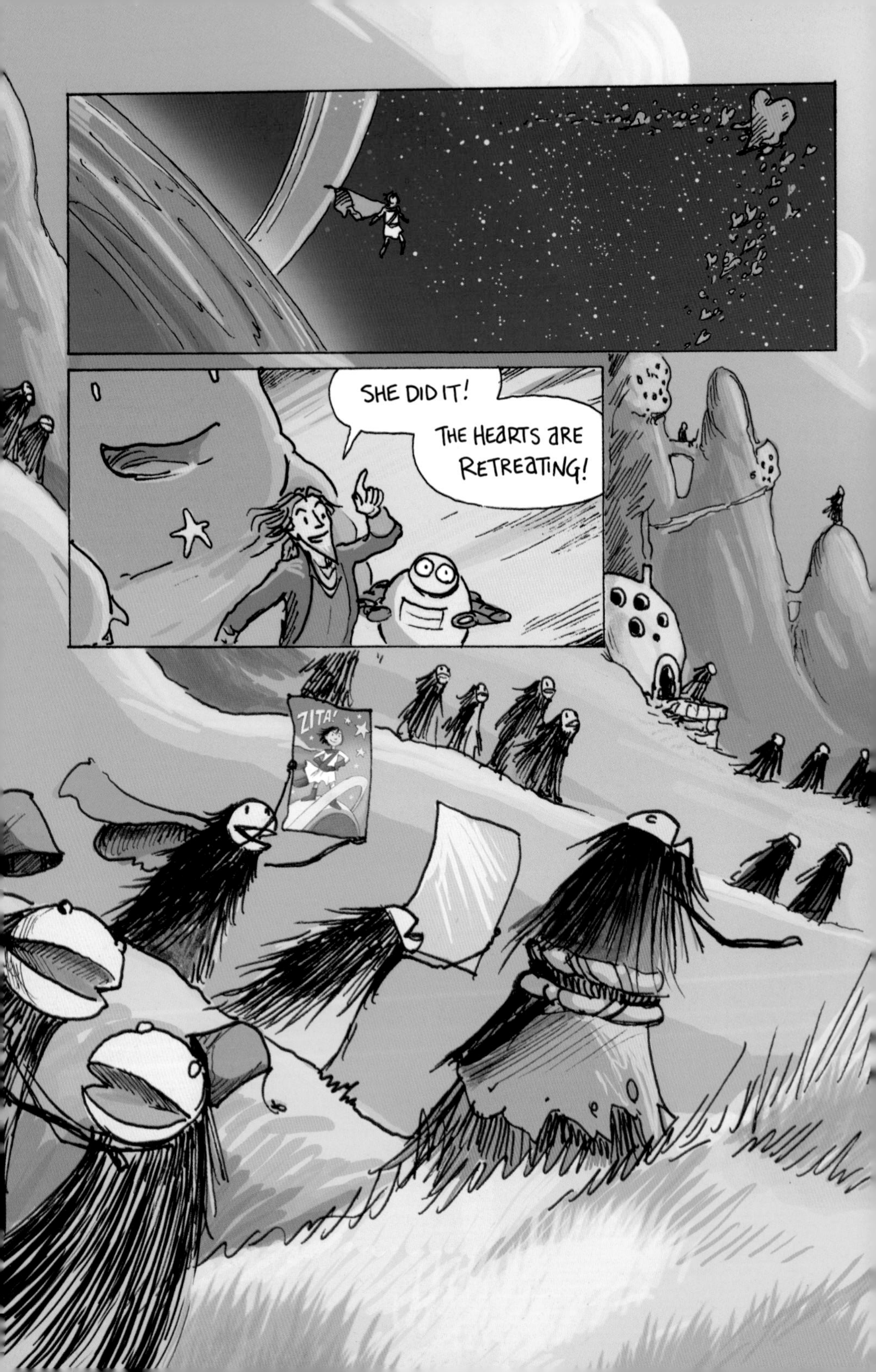
SHE DID IT!
THE HEARTS ARE RETREATING!
ZITA!

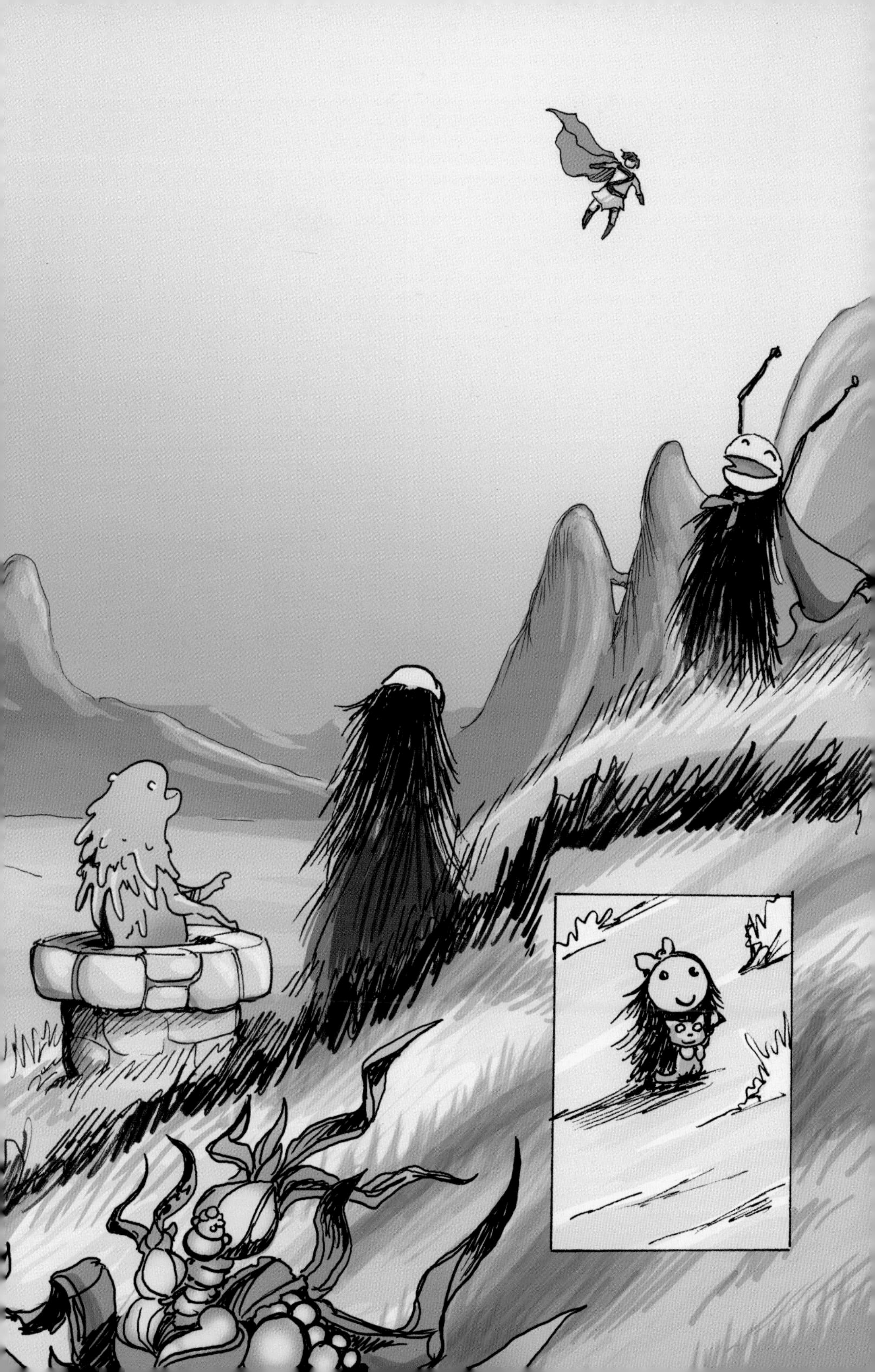

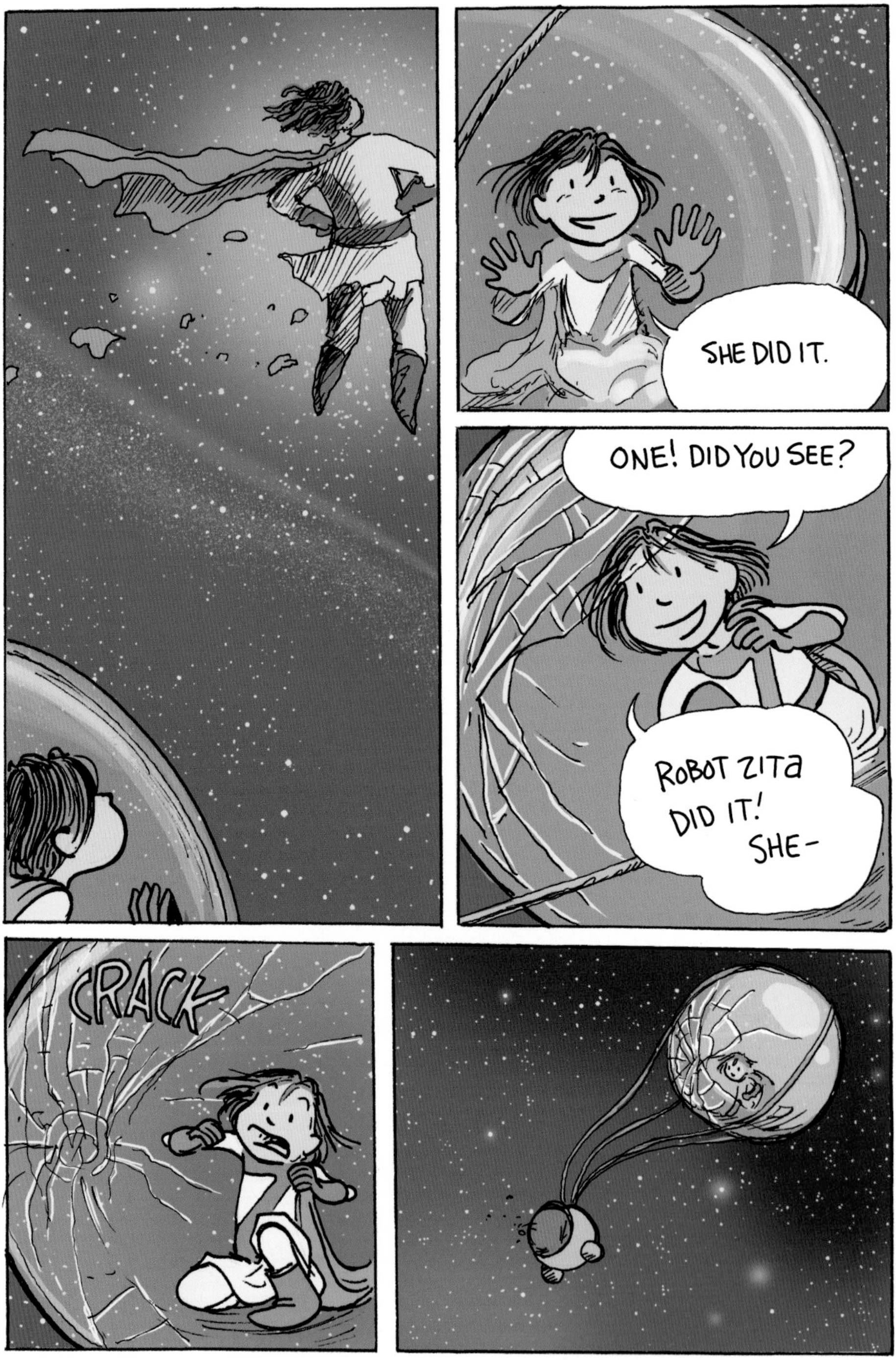
SHE DID IT.
ONE! DID YOU SEE?
ROBOT ZITA DID IT! SHE-
CRACK

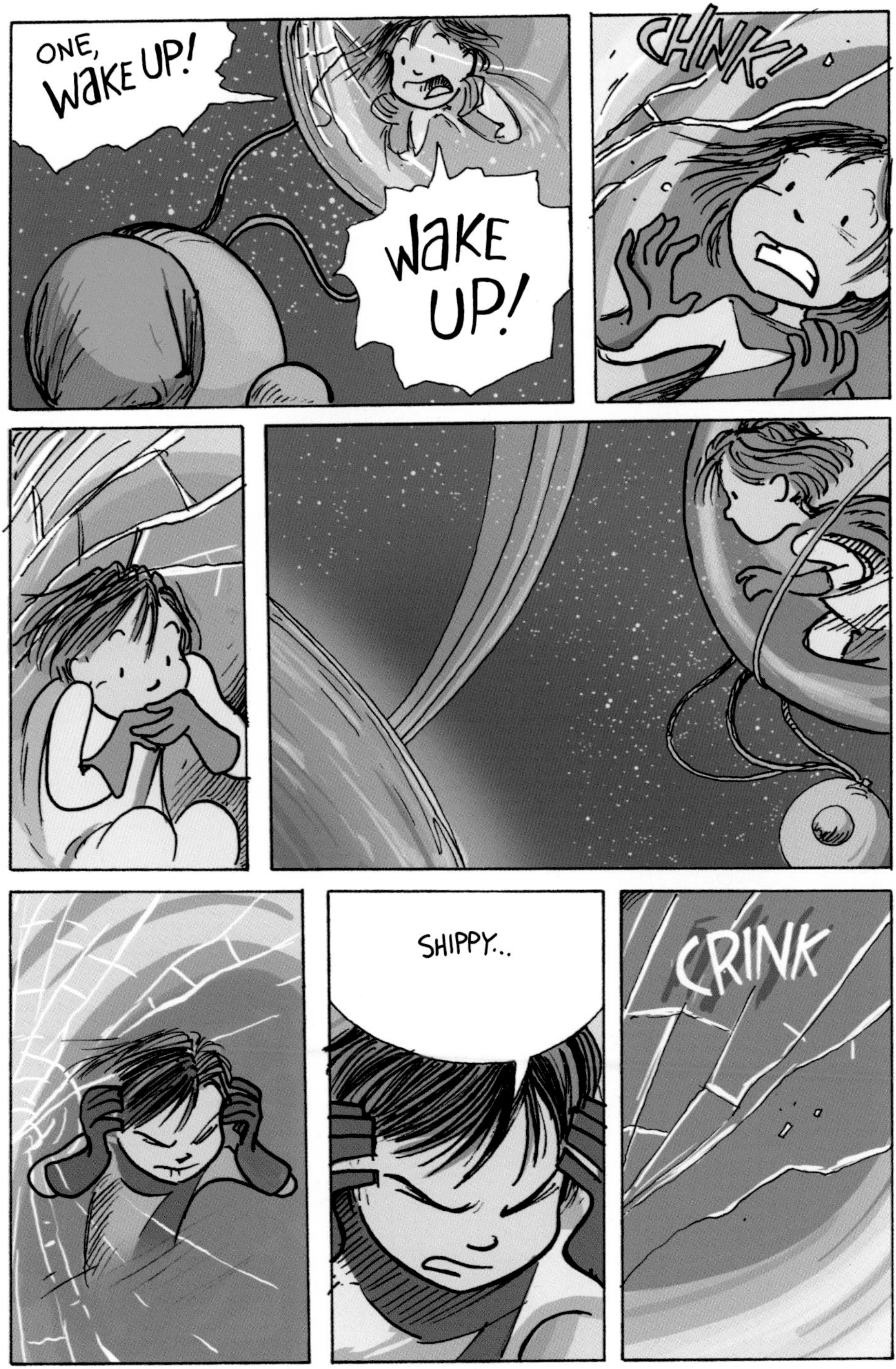
ONE, WAKE UP!
WAKE UP!
CHNK!
SHIPPY...
CRINK

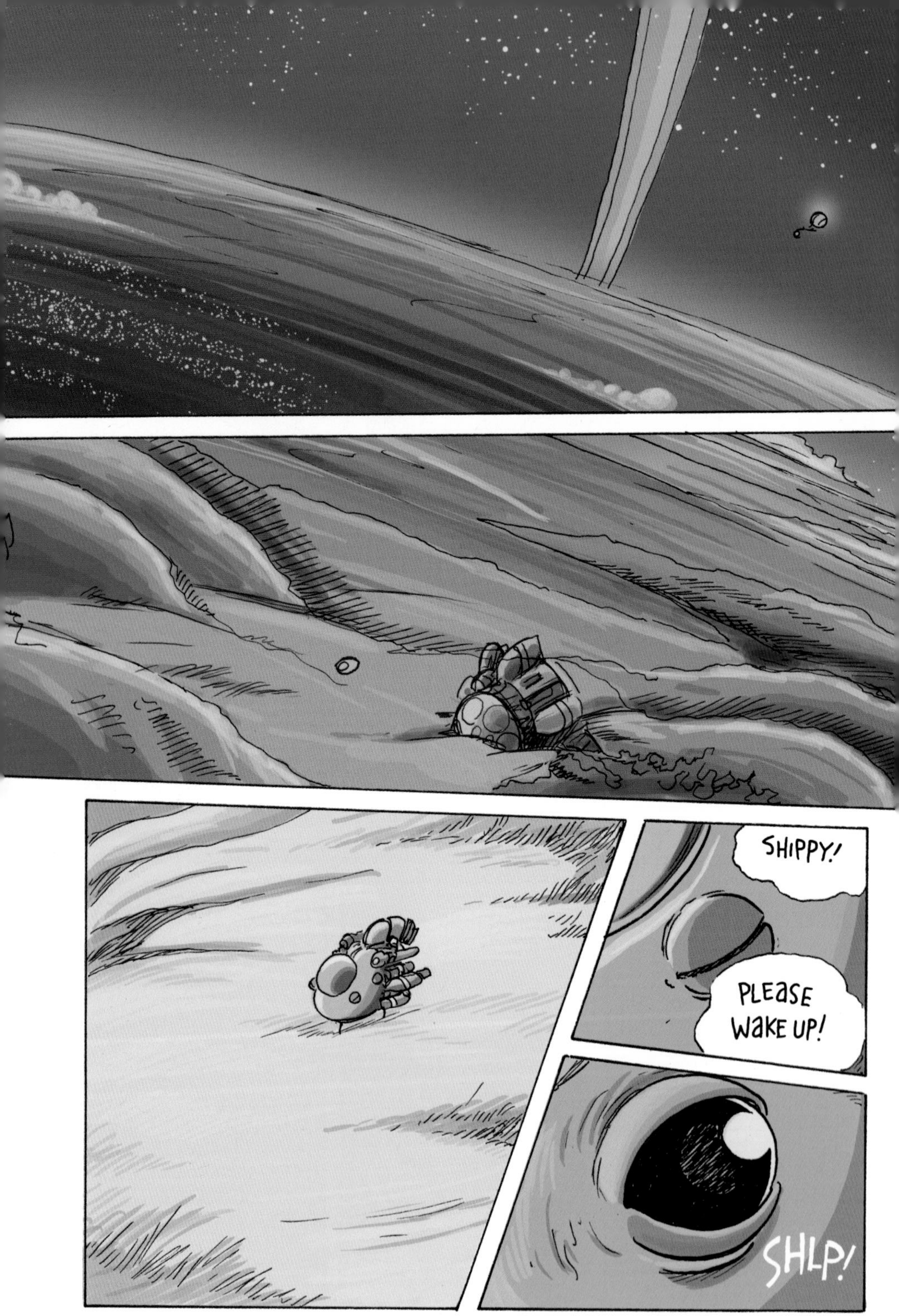
SHIPPY!
PLEASE WAKE UP!
SHLP!

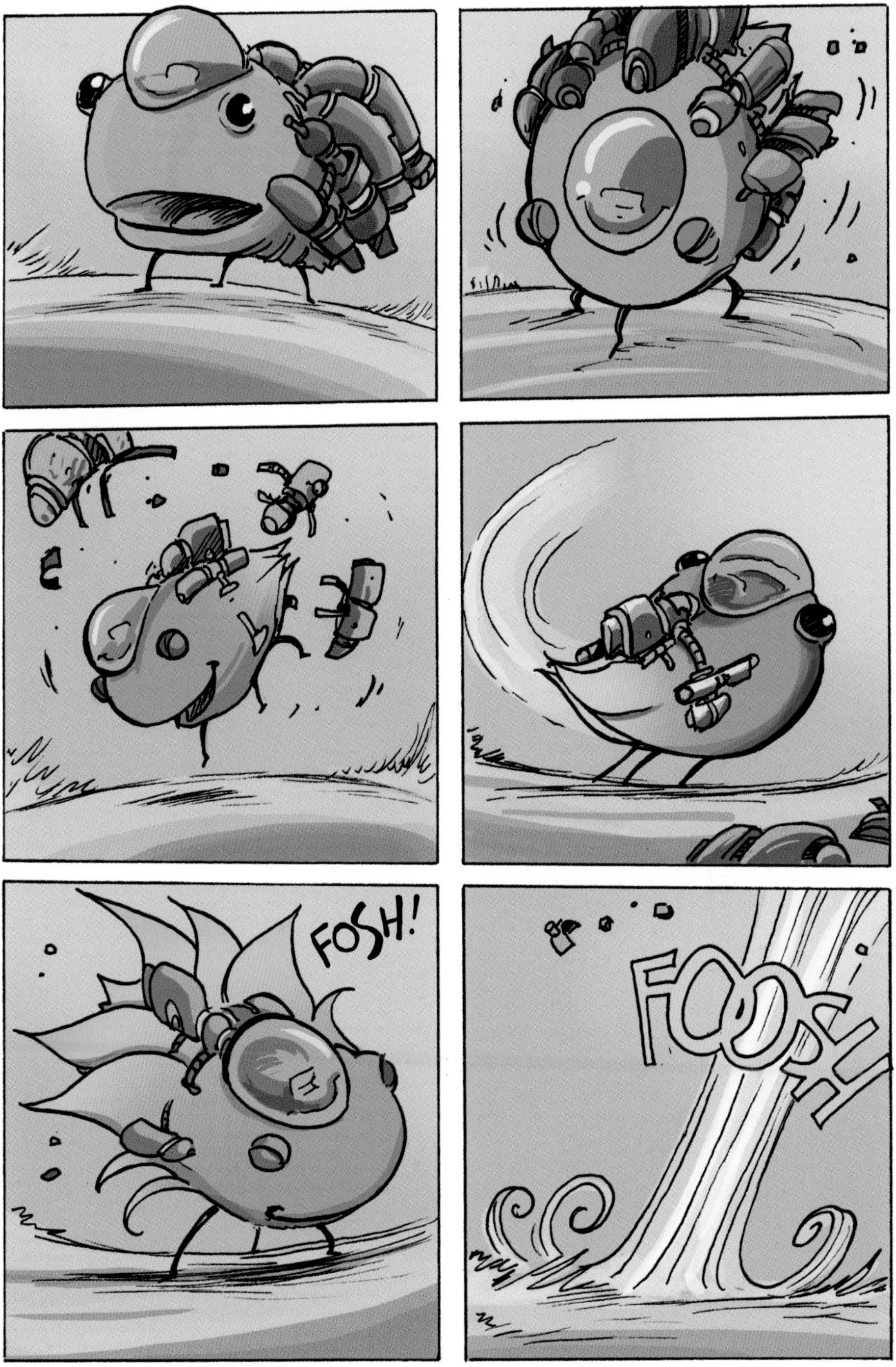
FOSH!
FOOSH

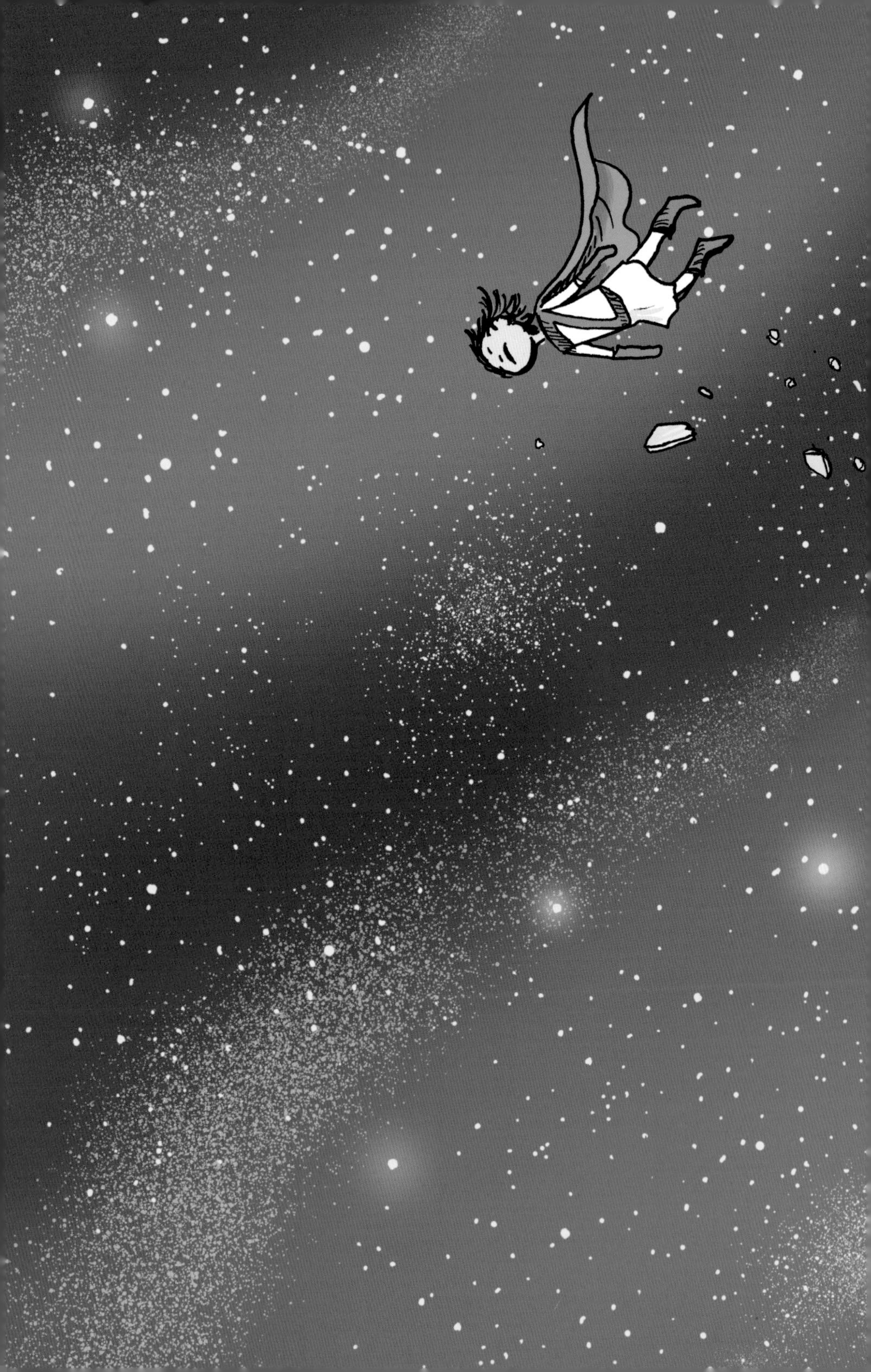

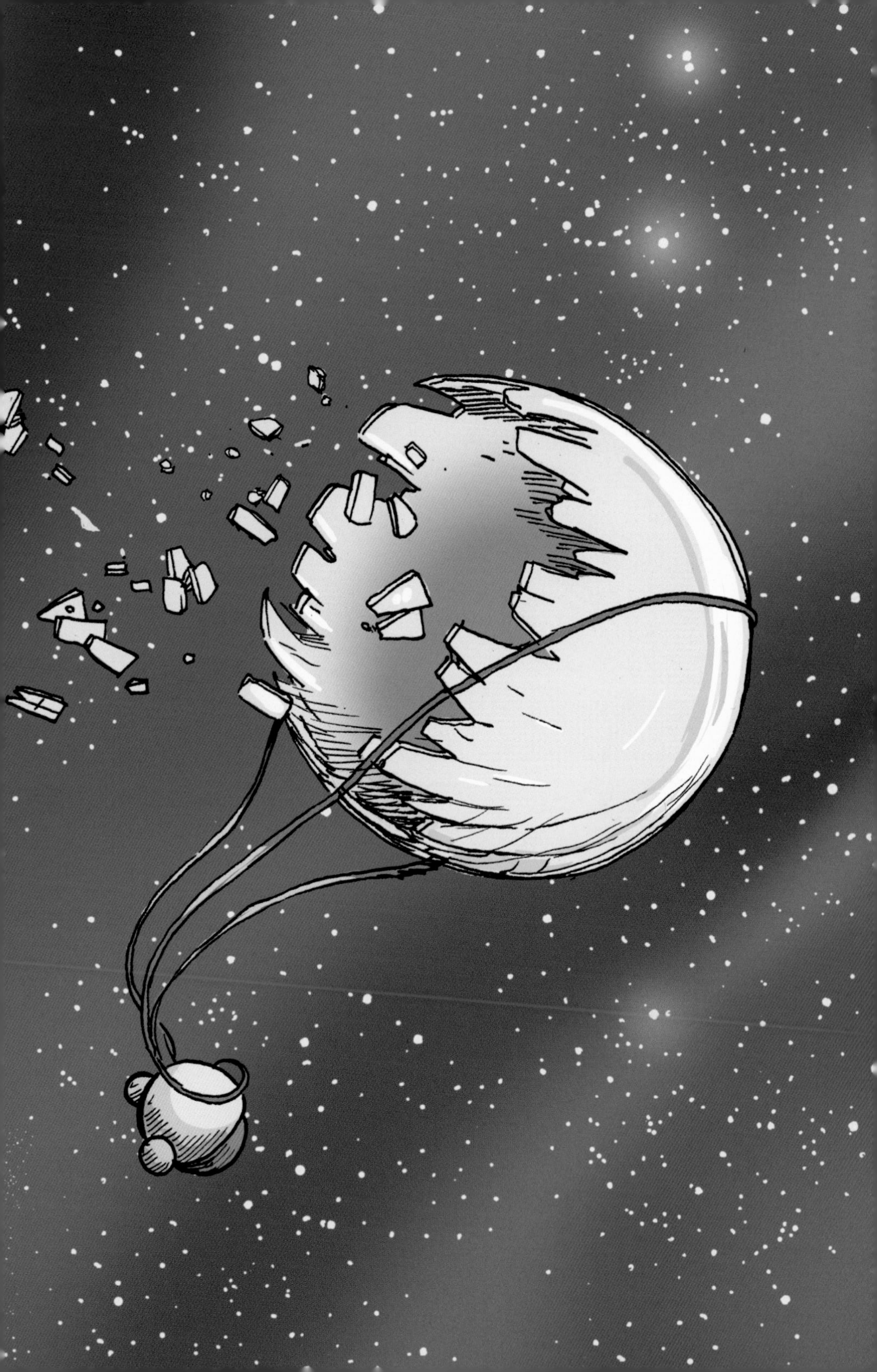

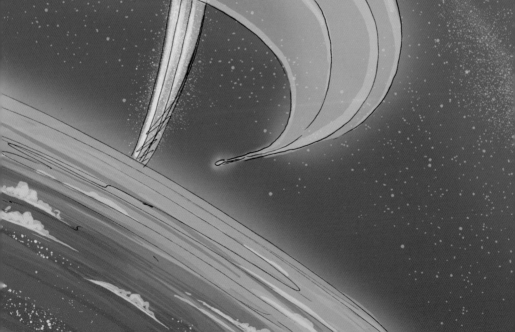

Chapter
Six

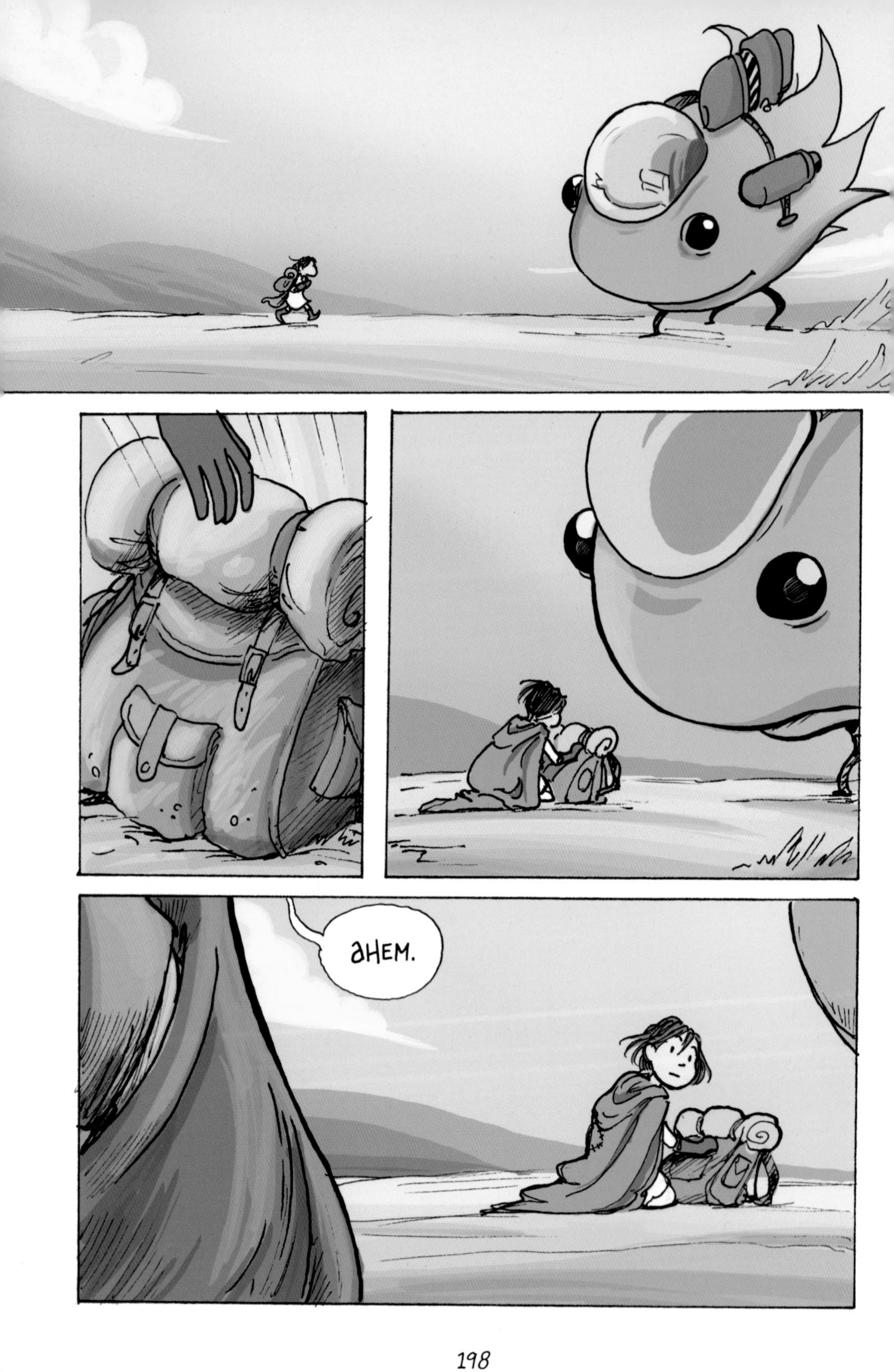
AHEM.

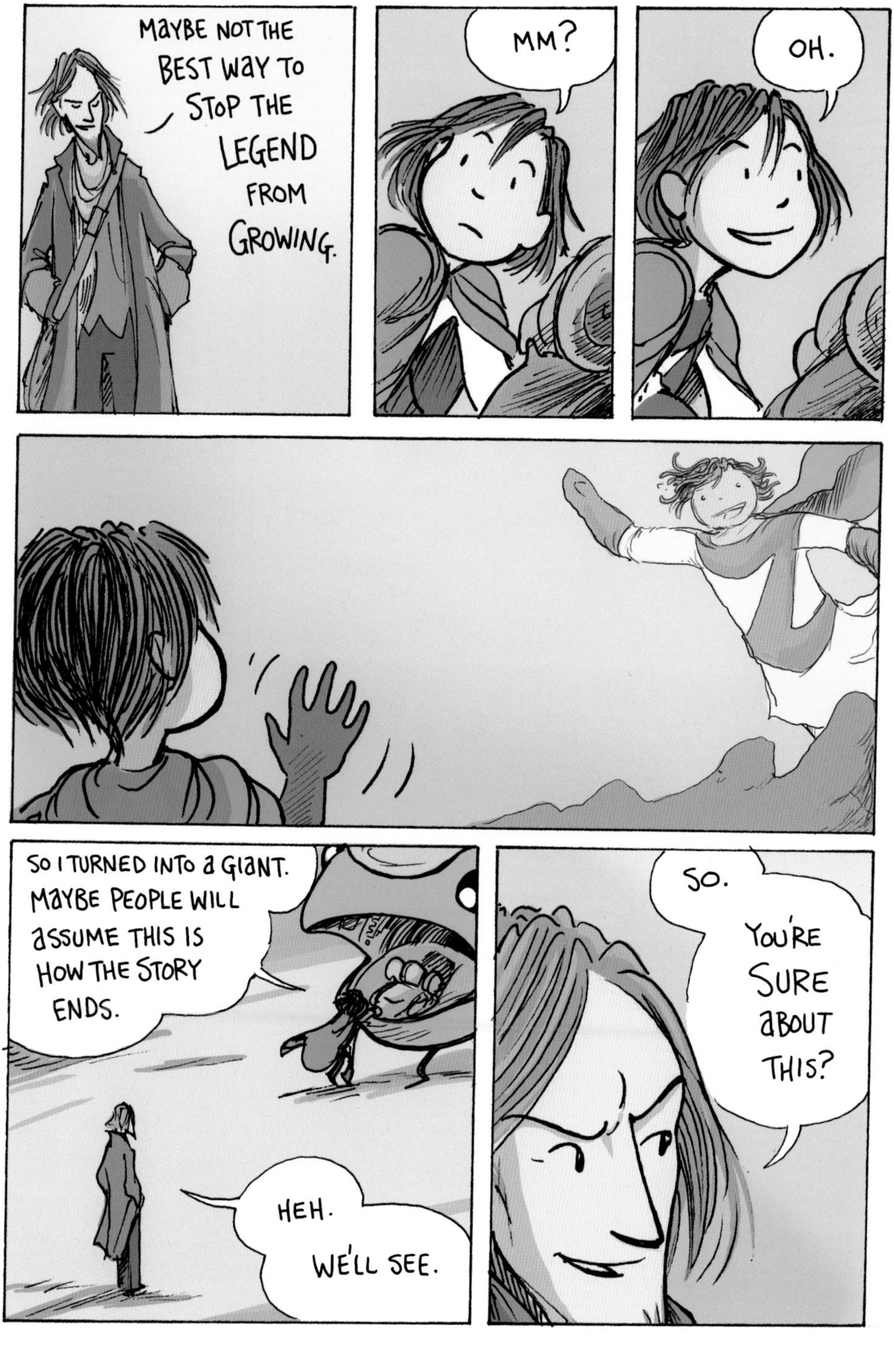
MAYBE NOT THE BEST WAY TO STOP THE LEGEND FROM GROWING.
MM?
OH.
SO I TURNED INTO A GIANT. MAYBE PEOPLE WILL ASSUME THIS IS HOW THE STORY ENDS.
HEH.
WE'LL SEE.
SO.
YOU'RE SURE ABOUT THIS?

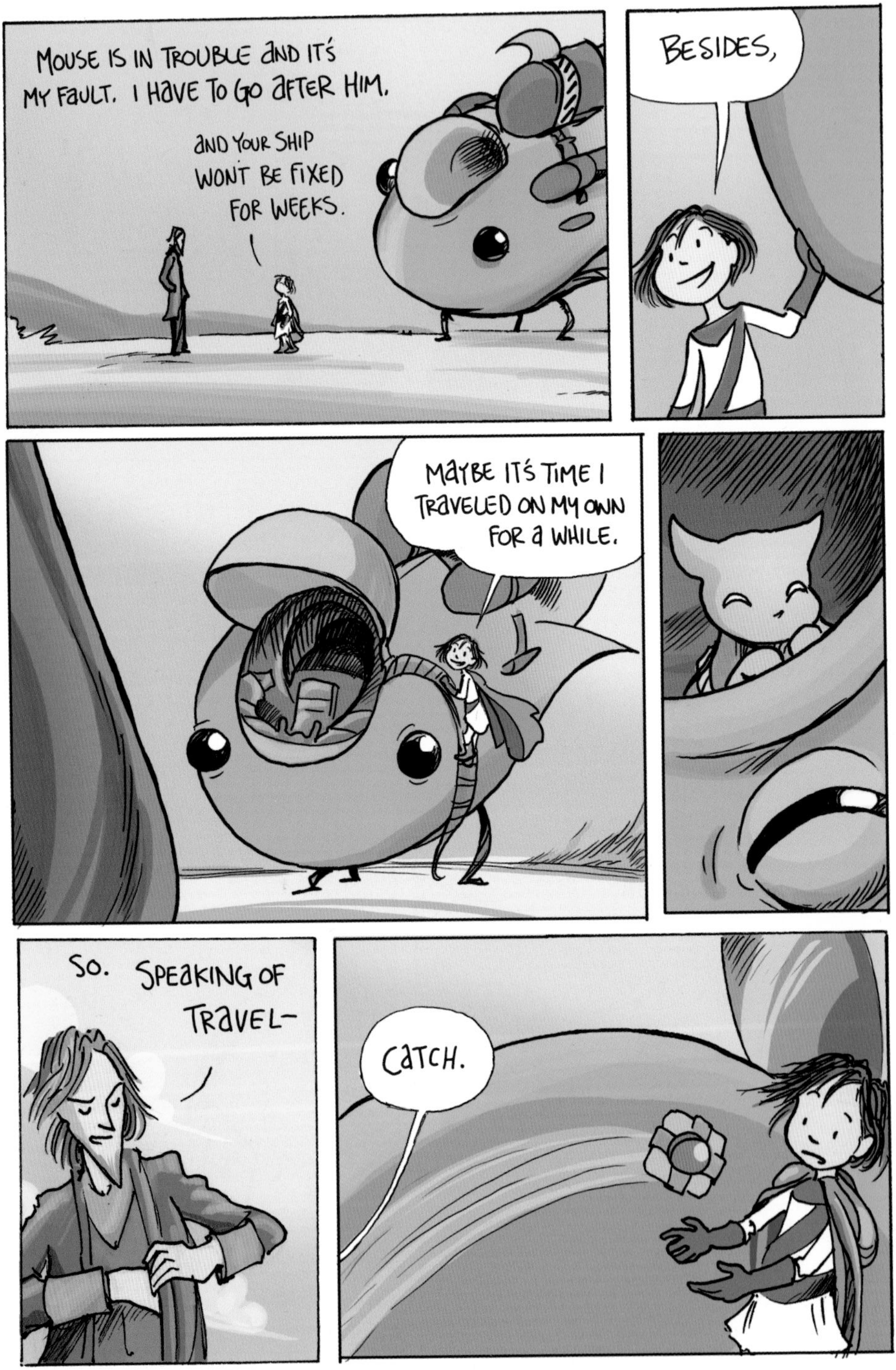
MOUSE IS IN TROUBLE AND IT'S MY FAULT. I HAVE TO GO AFTER HIM.
AND YOUR SHIP WON'T BE FIXED FOR WEEKS.
BESIDES,
MAYBE IT'S TIME I TRAVELED ON MY OWN FOR A WHILE.
SO. SPEAKING OF TRAVEL-
CATCH.

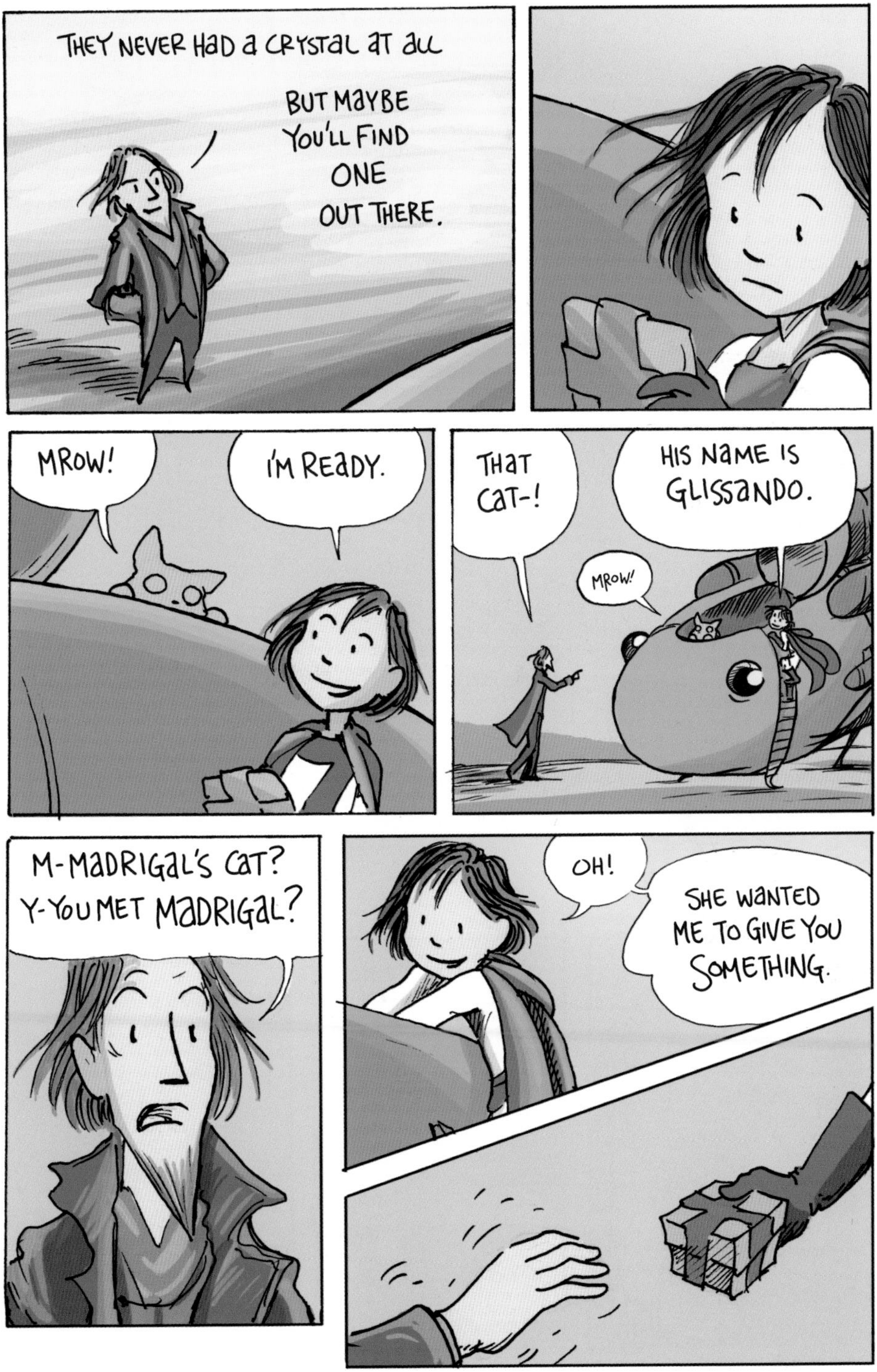
THEY NEVER HAD A CRYSTAL AT ALL
BUT MAYBE YOU'LL FIND ONE OUT THERE.
MROW!
I'M READY.
THAT CAT-!
HIS NAME IS GLISSANDO.
MROW!
M-MADRIGAL'S CAT? Y-YOU MET MADRIGAL?
OH!
SHE WANTED ME TO GIVE YOU SOMETHING.

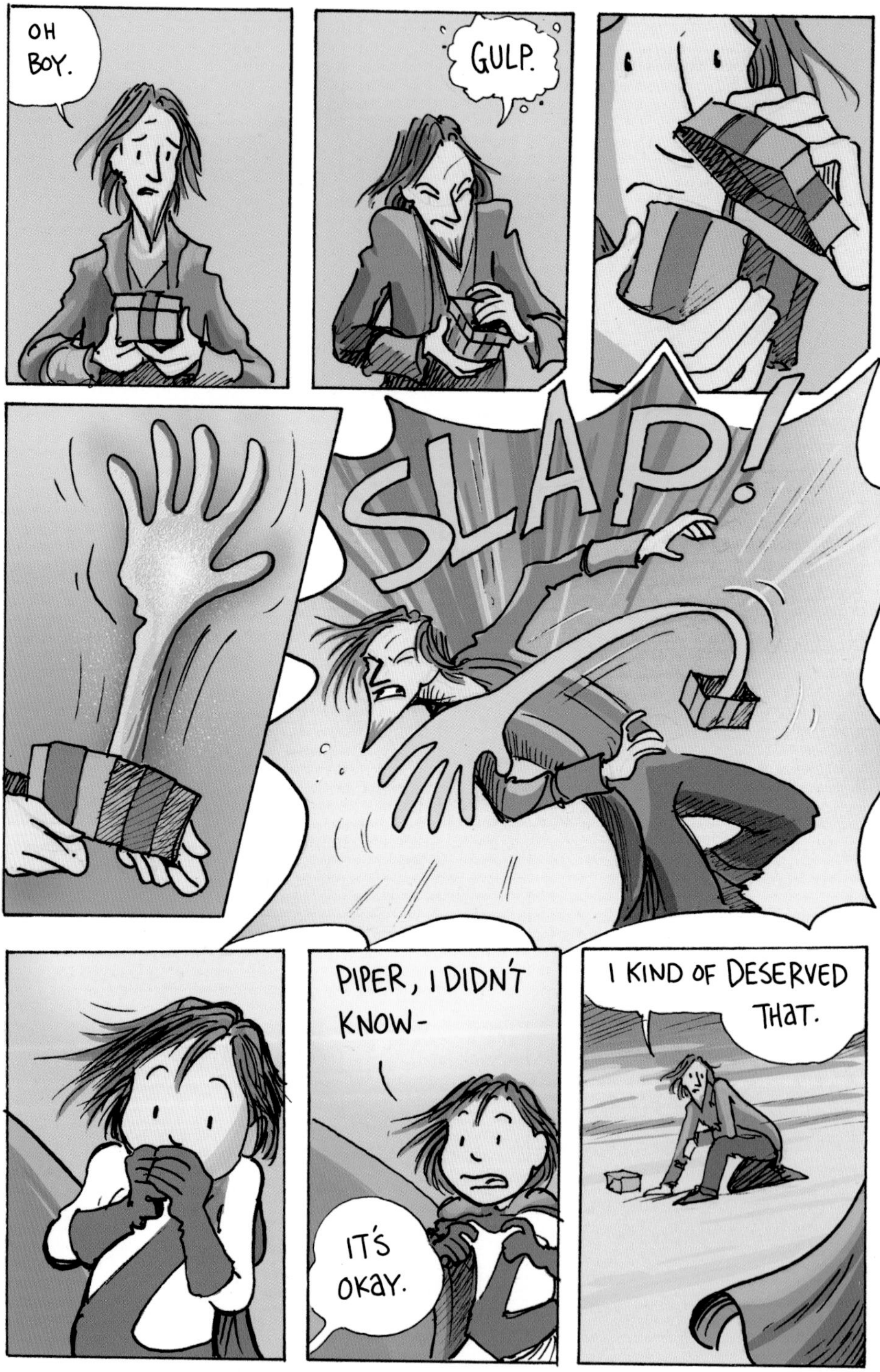
OH BOY.
GULP.
SLAP!
PIPER, I DIDN'T KNOW-
IT'S OKAY.
I KIND OF DESERVED THAT.

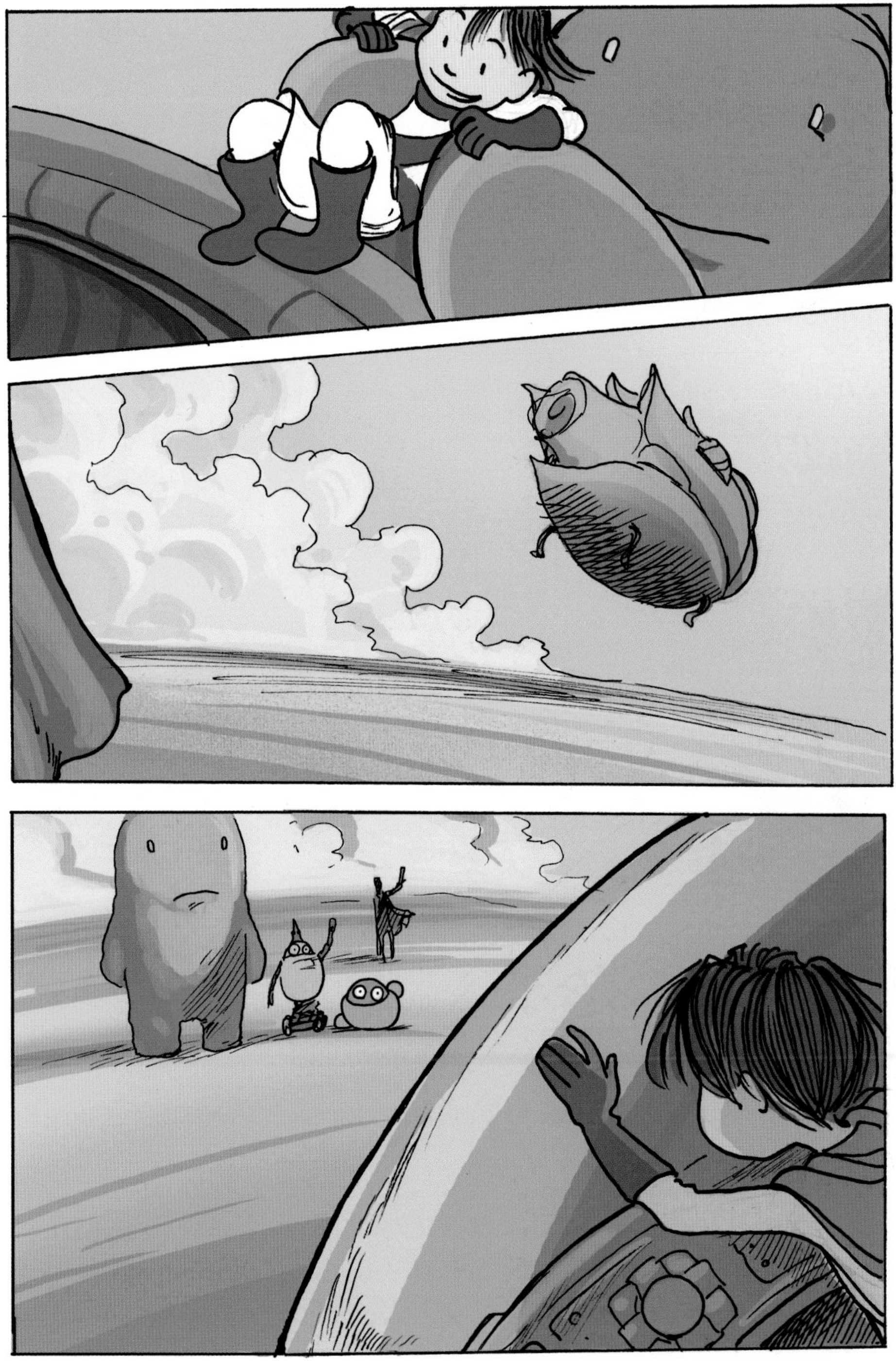

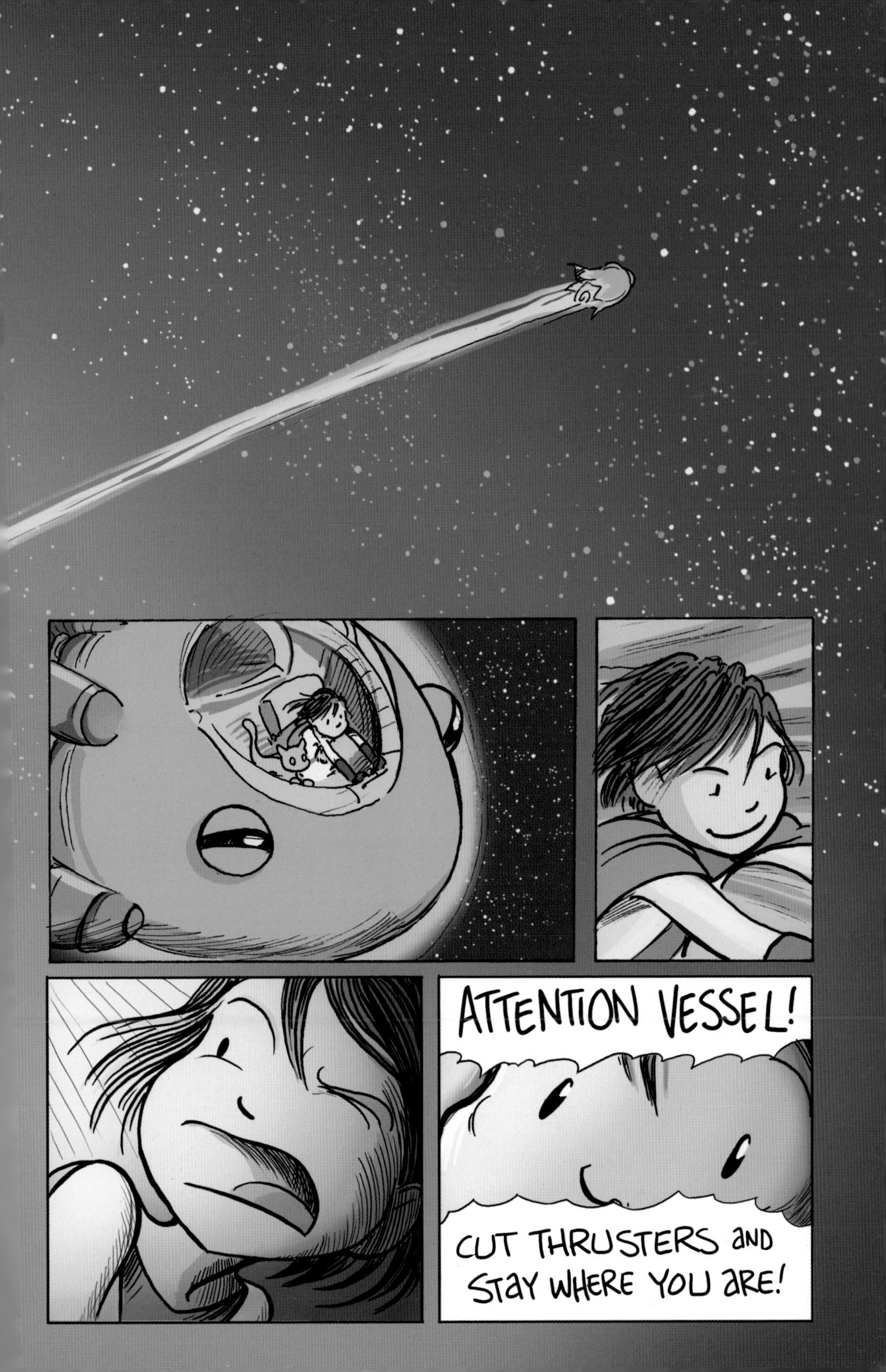
ATTENTION VESSEL!
CUT THRUSTERS and STAY WHERE YOU are!

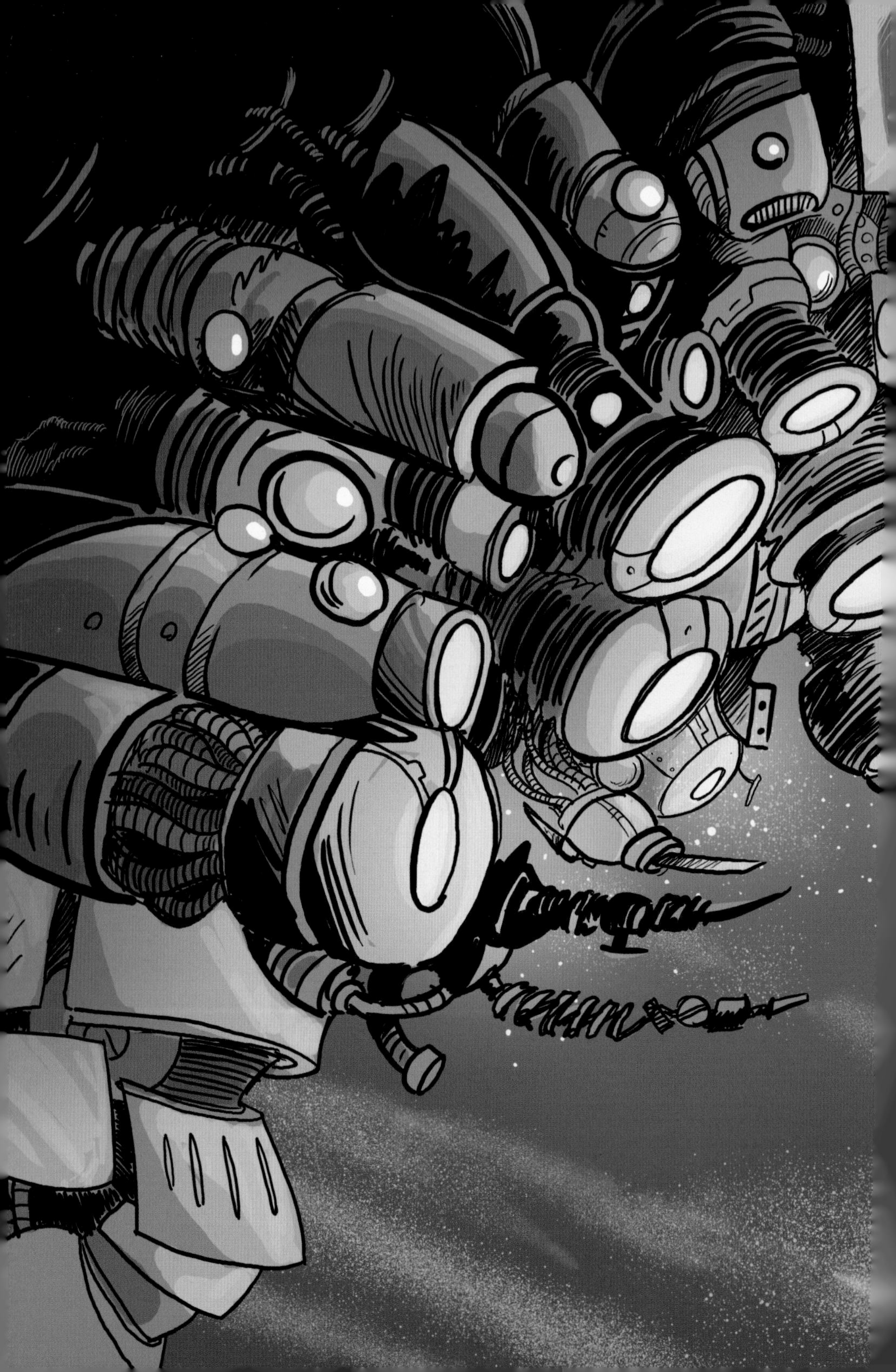

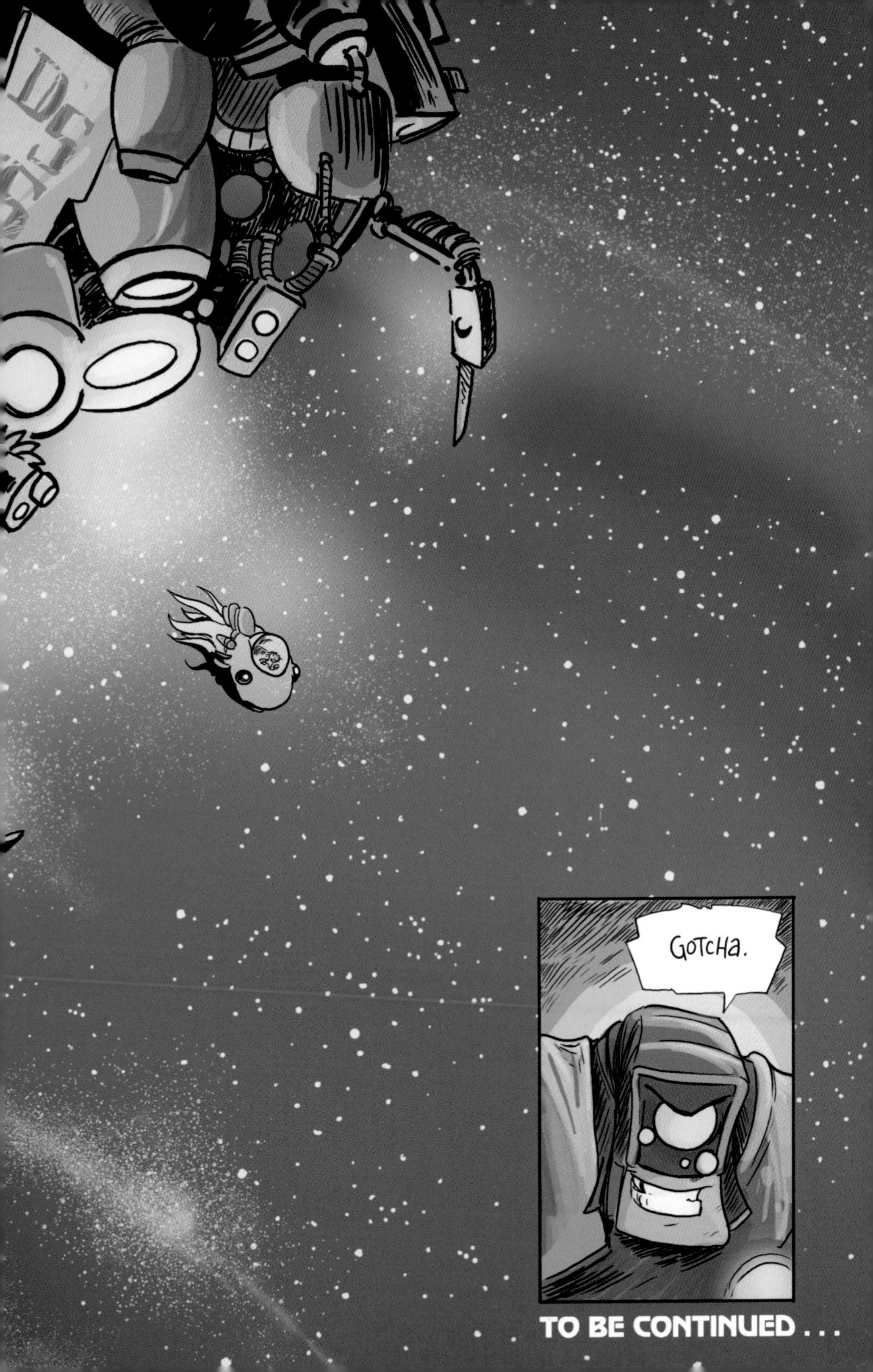
GOTCHA.
TO BE CONTINUED . . .

SKETCHES

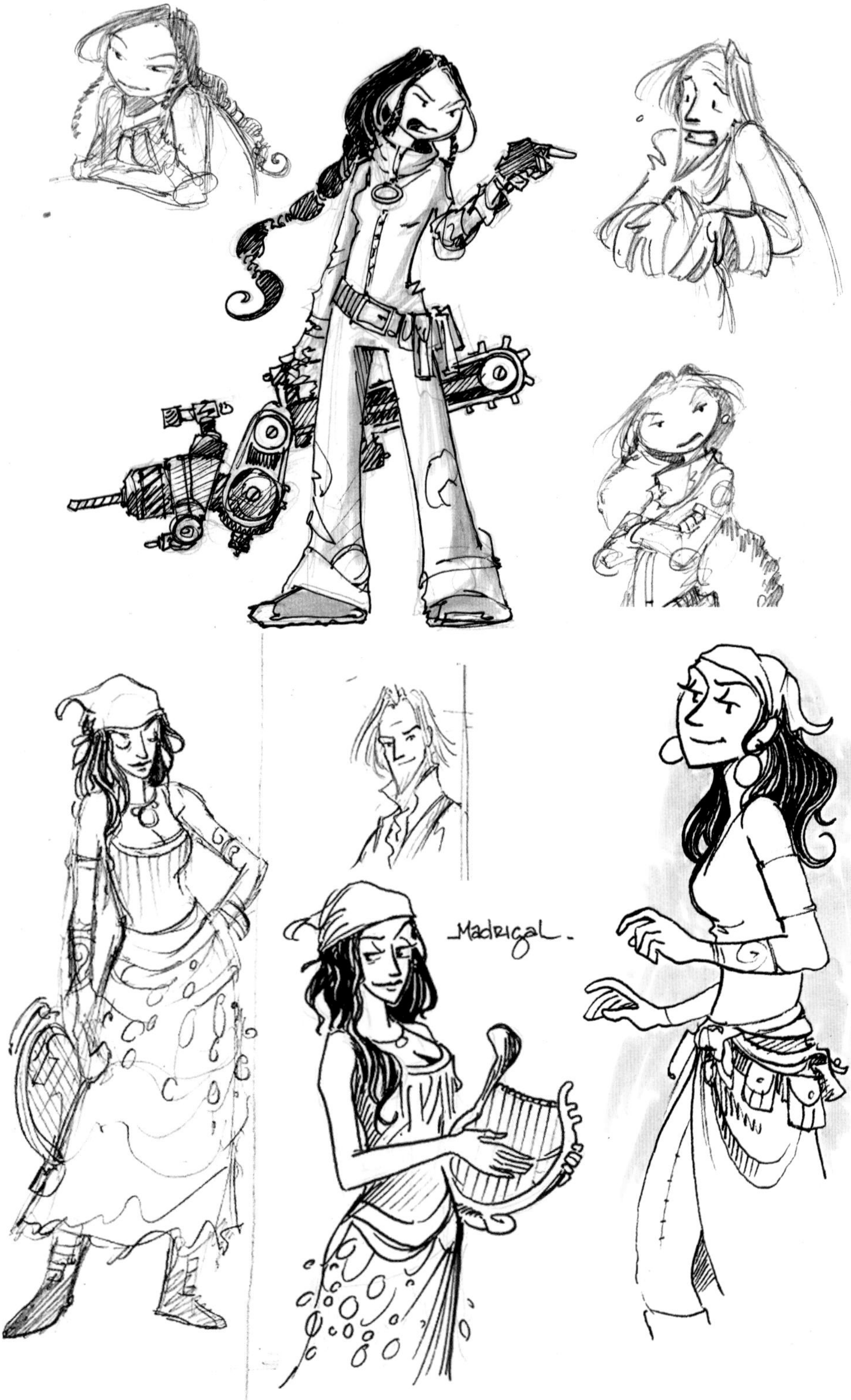
Madrigal

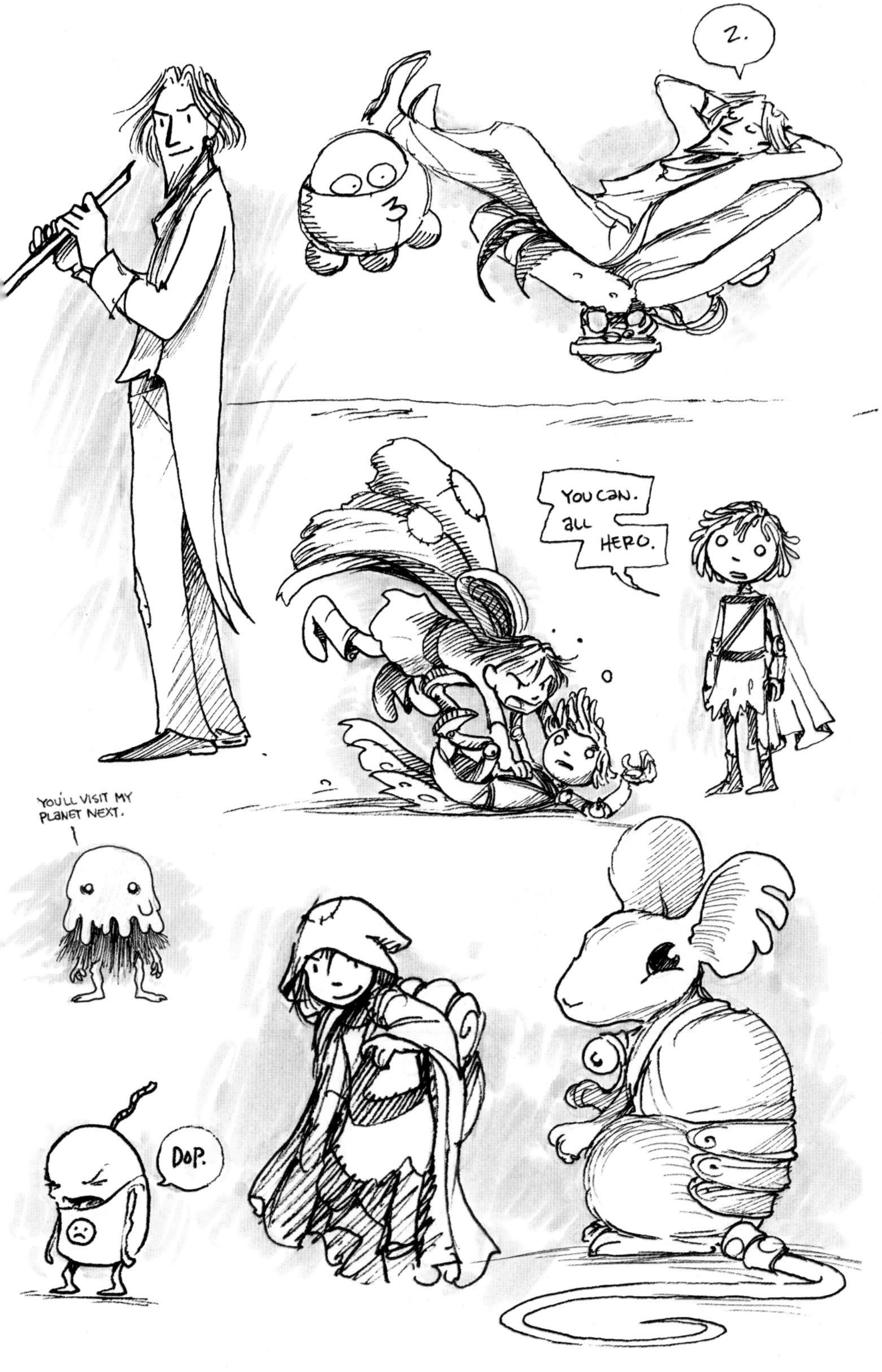

Z.
YOU CAN.
ALL
HERO.
YOU'LL VISIT MY PLANET NEXT.
DOP.

ACKNOWLEDGMENTS

First and foremost, special thanks go to my lovely wife, Anna, whose patience knows no bounds. Whenever I walk the road of sadness and self-doubt she jumps out from behind a tree of good cheer and throws rocks of encouragement at me. You're the best ever, Anna.

Thanks to my old friends Andy, Ryan, and Bill for reading early drafts. You guys are okay too, I guess.

Thanks to my ever-faithful editor, Kat Kopit, who knows so well how comics work, and thanks to her father, playwright Arthur Kopit, for one special conversation about stories. Thanks to my agent, Judy Hansen, for looking after me. And thanks to Mark Siegel for being not just a publisher, but a fellow artist and a friend.

Finally to my coloring crew! This book would not have made its final deadline if not for Kean Soo, Tory Woolcott, Anthony VanArsdale, Stephanie Yue, and Rosie ("the cat") Schmiedicke. You guys bailed me out.

Oh, and of course to my ever-inspiring daughters, Angelica, Zita, Julia, and Ronia. You four make life fun.

ABOUT THE AUTHOR

Ben Hatke has published comics stories for anthologies, including the Flight series and Explorer. He also keeps a comics journal online, which he gathers into yearly collections. This is his second graphic novel.

Ben lives in Virginia's Shenandoah Valley with his wife, four daughters, a flock of chickens, and a cat. He enjoys juggling, fire-breathing, doing backflips, and rolling 20-sided dice with his friends. Ben's art and journal comics can be seen online at www.benhatke.com.

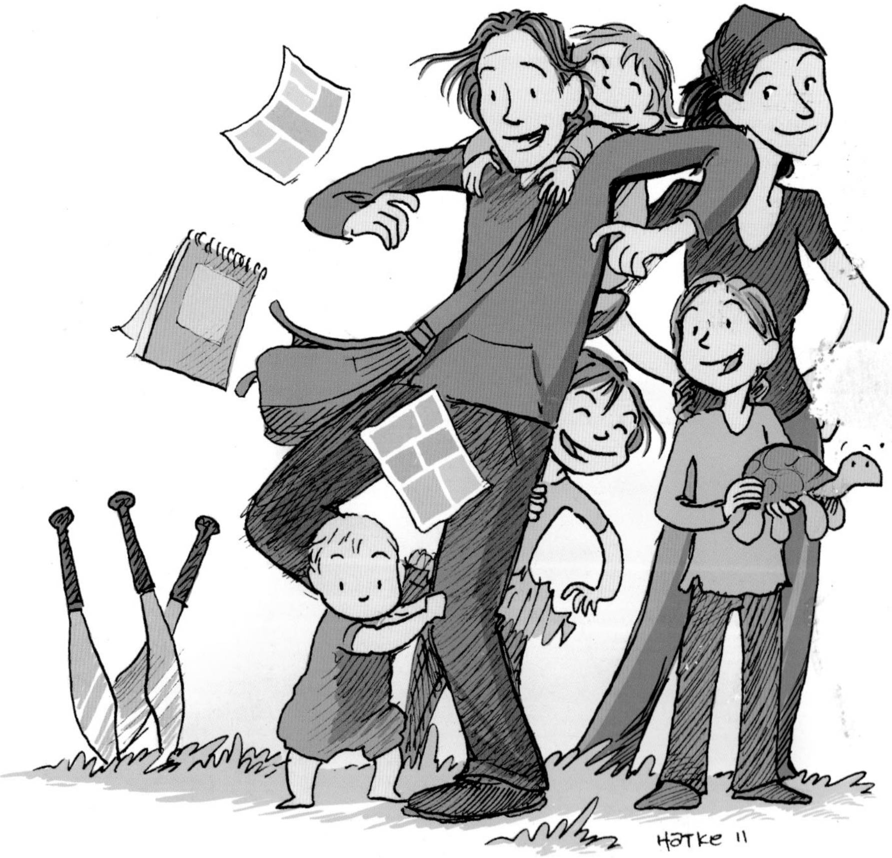
HATKE 11